EXCEPT THE LORD

Joyce Cary's "Second Trilogy"

PRISONER OF GRACE
EXCEPT THE LORD
NOT HONOUR MORE

Joyce Cary
EXCEPT THE LORD

A NEW DIRECTIONS BOOK

Manufactured in the United States of America
Published clothbound by Harper & Brothers in 1953
First published as New Directions Paperbook 607 in 1985

Library of Congress Cataloging in Publication Data

Cary, Joyce, 1888-1957.
  Except the Lord.
  (New Directions paperbook; 607)
  Sequel to: Prisoner of grace.
  Sequel: Not honour more.
  I. Title.
PR6005.A77E9   1985   823'.912   85-10601
ISBN 0-8112-0965-2 (pbk.)

New Directions Books are published for James Laughlin
by New Directions Publishing Corporation,
80 Eighth Avenue, New York 10011

TO MY GRANDSONS
*Lucius, Tristram Charles, Anthony Joyce,
Christopher, and John Tait Lunel*

EXCEPT THE LORD

1

YESTERDAY, an old man nearing my end, I stood by the grave of a noble woman, one of the three noblest I have ever known, my mother, my sister, my wife. If I draw back now the curtain from my family life, sacred to memory, I do so only to honour the dead, and in the conviction that my story throws light upon the crisis that so fearfully shakes our whole civilisation.

It is the story of a crime, of a soul, my own, plucked back from the very edge of frustration and despair. I was a poor boy, brought up among the poorest in our moorland hamlet, itself a poor place. We had not always been so—the first six years of my life knew better things. My father then farmed Highfallow in Devonshire, forty acres on the moor. He was an independent yeoman under the Duchy.

He came late to farming. He had been soldier and miner before he married, as they say, above himself, a schoolmaster's daughter—her savings had stocked the croft.

He himself, though self-educated, was a deeply read man. For many years he had been a lay preacher. Now at Highfallow, he attracted to himself many from lonely farms about, cut off for months at a time from the chapels of the vale. My father was one of those who waited confidently for the Second Coming of Christ, a doctrine appealing strongly to many lost and bewildered souls. They grew to like their minister and formed soon a permanent congregation. Often we had fifteen, even twenty worshippers, in our kitchen of a Sunday, and during the week, they would wait upon him with every kind of problem.

Some came not only for encouragement but to beg and borrow— few went from the door without help. I remember my mother coming to us one evening at supper with a small tin box in her hands. She opens it before my father and turns it upside-down. But I see that she is smiling and I am puzzled by the idea that anyone can laugh at my father, so much the greatest man in the world.

I recall with great vividness another scene. My father is going to market—five of our black-faced sheep are penned between two gates and I am flattered to think that I am guarding them while my father harnesses the mare.

Suddenly a huge red man appears from the hill—he speaks to my father, argues, begins to wave his great fists.

I know the man and fear him—a drunkard whose wife also drinks. And when they have fought he has a way of rushing from the house and going on the drink for weeks. He has been in the courts many times, for beating this miserable wife, for fights in the town, for debt.

Now he is shouting and his words appal me, "How about your Jesus then?" and then, "You set up for a Christian and let a man go to hell for ten shillings."

My father, a small figure, thin, already grey-haired, answers sharply, "If I gave you money, you'd only drink it. And what are you doing here?"

I am still more terrified by my father's anger. I have never seen him so angry—his moustache seems to bristle, his black eyes glare fiercely.

Suddenly the giant falls on his knees and begins to weep. My father calls my mother and says a few words to her, then sets off across the moor to take the runagate home. My mother looks after them a moment, then releases the sheep, and shoos them back to their pasture. She goes back thoughtfully to the house—we have missed another market day.

2

How cruel is that charge, of the selfish against the Christian, often poorer than himself, "You profess Christ, therefore you have no right to refuse me anything." In fifty years of politics, I have not known worse—it wounds so deep. But my father would have said, "The weak must be forgiven because they are weak."

2

Did we as children understand our fearful insecurity? It is impossible to hide anything in a six-room cottage. We knew of losses and debts, we heard talk of eviction and felt our parents' distress. And yet my only memories of Highfallow are of a great happiness, intense delights. We lived poorly, we had none but the roughest home-made toys—but we were two brothers and two sisters, we had each other and lived in that wealth of community, of instant comprehension and response, which belongs only to children in a closely united family. I will not say that I have never known such happiness as belonged to us—every stage in our life's pilgrimage has its own sorrow and its own appropriate satisfaction. But there has been none whose scenes are so deeply engraved upon my memory. I see again the moors under snow and it is part of the joy that we are cut off, no one in the world can come to us; and all these great hills, these sphinx-like tors with their crowns of granite capped with ermine, couched about us like a guard of monsters extinct in all the world besides, drowse like the beasts of an older revelation upon the bed of winter. Their broad backs and long ribs shine pale gold under a blue sky as deep as the time which buries their names, for our east winds on the moor blew always the clouds away, the sun came with the snow, and while our father with frozen hands, helped by my elder brother Richard, was digging out his sheep, we smaller children, indifferent to ten degrees of frost, quite unaware of fingers, ears and noses aching with the cold, would be sliding down the combe-side on a home-made sledge.

Then we are Eskimos, out of one of Richard's books—we harness the old sheep-dog to the sledge. But he turns round and jumps on us, sledge, dog, harness and ourselves fall in an inextricable tangle. He barks wildly, entering into our festival mood, as we roll in the snow, quite drunk with our own joy.

4

Even from our wars, our terrors, in that enchanted world of affection—from the impulses of evil that arise so irresistibly in a child's
heart, I have only memories that restore the soul. I am paddling in
the little shallow stream that runs through the orchard to the cow pool.
It is spring, the blossom is falling round me like snow, the sun is
throwing down its broad yellow bars between enormous clouds, but
the water is so cold that I jump in and out quickly with cries of mock
pain.

My sister Georgina, one year older but at least a head taller, is
beside me—she is performing what she calls a water-dance, a kind of
slow minuet in a pool, to the accompaniment of her own song which
in various keys and tones consists of the one word "water-ee—wateree
—wateree."

Suddenly she laughs insanely, lifts up her skirt, gives a high kick
and staggers against me. I push her over into the pool, and fly for
my life.

I hear her panting behind and scream, her long nervous hand skims
through my hair, I feel her other hand grab at the back of my flying
overall. I cry again but it is a cry of despair—I am going to be beaten,
slapped, shaken by this terrible sister.

Suddenly my mother appears at the kitchen door, she has come to
feed the chickens. I run behind her and she catches at the furious
Georgina—I hear her saying reproachfully that I am only a baby and
that Georgina is supposed to be looking after me. I am certainly not
to be beaten.

I dare say the whole memory, the blossom, the cool of the stream,
Georgina's vindictive rage, remain with me only because of that
escape, of the sudden triumph that came with my mother. It seems to
me that the column of her skirts was like a fortress against all pain.

My only memory of grief at Highfallow comes from quite another
source. I had committed some fault, and told a lie about it and not
been discovered. And I had been taught that bad children who do not
confess and repent will go to hell.

I do not remember anything but the terror—possibly for a very
short time before I was found out, and punished, and so absolved.
The fear of hell, the punishment of sin, how the modern parent revolts

5

from such teaching. Yet I will assert that far from doing us children harm, it was a sure foundation to the world of our confidence, a master girder in our palace of delight. For we saw its justice, we knew, in the common phrase, exactly where we were—the wicked would be punished, and the good should have reward.

3

IT was not the parasites who fasten on every generous man, or even farming losses, that ruined us at last, but a much more terrible misfortune—sickness. My mother, overworked as only such women of high standard and small resources can overwork, fell ill and slowly wasted away. In such a case, only one thing can save a family like ours, a daughter or relation capable of taking the mother's place. But Richard was ten, Georgina seven, and we had no available relation— our nearest neighbour was a mile away.

Neither were neighbours, then, willing to help. They looked upon the Nimmos as proud, our ruin as the just punishment of upstarts. For in such primitive communities, the smallest difference of habit, of education, is enough to bring suspicion and hatred.

It seemed to me on my visits to Shagbrook, our nearest hamlet, that every window hid behind its Nottingham lace curtains a watchful enemy saying, "There goes the Nimmo boy in cracked boots—I hope that will bring him down a bit and all his family too."

Will it be believed that even our names were subject of scorn— Georgina and Chester—who had ever heard such among cottagers? It was no excuse that the one came from my mother's mother, the other from my father's old colonel who had been my godfather. These were gentry, and to use their names was to claim a status above our rights.

I remember one who came to work in our fields, a decent simple woman with children of her own. She had just been paid and stood in the path tying up the coins in a corner of a cloth—my mother, who had been better during the autumn, was sitting in the doorway to enjoy the sun. My youngest sister, Dorothy, then a baby of three months, lay kicking in her lap.

I have few memories of my mother, but they are vivid. I remember her on that afternoon, no doubt, because of this incident. She had been reading while she nursed, now she had laid the book down on the bench to play with Dorothy.

7

It seemed to my memory that my mother was tall and beautiful, she was very fair with dark blue eyes, a great beauty. I am told that she was little taller than my father, and that her beauty was rather in her expression than any regularity of feature. But surely it is in expression that the most precious beauty lies. I have reason for my memory. She was by nature lighthearted, she would romp with us like another child, she taught us all our lessons, but chiefly by reading to us which we loved.

Now my brother Richard, coming in from some farm task, squatted down beside her, picked up her book and began to read aloud in a sing-song voice.

I cannot remember what the book was, but it had many difficult words—possibly it was by Ruskin, a favourite of my mother's, whom she had taught my father to admire also.

Richard read the hard words easily but with a certain comic exaggeration—the woman looked at him with an angry, alarmed face, and then at my mother. "What sort of book is that?" she asked, and my mother told her. She went away with a flustered air, and Richard gave a loud laugh. "She thinks you're a witch," he said. "In Shagbrook they say you talk Latin to the cat."

Richard liked to scorn Shagbrook. But it was a fact that, because my mother read so much, she was thought arrogant—a charge that did not long survive our arrival in the hamlet. Her simple goodness defeated all but the most malignant there—those who were merely stupid learnt to respect her and even to love her.

For all her gaiety, her humour, my mother was a dedicated creature. Her life was inward and she trembled before a God that judged the very heart. When I knelt in her lap and whispered my first prayers into her breast, I cannot tell what ideas that bedtime ceremony stirred in my infant mind. But was I wrong to feel that I knelt in a holy place and communicated with a spirit which was then in all its gentle and modest service truly one with the Most High?

Confused ideas they were in a small child, and more feelings than ideas. But all the deeper, all the more powerful to guard me long after that lap and that breast were dust.

4

DISASTER, for us children, came without warning, quietly as the fall of a leaf. One morning we were told that we were to move, the stock to be sold, the auctioneer was already in the yard.

A hay-cart was waiting for us—within the hour we were creaking away on the rough track. Richard and Georgina stood up to look over the tall side of the cart at the last of Highfallow. But when I asked them to lift me up to see too, my mother, propped up in her pillows, pulled me down in her lap and said, "Once upon a time there was a little boy called, what do you think?"

I answered, with a sense of deep penetration and cunning, my own name. My mother often told us stories in which we were the heroes and I especially revelled in them. The day was fine, the pale November sun shown on the boards, gulls were crying overhead, I had the consciousness, delightful to a child, of being on a journey. I gazed in wonder to see that Georgina, huddled against Richard in the opposite corner, had tears on her cheeks and that Richard himself looked pale and sad.

What amazement fell upon me to find myself in a mean cottage, one narrow slice out of a terrace in Back Lane, Shagbrook, with only a muddy road in front and a muddier yard behind. For days I wandered in a trance, which was too bewildered to be misery.

My father, meanwhile, thought himself lucky. The sale paid his debts and he had found home and employment within reach of his flock, who had begged him not to desert them.

True, the employment was uncertain—in the stables at Stonepit Farm, under the foreman, Paviour, at a labourer's pay. But work was scarce, especially for a man nearly fifty, my father's age, and cottages still scarcer. I heard my parents at evening prayers thank God for His care of us and my mother's amen came from her heart.

But we children were more and more depressed, we felt only our

9

losses, our ignominy. Every time we walked down Back Lane we had to harden our nerves against the village children as they drawled after us, Ches-ter Nim-mo, Geor-gina Hel-en. We could not realise our escape from the hell which might open then beneath a family without work or home, the workhouse, separation, destruction. We had not known dependence. How shall I describe the emotion, neither amazement, nor fear, nor anger, but partaking of all these, with which, a few days after we had entered our new house, I saw our landlord, the farmer, or rather farmeress, Mrs. Coyte, march in and shout for my mother.

Mrs. Coyte was already a name of power to us. Not only had she employed my father, but half the hamlet was dependent upon her for employment, especially for those casual tasks about a farm to which a countryman looks for that margin of income which makes the difference between penury and a living wage. Mrs. Coyte was an active farmer. There were always ditching, hedging, repairing of roads and dykes at one or other of her farms, apart altogether from harvests, and she would give the work only to those whom she approved. She preferred Wesleyans to Baptists, and both to the Church. She would bar a man or woman who got habitually drunk on any day but Saturday, and she would never give work to a certain S., our chief village sea-lawyer who had once summoned her son for not paying his men's wages in money. The Coytes would often pay their men partly in kind, in skim milk or potatoes, in spite of the Truck Acts.

I had already, therefore, a strange idea of Mrs. Coyte as a mysterious providence, and when I saw her now before me she was a sufficiently alarming figure. She would have been a very tall woman if it had not been for her remarkable stoop. She seemed as if her back were broken just behind the shoulders. Her height too was in her body, she had comparatively short legs, so that with her long thin nose, her big staring eyes, she resembled a buzzard. Her voice also was alarming to a child, deep and hoarse. She sometimes uttered sounds like the croaking of a daw.

My mother was bathing Dorothy in the far corner of the room nearest the fire. It was our bedtime, and I stood penned in the corner ready to be undressed. So I saw Mrs. Coyte come in and exclaimed

10

in alarm—my mother waited to quiet me and to wrap a towel about Dorothy before she gave attention to the visitor.

Meanwhile Mrs. Coyte, having perceived her in the dim light of the winter evening, had advanced to the attack—as she stood bending over my mother, rounding her great eyes and shouting that the house was the best house in Shagbrook, better than her own, that it had just been repaired and that she could not afford any more repairs, I had the shocking notion that she might do her an injury.

My mother had complained of holes in the attic floor, and especially in the stairs and stair rail, which she thought dangerous. Mrs. Coyte now marched upstairs stamping and bawling. She had as usual a thick ash plant in her hand, and with this she struck hard blows on the rails and steps, declaring that they were strong enough to carry a horse.

My mother's gentle manner and soft voice were deceptive—she was, in fact, a woman of good courage and determined will in any matter that seemed to her important—in religion, and in anything that concerned the welfare of her husband and children. Mrs. Coyte seemed perfectly astonished when, after all her shouting and beating, this pale dying creature pointed out that though the stair rail was strong, several banisters were entirely missing and others were quite rotten. Also that there were holes in the treads and in the floors above big enough to catch a child's foot.

Mrs. Coyte was not a bad woman, but she was a rough one. She had fought her way in a hard world. She had, too, some excuse for a grievance against us—she had not known that my father preached the Second Coming.

"None of your nonsense preachings in my cottage," she had shouted. "Who are you to go cutting and chopping around at the word of God?"

Mrs. Coyte herself was a Wesleyan and a regular chapelgoer, but I think that this only made my father's ministrations more repugnant to her. Like other orthodox persons she considered any deviation from her own scheme as heretical and dangerous—that is what she meant by "nonsense preaching."

Indeed, I believe my father and mother were put to great anxiety by her ban. They seriously considered whether it would not be better

11

to hold the meetings at Dollyford, four miles away, where one of the faithful offered a room.

But when they had prayed, there was no doubt in their minds that my father's duty was to testify in Shagbrook.

For the man with a message, opposition, even hatred, is a sign that he is needed precisely in that place where the most violent hostility is to be found.

He held his service as usual the very day after Mrs. Coyte's prohibition—it is perhaps not surprising that she showed some rudeness on her visit. Her answer to my mother was that if children were fools enough to fall downstairs they'd better do so and learn better. She added, "I know you think Slapton House wouldn't be good enough for your ladyship, but I ha'nt got it to give you, and if I had I wouldn't, for it would not be suitable."

Then she stamped out and called me to bring out a chair so that she could mount her horse.

But I would not take the chair, I think perhaps such was my feeling about Mrs. Coyte that I could not have done so. And it was my mother, reproving me for my bad manners and unkindness, who took out the chair and helped Mrs. Coyte, who was stiff as well as short in her legs, to mount the cart horse on which she was riding out to her pastures.

5

My father belonged to a kind still, I hear, not by any means extinct in the imperial army, the religious soldier. He was a light-built man, very dark in complexion, with a somewhat hollow face, and a long sharp chin. His moustache, once, so my mother said, short and waxed at the ends in the style of a smart troop sergeant, was now allowed to grow large and bushy. His figure and movements were quick and agile and proclaimed, together with a slight bow in his legs, the old light horseman.

At Shagbrook, indeed, perhaps because of the damp in our walls, he had begun to suffer attacks of rheumatism, that countryman's scourge, yet even when he limped he contrived to seem rather the active smart man suffering from a temporary defect than a middle-aged man declining into the stiff joints of age.

I see him still, proceeding with this rapid limp towards the farm or standing outside the shop—there was but one—in conversation with its owner, grocer G. That talkative and companionable man would never let any prominent citizen pass his door without running forth to hold him in parley. There they are fixed in my mind's eye, G in his apron, clean, part-clean or very dirty, according to the advance of the week, and a bowler of the dashing type he affected, leaning his short back and long neck forward and speaking at great speed with much expression—my father, dressed as usual in breeches and leggings of the smartest cut, relic of his yeomanry and last vanity of an old huzzar, listens as if to a communication of the profoundest importance, grave and alert.

So he would hear the most trifling statement from one of us children and ponder his answer. No one ever gave a child or some timid enquirer more sense of dignity and personal value.

It was not surprising that such a man, at once soldier and prophet, could not be turned from his mission by threats—I will not say that

13

he gloried in persecution, such was not his military character, but I have no doubt he believed it to be the proper consequence of his devotion and God's reward that his flock, which had been somewhat diminished by our move, now began to increase again. Perhaps it is impossible in England for any man of prophetic force to want followers, and some of these new recruits were men of importance: Major Udal, late of the Royal Engineers, from Dollyford, became one of the most devoted faithful, and brought his wife; Mr. Newmarch who farmed four hundred acres near Queensport, one of the biggest farms in the neighbourhood, would drive ten miles on Sunday to hear the word.

I remember this man because it was on his account that I first became aware of difficulties arising for us from my father's mission. For one Sunday he denounced Mr. Newmarch, from his desk, for separating from his wife, and Mr. Newmarch, an enormous red-faced man, got up in the middle of the service and, muttering to himself, left the room.

And after the service when I was standing in the back yard with Richard and Georgina, who had retreated thither to leave the house free for those who wished to consult my father after the service, I heard Richard say to Georgina, "Why had father to come down so upon old Newmarch—now he won't get that job either."

Georgina at eight quite understood the point—I think that I at seven understood it too, for I was instantly attentive and anxious. I had probably heard that Mr. Newmarch, the only big farmer among my father's flock, had promised to recommend him for a foreman's place.

And I knew for the first time the sinking down of the spirit—the sense, as it were, of a momentary interruption of life itself, which comes upon a child at the idea of a parent's danger or incompetence. I was not breathing as I looked from Richard, my wise and kind brother, to Georgina, already a standby, rough but reliable, in every crisis that could not be taken to my mother, who had spent all that January in bed.

And in Georgina's wrinkled brow as in Richard's downcast look

14

and raised brows, I saw the reflections of the same puzzle—how truth and sincerity were to live in the world of men.

Georgina answered that Mr. Newmarch had been cruel to Mrs. Newmarch and that father was quite right to call him to repentance. "You think of Mrs. Newmarch, but you don't think of our own mother," Richard answered, at which Georgina flew into a temper and said that Richard was a liar, she thought more of mother than he did.

Georgina would never hear any criticism of her father, whom she worshipped, but she was just as troubled as Richard by our gloomy prospects. Indeed, she was already helping my mother and knew very well the difficulty of feeding and clothing the family on the few shillings a week earned by my father, and Richard himself, at casual and temporary jobs.

On this occasion my brother's fears were not justified. Mr. Newmarch, whom we thought so gross and selfish, still had some Christianity about him—after only two weeks' absence he returned to the congregation. Moreover, though he never took his wife back and suffered many public rebukes in consequence, he sought to do us good and would bring us some vegetables or even a piece of meat from time to time, all very welcome to our larder.

15

6

How do the hearts of children fly into their eyes at the sight of excellence, of beauty, wisdom, courage, strength. I can know still in a moment the vision of my brother Richard at that time, slim and fair, with a peculiar grace in the poise of his small head on his slender neck. His eyes were dark blue like his mother's, and had the same expression, or rather, expressions, for they were very expressive. Often when he was silent they seemed to speak for him —but they did not say the same kind of thing as my mother's. Hers, for all her reflective habit, responded to an actual world of necessity —she was active with understanding, amusement—no one more instantly appreciated our jokes, however simple. Richard's glances were always tempered by enquiry—he seemed to look out of a private world and ask of ours, what exactly does it all imagine that it is doing?

He seemed to me the wisest person in the world—for my father did not belong to the world, dwelling as he did in quite another dimension—I seized upon and pondered his every word.

Richard was the hope of us all. We thought him a genius, and we were not deceived—many have acknowledged his brilliant quality. Already my parents were half reconciled to our fall because it brought us nearer to the school at Dollyford, so that Richard's journeys to and fro should be shorter. For, like all of us who took after my mother, like my eldest sister Ethel, who died at three, like my sister Ruth and the baby Dorothy, he was very delicate. The old people of the village had already marked him down for an early death. And if he cheated them it was not by his own care, he was an absent-minded boy who never seemed to know whether he was warm or cold. He would, so Georgina said, forget to eat if she did not pester him.

Richard had the best of all we could give him—he was the only

16

one who had a whole suit, unpatched boots. I do not like to think of the sacrifices of my parents to buy him books, but even I understood completely that this was right and necessary. My parents would have held it a sin against God's bounty not to cherish this special gift—Richard's light must not be quenched under a bushel.

The master at Dollyford, a real scholar, greatly excited us at this time by a visit to Shagbrook, only to make our acquaintance and tell us that he hoped to send Richard to Queensport Grammar School on a scholarship, and from Queensport he might even go to Oxford or Cambridge.

This was a rare thing in those days. It was ten years since a Grammar School boy had gone to Oxford—how dejected and alarmed we were when Richard himself said that he would prefer to be a farmer and live at Highfallow again.

"You would never work at a farm," Georgina told him. "You would simply read all night and forget to wash yourself."

Richard made no answer to such sallies from Georgina, he repelled all criticism with the same silence which seemed not so much rude as meditative, as if he had reflected on the answer and found it not worth utterance.

So he would submit without a word when on Saturday, relieving her mother, Georgina would wash his hair, abusing him for getting the soap in his eyes, to cover her own clumsiness and remorse. For next to her father she adored Richard, and she was closer to Richard because he would sometimes talk to her about his plans, even his work. It was through Georgina that we heard usually of Richard's wants—he himself never asked for anything. So we heard from her that he must have a Greek dictionary of his own and there was a second-hand one the master had seen in Lilmouth for only two pounds. Two pounds—it seemed to me a sum beyond imagination. Yet we gathered it and the dictionary was bought.

And this again was partly due to the energy and pertinacity of Georgina. In that spring, Mr. Newmarch, seeking to do us good or, perhaps, trying to make his peace with my father, recommended Georgina to his friend, the grocer G, as a useful assistant.

This man was probably the richest in the village, richer certainly

17

in money than our other magnate, Mrs. Coyte. He was an old sailor, a man of about my father's age, of middle size with unusually long arms and legs, very thin and hollow-chested so that he looked weak and puny. In fact he was very strong and had been a great wrestler and pole jumper—twice champion of the whole southern moor. He would still follow the hunt, and I have seen him jump streams of eighteen or twenty feet with his pole. He would drink with anyone, but no one ever saw him drunk.

I will call this man G because he bore a name that, in his son, attained to honourable distinction both in public and private affairs.

G was a very popular man throughout the moor, and especially with children. He would take the boys rabbiting with him and show them wrestling holds—he would romp with the girls. He would often give either a ride in his smart high gig to market or a contest of moor sports.

You may wonder how Mr. Newmarch could propose a child of eight for assistant in a shop, but Georgina was then nearly nine and tall for her age. Besides she could read and write and figure, and G was completely illiterate. Up to this time his son Edward had done his accounts, but now Edward, at fourteen, was to help his grandfather in a shop at Tarbiton, and G objected to paying more than a shilling a week for a secretary.

Mr. Newmarch and my mother thought this too little and also wanted fixed hours of work. G, like most of our people, was a hard bargainer—negotiations went on for weeks—it was Georgina herself who decided the issue by going to the shop and proposing to work a week for nothing to show her capabilities. G then offered one and sixpence, a good act because Georgina was ready to take a shilling or even less. She had enjoyed herself at the shop—what child does not enjoy responsible work?

So it was arranged that she should go every morning for an hour, after her housework, to serve in the shop at the busy time, and for an hour in the evening to write accounts and letters.

I see her now as she comes in on Saturday night and silently lays three sixpences on the table before my father. She is blushing with a

18

kind of shamed pride, her peculiar blush, a dark red. She hates to seek his praise—she loves him too much.

"I asked for good ones," she says. My father looks up from his book and murmurs, "Yes, so they are."

But Georgina's wages were not to be despised when my father's own pay was often not more than twelve shillings a week. Richard and I would win a sixpence now and then for bird-scaring or weeding but these gains could not be counted on—they were casual and seasonal.

And already in this new place, we were in the midst of new life. Looking back I wonder at the ease of that passage from our paradise in the hills to the dark three-room cottage in Shagbrook. I remember a sense of deprivation and of contempt for those who rejoiced in our fall. But the memory cannot be separated from these others of triumph and freedom—of Mr. Newmarch coming back to the fold—of Georgina in the shop, not much taller than the counter, explaining confidently to a large fat housewife why rice was dearer that week—of my own first earned shilling, brought to my mother's bedside. I was quite ready to look for praise and I knew where to find it.

But earning was for me a trifling pleasure—I had keener delights. Now at eight, I was at the age of wandering, of enterprise, I was irresistibly attracted to boys, almost any boys, rather than sisters. I ran with a gang. I would spend whole days on the moor with four or five village boys, and a dog, hoping to surprise a rabbit, or shooting at birds with a catapult.

I worshipped for leader a certain young Cran, three years older than myself and a relation of the Coytes, who used to invite him for summer and harvest when he could be useful. He was a London boy, a foreigner, and started among us at that disadvantage, but he conquered this at once by his stories and his ingenious tricks.

It was he who organised our poaching raids and a big foray for apples at a place beyond Dollyford. It was he who taught us to carry out such enterprises at a long way from home where we should not be recognised. It was he who discovered that poached trout could safely be sold in any town at the back door of quite respectable houses. Lawyers and doctors would pay well and ask no questions.

19

Cran was my hero, my joy. Why, you ask? Why did I, a child so carefully brought up, fall under the influence of this trickster, this petty thief? Because, in one word, to defy the law was brave and free. And how I worshipped that master of arts. If I had been asked now whether I regretted Highfallow, I might have been puzzled to remember it. I could not have imagined it without father and mother, brother and sisters, who were here with me.

However wilefully I avoided them now, however I grieved them by my new wild ways, my torn clothes and scratched limbs, my coarseness and loudness of speech, and triumphed in their pain, I was one with them. Even when I was most unaware of them upon some marauding expedition in a distant orchard, I took with me the sense of home as I took my very flesh, and it was my own home where I should find again love and a scrupulous regard for what was good and right. However much in my new exultation of independence I insulted that authority, I rested my very joy of rebellion in it as the puppy, tugging at his mother's ear, exults in confidence that he is not only brave but safe.

7

THIS was a time of increased anxiety for my parents. The foreman at Stonepit, after a quarrel with Mrs. Coyte, suddenly threw up his job and departed from the place, leaving a good post and an excellent cottage empty. Mr. Newmarch, a man of influence and a magistrate, who knew Mrs. Coyte very well, and G, who had joined in many deals with her, at once urged my father upon her.

The support of G was unexpected. It was due apparently to his appreciation of Georgina's services, and even some affection for her. Besides, as an old man of war's man he would come up to my father in the street and discuss such news as reached us from the last campaign—they were the only two service veterans in the place.

Mrs. Coyte, for answer, let it be known that she had kept on my father only to please Paviour, and that she had no intention of putting any nonsense preacher in charge of her farm. The sooner, she said, he was out of Shagbrook, the better, our family had been nothing but a nuisance in the village.

No doubt part of this answer was due to Mrs. Coyte's indignation at receiving any advice from anyone about her business—she was not used, she said, to such a thing. But it would be foolish to suppose that her charge was quite unfounded. We had certainly been a nuisance in the village, no newcomer, much less a preacher, could avoid causing disturbance in a small hamlet of that time and remote place. The rare visitor driving through towards the high tors might think Shagbrook a mean collection of cottages scattered on a hillside, but he would be very wrong—it was a highly complex and delicate balance of personal relations between families and persons, who were obliged to live so close together that the whole of everyone's actions, and almost his thoughts, was open to inspection by all the rest. There was no such thing as privacy, for though a general discretion caused every prudent person to be careful of what he said, in public, each had intimates to whom all was disclosed. Thus everything was known, all scandals circulated continually beneath the smooth surface of mutual caution.

God forbid that I should libel my countrymen, as good and true a people as exist anywhere, I am not describing faults of character but of circumstance—the poverty that deprives, the crowding that degrades, the tensions that wear the nerves. How many gentle considerate souls were tortured day and night by the innocent exuberance of neighbours deaf to noise and blind to dirt.

We had, too, our proportion, not large but momentous, among no more than two hundred persons living in closer quarters than many gaols, of drunkards, queer fish, touchy and quarrelsome people looking, as it is said, for trouble. And some degree of quiet and decency could only be maintained by a reciprocity of obligation and reprisal, a balance of powers in which true charity and fellow-feeling, conscience and self-respect—in short, Christian tradition and example, more or less recognised as such—were mingled with what I must call real politics, a system established over years of trial and error. For instance, we found at once in our new home, with its thin walls, that we had a week-end drunkard next door who amused himself during my father's Sunday services by beating pots, blowing a tin trumpet and howling lewd songs.

Almost everyone in the village strongly disapproved of these actions as not only unneighbourly but blasphemous. Even those who most strongly disliked my father's tenets considered it wrong to interrupt a religious service. But no one cared even to remonstrate with the fellow; he was dangerous in drink and persistent in revenge. He would carry on a feud for years with great enjoyment, resembling thus those elements in all countries which exist only to stir up hatred against others—usually their next-door neighbours—people who compensate personal insignificance by the sense of power given by fomenting strife.

There seemed no cure for a nuisance which threatened to destroy my father's lifework, until the housewife on our other side, a Church of England woman but a good neighbour who had grown much attached to my mother, took the matter in hand.

22

It seemed that she was the possessor of a small Dutch oven in which she was accustomed to cook a piece of meat once a week for the drunkard's old mother at the other end of the village—she did not turn up one week and explained that the son's noise had given her a headache. So by a long and elaborate approach the mother was induced to speak to the son, and the son no longer howled throughout the service but only looked over the hedge with a satirical expression and muttered something about Methodists. He was Church of England and, so he told us, proud of it. What's more, he had been fond of the former tenant and they had gone drinking together.

The whole village was such a tissue of interests that a single foreigner was in fact a disturbing factor, even if he did not preach against drink and lie with his children under the imputation of superiority, pride and education.

A new objection, and perhaps an even more forcible one, against my father in Mrs. Coyte's eyes was that he had lately been asked to act as treasurer to a miners' friendly society set up near Dollyford. This was a common request to a man in my father's position, an evangelical preacher—a natural one to a man who could not only be trusted but could keep accounts. It was made by two leading men among the miners themselves, both members of the congregation. It was my father's obvious duty to accept. But Mrs. Coyte and, indeed, G also, hated anything like a trade union—she remembered, and would remind anyone on any occasion, of the outrages of Captain Swing thirty years before in her own childhood, and even more recent outrages among the cutlers in Sheffield.

My parents were perhaps too patient in face of Mrs. Coyte's wrath against themselves, but in the way of parents less than patient of her charges against us. They were indeed very angry when one day she came to the cottage on her horse and shouted for them to come out, and said that the Nimmos were a disgrace to the place, that I was a thief and that Georgina had nearly knocked her son's eye out.

My father denied the facts with such warmth that the woman rode away in doubt.

Yet her charges had some foundation. Cran and his gang, including myself, had certainly taken rabbits from snares set by her men, and it was quite likely that Georgina had thrown stones at Fred Coyte.

We regarded wild rabbits snared on the moor as the property of the first comer; and as for Fred Coyte, he was a big fat man of twenty-five or thirty well able, we thought, to take care of himself. Moreover, he was a village butt, and so, we children thought, legitimate mark for stones, a creature without rights.

8

I DARESAY you picture my sister Georgina as a little mother, a girl responsible beyond her years, and this was true, though Georgina was not more responsible than other girls in the village of the same, or even younger, age. There was one of seven in sole charge of a bed-ridden grandmother, and very well she fulfilled her task, I have often thought that children seem irresponsible only because they haven't had the chance to show forethought and intelligence.

Georgina had both, but outside the line of her duty she was still a child of ten with a strong taste for amusement of any kind, especially the most active kind of amusement, like shouting, swimming, tig, dancing, fishing and poaching—she had a passionate temper and no fear of anybody. She was perpetually in and out of alliance with the village boys and when she quarrelled with them she claimed the right to fight like a boy, squaring up with her fists and then closing for a fall.

One of her fights at this time caused gossip, even beyond Shagbrook. I tell the story here for nothing could better show my sister's nature as a child and her relation with my father.

Imagine, then, Georgina and me on an autumn morning coming from the shop together. It is Saturday, the wind is blowing, enormous clouds are rolling up the sky, but the sun falling between is still hot and we expect at least a fine morning. All round the brass-coloured moors are splashed with the round brown shadows which run over the crests as if in full and joyful hunt after some unseen quarry.

I have been sent to the shop to meet Georgina, because on the Saturday she will have a heavy bag of groceries and she is just out of bed. Georgina, though so dark and wiry, had lately had influenza, and a touch of pleurisy, and the doctor when he came to see my mother had warned us that the girl was worked beyond her strength.

I had planned that day to be out with our gang. We had meant

25

to use the fine morning for a visit to a warren beyond High Tor with a borrowed net and Fred Coyte's ferret. Cran had promised us that if he could not borrow the ferret, still he would take it. But I, having been ordered to help Georgina who would not be free till at least half past nine, had to stay behind. I understood that this was right, that because of my mother's illness, Georgina had a hard life and so must be helped—on most mornings I swept floors and washed pots and I did not complain. But I was enormously disappointed that morning and Georgina knew it, as she knew most of my moods. So as we came from the shop, each grasping the sack by one side and straining away from each other to hold it up from the road, she fired a mixture of accusations and warnings at me.

"You needn't have come for me—I'm sure I could have done it by myself. I'd rather you'd gone with that nasty Cran—it's something to have you out of the house even if you do come back a mask of dirt."

"Oh, go on, Georgy," I said. "You know you've been bad and father said I was to come for you and the sack."

"Then don't go on glooming at me as if you wanted to bite me—I'm sure you're the crossest boy in the whole moor."

I may say that this exchange would have been quite incomprehensible to a stranger. We children together, and often our father, talked the broadest Devon, or, as Richard called it, moorish. But I deliberately refrain from dialect. I have not chosen anywhere in this record to set people apart by their speech, for that speech was the expression of their feelings, their anxieties, which would only be hidden from you in dialect, and I do not deal with a world divided into classes—of gentry and yokels—but one of human creatures under the same sentence of life, their doom and their delight. My sister and I, tormenting each other on the moor road, were as unhappy as persons of the most refined London accent.

Georgina's fiery pride could never bear to ask a favour, and I as strongly resented the expression of that pride heaped upon my deprivation. I told her she was the cross one, and she answered that she would drop the sack in the road if I did not leave go of it. She would take it herself or not at all.

So almost in tears we staggered along, bound together as much

26

by our anger as our affection and our duty, for neither would give way by doing what the other even pretended to wish.

Shagbrook is divided into two parts by one of the Stonepit fields—the lower cottages in a dip or dent on the hillside where we lived, and an upper larger group scattered over the skyline, at the opposite end from the farm buildings. The shop was placed strategically between the two sections, but still on higher drier ground than Back Lane. The inn, called the Green Man, was lower down and closer to us. So that in going to the shop we passed the inn twice, on our way out and our way back.

As I had gone out, the high road opposite the inn had been, as usual at such an hour in the morning, quite deserted. But now, as Georgina and I came round the slight bend from the shop, we saw outside it a group of Battwell girls just arrived by brake and intending some junket on the moor, or perhaps a local fair. Their brake had suffered some mishap and so they had taken the opportunity while it was put right of having a drink. This was a startling sight to us—the girls were brightly dressed, in their holiday frocks, far more gaudy in colour than anything approved in our parts, and they were drinking beer in the open air and talking together in what seemed to us a very loud and bold manner.

These Battwell girls came from the cloth factory there and were renowned for roughness. Even in the mining villages they were looked upon as rough and they were wont always to travel, as we saw them that morning, in parties of formidable size.

As I look back now, I think that our views were coloured by that feud, by those jealousies which so commonly subsist between neighbouring villages. We of Shagbrook were certainly hereditary enemies of Battwell, and seeing again in my mind's eye that group of brightly dressed noisy girls, with their stout bodies, their red cheeks, and hearing again their shouts of laughter and loud jokes, I think that their sport was innocent enough and their famous roughness little more than the high spirits of country girls on holiday, with a touch of that brutality which belongs to those who, enduring themselves hard conditions of life, do not imagine in others more sensitive feelings.

But at that time both Georgina and I, as Shagbrook children, scorned and hated the factory girls. No doubt our hatred was mixed

27

with fear, for when I saw this group spread across the road from the inn I proposed: "Those are the Battwell girls. Let's go home by the path." This path turned aside from the road before the inn, to follow the edge of the inn paddock into Back Lane, so that by taking it we should have avoided our enemies.

But Georgina answered only in a scornful tone, "I'm not afraid of them," and walked straight forward—I, holding the other side of the sack which held our stores, was obliged to follow.

I do not know now if Georgina deliberately collided with one of the loudest and biggest of the girls. She has always claimed that the weight of the sack and a stone in the road together caused her to stagger. But what I suspect is that Georgina's impulses of aggression were often beyond her control, and that her stumble was due simply to her indignation against those whom she regarded as intruders on our peace and despised for their bright dresses and noisy manners. In any case, the collision took place, the Battwell girl turned round and in a good-natured manner pulled the child's hair, addressed her by the name of rat tails, and advised her to mind where she was going. Georgina instantly dropped her side of the bag and flew at the woman, she managed to knock the pint pot out of her hand, splashing her with beer. The woman then caught her in her left hand and smacked her face, and pushed her away so that she fell. Georgina at once jumped up again and flew to a second attack. Two or three of the women had now turned round. They were laughing and also in a punishing mood. They were well aware of our hostility in Shag-brook. Indeed they had been defying that hostility by the loudness of their laughter and coarseness of their jokes. Probably they looked upon this white-faced, black-eyed little girl, in a sack apron, as a moor-land savage who needed to be taught a lesson. One of them seized Georgina by the arm and the other, the original victim, smacked her face on each side alternately. This was a cruel punishment. The smacks were those swinging blows given by an expert—Georgina's own furious struggles, with face turned aside, perhaps exposed her to unintended damage—but, in a moment, her eyes were closed and the blood was running down her lips. Yet, when again the girls pushed her away, she rushed at them blindly trying to beat them with her fists and claw them with her fingers.

9

GEORGINA had always claimed the status of a boy. She fought like a boy—it was understood that she must fight alone and unsupported. For this was the rule—if Richard or I had gone to help her even when she was overmastered, then all the boys of the village would have descended upon us to vindicate our laws of war, and Georgina herself would have been more infuriated by our intervention even than by the most humiliating defeat. But the same laws of war now entitled me to go to Georgina's help—so as soon as the second girl caught Georgina by the arms, I also flew to battle. But as I was not only much lighter even than Georgina, and also, I suspect, so terrified that I scarcely knew what I was doing, I was swept at once into the ditch with one careless swing. Georgina was now thrust down on top of me and held there by the big girl who now seemed both puzzled and remorseful—she kept on asking her companions what she was to do with the little ——.

At last, to the great relief, I think, of the Battwell girls as well as ourselves, a certain labourer, a neighbour of ours called Sam Weaver, a tall and powerful man, came by and asked with some indignation what they were doing with us, and heard the story. It was corroborated sufficiently by the beer on the girl's frock, and scratches not only on her hands and cheek but on the hands of the girl who had held her. Sam, a just man, then apologised for Georgina, tucked her under his arm, picked up the sack in the other hand and conveyed both away, not to our cottage, for, as he said, he would not pester that poor sick woman with her bad children, but a hundred yards further to the Coytes' stables where he judged my father would be found.

There was reproach as well as pity in the tone of good Sam Weaver when he spoke of my mother as pestered with bad children. For it was held by most people in Shagbrook that our parents spoilt us. My father, for instance, had never yet beaten any of us under the strongest complaint.

29

And this was an extraordinary thing at that time when children, both boys and girls, were beaten for quite small offences as a right and proper thing, for it was a punishment directly enjoined by Scripture.

No one can estimate the power of authority among poor and uneducated people in a world whose problems confuse even the wisest. I have heard the roughest quote the Bible as warrant for their action and their thought.

But also there was scarcely any other sanction open to our cottage parents. They could not deprive their children of pocket money because most of them had none, and beating was a punishment that could be graded from a random cuff administered with some half-joking objurgation, through a hard smack, to a formal slippering and finally execution with strap or whip, which could be of a cruelty commensurate with any crime.

Sam Weaver, occasional attender with our congregation, was convinced, like the rest of Shagbrook, that Georgina was a limb of Satan who urgently needed correction. I was commanded to follow behind as part sharer in the guilt, and so I saw and heard the charge delivered. Sam planted my sister, a truly miserable object with her swollen bloodstained face, her mud-covered clothes, before my father and related the crime.

My father was harnessing the waggon. The corn stacks were still out and as the weather seemed to threaten a break it had suddenly been decided that morning to bring them in for threshing. Diamond and Pearl were already chained to the pole, and as we entered the yard my father was in the act of hooking the trace. With his long whip in his hand he stood listening in silence to the tale, which ended with Sam's proposal that Georgina should there and then receive a proper hiding and be taken back to tell those Battwell girls that she was sorry.

Georgina, like my father, uttered no word until the end of this speech, when she screamed out suddenly that she would not speak to those —— ——, using words so bad that Sam uttered an exclamation of surprise and disgust.

30

Do not think him prim and priggish. All of us knew all the words, how could we help it in that close community?

But the good and evil conduct, good and bad words, stand much more luridly before village eyes. A foul-mouthed oaf, a drunken labourer lying in a drain, a beaten wife with blackened eyes and torn clothes, cannot be made romantic to a child who sees how other children suffer from bad-tempered parents, from drunken fathers or termagant mothers.

"There, Mr. Nimmo," said Sam Weaver to my father, "you see what it is, she has grown real wicked—it is beyond anything, I wouldn't like to say it isn't too late already."

But my father propped his whip against the wall, sat down on a bucket, and asked Georgina in a stern but reasonable tone what had come over her to do and say such things.

Georgina made no answer, holding herself rigid with clasped hands and looking her most sullen. Yet I could see her arms quivering at her side, making her apron shake.

But Georgina would shake with rage as well as fright. I daresay she herself could not tell what made her do so at the moment.

My father looked at her for some time with a perplexed air, and asked her then if she did not think she ought to be beaten when she was so wicked and so sullen. When she did not answer he shook his head and said, "Ah, my poor Georgy. So that old devil is back within 'ee after all our prayers—and worse than ever."

And when Georgina remained silent, locked in her pride, he sighed and said that still he knew how she had tried to fight that devil and so he could not find it in his heart to beat her. In the name of Jesus who had put grace into her heart before when she was at her wickedest, he would pray again for her poor soul. So let her kneel down with him and they would pray together.

My father was such a believer as you do not meet in these days, perhaps not in all the land. For he had lived in the idea and the very knowledge of God's presence all his life. Even as a young soldier in India he had carried his Bible, a thing not so uncommon in those days when the colonels of regiments would take the service and preach to their men.

31

To him the battle in Georgina's heart between the devils of her temper and her passions, and the grace of God's love, was as real as any fight upon a fair day.

Georgina stood stiff and unrelenting, but the nervous shake in her arms had now communicated itself to her body, she was quivering all over like a plucked string, and my father said, "Ah Sam, see how it shakes the poor little maid, her soul is all torn with the fight." And he drew her aside and knelt down on some sacks next the wall, and suddenly before he could speak, Georgina gave a cry and threw herself down on the ground and caught him round the ankles. She was weeping so violently that her body seemed to jump on the stones.

My father said, "There, there, now, he's out of 'ee, it is all over. Take your time, my dear, and don't be frightened."

And he stroked her head and made those noises with which he would soothe a frightened young horse or filly foal.

I think perhaps that my father's method with Georgina, which was less the fruit of method than conviction, was the only one which would have kept that stormy and impulsive spirit within bounds. For she dreaded nothing so much as his displeasure, and a few words of reproof from him would bring her to repentance that no violence, no defeat, could wring out of her pride.

When he told her then to go back with Sam Weaver and apologise to the Battwell girls, she rose obediently and took Sam's hand.

But perhaps it was lucky that the brake had been mended and the girls had gone, for though my father would always assure Georgina that her devil had left her, it was always liable to return again at a moment's notice. As I say, away from her duty she was still a child and had little foreknowledge or self-control.

10

THIS was not the last of Georgina's scrapes. Not many days afterwards she took a fancy one midday to join with a certain ragamuffin friend or hanger-on of Richard's, a boy called Wilson, to ride into Tarbiton, twelve miles away on the shores of the Longwater.

It was with something like stupefaction that I saw her mounting a bagman's gig just outside the inn. I called out to her, "Where are you going, Georgy?" Her only answer as she sat holding Wilson round the waist with one hand and the gig rail with the other was to toss her hair at me and make a face meaning, "I don't care what you say."

She was not seen again till twelve o'clock at night and her only excuse was that the bagman had promised to bring them both back again. Privately she let me know that Wilson had offered to show her wonders in Tarbiton, which had turned out to be only a two-headed calf dead in a back yard, "Just what you'd expect from Will Wilson— I never could bear the nasty dirty boy. I always hated him."

But I thought that Wilson had had little to do with the matter, that Georgina's accusations against him were due to nothing but jealousy, for she did not need anyone to tempt her to go wandering when the fit seized her.

Wandering, seeing the world, was a passion with us both, but Georgina, characteristically bold, had already promised herself a voyage to China. G had fired her with his stories of the beauties of that country, especially the silks and satins of the ladies' dresses. About this time Georgina obtained from the shop a Chinese picture from a tea packet, and from somewhere else, she would not tell us where, a fragment of embroidery on red silk. These were her greatest treasures—nothing made her more furious against us than a slight cast upon them or anything Chinese.

But whatever the impulses of wandering drove my sister to climb on a bagman's gig and be carried recklessly away from her family and work, or to imagine voyages to China, soon after the flight to Tarbiton and the sea her responsibilities were suddenly increased. My mother who had till now always been able to supervise the work of the house, became too weak to do more than move from her bed to a chair. It was indeed surprising that she lived so long, for she had not only her illness to contend with, but ceaseless anxiety for us all, for what Sam Weaver had called her bad children.

And it is true that we had run wild and that no reproaches from her and from my father, no resolutions on our part, would keep us steady. Richard, Georgina and myself had all been thrown suddenly by what I might call the social revolution of our lives into an alien and a critical world. The wise Richard did not resent his lot. But he used his wits to escape from it, and his escape was into new friend-ships at his school, a new enlargement of thought and ambition, a new reserve in his own family. His mother felt the growing distance be-tween them, and could not but be fearful for this clever and wilful boy, now thirteen, who claimed already the right to order his own existence.

As for Georgina and myself, we were backsliders of the common type, and yet it was always a surprise to me to find myself a nuisance. The urge to fly out of Shagbrook away from grown-up observation in the delightful company of Cran was too strong for a lad of my age.

And though I was now sent regularly to school with Richard, I would play truant almost at will and without discovery. For Richard would never tell on me, and the school authorities were far too busy and worried to report me. Besides, even if I asked leave of absence, I could always obtain it on the ground that I was needed at home or to help in some necessary farm work. There were boys of twelve and more in Shagbrook who had never been to school at all, and these were not always children of parents who hated schools, but simply of very poor or sick people who needed their services and earnings. Most of our families were too poor to do entirely without their children's earnings—one reason why I was now free to go to school was that my earnings were no longer considered so important to our budget. For at the beginning of this year, Mrs. Coyte had sud-denly promoted my father to foreman and given him the foreman's cottage, not only a much superior dwelling to any in the Back Lane, larger and drier, but possessing a large garden behind, where vegetables could be grown.

The reason of this action by our mistress was not apparent and she gave none. Like other persons accustomed to absolute rule, she seemed to enjoy doing even a kind and good deed in an arbitrary manner—perhaps in order to maintain a certain atmosphere of helplessness and terror in the dependent. So she had no credit from us for what was a good deed—good from the point of view that she need not have gone to the expense, for she had had my father's services, a foreman's services at a hind's wages, for more than a year, and my father in his difficult position would have been glad to continue in the same way.

Fred Coyte indeed, her son, claimed the credit for her benevolence, and Fred had recently begun to frequent my father—several times when his mother was away on a Sunday he had even slipped in to hear a service, he would sit at the back near the door with his usual sly foolish grin on his face. Richard would say that this great oaf came only to annoy his mother and understood nothing of the sermons, but my father declared that on the contrary he was very intelligent, and was especially good at following the argument for a Second Coming.

But we knew that my father could seldom see any fault in one of his disciples, and as for Fred's claim that he had persuaded his mother to do, as he said, the fair thing by him, the whole village knew that Fred loved to boast—indeed he was one of those leaky vessels who would tell all his thoughts and troubles to anybody.

So he told how his mother smacked him for smoking and how she would send him to bed without supper. For Mrs. Coyte still treated this six-foot man of thirty as a small boy and would claim that he was not fit to be trusted.

We doubted Fred's boast, and yet I believe it was partly true that his mother had been moved as much by his representations and his attachment to my father as by her own conscience. For she not only loved Fred—he was her chief treasure—she was a conscientious woman, well known for fair dealing and truthful speech.

35

My father's rise of pay was timely—we needed every penny to pay for the port wine and arrowroot which were then thought specific to my mother's illness.

No one nowadays can conceive the ravages of consumption in our country districts, there were few families in Shagbrook who had not lost members by it. One gaunt old woman living alone in Back Lane was the last survivor of a family of eight, a sister, two brothers, her husband and four children. I daresay all of us were touched by the infection. Georgina and I were both wont to suffer mysterious temperatures, my younger sister Ruth, who was acknowledged to be in danger, would be kept in my mother's bedroom for weeks at a time in cold or misty weather.

This was before the days when consumptives were sent to the mountains—warmth, not cold, was the accepted cure. So one of the daughters of a local magnate, Lord Slapton, had been sent the year before, after the birth of her first baby, to Italy. I cannot say now if her illness was truly tuberculosis, or merely some form of anaemia combined with cough and fever, but it was accepted then that she had had the same distemper as killed dozens every year in our villages. We certainly understood that if we had been able to send my mother to the South of France she could have been saved.

But not my father, not one of us children, except perhaps Georgina, even perceived this difference as an injustice. So that when Georgina suddenly exclaimed one day after the doctor's visit that his medicine was no good, the only proper medicine was some money so that "mother can go to France and be properly warm and drink plenty of wine," we stared at her in surprise. And before we could reflect on her meaning our father said shortly, in the common phrase, that wishes never put shoes on a horse or meat in the pot.

And then as if he had suddenly understood the desolation in our minds, and that deep question and anger half articulate in Georgina's exclamation, he raised his head from his book and said in a stern manner, "It is not for us to question the work of Providence, the Lord gives and He takes away. You did not earn yourself, Georgy, and you would have no right to cry if you were crooked."

Georgina, as often when she was reproved, muttered to herself and

36

turned pale. Then she went suddenly out to the yard, and we heard her for some time scouring her pots and banging them about with such vigour that it was a wonder she did not break them, iron as they were.

And this, even in our grief, amused us. Richard smiled covertly at Ruth. I daresay I felt, too, that secret satisfaction which affects one who is calm even when his calmness is not a merit.

But even Georgina, though she felt so strongly the want of money which deprived her mother of the chance of life, was not embittered against those who had it. We were not an envious nor a resentful community. I think none of us as children felt malice against those richer than ourselves, much less against the wealthy. The real rich belonged to a world as strange and romantic to us as fairy tales. We had perhaps even less desire to enter that strange and elaborate world than hope. No one in the village seemed even to resent the predominance of our richer neighbours, the Coytes, and the grocer whom I have called G. We discussed his sharp practice and his extravagances, but without rancour, and my hatred of the Coytes was a personal feud. I did not hate them and rob young Coyte's snares because they were richer, but because Mrs. Coyte had, in the common phrase, set down my mother before me and made me feel humiliation and fear.

There was a time within the next years when the hatred of social injustice and of the fearful inequalities of our society became an obsession with me and Georgina, a pressure that tormented us even in our dreams. And more than half a century has passed before I have reached again the deeper wisdom of my father in his simplicity. "The Lord provides and the Lord taketh away," and that profound saying, so characteristic of him in its homely penetration, "You did not earn yourself, Georgy, you would have no right to cry if you were crooked."

11

My mother had been ill for more than two years when she died, and at the end she was wasted to a fearful thinness. Yet her death which had been so long in our fears struck us with the force of unexpected and overwhelming disaster. She was conscious to the last, and so we saw in her that anxiety which had lain upon her for years grow to agonising intensity. A mother who leaves behind her young children cannot but feel a fearful apprehension. Who could dare to estimate the depth of her longing, the earnestness of her prayer as she looked from her death bed on our five alarmed faces and asked God to watch over us—to watch, how much understanding of a child's daily need is concentrated in those five letters.

I say we were alarmed as we stood at the bedside of our dying mother. But that is a poor description of the panic in our souls, the sudden knowledge of tragedy that cannot be remedied, and our mother's helpless anguish—the sense already impending over us of that new dangerous world without her love that was opening now before us like the wilderness before some band of exiles.

I cannot forget the look of confusion on my young sister's face as she stood beside me supporting herself by the bedclothes. At eighteen months she had only just begun to stand, and she would crawl to my mother's bedside and pull herself up and clamour to be taken in by her side.

But now, even in her infant mind, bewilderment as it seemed was mixed with misgivings so deep that she did not even cry. She stood gazing at her mother's face with round surprised eyes which asked the questions she could not form of her who could not answer her own.

Though she stretched out her arms, she did not complain that she was not noticed. It seemed that she understood, however vaguely and uncertainly, that my mother, as she lay too weak to raise her head, could neither see her nor respond.

As my father began a prayer for the soul passing in its agony, and we, terrified, fell on our knees, the baby still reached out her hands to her and made the gesture of climbing which was only the habit of her childhood repeated in this trance of wonderment.

They say that among African tribes the death of a mother means almost certainly the death of any child under three. I do not suppose that among the English poor, even in those days, this was always the case, but certainly the chances of survival among babies of Dorothy's age were much lessened, and Dorothy began to fail almost from the day of my mother's death.

She was not neglected. The two elder girls did their best for her. My father showed her especial affection for her mother's sake, but she pined. Where can one find a profounder desolation than in the poor child who has lost its mother? For with all our goodwill, the baby had to be left much alone. My father was away often before dawn. Richard and I were at school, and when we were not at school we were pursuing eagerly our own lives of exploration and dream. Ruth, at nine, was now doing much of Georgina's rough work about the cottage, for Georgina had to earn at the farm as well as the shop. We were deep in debt, not only after the long illness, but to pay for the funeral.

It was, I think, five years before we paid off the funeral expenses. My father loved and honoured my mother too deeply to give her a cheap funeral.

Do you tell me that funeral expenses are the curse of the poor everywhere on earth, that they are wasteful and unnecessary, that they are the price of foolish ostentation and a display that is less an evidence of grief than a vulgar travesty of those pompous obsequies where no grief is?

I have thought so and said so myself. In my fourteen years as a preacher of the gospel, I held forth many times to this very purpose—after half a century the words come again to my lips: ostentatious folly, a mockery of the dead.

I had not asked myself then why, throughout all the world, a family

39

may still spend all they have, and more, on the funeral of a parent, wife or husband; I had not asked myself, in short, why mankind, even the humblest, set certain responsibilities of the soul, certain duties of the heart, above expense, even when that expense may bring them years of real want—and why, too, those who know how to honour goodness and truth in their hearts feel it laid upon them to make those reverent feelings known.

I have never known a man less inclined to ostentation than my father. He was, if anything, as we shall see, too indifferent to the opinions of others, too independent in his living. The sum he spent, largely on credit, on my mother's funeral was not only his statement before the world that my mother was worthy of honour, but also, in the mysterious domain of our spiritual life, an act of gratitude and worship towards the dead. And how better to measure that gratitude than by a personal sacrifice?

My sisters, working ten or more hours a day from childhood, never found any fault with an expenditure which condemned them to years of scraping.

Yet that cost, too, weighed upon the youngest, who did not know what obligation was. When both the girls were out earning they left her with a neighbour, kind enough but equally busy, and she could not comprehend this new world; she died within five months, according to the doctor of pneumonia, but truly I think of a loss that could not be repaired—the company of those she loved.

12

DEBT, this was the terror that overshadowed all my childhood. For the poor it is a fearful risk, they stand always close to the precipice. To do G. justice, he was not a hard creditor. But for his own security he could not allow a bill to run beyond a week or two. All our savings and more had gone on the funeral—we looked anxiously for any means to earn a few shillings.

It was now that Georgina began to do housework at the farm—she was delighted when Fred said that he needed her help at the market stall.

Mrs. Coyte, though ranking as a big farmer, did not consider it beneath her dignity to keep a market stall, but once the stall had been set up she preferred to gossip or march about the town square looking at other people's wares rather than to sell. This duty now fell largely to Georgina.

But these earnings, with the occasional shilling that I could gather on days when I played truant from school, barely paid current expenses and could not reduce our debt.

Georgina's watchfulness of expense, so unnatural to her impulsive and rather reckless character, led to continual quarrels. She was not only too young for such cares, but she was in the difficult position of all such elder sisters who have to take a mother's place without a mother's natural authority. Even with the polite and reasonable Richard she had differences, the more bitter because she was so fond of him.

One of these quarrels had a serious consequence. It began one evening on the subject of candles. We had been sitting by the fire to use its light, Richard on a stool, which obliged him to hold his book high and bend his head sideways in a very uncomfortable manner; I upon the floor with a slate and a hard pencil whose every scratch caused Richard to raise his eyebrows; Georgina crouched down on the hearthstone sewing with quick impatient stitches. Georgina hated sewing and did it badly—and hated to do it badly. And perhaps some of her exasperation in this troublesome duty invaded her voice when she suddenly asked Richard if he had not better do some of his Greek instead of reading that silly story as he had been doing all the week.

The silly story was, I think, one of Scott's romances—Richard at that time was fond of Scott.

Richard made no answer and seemed not to have heard. Yet as my pencil skreeked again—his own name for the sound—his fine eyebrows flickered again, though without any other change in his calm absorbed expression.

We all knew that he had heard Georgina's protest. She frowned angrily, but he had all my sympathy.

Both Richard and I resented her attitude towards our work, we did not acknowledge her right to drive us to our books, though, in fact, on that very evening I had been obliged to bring her my sums because I could not understand them, and because the mistress at Dollyford had begun to pick me out for questions and make me look foolish if I could not answer them.

This too, though I did not know it then, was Georgina's doing, for she had leagued herself on some visit to Dollyford with this woman to keep an eye both on Richard and myself. It isn't surprising perhaps that when we discovered this it made us furious with Georgina. We called it a sneaking act and asked what right had Georgina, who could not even make a good pie, to govern over us.

For you must understand, in some excuse for our attitude, that Georgina was by no means an efficient or careful housekeeper. In some ways she was more childish, more slapdash, more impatient than Ruth, three years her junior. It was Ruth whom we relied on when anything was mislaid, or when we had any special commission at the shop. She had an extraordinary memory and great neatness of hand. Georgina at that time would break off in the middle of one task when she remembered another, and leave them both half done. And she was still capable in the middle of almost any duty of rushing out of the house to see a dogfight, or the hunt passing down the road to a meet, or even a strange carriage.

42

Her severity in fact was more like that of a child who hectors other children in a game than that of the housemistress who insists on tidiness and punctuality for everyone's convenience.

Georgina herself was not tidy, and yet she demanded tidiness in us, and we thought to see in this demand, as in all her authority, an imitation of her mother. I daresay, indeed, that Georgina did copy her mother, without the gentleness. What other model had she? It did not strike us that, in making rules after our mother's pattern, she had the same purpose of our welfare.

On this evening therefore, while I sat in the firelight with my slate while Georgina instructed me in simple division, I was not less exasperated than she, and showed it in my drawling tone and slow responses.

She took my slate and spat upon it and wiped out my figures with the top of her stocking, telling me to start again and write so that my figures looked like figures and not like Shag wood after the fire. Then, as she handed it back to me, she said to Richard, "I don't care if you don't get a scholarship, so don't think it. It's only father who might be disappointed."

Richard again made no sign—he turned a page and his eyes flew along the lines.

Richard was often seized with such idle fits, when it seemed that he could not lay a book down, when for days together he would be absorbed in some tale and would even play truant to go on with it. But only I knew of the truancy because we went to school together. When Richard wanted to read in peace he would go to the dockside in Tarbiton where our mother's cousin, a marine store dealer, allowed him the run of his loft full of ships' lanterns, and coils of rope, bolts of sailcloth and swinging chains of blocks.

Georgina did not know of Richard's truancies, but she knew well every one of his moods, and when he had an idle fit she always told him so. For her he was a genius, the hope of the family, and she could not bear to see him waste his time. The result was that Richard, who would never quarrel with anyone if he could help it, avoided her.

He got up now, after a suitable pause, and Georgina said in an angry voice, "All right, if you don't want to stay with us I am sure we don't want you." Richard made no answer to this, but turned away and made for the stairs.

Our new cottage not only stood by itself in its own ground, it was much larger than the old. The kitchen, which filled the whole ground floor, was quite eighteen feet long—it was lighted by two windows in front and one behind. At one end there was an open staircase, at the other the large chimney breast projected some way into the room, making two recesses on either side. Cupboard doors, flush with the walls of the chimney, hid these recesses by day in which there were two built-in bed-places, mine and Richard's. At the north end of the room the staircase slanted across the wall through the beams of the ceiling, which was unplastered. There was a trapdoor to cover the opening, as not uncommonly in old cottages, but it stood open for weeks together.

Above there were three rooms, of which one, the largest, was my father's, and the other two opening into each other belonged to the girls.

The girls had, therefore, what was then the rare luxury of rooms and beds to themselves, but this was due chiefly to the fact that neither of their minute apartments was big enough for more than a cot. In the same way, Richard and I enjoyed separate bunks in spite of the extra expense for bedclothes, because our beds were too narrow to hold us both.

Richard's books, clothes, all his private belongings, were kept in two deep drawers under this bunk, and two shelves above, so that he had no reason now to go upstairs. But since my mother's death he had formed a very close alliance with Ruth, and so when he wanted to read by himself he would take refuge in her room.

"Go and spoil yourself if you want to," Georgina called after him, "but you have no right to use the candles."

Richard, perhaps because he hated quarrelling, would fly out at those who forced a quarrel on him, and now from the level of the ceiling, stooping down his head to make himself heard under the beams, he answered in his usual conversational tone, "At least they are not G's candles—I wouldn't use any of the things he gives you."

These words seemed to startle Georgina very much. She sat for a

44

moment and then answered in a fierce and threatening tone, "You don't mind eating his jam and bacon though, nor his sugar and bread."

Richard said that he had thought we paid for such things.

"We will when we can," Georgina said. "You thought—you never think how we manage."

"I think how people say we manage," Richard said.

Georgina then threw down her sewing and flew across the kitchen. This surprised me very much, for I did not understand the implications of Richard's speech. But Georgina had understood at once, and I have seldom seen her so enraged.

Georgina, as I realise now, as any man can realise who has had a daughter, was at that age when girls are a strange mixture of the child and the woman. Sometimes all woman, sometimes all child, and sometimes, in a more perplexing way, both at once. So that the childish playmate looked at one suddenly with a woman's eyes; and the woman in the act of showing a woman's thoughtfulness suddenly, as if to mock her own gravity, played some childish trick. With Georgina these alternations were unusually violent, partly I daresay because of her headlong nature, and partly because of the new burden that she was carrying.

Georgina was already isolated among us. As a child not yet twelve she was shut out from all our councils. Richard whom she loved so much was Ruth's friend, and I, too, confided in Ruth when I told anything of my mind within the family. And Ruth, reserved, gentle, delicate like Richard, already very pretty and much pitied by the village, even by Mrs. Coyte, had never been at ease with her impulsive and temperamental sister.

Georgina had felt her solitude, for great bitterness was expressed in her remark, "Very well, go away from us if you like." She was too proud to say "from me," but that was what she meant, and that was the jealous thought that burned in her soul.

And now as she rushed down the kitchen she seemed in a frenzy of rage, and screamed at the top of her voice something to the effect that she was not afraid of G or anybody, and that she would kill Richard. Georgina in a temper would often threaten to kill people, but now there was something terrifying in her anger.

45

Richard had already gone through the trap. He now closed it after him and stood upon it, but Georgina beat upon it with her fists and kept on screaming that it was lies about G, that Richard would not get away from her, she would wait for him and then she would kill him.

She did not stop till some minutes later my father came in and asked sternly what was going on. My father, so patient and self-controlled, was severe upon any of us who showed a lack of self-control, especially upon Georgina. He saw in what he called her devil the chief danger to her peace and welfare.

"What are you doing?" he asked. "What is this about G—what has Dick said to you?"

13

My father had never lost his temper with us, never beaten us, but we had for him that feeling often described as fear, which is something quite different and far deeper than alarm. It was that sense which, without irreverence, I have thought to find expressed by the great evangelists when they speak of the fear of God. One does not fear God because he is terrible, but because he is literally the soul of goodness and truth, because to do him wrong is to do wrong to some mysterious part of oneself, and one does not know exactly what the consequence may be.

So we feared my father. And so Georgina, hanging upon the rail of the stair, sobbing with rage, gazed at him as at an apparition of the Judgment.

My father called out loudly, "Who is up there? Open the trap, come down at once." And when Richard and Georgina had come down to the floor and stood before him he asked them, "What is all this, what was it you said, Georgy?" And then when they stood silent he turned to me and asked me why they were fighting like beasts that perish.

And as I did not truly understand the cause of Georgina's rage, I thought to make things easier for all parties by telling part of the truth, "It was only the candles."

"Candles," my father said, "what about candles?"

"I was going to read by a candle," Richard said.

"What did I hear about G?" my father said. And then taking Georgina by a shoulder he said to her abruptly, "What has G been doing to you?"

"Nothing, father."

"But I heard his name. Did you not say that you were not afraid of G? Why should you be afraid of G?"

Georgina hesitated a moment looking up at her father, and then

47

answered that she had said nothing about G. She spoke as a child speaks when suddenly resolved to tell a lie, with a gulp and a rush.

My father seemed taken aback by the lie. He paused a moment before he answered, "Then my ears deceived me, for I heard those very words, and I never thought, Georgy, you would tell me a lie. That has never been the way of your wickedness, that is why I have hoped for your salvation. I knew there was truth in your soul."

I had never seen Georgina so pale, and her chest was heaving now as if she would weep, but she did not answer. My father put his hand on her head and said, "Tell me the truth and I'll unhear that lie. Come, my poor maid, you are never afraid of the truth. What is this about G? Has he done anything unfit to be told? If it is unfit to be told, it is unfit to be borne too. I will take 'ee away from that shop."

But Georgina answered that she had said nothing about G, that G had done nothing to her. And then, apparently quite composed, went to fetch my father's supper.

My father seemed too much astonished by this effrontery, and the girl's sudden recovery of her nerve, to say anything more. But he kept on looking at Georgina during the whole evening, and at our evening prayers he prayed for Georgina by name that she should be saved from the lie in her soul. For, he said, "If we do not own to ourselves that we are guilty before God and not fit to stand in His presence, if we deceive ourselves, then we have the lie in our soul. The lie which feeds on the spirit as maggots feed on a dor beetle till all is hollow, black and empty within a painted shell."

At prayers each of us knelt at our own chair, and afterwards we would say good-night. But on this night Georgina got up quickly from prayers and went away without wishing us good-night. I daresay she was weeping, or if she did not weep she would not dare to speak or show her face in case she was caused to do so.

The next day she seemed as usual, only I thought a little paler, a little more impatient, and nothing more was said by any of us about that tremendous lie. I daresay even my father understood that Georgina had some reason for it and was suffering for it. It would be tempting to say that that battle with my father changed Georgina from a child to a woman, at least in spirit. That the woman's anxiety about household bills, about feeding her family, forced upon her a decision far beyond her years, to bear with G as long as she could. And that like a grown woman she perceived too that she must make a decision alone. That her men, even her father and her own brothers, would not understand the situation as she did.

It would be tempting, but it would not be true. No one grows up in a moment under any stress that I have known in a very full life. I have thought even to see the traces of the child in one of Her Majesty's Cabinet Ministers not far short of seventy years of age. It was many years before Georgina could be called a complete woman.

But that decision taken so suddenly, and supported with a resolution so astonishing in a child, did profoundly affect Georgina. It changed her relation with her father. She had always worshipped him—that is, her love for him had been quite unlike her devotion to Richard. For Richard she had a brooding maternal love, mixed with a younger sister's admiration, and also with a sister's critical anxiety. But up till now she had never dreamed of criticising any of my father's least words or acts, there was between them a tie so close that it seemed a wish of my father's became at once Georgina's without passage through her brain.

But from this time he became to her a person who, like ourselves, sometimes needed to be handled, managed, who could not be trusted to know his own advantage.

All of us were aware of this change, we would see Georgina looking at our father with an anxious doubtful expression as if wondering what was going on in his mind—if he looked then at her, she would colour and turn away her eyes. She did not forget, neither of them forgot, all their lives, that immense lie that had come between them.

Now, too, she studied his needs with a tenderness of which we had not thought her capable. She had been, and still was to us, a slapdash housekeeper; for him she was tidy and careful. She took trouble to see that he had what he liked to eat, that his clothes were mended and weather-proof, she became like a wife to him.

Yet like a wife, as we soon saw, she was still firm in her own line of conduct when she thought it justified by family duty. For in another few weeks, just after her twelfth birthday, she suddenly declared her intention of leaving the shop and taking up work at the inn, the Green Man. This inn, our only inn, was kept by G's wife, Bella.

Bella G was a very handsome woman, tall, dark, with the face, so Richard said, of a Roman empress—a woman born to rule, that is to say, superbly indifferent to the clamour as well as the admiration of the crowd.

And who shall say that her strength was wasted? How many of those who knew her, how many who passed only once through her bar, got from her a new impression of the dignity which belongs to the morally fearless—to those who will not bow to the mob, who are not seduced even by the cry of the fashionable rebel. It is such impressions, much more than any exhortation, which turn the soul that is already half lost between disgust at conventional paths and the bewilderment of the trackless moor back to the dusty high road of common obligation.

Mrs. G was the only daughter of a shopkeeper, a well-off man in Tarbiton, and remained always a stranger in our village, an enigma of the moor. She made no friends among us, and did not attempt it. Speaking to us, and even to her husband, she had the brisk manner, the sharp, cool look of an official who does his duty because it is a duty. Her friends were in Tarbiton where she visited often. Yet she was attentive in the beer-house where she was absolute ruler of the bar. No one was heard even to swear in the presence of Mrs. G. This strangely assorted couple had one son, Edward, who at a later time was my chief friend. But he was then very shy and awkward, but also capable of the boldest feats. He would be seized with fits of daring when he would astonish us by climbing some sheer crag or invading some guarded orchard known to be highly dangerous to boys. I need not say that such orchards were not Mrs. Coyte's. Village boys do not steal in their own village. Young Edward G, though six years older than myself, was still a follower where I led, and still more where Georgina led. It is not too much to say that he adored my sister and, indeed, his most dangerous feats were accomplished in an admiration of her own and to win her applause, and she would praise him more than any of us. She understood this nervous anxious boy better than any of us who despised his weakness and his timidity. She would say

50

that he would be a great man when we were nothing, and she would point out that if he said he would do a thing, it would always be done at any cost or danger.

But Edward was despised by his own father and coldly treated by his mother. I am convinced that this strange woman passionately loved her only child, but for that very reason she could not bear his ugliness and his timid ways. She showed him no affection because she wanted to make him bold and free like his father.

Yet she was virtually separated from G. She was never seen in the shop, and G was never seen in her bar. And as she was helping her father in the Tarbiton grocery as well as keeping the beer-house, she spent three or four nights a week away from the village.

We had not supposed that Georgina had so much as spoken to this woman when she proposed to work for her. But Mrs. G herself now paid a stately visit to my father and asked for her services, offering five shillings a week, which was a shilling more than she was receiving at the shop, indeed high pay for her age. Besides, Georgina was to be paid all in cash instead, as often at the shop, more than half in goods.

14

One Monday morning in spring Georgina, instead of going to the shop, mixed a bucket of limewash and set about the annual whitening of the cottage. She seemed in high spirits and allowed me to help in a task that every child enjoys, telling me only not to splash the windows.

I presumed like all the family that G had given her a holiday; what was our surprise to see G, in his bowler and a clean apron, coming down the road at this time in the morning. My father, who had stopped in his cart to admire our work and advise a little more blue in the mixture to give the true dazzling effect, gazed like us.

G, with his peculiar slouch and grin, came up to us, nodded at the wall as if approving the colour, and said then, "An't you coming to-day, Jo?"

"No," Georgina answered, dipping her brush.

"Look at that now," G said, grinning at us. "She takes a holiday just as she pleases."

"It's not a holiday—I'm not coming any more," Georgina said. "I told you on Saturday."

G appealed to us again, "She's obstinate in her tempers, your Jo."

Georgina then turned on the man and said, "It's not temper and I'm not coming. So go along now."

And when G went on saying that it was silly of her to be so obstinate, she took up the bucket of wash and threatened to throw it over him.

He knew very well that Georgina was capable of this violence and made his retreat with another joke about these women and their cranks.

Georgina never told us, or anybody else, why she decided to leave the shop, but even my father did not ask her any particulars. Since that lie, he had drawn a little away from Georgina, as if from one who had withdrawn confidence in him; and perhaps he felt that the girl must be her own mistress.

52

At that time, you must understand, even half a century ago, the world was a much rougher place than it is to-day. There were many places where no woman could go unprotected, and almost every woman, except among the most sheltered class, was accustomed to incidents which would now be thought fit for a police court. It was not for nothing that ladies did not venture even down the street except with a maid or a footman, and that their menfolk so fiercely maintained what is called Victorian morality. That moral system which has been compared with that of Eastern potentates, whose women are guarded for their whole lives in the fortress of a seraglio, had the same end and arose largely from the same necessity to protect and maintain their refinement and their chastity in a world inconceivably brutal.

Our women, even on the quiet moor, seldom went anywhere alone. They chose to go in parties and if they went far from home they liked to have some of their menfolk with them. And any man upon the moor or in our western towns was prepared to defend his woman with his fists and his body. Not that the women were not prepared to defend themselves. Mrs. G herself, when two of those tramps who then infested our roads stopped her on the moor, so battered them with the butt of her whip that one was left unconscious, or pretending to be so, and the other ran all the way to Dollyford while she drove and lashed at him from behind.

All this was taken for a matter of course. It was the way things were and always would be. Nature, we thought, had made them so and those who could not make their own way in such a world must go under. So Georgina's silence as a child of eleven about what happened in the shop was respected and approved. It was felt that she was a girl of character who did not make a foolish fuss, and knew how to keep her self-respect without the indignity of public accusations or the unreasonableness of bringing G to public shame. For the view in the village was that G was G. There was good and there was bad in him and it was the business of those who had dealings with him, young or old, male or female, to reckon with both.

And though Georgina so abruptly left her employment at G's shop and took that other work at so much greater inconvenience, we still shopped at G's. She would still return his greeting in the road. Indeed, as we all noticed, she would sometimes speak to G in a very peremptory manner. She would say in the shop, "Don't cheat me as you did last time," in a voice that startled those who might perhaps say such things to G but only in that tone of raillery which he himself had used.

And G himself, when so challenged, would laugh and make a joke of it, saying that Georgina was too sharp for him and that he would like to see the man who dared to cheat her. To which she would remark only that she had been cheated before often enough and would be cheated again. Neither would she ever again accept any of those little presents that G would hand out so freely, of damaged sweets, stale bars of chocolate, bruised oranges, windfalls. It was surprising, indeed, that G would go on offering such things to the girl in face of consistent snubs. But G had that kind of impudence which belongs to such a character. The man sure of his power, confident of his position, a man who knows that everything about him, the very worst, is known and discussed, and for his own glory will never admit shame.

But though my father did not question Georgina about G's dealings with her, he was much opposed to her taking employment at the beer house. He was a very strong teetotaller, like most of the leading members of our chapels, and he said that no child of his should ever work in such a fly trap of Satan as an inn.

My father, as I say, was a deeply religious man, of profound faith and strong conviction. It would be a great error to set him down as narrow or bigoted.

But drink, in those days, was an evil inconceivable in ours. The fearful uncertainty of life, unemployment, the appalling squalor of slums, drove millions of the weaker nerve to drink.

Wesley has described the state of our mining villages before their conversion—there were still towns all over England where great regions containing millions of souls were nightly given over to scenes whose bestiality could only be surpassed by their hideous rage against everything that dignifies humanity—vice delighting in foulness only to express the spite engendered by its own despair.

Hatred of drink and the drink traffic, in my father, was not fanaticism. He was an enthusiast but no fanatic—he acted not from the impulse of passion but from reasons which he was always prepared to

54

defend. His reasons, in some matters, were not such as would be accepted by professors—he was self-educated and had had no guidance among the wilderness of books. He had not learnt to read until the age of seventeen, and yet that effort in a ploughboy son of illiterate parents who had not a fragment of print, much less a book, in their one-room hovel, was itself a remarkable feat. And now he would quote from Ruskin as well as Bunyan, he read in the masters of theology as freely as in the little grey pamphlets that arrived monthly by post from the headquarters of the Adventist movement.

He could defend his faith there too, by mathematical argument, as he would say of drink that no doubt it did no harm to those who could control their appetites, but it was the duty of Christians to consider their weaker brethren and to forgo a slight and transient pleasure for a great and lasting good. And the good should be to their own salvation too, in the discipline of their flesh.

Do not be deceived by these old-fashioned words, soul and flesh, appetite and brethren—only fools can trifle with the things they mean —in his battle with Georgina my father was fighting for the salvation of a nature in which there was as great power of evil as good. To him the girl's choice of task was a fearful danger to her spiritual health— and quite apart from his faith no one knew better than he how much her happiness in a cruel world depended upon the cast of her soul.

And on this occasion Georgina did put forward her case. She said that we needed the money, and that there was no other employment in Shagbrook which offered itself even at half the pay. It was the shop or the inn, and she would not go to the shop.

My father's answer, of course, was that no one needed money earned in the service of the devil, and that we should not starve for want of five shillings a week.

Here, of course, Georgina again was on ground where she had to stand alone. Five shillings in those days bought ten times what it would buy to-day, and especially all those small comforts—sugar and tea, my father's tobacco—which we accepted as basic necessities, and of which even my father did not count the expense.

He would instantly have abandoned them if he had understood how much they cost in our budget. But Georgina did not choose that he

55

should go without his tobacco, or that we should lose our jam and our occasional saffron cake. And yet she could not tell him so. Therefore, once again, she became dumb, and with that obstinate peaked look, which we knew so well, refused to argue the point. She repeated only that Mrs. G had promised not to set her behind the bar, that she was needed only to mind the house, and that she had given her promise.

This battle was far longer than the other. My father prayed at Georgina for many nights. For many nights, so Ruth has told me since, she lay awake in tears, and yet she never wavered and in the end it was my father who was defeated.

Which was wrong in this battle between daughter of twelve and father of more than fifty? I cannot but say that both were right. Yet it was unnatural for a child of that age to know such a triumph. Victory is a burden for the strong who alone should win it. Georgina did not want it, and having it, found it a torment—her pride saw my father humiliated—his humility considered only Georgina's special temptations.

Georgina to us became now still more peremptory; in despair of our liking, she seemed, like other autocrats, to find a pleasure in abusing her subjects.

15

THE work of the herdsman, how romantic it seems; the party from town in the car passing through winding lanes among banks full of wild flowers, under trees in full leaf, meets the farm boy dawdling from sun to shadow with his beasts, and cries, "Lucky boy—delightful work for a summer afternoon."

But how we hated that task, especially on the Dollyford road so famous for its beauty. There we were bound to meet carts and gigs, which meant that every moment we had to run up and down shouting and waving sticks at our stupid charges to make them clear the way. Meanwhile some impatient bagman or farmer, some coachman with a family carriage, would be shouting at us to know if we were asleep or if we supposed we had bought the whole road, and driving by would throw us at best a scornful glance, at worst a curse—even a flick of a long whip. All this in spatterings of mud or clouds of dust which made us cough and blinded our eyes.

So on an August day Georgina and I were bringing some cows along from market; we were in the last stage of heat and exasperation—Georgina had just hurled a curse after a waggoner even louder than his own—when a man on a horse suddenly emerged from in front, out of the great tawny cloud raised higher still by the waggon team with their great hooves.

This man, very smartly dressed, like an M.F.H. in summer garb, out on a hack, told us to take our d—— brutes out of that and actually aimed a blow with his whip at a heifer. This was a breach of road law—no one is permitted to strike at another's beast—I was quite taken aback by such conduct—Georgina rushed forward, stick in hand, with a cry of wrath.

But at this moment a large grey mass came reeling slowly after the horseman—we found ourselves staring with feelings that surpassed analysis or description at what we knew to be an elephant.

57

This wonder made all the wildest fairy tales on earth perfectly rational to me, in one instant all my faculties of imagination were enlarged by ten or twenty times, as if my soul had said, "If God can make an elephant and send him along the Dollyford road, then His powers have been underestimated and undervalued." I don't even mean that at that time I put any limit to the powers of God, but only that my conception of those powers in action was suddenly increased.

This astonishing creature, as he slowly bore down upon us, forcing us to the very verge of the road, carried on his vast flank, curving upwards and away into the sky, a scarlet housing about two yards each way on which was embroidered in huge gold letters LILMOUTH GREAT FAIR.

The driver on his back—an Indian or one dressed like an Indian—now put a coach horn to his lips and blew a call. Upon the long note and the echo among the trees, a mournful comment on all afterthoughts, the dust closed and we were alone again on the too familiar Dollyford road with three miles of driving before us.

Georgina and I had fallen back against the bank. I felt Georgina press tight against me in an excitement that caused her to grasp my hand. I looked at her now in my own excitement, sure of her sympathy, but she was staring after the elephant with round eyes and tightly compressed lips.

No one had more expressive features than Georgina at that time. She was fearfully thin, almost emaciated, so that all her bones showed. Her small hard beak of a nose shone with the stretched skin, her cheeks were hollow, her great black eyes seemed to protrude from the thinness of the cheeks, and her small rather thick lips had a perpetual pout from the same cause.

Already one could see fine wrinkles in her forehead and by her lips. In thought or depression she sometimes looked like an old woman.

At the moment she was burnt as dark as a gipsy—with her dusty black hair falling in wisps across her eyes she looked as rough as she probably seemed to many of our neighbours.

"Shall you go to the fair, Georgy?" I asked her.

Thus recalled to my presence she looked sharply at me, withdrew

58

her hand and jumped upright. "Why shouldn't I go?" she said. "Why not?"

"It'll need a lot of money," I said.

Georgina made an impatient gesture with her stick. "If it keeps on like this," she said, "there'll be the harvest money." And then as if arguing with herself, she said, "Father wouldn't mind, he took me himself last time. Of course I'll go."

This answer gave me great satisfaction. It was the one I had sought. I knew that if Georgina went to the fair that I should go, for she would feel it wrong to take any pleasure not accorded to her family.

But I wished to involve her in a promise while she was still in the mood of excitement produced by the elephant. All of us, even Ruth at nine, were experts in Georgina's character, the subjects and courtiers of an Empress Catharine could not have studied her moods so closely.

"Do you think I could go too?" I asked.

"Of course—we'll all go."

"Is that a promise?" I said, knowing that for Georgina it was a promise. I wanted only to fix it in her memory.

"Of course it's a promise."

A shout from the road in front brought us to our duty—the cows were scattered over fifty yards on both sides, two were moving into a field. Both of us rushed forward with loud cries of "Hi—Hi up," and it was five minutes before, panting and sweating, we met again.

But now we did not find the way tedious, the afternoon boring, we could not talk fast enough. No sooner had Georgina gone forward to turn the wandering beasts from a side lane than she thought of something more and ran back to tell me that elephants lived two hundred years, or that Indians could eat fire, or that once upon a time at Lilmouth fair there had been a theatre with real plays. Her mother had seen the actors.

I contemplated with hopeless passion the idea of a play. I knew the answer before I asked, "Could we go to a play?" Georgina answered with impatience that I knew we could not go to a play. Plays were wicked. But we might see the actors, it was the custom for them to come out on a platform in front of the tent and show off their fine clothes.

This spectacle, she said, was allowed because it was not acting—besides no one could stop you walking past. "And they're certain to be there," she said, "because, you know, this is a special fair—the real Great Fair. That other one was nothing—nothing at all. It hadn't a theatre or nothing—not even a lion."

She was speaking of a former Lilmouth fair to which we had been taken some years before. Lilmouth Great Fair had always been one of the most famous in the west, but for several years past it had been much diminished in grandeur by a quarrel with the town authorities about the rights of the showmen to pitch their tents on common land. This had now been settled, and all the west country heard with great satisfaction that the fair would once more reveal its old splendour.

None of us had seen it in its glory, and now we had Georgina's promise, extracted by my cunning diplomacy, that we should go—that is, that the necessary funds would be found. This was important—Lilmouth was sixteen miles away and we should have to go by railway. Also we should need money at the fair itself—notoriously fairs were expensive. But now both Richard and Ruth offered help. Richard had a prize from his headmaster of two shillings—Ruth revealed a store of Saturday ha'pennies saved to buy a wax doll; both paid their treasure into the common fund.

Ruth and Richard brought this news to us one day at teatime; but just while they were enjoying the triumph of their generosity and I the prospect of the fair, Georgina came in from the Green Man. She was in her most concentrated mood and accused Ruth, as often, of making the tea with cold water.

Ruth coloured as usual under reproach, but made no answer, and immediately Richard, to take attention from her, told Georgina about the money. "It's nearly ten shillings. That will take us there at least."

Georgina answered that the tailor was coming, and that another baby had died in Ranstone—that was to say, a striker's baby.

There was a tin miners' strike at Ranstone, now some weeks old, which was giving our father much anxiety as treasurer of the fund. He had been collecting for the men as far as Dollyford, but we knew that things were bad in villages that depended entirely on the mines.

We sat silent and dismayed. I will not say that we were quite sur-

60

prised at Georgina's announcement, but it alarmed us very much. I think we had all felt our father would not consider it right to spend money on pleasures while fellow creatures were starving within a few miles.

Richard said at once that the tailor came twice a year and that we had already promised half our harvest money for the soup kitchens. "And that's a good deal more than anyone else here is doing."

"I know," Georgina said, "if it weren't for father no one here would do anything."

"What has the strike got to do with the fair?" Richard said; and then using an argument familiar to every old parliamentarian—"I suppose everything can't be stopped because of the strike."

"Father gave five shillings last week, and we owe G nearly a pound," Georgina said. "So I don't see exactly how I'm going to the fair." And then seized with that foreboding which was always apt to fall upon her, she said with great bitterness, "I knew all the time I wouldn't."

All of us looked at her with rising indignation. It may seem unjust that we should be angry with Georgina for expressing our own doubts, but that of course was just why we were angry. She called up the fearful obstacle of conscience, and we did not forgive her because she was simply representing our father's probable wishes.

I exclaimed with great wrath that I could see Georgina wanted to stop us from having any fun at all.

"What a lie," said Georgina, jumping up. "I'm sure I don't care what you do ever, and you know father won't even ask." And she left the table to go back to work.

"Georgy doesn't realise how important it might be for us to go to the fair," Richard said, advancing as usual an unexpected but somehow characteristic point of view. "Ruth has never seen a lion and has no idea of an elephant. This is her only chance to see the real thing and find out how she feels about them. And Ruth didn't make the strike."

Richard argued that if the strikers were starving it was their own fault. This was a view held by many in Shagbrook where the miners were not popular—they were regarded as rough and vaunting people who made too much money and looked down on poor labourers. In fact

61

I believe the real truth of the dispute was that prices had fallen and the poorer mines had ceased to pay—what was wanted was reconstruction. My father himself urged this solution, but meanwhile he held it a duty lying on all citizens to support the soup kitchens which kept the strikers and their families alive.

This had already brought down on him and his fellows, including most of the ministers about, and even the vicars at Battwell and Tarbiton itself, some bitter attacks. The owners and shopkeepers, already half ruined, said that it was these collections which kept the strikes in being. Here is a war, they said, a battle for survival in which we are being driven into bankruptcy, and you are taking sides against us. Why should we go to church and chapel and put money in the plate?

I am not going to enlarge on this subject from an economic point of view, so full of bitterness and confusion. What I want to point out is that there was religious feeling on both sides. As I say, my father had been chosen as treasurer of the friendly society simply because of his religious standing.

The friendly society itself—the union—was profoundly religious in idea. I have before me a union card of that date. It is surrounded with religious emblems; God the Father at the top dispensing His benefits to all people; Christ at one side receiving the children; and the Holy Ghost sending down the flames of His spirit upon His preachers; and below one read that the labourer was worthy of his hire. Only a week before this time my father, bringing Richard and myself from school in the cart, had drawn out from the road on a patch of moor and tied the horse to a tree, then he asked us if we would like to wait there or come with him—he had to see Dr. Leddra.

Dr. Leddra was the Baptist minister at Tarbiton and a family friend. We were surprised to hear that he was to be found on this deserted part of the moor—he was an old man and infirm—but we asked for no explanation and my father did not offer one. Not that he was a secretive man, he was merely preoccupied.

We followed him therefore across the moor and came soon upon an unexpected combe, or rather a semicircular valley at the mouth of a combe. Here we found a meeting in progress. Perhaps a hundred men were gathered on both banks of the stream listening to Dr.

62

Leddra who stood on a rock above the fall. It had been a dry summer; the brook was brought down to a runlet but a few inches deep, and the fall itself made a tinkling noise which seemed rather to carry the speaker's words than to obscure them. We recognised the gathering at once for tin miners, by their dress, and realised that they had chosen the place here at a spot equally distant from their own villages and Tarbiton, to avoid notice.

My father took his seat on the hillside to wait for the conclusion of the meeting and motioned to us to do the same. His calmness startled us, we did not realise that he was accustomed to such misery.

I myself was well acquainted with poverty, I had seen friends changed in a few weeks by some family disaster from plump and gay comrades to waifs, thin, anxious, ragged. But living in a small hamlet of farm workers, I had never known a general distress.

Now suddenly we found ourselves among a crowd of men and women of whom there was not one who did not carry the marks of long privation. The men's clothes, unnaturally clean, hung upon them, the hollow cheeks and bright feverish eyes turned in silence upon the speaker were those of famine.

The women in a smaller group stayed apart, some sitting in a close group on the rocks beside the stream, others standing on the hillside. Many had brought their babies. The young mother then, like an African native, would carry her baby with her wherever she went, not trusting it out of her sight. And if the men seemed starved, I had never seen so thin and worn a crowd of human beings as those women. It was once explained to me by some factory owner during an industrial dispute that my sympathy for the suffering of the women was somewhat exaggerated. Women, he said, have small bones, and a week or two of short commons will make them seem almost transparent. I said to him that I admired his transposition of starvation into short commons, and that women should starve and their babies starve in a dispute between men seemed to me at the least an anomaly.

And yet we heard Dr. Leddra say to that desperate and broken multitude there that they were Christian men and, in the name of Christ, he beseeched them not to use violence towards their enemies.

63

He spoke of some fight and denounced those who had brought shame to their cause; he called on them to kneel down and to pray for God's forgiveness and mercy, and after the prayer they sang the hymn—

> O God our help in ages past,
> Our hope for years to come.

I have never forgotten that scene upon the combeside; the sky above full of July sunlight, the stream glittering among the stones, a bird flying over and turning aside in alarm at the sight and sound of humanity in this quiet place, and the ragged crowd about the minister, men threatened with the ruin of their lives, raising their voices in chorus, hoarsely indeed, but with earnest appeal in that hymn of prayer.

I noticed, indeed, that many of the women had not prayed and none sang. Perhaps as they stood aside from the meeting of the men, so they did not feel part of the service in prayer and hymn. But I think, too, that among the women, as in Georgina, there was always a deeper rebelliousness. For women in those days, the break-up of a home was often a break-up of their lives. Many a girl in the bad times passed in a year from bridehood and motherhood to the workhouse or the streets. For the men would move away following the work where it was to be found. They were expected to do so. Was it not a law of the economists that labour seeks its market at the place of production? So the children of starving cottagers had poured into the towns for work in the new factories, and so when some industry was ruined the workers would travel hundreds of miles to some newer and more prosperous trade. What happened to the iron workers of Sussex or the cloth weavers of Somerset was happening all the time. Labour was always on the move, leaving behind it broken homes and deserted villages, as well as ruined factories.

Such economics in those days were not only the tenets of the rich, I have heard them from the lips of poor men. My own father, so far as he took the least interest in a subject so remote from his own deeper preoccupations, held something of the kind. They were indeed implicit in the very centre of the evangelical creed, that all was in the hands of the all-wise providence.

But God had also commanded charity and mercy among men, and so those who suffered by economic law must be saved if possible from the worst consequences.

How many clever men have sneered at this confusion, saying—"So the same God that sends economic war in order to secure cheap production also enjoins charity to make the war ineffective."

My father accepted the position without question—he did not concern himself with logic in such a matter, he presumed that God knew what He was about and simply did his duty as he conceived it.

That was something he understood quite clearly—on the one side no violence, no hatred, on the other charity and mercy.

After the meeting he had his conference with Dr. Leddra—it was about a strikers' representative on the fund committee—and took us home. He did not speak to us about the need of funds for the kitchens, he said only in a general way that they were nearly exhausted and that it was surely God's will that everyone should give all they could spare to such a cause.

Ah, I hear you say, a typical Victorian despotism, a hypocritical theocracy in which children were robbed of all freedom and joy—even of their own earnings—in the name of a Divine Providence that was in fact the whim of the paternal autocrat. Nothing could be more untrue; I doubt if that parent ever existed except for the purposes of professional novelists—a not very reputable tribe, eager, as our friends in America put it, to "cash in," on the usual reaction of every age against the last.

I do not pretend that we did not suffer as children from belonging to a Christian household—we were often bored to distraction in long Sunday services—we resented certain prohibitions, for instance on Sunday games—we hated to see other children even poorer than ourselves, from households deep in debt, spending their twopences and their chance earnings, when we felt ourselves obliged to give all up to the payment of bills, and chapel collections.

But none of this was demanded of us, in all his life I never heard my father say that we must give. No force was at work but that of conscience, and the sense of family honour. We had to pay our debts because we were Nimmos—we had to give to missions and soup

65

kitchens because they served people whose need was greater than ours.

And our freedom was real. When I had a boon of sixpence for picking up a gentleman's whip dropped by him in riding through the market and spent it on a singing top, which was then the admiration of us all, no one, least of all my father, suggested that I should have handed in the money or any part of it. One year Richard kept all his harvest money for some mysterious purpose—we wondered but did not ask what he had done with it. In fact this freedom of choice made our problems more difficult—we were always faced by a conflict of duty and inclination. When Richard said now that all the same we should go to the fair, he was already involved in the battle.

"It would be quite enough if we gave half the harvest money to the soup kitchen."

"Of course it would," I said. But I could not forget that starving crowd in the combe, and so I said that the strike would probably be over before the fair.

"Not a chance while we feed them," Richard said.

Richard was extremely gloomy, and suddenly he said, "Georgina needn't go if she doesn't like—I don't see that it's our business."

But even I could see that even Richard was wavering; I was scarcely surprised when on the next day at breakfast he said to Georgina, "Do you really mean that you won't go to the fair?"

"How can I?"

"Of course you could if you liked."

Georgina said nothing to this, and I said, "You know if you don't go we can't go either."

"Why not, you've got the money?"

"You know we can't," Richard said in a sharp tone.

Georgina then flew into a violent rage and shouted, "I tell you I won't—I won't—and no one's going to make me."

We all looked at her in silent disgust. I need not describe our feelings at this situation from which there seemed no escape. Then Richard got up, went to the drawer under his bed and took out a small canvas bag—it was one of the bags Mrs. Coyte used for

66

samples of corn. He brought this to Georgina and handed it over, saying, "It's eleven and fourpence altogether."

This dramatic handing over was meant, of course, to make Georgina feel our indignation, and so, of course, she showed no feeling at all. She carried off the bag to her room, and we did not see her again till bedtime.

In fact Georgina's coolness succeeded in giving us the impression that she was not troubled by our anger. She affected so successfully the calm aloofness of the person in authority that our resentment became less violent, or rather fell into the general stock of our irritation.

I daresay, too, that we did not quite believe yet that we should never see the fair. For children, to want anything very much is almost to be certain of getting it. And as usual we had plenty of distractions. Do you suppose from these reminiscences that we were an oppressed and unhappy family? On the contrary, my recollection of life at Shagbrook, as at Highfallow, is full of excitement and fulfilment. So, indeed, that to make a complete picture I am obliged to enquire, as it were, into different parts of my experience which seem to exist almost in different boys. No doubt at that time, like other children, I lived in half-a-dozen places at once, and each of these places— home, the moors, the streams in the deep combes, school at Dollyford, dockside at Tarbiton, the great farmhouse kitchen with its smoky ceiling and the gun above the fireplace—has its own chain of experience. So now it is only by a deduction of dates that I can put our battle with Georgina over the fair money in the same month with that year's harvest, memorable for the first appearance of the two-horse cutter.

16

THIS was a good harvest among bad years, and I received regular harvest money for tying sheaves instead of a mere dole as in previous years. So, too, I attended the harvest feast when we brought home the corn-baby to hang in the kitchen for another year—among such delights the doubt about the fair was no worse than the frozen nose which had not hindered us at Highfallow from the joys of the Eskimo.

It was on the day after the harvest feast that Richard and I, about eight o'clock, came in late from the field where we had been gleaning for our chickens, and noticed Georgina sitting by herself in the dark corner of the room under the stairs, an unusual place for anyone to sit, as it was unusual for Georgina to sit anywhere during the day. We paid no attention to her, nor she to us, and took our gleanings at once down the back garden where Ruth was shutting up the chickens for the night. And then as we stood there looking down at the Shag beneath our garden fence as it poured away through the combe, Richard said suddenly, "What was Georgy doing in the corner?" I suggested that it was because she was not well, Georgina had been feverish for a week past. But Richard answered that Georgina was always ill when she was angry, and neither of us said anything to this—we perceived that Richard had something on his mind.

"We treat Georgy very badly," Richard said then. "I wonder why we treat her so badly."

At once both I and Ruth perceived that we had treated Georgina badly. All three of us stood contemplating this revelation; it was not less a revelation because we had known it all the time.

I suggested that it was because of her temper. Richard agreed with this but pointed out that it was we who had put Georgina in a temper.

68

"She's very unhappy," Ruth said then. "She was awake all last night. I heard her walking about and talking to herself."

"After all," Richard said, "we needn't have given her all the money. I am going to tell her that we are sorry about it."

We then went back to the house, feeling both surprise at this sudden change in our ideas and pleased with ourselves for our resolution to apologise to Georgina. And as soon as we were in the kitchen again, Richard went up to Georgina and said that she had been right about the fair, it would have been wrong to spend money at the fair when it was needed for the house.

The result was disappointing. Georgina looked up at the three of us and made no answer. There was an embarrassed silence—Richard was obviously surprised by this lack of response.

We were relieved when my father came in, a moment later, and sat down as usual by the front window.

His book lay open on the window sill with his spectacles on the page, and after a little meditation and a sigh, probably from weariness, he took it on his knee, put on the spectacles, and began to read by the light, already fading, of the sunset—Georgina, also as usual, went to take off his boots.

And afterwards she went to help Ruth with the supper. Neither did she speak a word to us, at that or any other time, of reconciliation.

It was not for many years that Georgina told me how, that evening, she had thought of killing herself. She had had in her pocket, as she sat in the corner, a bottle of spirits of salt which she had taken from the inn—Mrs. G was accustomed to use it for cleaning the sinks.

"I stayed in the corner because I hated you all so much that I didn't want you to speak to me again, and I hated father too. But I could not bear that anyone else should take his boots off, and so I waited for him. I knew he wouldn't speak to me, because he never did—I don't think he would have noticed if I had never taken off his boots. He wouldn't have known that he still had them on until he went to bed."

Georgina said this with a kind of pleasure—even when she was a child we realised that she did not blame my father for his absent-mindedness. We all understood that it was rather present-mindedness, for his mind was always concentrated and active. It was this activity, this concentration upon those studies whose importance was so great to him, that caused him sometimes almost to forget the existence of his family.

And since he believed that the end of the world was due within the next few years, and that it was possible by careful attention to the authorities to ascertain its exact date, his absorption in learning, his aloofness from the small details of family life, are not surprising.

As for gratitude to those who served him, did he not thank God every night, in our own presence, for his children, sent to him for his comfort and blessing? True, he did not much distinguish between us as blessings—his own life was so entirely given to others without regard for return that he hardly noticed the difference between the labourer who, like Georgina, worked all through the day, and those like us who came in at the end of it and did comparatively little. He had that blindness to common justice between man and man which is not unusual among saints, who see all men as sunk so deep in obligation to God that their various merits are as corn to the height of the sky. One reed shaking in the wind may be some inches taller than another, but what are inches in the abyss of the eternal contemplation?

17

GEORGINA said that when we had spoken to her that evening, she was only the more furious with us because she saw then that she could not kill herself. "You would simply have said that I was as spiteful as you thought, and good riddance." I said that it had been we who were spiteful, and that we knew it—we had confessed it to each other in the garden that very evening.

But she answered that I did not know how full of hatred and spite she had been in those days, and how she had loved her hatred—even for her father.

"I knew it was hatred—I knew it was wicked—that's why I was ashamed to have father and all of you say that after all I was no good for anything. And so," she said, smiling at me as if to say, this will tease you, "if it was the everlasting arms, I did not say thank you for them. Perhaps God did save me as father said he would—he saved me over and over again in that miserable time after mother died—but not quite as father meant it. He saved me by my own pride and wickedness."

I answered that I could not agree. This conversation took place at the time when I had just begun to preach—when I was once more strongly under my father's influence—and I did not like to agree that anyone could be saved by pride. I said that Georgina had always undervalued herself, perhaps because of our lack of appreciation when she was a child, and what had saved her was not her pride but her knowledge of right and wrong. "You knew what was right and you did it, although you got no thanks for it."

But Georgina insisted that she had been dutiful from the worst of motives, and if she had been saved from the final wickedness of a spiteful suicide it had been because of our impulse of forgiveness and not anything good in her. "You don't know how furious I was with you for taking away my chance of revenge. And think how father

71

would have suffered—it was really a wicked plan. And I haven't for-given you yet after all these years." And then looking at me with bright eyes she said, "Yes, I hate Dick even now, and you know how I love him too. I would do anything for him, but of course he does not need anything from me or anyone else, and I hate that too."

Georgina always looked upon herself as a lost soul. Even as a grown-up woman she would say that she had never been converted like Ruth and myself—because there was something in her that re-fused to give up her anger. She liked to be angry. I shall be told that this poor girl was so filled with guilt, had such burdens laid upon her, body and soul, before she was fit for responsibility, that her whole life was spoilt. But I dare to say that Georgina in her position could not have escaped burdens, fate had laid them upon her, and fate too had given her a temper which made them hard to bear. Ruth, in Georgina's place, would have been both happy and respected, Georgina felt her-self deprived, even of our love which she would not stoop for. And as she said herself, without that discipline of my father's teaching she might have made a total wreck of her life.

18

AFTER all, it was because of the strike that we got to the fair. Cran was now paying his annual visit to the farm. He came usually for harvest which he seemed to enjoy, and he assumed as a matter of course that he would not only go to the fair, but take his friends, including myself. He therefore set his London wits to work and discovered that because of the strike a Dollyford carrier who took miners to work had nothing to do. Cran proposed to this man to take a party from Shagbrook, at sixpence each, as far as the railway halt between Dollyford and Lilmouth. As for the railway fare, he said there was an excursion train and he would provide the tickets. What's more, hearing that Richard and the girls had no money for the fair either, he invited them too. Richard, who liked Cran, accepted at once; Georgina refused and asked Cran where he had got the money for the tickets.

Cran, who was never put out by anything or anybody, answered cheerfully that he had got it, that was all that mattered. Whereupon Georgina said, "I suppose you stole it."

Cran laughed and asked her again if she wouldn't come to the fair. He seemed to like Georgina, and especially he enjoyed teasing her.

But she made no answer and walked off. What's more, she persuaded Ruth also to refuse Cran's offer.

Georgina had always fought with Cran, but I think she was ruder to him than usual on this occasion because he had suggested a scheme by which we hoped to go and come back from the fair without our father's knowing anything about it. Cran pointed out that the third day of the fair coincided with Tarbiton monthly market when Mrs. Coyte met friends from distant farms and often stayed very late. My father therefore, in attendance as driver, was also kept until a late hour. If we waited for the third day of the fair we could be home before my father.

73

Georgina said nothing against this plan, but I've no doubt she thought it very treacherous and deceitful and was not going to have anything to do with it. As for us, we were delighted to avoid having to ask our father for leave to go to the fair—not that he would have refused us, he never refused any reasonable request, but he would have been distressed by our wanting to go to the fair at such a time.

Cran himself was going on all three days, he did not need to alter his own arrangements. And so on the Wednesday we got up a little earlier than usual as if to start earlier for school, walked down the road as far as the Green Man and climbed into the van with a dozen other village children—a dozen more were going by waggon with their parents.

For most of Shagbrook went to the fair—it was the time when most houses had cash earned in harvest—and, as my father had said already, the fair came at that time to reap its own harvest. "If the labourer is worthy of his hire, I suppose the circus is worthy of the labourer's hire."

My father had a certain unexpected humor of his own, usually turning on the tricks of fate and the uncertainty of life. I have noticed a similar vein in other evangelicals deeply convinced of the human fallibility.

But our anticipation had now reached such a pitch that I doubt if any obstacle or prohibition could have kept us from the fair. The news, on the evening before, that the strikers' committee in Lilmouth had talked of attacking the fair, because they had been forbidden to collect funds at the gate, merely provoked us. Even Georgina had said severely that the committee was stupid to annoy people when they were on the strikers' side already, and she was sure no one would allow the fair to be closed.

The rumour, indeed, only added to our excitement at our departure. We were prepared to protect the fair against all comers—magistrates and strikers. It had become our fair, by mere imagination.

We had taken a boy called Doan in place of the girls, and when we reached Crow Halt, we four boys were invited, by acclamation, into a carriage already jammed to the windows with Dollyford boys. They set up a shout for us, as soon as we were seen on the little platform. They were not particular friends of ours, indeed as Dollyford

74

boys they ranked as local enemies. But in a train full of people from Queensport and Longbridge, and a score of hamlets, they recognised us as allies. Thus at the fair we wandered among the booths like a group of visiting tribesmen in a strange city, gaping at the sights, but also, to keep up our prestige with each other, jeering at them.

Continually we met other groups from other parts of the moor, from places a hundred miles away in Somerset, or even Dorset, who seemed to speak a different language. And then, too, we gaped and jeered. And when two tribes met in the crowded alleys they would not give way, but pushed against each other. And while we pushed, full of valour in community, we shouted to each other trying to frighten the enemy with our noise and violence.

I have always thought that what was strange about those fairs was the sense of lawlessness, the pushing and shouting, and yet the good behaviour of most of the people. It was seldom that tempers were lost. There were, I think, no more fights, less real brutality, at the fairs than on ordinary market days. True, in the evening the hustling grew rough, and sometimes a booth was attacked. The fairmen were always ready to defend themselves, their sticks were never far from their hands.

But even at night the crowd, of which many in both sexes were now more than half drunk, was extraordinarily patient. It seemed that people were too happy, too pleased with their enjoyment, to take offence even when robbed, pushed, shouted at, herded like cattle.

This was the last day of the fair. Everything had a worn battered look, and the showmen and showwomen standing at their stalls, at coconut shies and rifle galleries, Aunt Sallies and penny-rollers, seemed like soldiers after a long battle. Many of the men were stripped to the waist, the women wore a single garment. The men had not shaved, the women's hair was in tails. Their faces, too worn and too dry for sweat, still had the leather look as if tanned in perspiration. They stared at us with red-rimmed eyes, and held out balls or guns in silence. And those who could not keep silence—the cheapjack men, the barkers outside the animal booths, the freaks and the flea circus—had voices so broken that they no longer sounded human. They were like the croaks, bellows, trumpeting and screams of a furious zoo.

75

And these voices, too, belonged to a sorcerer's world, the world of the great fair where anything was possible and everything was strange, exciting, violent—where there were to be seen at all times "Juglers, Cheats, Games, Plays, Fools, Apes and Rogues," as well as "False Swearers and that of a Blood Red colour."

I have wondered, indeed, if Bunyon did not take old Lilmouth for a model of his Fair, for we were in actual fact of "a Blood Red colour." Over all hung clouds of Devon dust which covered everything—booths, faces, hair—with a thick coat of reddish powder, so that we grew more and more like Red Indians, and the sun blazed down on us through sparkling layers of bronze as in the missionary pictures in my mother's Bible representing the children of Israel in the desert.

But this comparison was an afterthought, no such reasonable fancies entered into my bewildered, intoxicated senses while I drifted through the heat, the noise, the whirling roundabouts, the crack of rifles, the hollow thump of wooden balls against canvas, the ear-splitting blare of steam organs, the strange rasping noise of thousands of iron-shod boots scraping hard earth, and the ground bass of voices like the rumble of waggons over new macadam.

But it was night time which overwhelmed my last remnants of sense. In those days there were but two illuminants for the showmen, the candle lantern—ruby, emerald, lemon—and the naphtha flare, a great naked flame, deep yellow and orange, leaping and curling and throwing up dark twists of smoke. In my memory both have seemed to be much more beautiful than the strings of electric bulbs which now puncture with still points of light darkness made impenetrable by the glare of limes.

No doubt I am deceived by my memories, and yet it seems to me that the quivering lanterns, the jumping flames, were one with us in our moment of violent life, that they gave an elation to our saturnalia that would not have been kindled by frigid festoons of wattage and the cold eye-burning glare of the limelight. It is, I believe, no sentimental illusion that mechanism is everywhere the enemy of joy: no less than the mechanical centralism of bureaucratic Utopians is the enemy of true citizenship.

76

19

But this is a digression. The reader must forgive the old war-horse in whose stiffening limbs and rather shaky heart the "fire is not yet quenched." I was relating that event, central in my history, of Lilmouth Great Fair.

I did not know by now how or where I was going. I was carried along by the crowds, now greater than ever and more boisterous in their resolution to enjoy the last hours of the last fair day, the last for a whole year. Tomorrow hung over them already with chains in its hands, the gaoler, the slave-driver of their daily work, but while they were so free they would make free. In the darker alleys one heard the laughter and screams of the girls. In the main walks there were conflicts of pressure which broke into challenges of defiant yells and some hard swearing.

So I found myself often actually lifted off my feet as our group, now reduced by mere attrition to Richard, Frank Doan and myself, made our way slowly towards the gate. It was still early for the train which left at half past nine, but Richard feared that as we began to make our way thither we should be so hindered by the crowd as to miss it.

And towards the gate as we expected the crowd grew thicker, for at the gate, the most favoured spot as being nearest the town, there were the two chief attractions of afternoon and evening, the boxing booth and the theatre tent.

I had several times urged a visit to both—I have never forgotten for a moment Georgina's picture of the actors displaying their wicked persons outside their booth. But all my companions had been strangely indifferent to these delights; Cran had said he saw real theatres in London, Richard satisfied himself by saying that we should have to see it before we went—he spoke as with regret. Richard seldom shewed any enthusiasm for my fancies. And now he sighed in my ear, "I knew there would be a mob."

The mob for me was part of my excitement, I was breathless not only with the buffeting and the contending tides of people which bore us here and there. When suddenly I found myself at gaze, between a woman's fashionable head, a tower of hair and feathers, and a labourer's vast pink ear, at two men, a young and an old, who stood upon a staging with crossed arms, my first wild notion, those are actors, gave me a sense as if the blood had run out of my heart.

The men were both stripped to the waist, they were squeezing their arms to push out their biceps. The old man had huge hairy arms full of swollen veins, the youth's arms were so thin and flimsy that the muscles seemed only like a fold of skin. An old gipsy beside them bawled his challenge to all comers—a minute had passed while I gazed and listened before quite slowly some intelligence flowed back into my mind, and I perceived that these were not the actors.

But the crowd was moving again, a surge turned me half round—the fashionable hat and its curled feathers were carried some yards away, the great red ear was replaced by a baby in arms. It was sucking calmly while its mother, a red-faced woman streaming with sweat, fiercely elbowed her neighbours back, and I caught my first glimpse of striped canvas, lights brighter than all the rest, and a man in a shining tall hat, a dress suit and white waistcoat—the two latter articles were the first of their kind that I had ever seen—who was working his jaws and his arms in an extraordinary manner.

I could not hear a word, he was still ten yards away, but I knew at once by its mere magnificence and strangeness, the stripes and the waistcoat, that this must be the theatre.

Both were at once hidden again by another convulsion in the crowd, but it was towards the theatre that the strongest current was setting. The most powerful waves, I perceived, were caused actually by audiences coming out and going into the tent. After about twenty minutes, a third immense and long-sustained drive, which I thought at one moment would finally crush out my life, discharged me like jetsam from a wreck, to my amazement, almost beneath the platform. I could have touched the barker's patent leather toes as he stood above, roaring out his tale of seduction and murder. The play, he told us, was the most famous ever performed in any country, it had been specially commanded by all the crowned heads in Europe, its name was *Maria Marten*. It was the most exciting, the most terrible, the most dramatic piece ever performed—above all, a crowning attraction, it was true.

The man's face was crimson and dripping with sweat. His shirt was grey with moisture, his voice was that hoarse grating screech which makes one wonder how long a throat can survive, but every inch of his body was in action. Sometimes he banged on a great drum, then he would blow a post horn, and with great sweeps of both arms he would introduce to us the actors. Maria Marten, dressed in a sunbonnet, with a frilled collar and many skirts, carrying her baby in long clothes, tripped across the boards and smiled at us. Then her old father in smock frock and leggings hobbling on a stick. Then Tim Bobbin, a farm worker and a comic character, as we could tell at once by his enormous boots, his shuffle and his sly idiotic grin. And then old Mrs. Marten in a poke bonnet with white frills, and a blue apron. Gipsy Lee, dark and fierce, the picture of Nemesis, in a black slouch hat. And, finally, Corder himself swaggering in the dress of a smart young squire, in a cutaway coat, buckskin breeches and boots of the most brilliant polish.

I need not further describe these characters—*Maria Marten* is indeed a famous play, though hardly in the manner assumed by the barker.

That mysterious passion which had seized upon me ten days before, to see an actor, was not disappointed—I stared with eyes and mouth at once—I craned upwards till my neck ached.

What is it in the actor, the stage, that casts so powerful a spell on the young imagination? I still feel in my old nerves the vehement tremor of that night. Is it that impersonation by itself has some secret and immemorial power over the growing spirit—some primitive urge older perhaps than humanity itself? I could not take my eyes off these strange creatures as they passed mincing, hobbling, and strutting across the boards, and disappeared again into the tent. My eyes followed them to the last coquettish flick of Maria's skirt, the last twirl of Corder's spurred heel.

No doubt it was precisely because of this fascination that the showman brought out his performers. One would have thought a priori that such a premature display would be impolitic, that nothing would be more likely to discourage, to put off, the audiences than the sight of the puppets themselves, merely as puppets, apart from their play, in the crude flickering light of naphtha lamps, passing before us in silence, anomalous beings neither natural in our world nor real in their own.

Fair showmen are not fools, they know much more of human nature than many psychologists, it is their livelihood. And certainly having seen their puppets, dumb as they were, I felt such a longing for the play that it was like the hunger of starvation. But as I gazed with this fearful longing at the tent which hid I knew not what miracles of art, I had not the faintest hope of entering.

The price of entrance to the pit was sixpence and neither Richard nor myself had a single farthing—nothing was left us but our return tickets. A more important reason still in my mind then; the theatre was absolutely forbidden to members of our church and, moreover, I felt its evil. I had never felt it more strongly than at that moment when I was seized by an immense longing to follow the actors and actresses behind the canvas of that mysterious tabernacle, the temple of Satan.

It was then that I heard Richard's name, and looked up and saw standing over us a great red-faced man whom I knew for a small horse-coper in Tarbiton. He was dressed in a tweed coat with large checks, and corduroy trousers, a combination of the sporting gentleman and the labourer, which represented pretty accurately his mixed status in society. He was half drunk, or, as they would say now, squiffy. But as he teetered over to Richard he grinned with a peculiar knowing air and put his hand in his pocket. "Ah, you'm Dicky Nimmo," he said to Richard. "Like to see the show?" And he pulled out a coin and gave it to Richard, saying with a wave of his hand, "Go on in, it's worth it. It was a real murder you know." Then he gave Richard a pat on the shoulder and said, "Tell your dadda how you saw me," and pushed away towards the boxers.

Richard looked at the coin in his hand, and I turned it over and remarked that it was a big shield, half a crown.

80

"There's no time to go in," Richard said, "we'd miss the train."

"Would you go in?" I said, astonished by Richard's assumption that such a thing was possible. And he answered, still more to my surprise, no, that he had seen proper plays already. "We act Shakespeare at school." And to my gaze of wonder he added, "At Mr. Lakin's."

Mr. Lakin was that master who had suggested that Richard might be a scholar—he had since given him much special instruction.

For a long time now Richard had been withdrawing from me and, indeed, from all his family. I do not mean that his manner to us had changed—he was always gentle and considerate—but simply that he was passing into a world where our imagination followed with difficulty. We simply did not know enough of the facts, we had not furniture sufficient to set the stage. This casual remark about acting Shakespeare took him a great leap further into this mysterious realm where he lived so calmly. My response was quite inadequate. I murmured only, "You never told us."

"No, it would only worry father for nothing—and Georgy too. They'd think I was going to the bad. Why, last time I was Cleopatra, and they painted my face."

I did not know who Cleopatra was, I could only stare at Richard's cheeks as if to see there the traces of this daring iniquity, whatever it amounted to.

Richard asked me then with mild impatience to make up my mind, did I want to go to the play or not? He held out the half-crown.

"There are two more trains after this one, but you'd have to walk from Crow Halt."

I could not touch the coin and said, "But half of it is yours."

"Don't wake us if you come late," Richard said. "I'll leave the door open."

I answered him with a question, was the story of the play really true? Had there been such a murder? And Richard answered that it was so.

I remembered this exchange afterwards—I can perceive how my mind was working. Our whole education as children turned on respect for the truth—falseness was a sin and falseness had a very wide

81

meaning. Any kind of pretence, any kind of conduct having the least tincture of hypocrisy was not only a sin but a deadly trap. How often had I been told that the lie corrupts and poisons the very soul?

This was the principle that lay at the root of our objection to plays and players—they dealt in falsehood. Call this bigotry, but how much does England owe to such a faith? It is such ideas planted in the mind of a child that makes the man, even when he does not perceive it.

I have thought, indeed, that when Georgina spoke of the everlasting arms which, in her day of despair, held her from death, what really enclosed her was not only the idea of goodness and love, but of truth. She could not offend that spirit by a deceitful gesture while it stood before her. For we had from childhood not only the experience of love and truth common to all family life, but the idea of them embodied in the person of Jesus, a picture always present to our imagination as well as our feelings.

20

Temple of lies, where men and women practised feigning as an art, to deceive and confuse honest souls—I gazed from it to my brother and said to myself, "But this story is true. There is no sin in a true story truly represented."

Richard looked down at me with his calm patient air—at last he murmured, "I don't want to miss my train." Then suddenly with one of those quick unexpected precise movements which reminded us of our mother, he caught my hand, pressed the half-crown into the palm and closed my fingers upon it.

"Here you are," he said. "If you really want to see the thing, why not see it?"

I was as much astonished by this statement of the case as by Richard's reading of my thought—and the enormous gift. I could only stammer, "He gave it to you, Dick." Richard waved his hand like a prince renouncing a kingdom and said, "You can have it."

Already I had allowed myself to be pushed away from him, to be carried off by the stream now moving slowly but weightily like a glacier towards the entrance, and I did not see Richard again that night. And now I added my weight to the stream, struggling even to slip in front. My ideas of a theatre were based only on experience of a show tent where horses are displayed for sale, that is, an open floor about a roped-off enclosure. I knew that in such a tent small boys had much difficulty in getting a good view.

I cannot tell how I passed through that magic doorway—I have no recollection of paying the fee, although afterwards I had the change in my pocket. I imagine that in such a crisis of conscience fear and appetite divide the human soul so completely that there is no central point of reflection; there is no directing will within the person, and he has become a mere toy of events. I say I recollect nothing of my passage till I found myself in the third or fourth row of the audience gazing at the stage—a high stage brilliantly lit by strong footlights which made the tawdry curtain of plush, decorated with tattered gold stars in appliqué, seem dazzling in its beauty.

In front of this stage there was indeed a semicircular space roped off, in which an upright piano and a wooden kitchen chair stood on the bare earth among tufts of coarse grass left by trampling feet.

There was a row of chairs within the enclosure on which already some favoured spectators, men and women, were sitting. The price of these seats as announced on large placards, hung from the poles of the tent, was a shilling, yet I did not dream of taking one, for I perceived at once that they were reserved for a superior class of persons, large farmers, clerks. I recognised even a Tarbiton bank manager.

The crowd was not yet tight-packed, so that by alternatively jumping and stooping I could see these details, and the height of the stage gave me a full view of it at all times. Yet, attracted by its magnetism, I began to creep and worm my way forward, and this process was helped by bystanders who recognised my right as a small boy, short for my age, to be in front. So that at the last I was admitted by a stout motherly woman in a shawl, and her equally stout husband in his corduroys and white pea-jacket, to stand before them actually at the ropes.

I was just in time to see Maria Marten appear without her bonnet and in a long black cloak, to judge by appearances her private cloak, sit down at the piano and begin to play the lively air of "Villikins."

I had recognised her at once, and also perceived that for the moment she was not appearing as Maria Marten. I saw also with the village boy's experienced eye that she was far gone with child. But these circumstances again merely added to my sense of wildest expectation—I was beyond reflection. I was, so to speak, all exposed surface.

It was without any conscious addition to my state of wonder that, looking aside at Maria when she struck up a new tune, I saw just beyond her, at the ropes on the far side of the tent, Georgina's face thrust itself out suddenly between two men in the front row. The men, both large and heavy, were dressed in the dark suits common then to clerks, so that Georgina's pale face, seeming suspended in the air

84

against this background of broadcloth at about the level of a man's elbow, was very conspicuous. Her expression was a strange mixture of violent curiosity and alarm. Her eyes enormous, her forehead wrinkled, and her hair even more disordered than usual—long black locks streamed down her forehead and hung below her chin.

Her eyes were darting about, first at the woman playing, at the stage, the footlights, the festoons of painted cardboard at the top of the proscenium; then with a defiant suspicious frown at the circle of spectators as if to see if anyone there might recognize her, and to say, "I don't care if you do." She did not see me beneath the shadow of my fat farmer's wife. I stared at this unpredictable sister—my senses recorded only her presence—yet it had a strong effect upon my expectation, for Georgina, if I disliked and feared her government over me, had all the prestige that goes with authority. Her unexplained arrival at the fair, her still more extraordinary appearance at the play, to commit a sin against all her father's teaching, made the occasion even more portentous, more exciting than before.

The tent was now full, the attendants at the back were shouting, "Move up, ladies and gentlemen, plenty of room in the front, ladies and gentlemen," and I was pressed so hard against the rope that only my thigh bones prevented my stomach from being divided completely in two.

A loud voice from the middle of the crowd, speaking the broadest Devonshire, now shouted that that was enough of pushing folk about, he wouldn't stand any more of it. Immediately it appeared that this bold leader represented a strong popular movement; shouts rose from every part of the tent, and still more angry complaint.

The attendants hastily called that the play was about to begin and begged for silence. The drum outside, till now beat at every second minute, stopped. The barker appeared suddenly in front of the curtain and told us once more that the story was true, that the production was straight from the Lyceum Theatre in the West End of London, and that it was performed by London actors and actresses of the first rank engaged at enormous expense only for this season.

Maria Marten had meanwhile risen from the piano and returned behind the stage by a step-ladder at one side.

Immediately the barker followed her and the curtain rose, showing

85

a backcloth, brightly lit, of a village with thatched cottages; Maria, rather breathless, but in her former dress complete with bonnet, came in with Tim Bobbin, a village girl, and her old father.

The three young people took hands and danced in a ring while the father clapped the time.

At this moment Corder strutted in, whip in hand, stared at the dancers for a moment, came down to the footlights, slapped his trousers with the whip and said to us in the audience, "Ah, that girl once more—the prettiest girl in Polestead. I'll have her yet or my name's not William Corder."

21

I DON'T suppose anyone nowadays knows the story of Maria Marten or The Murder in the Red Barn, or has seen any of the scores of plays founded upon it. An actual murder, I believe, did take place about 1830. It arose, I am told, from the sordid enough liaison of a dissolute farmer's son with a village girl who was already the mother of several illegitimate children. This unsavoury Lothario killed his paramour when she attempted to blackmail him into marriage, ran away to London, was quickly traced, arrested and duly hanged. The case owed its celebrity, apparently, to one sole circumstance; the girl's mother, Mrs. Marten, testified at the trial that she had seen in a dream both the murderer and the burial place of the body in one of Corder's barns called the Red Barn.

In fact Maria's body was found buried in the barn, and this discovery led to Corder's arrest.

I say that the story was sordid enough. Corder was a common type of village blackguard, and Maria Marten a girl of loose character. But the play of the evening, like, I believe, all the popular versions then in circulation, was very different. Maria on the stage became the virtuous child of poor cottagers, and Corder a rich gentleman, son of the squire who was the Martens' landlord, his liaison with Maria was no longer a common intrigue with the village Jezebel, but a deliberate seduction by a villain. One might say, indeed, that it was rape; for Corder, as we saw him that evening, forced Maria to surrender by threatening to raise her father's rent by an impossible amount, and to evict him if he did not pay.

That is to say, the drama we saw, and that millions had seen, was a story of the cruelest kind of wrong inflicted by the rich upon the poor. Throughout the play everything possible was done to show the virtue, innocence and helplessness of the poor, and the abandoned cruelty, the heartless self-indulgence of the rich.

And this was one among hundreds of such plays. I have wondered often how such propaganda failed to bring to England also, as to France, Italy, Germany, almost every other nation, a bloody revolution. For its power was incredible. As I say, it was decisive in my own life.

With what heart-moving sympathy I watched the poor village girl as the brute Corder marked her down for ruin. I knew also the power of the landlord to oppress, and the weakness of poverty in self-defence. I wanted to cry out a warning, and when Corder himself appeared, the very picture of arrogant wealth, how I hated him. Hatred is far too mild a term for a feeling which would not have been satisfied merely to kill. I longed to see him torn to pieces, to be tortured to death.

I was trembling all over. My face was wet with tears and sweat. I heard myself utter groans and smothered cries. It was all I could do not to shout out my sympathy and my rage. In fact cries of anger and exclamations of horror did continually break out from the audience throughout the whole performance. The women, especially, gave vent to their feelings. The old wife who had admitted me to the ropes never stopped muttering to herself, "Ah, poor thing—poor old man—listen to the brute, and he a gentleman born." One girl, also near the ropes, broke into loud hysterical sobs.

I suppose no one in that tent, however inexperienced and ignorant, failed to realise that the play was a made-up thing, an artful construction whose whole object was to work upon our feelings. Yet our feelings were stirred more violently than by any truth, by any tragedy of our own lives.

But how is it possible for me to convey the effect of dramatic art upon one who had never seen such a thing before, who had never, for instance, seen even amateur theatricals or a school performance? I have heard it said that a man's first experience in the theatre opens a new world to him—it would be better to say that it destroys the old one. That half-hour in the booth at Lilmouth, crowded among farm labourers at the rope which alone divided us from the strange beings of the stage with their flaring paint and loud voices, their bold gestures, was a decisive event in my life and, I believe, in Georgina's.

88

And why in retrospect should I be astonished at such events? Is there not an element of drama still not only in our churches, but in the ritual of government? You may be sure that what has survived from centuries in spite of criticism has powerful motives for existence. Believe me, art, and especially the drama, above all the popular drama, has a fearful power and responsibility in the world—it acts directly upon the very centres of feeling and passion.

For me Maria was an epitome of helpless innocence and simplicity; and when her murderer stood before me, actually in that small space, within a few feet of me, my heart seemed to falter at the terror of such guilt. How, I felt, could any human being commit such villainies and stand there before a crowd of his fellows and own it—act it?

And I felt these overwhelming emotions although I was perfectly aware that Maria was an actress performing a part, and that Corder was merely a poor player whose livelihood it was to give any representation required of him.

Still stranger and more terrible truth, even in the midst of my horror at this monster in his blood guilt, I was aware of a fascinated admiration. When in his soliloquies at the front of the stage, his eyes, roving over the audience, seemed to meet mine, they sent forth an indescribable thrill—it seemed that something flashed from the very centre of evil into my deepest soul.

22

My father used to say of Milton that he made Satan too grand. When he would read Milton to us he would warn us against the charm of that devil, pointing out that the conflict in that great poem is between a real good and an evil so terrible that it could scarcely be conceived—the absolute government of cruel and lustful egotism—the utter destruction of the very idea of liberty, of love and truth. How, he asked, should we like such a world? I agreed with my father—but Satan still carried an irresistible appeal.

Is it fanciful in me to discover in Corder, that cut-throat of a booth drama, some tincture of the Lucifer who took upon himself all guilt and defied the very lightnings of Heaven? Or to find in that powerful experience of my young spirit some clue not only to that crime of which it is my purpose here to trace the source and nourishing, but even to the ruin and confusion which has fallen upon the world?

Let us confess it—power itself has a fascination for the young soul in its weakness and dependence. And when to power is added the guilt of blood, some horror of cruelty, its force can be hypnotic. Looking back on the event of that evening—upon the boy I was—I have come to see a dire significance in his excitement—the more so that he was a simple, untutored son of the moors, unable to falsify his own experience.

Pure awe indeed fell upon him at sight of Maria as she appeared in her mother's dream to reveal the place of her grave—pure terror when she rose through the very stones of the condemned cell, a ghost with snow-white gleaming face and shift all dabbled with great gouts of blood, to stand in silence before her murderer.

She represented for him then not only a supernatural being but the Rhadamanthine judgment of Heaven—the inescapable vengeance of the Most High. But did not terror itself bring with it a sense of fearful glory in the man who had defied that vengeance?

90

How that boy's very bowels shrank within him at the sight of Corder on the drop, between chaplain and hangman—with bound hands and the noose about his neck. I remember how he tried to turn away his head when the hangman drew the white cap over those staring eyes, that pale haggard face—and failed. His eager glance devoured to the last moment of his existence the villain, the devil—and the hero.

23

It was in a state resembling that of the sleep-walker obsessed with a dream, or one who has seen "things too wonderful for me which I knew not," that I allowed myself to be borne away towards the entrance. All at once we seemed to be surrounded by fair attendants who thrust at me with powerful flat hands, and shouted, "Move along, ladies and gentlemen, move on there."

I was not at all startled in this condition of trance to feel an arm about my waist and to realise that Georgina was beside me. She had seen me long before, and perceiving that I was alone, alarmed that I should get lost, had wriggled her way towards me.

In a moment we were ejected into the open air, and turning as if by one will passed out of the fair into the road. We felt both that the fair could hold no more for us.

Neither of us spoke; and so reaching the station we were again herded by weary porters towards a train so crowded that we did not try to find a seat. And when at last we climbed in, there was no place to sit for our carriage was a cattle-truck. Such trucks were often provided then on excursion trains returning from popular festivals when a good proportion of passengers might be roaring drunk. In fact there were many drunks, men and women dancing and singing all over the platform, to snatch at the last moments of joy in their one day holiday from hard and narrow lives. Yet it was a good-natured crowd. Once in the train, pressed together in a solid mass, we were not only in security but comfort—so well cushioned against the violent jolting of the truck that we did not feel the weariness of standing.

And such was our continuing state of mental tumult that neither of us perceived our destination, we were carried past Crow Halt to Dollyford and arrived after that long circuitous journey at past midnight.

Even Georgina seemed to have forgotten the extent of our grow-

92

ing delinquency. Not yet had I even wondered how Georgina had reached the fair—it was days before I found, and then by chance, that she had simply gone to G, apparently on impulse, and commanded a place in his gig for both Ruth and herself. And as she would not take money from him, she had accepted two shillings from Mrs. G, who had joined them on the way.

All this was of no interest to us on that night—as we stood on the platform among the dispersing crowd our first words were about the play. Georgina said to me abruptly and fiercely, "All the same I'm glad we went."

I agreed warmly and put in my old plea—"It was not a real play, it was true. Father couldn't mind us seeing a true story."

But Georgina would have none of this casuistry. "Of course it was a play—it was feigning—with real actors." She said this in a tone of strong indignation. "But I don't care."

We were already in the main street and now turned up towards the moor. We took, as by tacit agreement, a short cut used only by moor folk—it was the one advantage of our being carried to Dolly-ford that we could take this track and save a mile. We had perhaps four miles to go, but it was through the narrow Battwell combe along a horse path full of loose stones—a terrifying place even to moor children, for you must not suppose that moor people learnt indiffer-ence to the vast solitudes and bare hills of their wild domain. I have thought that they were apt, at least in those days, to be even more affected by them than foreigners, for their terrors were based upon more accurate images, more concrete fears. For them the moor was full of named spirits and authentic ghosts.

Yet Georgina and I were still so burning with our new imaginations and discoveries that I do not think we even gave a thought to mur-dered smugglers and headless horsemen, the death coach of the Slaptons, or the suicide at the Battwell crossroad who was to be heard shrieking and moaning from her grave under the broken sign-post which was thrust through her body.

Hand in hand we laboured up the steep track, clambering and slipping among the stones, and anxiously guarding each other from falls. For now, as it seemed to me, I loved and admired Georgina beyond anyone else in the world. She was not only my brave and wise sister, but my closest intimate.

Such sudden changes of allegiance are, of course, common enough in family life, where daily cohabitation provides in a few days incidents and emotions enough to furnish out an ordinary friendship for years. The allies of yesterday are implacable enemies of today, and after a long history of events friends again tomorrow. But this new relation of mine with Georgina was founded in a new understanding, a new reciprocity, and never again sank into indifference or blind hostility.

Georgina has suggested since that it was based originally upon our community of guilt, both of us had given way to the same overwhelming temptation. But I cannot agree. For one thing, our guilt was of a different order. Georgina, as it appeared now, had not meant to go to the play—her overmastering desire was to see the animals, and especially the elephants, billed to parade with howdahs on their backs and jewelled rajahs in the howdahs.

But Mrs. G, a stern Wesleyan, had seen the play herself on the previous day and now, to Georgina's surprise, advised her also to go, saying that it was of high moral value to any young girl. Georgina, shocked, had refused. But the seed of possibility planted by her respected mistress had grown so fast that she had turned back even before she reached the gate, handed Ruth over to Mrs. Doan who was catching the earlier train, and having no money left entered the tent actually by creeping under the canvas beneath the side of the stage.

Georgina could not explain her yielding to temptation, but she did not wonder at it. She put it down to her natural born wickedness, and she repeated over and over again in the same indignant gloomy tone that all the same she was glad she had gone. She was glad she had seen Maria, she was especially glad to have seen Corder hanged.

For now we had come out of our tranced silence, we could not talk fast enough.

What is more delightful in this world than the new-found sympathy of two full souls?—we were aware of it, we exclaimed at it even in the midst of our talk. Georgina would cry, "Oh, it was so nice to

94

see you there too." And I would agree with all Georgina's judgments, saying, "Yes, yes, that's what I think. I am so glad you think that."

And yet so strange are such rapprochements that even while I cried yes, and pressed against my sister in the delight of affectionate sympathy, I was often unaware of what Georgina had said last. I was still beneath a different spell—a feeling, an illumination that I could not describe, preoccupied my mind. I quivered still to the mysterious power of the actor. I do not say that I desired to be myself an actor—that is a story invented in these latter days to fortify a case, the trumped-up case against all of us in the old generation who honoured our people enough to give them prepared speeches. Not so, one consequence of that evening's experience, and not the least significant, was that I did not again enter a theatre for more than thirty years. I felt the evil of that power and dreaded it. But I also understood a power that I had seen exercised by my father also—though in a lesser degree—the spell of the orator.

For me the actor had revealed a fearful, an astonishing power—one that entranced my boy's soul not only by its imposing solitary glory, but perhaps even more profoundly by its defiance. And this was a power that could be achieved by anyone with the will and a voice, anyone capable of learning this art of stringing words together in poetic form, and striking the right attitudes. For Georgina he was a rich and selfish squire's son, a cruel brute, as the Martens represented the deprived and suffering poor.

She showed all at once that hatred of the rich that I have described as an obsession.

It was obvious even to me at that time that these ideas, poured out among the darkness of the combes under the steel-blue night sky of September full of stars which seemed to give so much light and yet served only to darken our eyes, were not new-found. She had brooded them for years, probably from even before my mother's death.

Girls are more precocious than boys in observing and moralising upon family events. Georgina, it seemed, had never forgotten the loss of our farm, and for her it was an unjust poverty that had killed our

95

mother. "They killed her," she said several times with indescribable rage, "and they ruined father. Lord Slapton has ten thousand a year, and you know how he spends it, on drinking and fornications. Father is worth ten Lord Slaptons, and he has not even money to buy books."

Once she turned fiercely on me, "What are you smiling at?"

Hastily I answered that I was not smiling. How could she imagine such a thing. I agreed with all she said. But I had not heard her for ten minutes past.

What are the best arguments in the world if they do not strike the time and the heart? I had not come to my moment of illumination, I had lived with inequality all my life—for me still the cruelty of social injustice was swallowed up in a vaster, more dramatic, more immediate fatefulness of life itself, of arbitrary death.

One child was born crooked, another straight; one to bad parents, another to good; one man was stricken, another left.

In that same year, that giant, Sam Weaver, who had carried Georgina to the judgment—a true pillar of the chapel, as the minister liked to say, a Samson who could indeed lift up the gates of the Philistines and let in the army of the Lord—in that spring Sam took what we called fever and died in three weeks of a pleurisy. And the Weaver family had broken up within a month—its place, in the fearful word of desolation, knew it no more.

We could not blame Lord Slapton, or that vague entity the rich, for such catastrophes as these. They fell upon my imagination as the deed of forces beyond my understanding, the decree of a God whose ways were not my ways.

And while Georgina raged at those who had injured her loved ones, I walked in a dream. Something moved in me that was not yet even an ambition—the mere ghost of aspiration. It was true that I had smiled. At what vision, or rather sensation of proud independence, I could not tell. Who shall set bounds to the secret unconscious appetites of a young soul starved of hope?

I was a king, a hero of the revolution. But without wrath—without even revolutionary principles. I could not be troubled with indignation on this wondrous night.

96

24

THE foreman's cottage at Stonepit is the most northerly building in the straggling village, except the farm itself a hundred yards beyond. But approaching from the side by the horse track we saw it from some distance standing by itself in the gap between the cluster of the hamlet and the farm steading, and we were startled to see lights in the windows. We had not, in our excitement, even reflected on an excuse to our father—we did not dread punishment so much as his disappointment. So as we stopped, and I exclaimed, "They're still up," I felt in Georgina's hard clasp a tribulation even more violent than my own.

But when we entered the kitchen we were still more taken aback by emptiness and silence. The stable lantern hung from a bacon hook in the beam, but my father's chair was empty and there was not a sound.

Richard's bed-place had been opened, and the drawing of his curtains showed that he was within. Richard, for some reason of his own, had laboriously fitted curtains made out of an old petticoat to his bed-place, and drew them across when he went to bed. Georgina now flung aside the curtains and shook Richard by the shoulder. He was a light sleeper, and as soon as she touched him he sat up and was immediately wide awake. "So there you are at last," he said, putting down his bare legs from the bunk.

Georgina asked him if her father knew where we had been, and he answered, "That's just it, father hasn't come home yet."

This news had a stunning effect on us both. It was completely unexpected, and Georgina at once imagined some disaster. She burst out at Richard, "Not come home, but why, what's happened? Have you done anything? Has Mrs. Coyte come home?"

"I don't know," Richard said, "I thought it better to wait for you."

Ruth had now joined us, coming downstairs wrapped in an old cloak of her mother's which she used for a bedspread. Like Richard she showed a placid face, highly irritating to Georgina and myself. Yet it was obvious that both Richard and she were alarmed. Her coming downstairs to us was proof of that, and she said now, "If there'd been an accident Mrs. Coyte would have told us."

"An accident," Georgina said, "how could there be an accident with old Diamond, she knows every inch of the road." Then suddenly she exclaimed, "I'll ask Fred."

Though Fred was an enemy of mine, he had with Georgina that jesting relation which seemed to be the rule in her dealings with the older men of the village. Like G, Fred Coyte had admired and laughed at Georgina when she had been famous for her fights, and still liked to pretend that she was dangerous.

And though Georgina treated Fred as she treated G with contempt, she would also use him if it suited her. She did not hesitate, therefore, to suggest this call upon the man in the middle of the night. She ran out of the door as she spoke, and in the absolute stillness we heard her a moment later rattling the little iron side gate which led from the road up to the front door of the farmhouse. This gate was always kept padlocked to exclude wandering cows and prowling boys —the front door of the house was never used except for entry to the front garden. But the regular entrance by a back door was actually through the wall of the stable from the main yard, a door that seemed to have no connection with the house. Georgina no doubt thought that knocking on this door would not attract Fred's attention so quickly as the clanging of the gate—he slept in a front room facing the road and immediately above the gate.

After what seemed a long time we heard a man's voice, a sleepy shout, and then Georgina's shrill voice speaking fast and apparently scolding. We did not hear Fred again, but in a moment Georgina put in her head to say that there had been a fight in Tarbiton between the strikers and the police, and that our father was somehow involved. Fred was putting the horse in the trap, and if she did not get back that night, Ruth was to make our breakfast.

She then disappeared again in the darkness—ten minutes later we

98

heard the trap rattle past on its way to Tarbiton. We sat in silence round the ashes of the fire, unable to find a word even for each other. I still remember the apprehension of that night, the sudden discovery of what it would mean to us if we lost our father. As I say, we had all seen such a catastrophe happen in the village. It was not two months since Mrs. Weaver had gone to the workhouse with her two youngest children, and the eldest, less than a year older than myself, had simply vanished out of the world. Certainly no one in Shagbrook knew his fate.

It was, I think, the depth of our apprehension that made even Richard so curt when at last Ruth began to cry. He told her, with unusual roughness, that crying would do us no good, and that she had better go back to bed. "In fact," he said, "we'd all better go back to bed." And I think both Ruth and I were glad to find that there was still someone in the house to command us.

25

My biographers are fond of dividing my life into three periods —that of the agitator, the preacher and the statesman, each of which, they say, led naturally to the next and contained all the former, so that they were rather chapters in a complete story than episodes in a broken career. The agitator who learnt the art of rabble-rousing from his father passed naturally into the revivalist preacher, the preacher with his extreme Protestant and dissenting creed naturally opposed himself to privilege and entered politics to achieve his ideal of equality. And then again he used the methods of the demagogue. They quote my early speeches to show that I was one of the first "to dangle before the mob the offer of something for nothing, pensions and doles, buying their votes with subsidies which must in the end ruin the national economy and confound poor and rich, industrious and lazy, the parasite and the worker, in one common disaster."

The reports are accurate—but the inference is wrong. I did not advocate old-age pensions and insurance as a demagogue, a buyer of votes—I agree that buying votes would be disastrous to any state and first of all to freedom—I spoke as a Christian and a Protestant. And in proof I quote from a letter to my wife contemporaneous with these speeches—it was written just after the birth of our first child and the original can be inspected at the British Museum. "True religion (I wrote) centres in the family—for the Protestant, priesthood resides in every parent responsible for a child's upbringing. That is why we are bound to stand for any state policy that can secure the family unit as a unit. For it is only in family life that the freedom and dignity of a responsible citizen accords with his religious duty, and who shall say that one, who knows the burden of authority over helpless dependents, is thereby weakened in responsibility towards the state that is a father to its people."

I stand by that letter, so fortunately preserved by the careful piety

100

of my dear wife—I can fairly claim that it was not the utterance of a rabble-rouser. The picture of my life as a continuous line is in fact quite false—it resembles rather the iron crook called by shepherds a Hampshire crook; a long strong socket and a long loop ending in a sharp backward curl. The loop begins from my poverty-stricken childhood, and curves naturally, rapidly, into the phase of agitation. But the next turn, the curl, cannot be anticipated, it does not follow. The curve was broken when I turned back, and I became a preacher not because I had been an agitator, but because I had been brought up to evangelism.

Above all, it was not from my father that I learnt rabble-rousing, he was rather the strong socket of my whole life, there was in him no trace of the demagogue. He took no party sides, and that was his crime, he spoke the truth as he saw it, and that was his danger. Angry men do not like truth, they want to be flattered. He tried to save others from injury, and that was his own, because the others were not afraid of injury so long as they could injure each other.

Some of the younger strikers and their wives, accusing the committee of slackness, had set up their own committee and gone collecting for themselves, but they were violent and rough. On that market day in Tarbiton they had held up traffic and abused the passers-by—there was a fight and a riot, waterside hooligans joined in, and the strikers' official leaders finding my father in the market asked him, as a respected citizen and a man well regarded on both sides, to intervene.

He went at once and succeeded in drawing away many of the more sensible men and most of the women, simply by going among them and appealing to them personally. But there was a minority too excited and too prejudiced to listen to him. They continued the fight with the police, and while he was trying to get between the parties he was knocked down and trampled—he had been lucky to come out alive.

Police reinforcements had now arrived and cleared the street in a succession of charges. My father was picked up with other casualties But as soon as he was recognised he was arrested, as one of the miners' leaders, and carried off to the prison infirmary.

101

It was here that we saw him that morning—in a damp cell lighted only from a street grating. I cannot describe the depression of spirit with which we children stood about our father's bed in this dismal place, and heard him explain that he might yet be sent to prison. We heard also from the constable, who remained throughout the interview, that his leg was badly broken, and that in any case he would be taken to hospital.

This was said no doubt to console us, but it could not have that effect. In our situation a father in hospital was little better than a father in prison.

And the danger was real. The magistrates, representing for the most part Tarbiton shopkeepers, were very bitter against men whom they regarded as foreigners in the town, the wanton disturbers of their peace. As usual in such cases, it was impossible from the evidence to know who had started the fighting, and who exactly was guilty of the damage done. The most effective witnesses, therefore, were the injured themselves. Policemen with bandaged heads and blackened eyes were stronger proof than any amount of hard swearing.

The police actually opposed bail for my father on the grounds that he had been a ringleader in the fight. No doubt they believed it, he was a well-known man and an official in the miners' society. A known name always attracts a charge.

We had no lawyer—my father refused, on principle, to use the strikers' money on legal fees, and he had none of his own—Mr. Newmarch and Major Udal arranged his defence.

We relied very much upon these friends—Newmarch himself was a magistrate at Queensport; the Major was a distinguished veteran and connected by marriage with Lord Slapton, the chief landlord of Tarbiton itself. That is to say, he belonged to the same class as the prosecution and we assumed very reasonably that he would have means, private or public, of putting pressure on the bench. The world, as we understood it, was a tissue of private and hidden relations—had we not daily experience of it even in Shagbrook?

And who shall say that we were wrong as to the main fact?—we mistook only in the application of our rule. We did not understand its more complex workings within the Major's class.

102

Both Mr. Newmarch and the Major offered witness of my father's high character and hatred of violence. Unluckily the Major, a great enthusiast for my father's teaching and quite fearless before the magistrates, took the opportunity of finding himself in the witness box to point out that anyone who condemned my father put himself in great danger of divine punishment, and that the danger was by no means remote. For the world of human law was coming to an end actually within the twelvemonth, and the fact was proved not only by the works of the Duke of Manchester and several bishops but my father's own calculations.

All this was received very coldly—the conservative and Church of England instincts of the bench were much stronger than their class solidarity. Or rather, as I have observed since, that solidarity was itself founded in conservatism and therefore rejected the Major twice over, as a religious crank and a traitor.

Even the Duke and the bishops could not prevail with those bankers, doctors and merchants—they were country Tories whose grandfathers had been Jacobites to a man, they would have turned out the Queen herself in defence of their principles.

I have no doubt my father was in real danger of prison. A man called Brodribb of the dockers' union, who had even less to do with the riot, who was not even on the spot, got nine months. But now Mrs. Coyte marched into court and insisted on giving evidence.

"It's all because the tinners were too much for your coppers, and I'm not surprised," she declared in her shrieking voice. "Nimmo had nought to do with the fight except he tried to call his chaps off."

This startled the Tarbiton magistrates, but not so much us from Shagbrook. Mrs. Coyte was the nearest thing we had to a squire and she valued the position. She was, indeed, a little too eager to make a case, she swore she had seen the whole affair. And when this was proved untrue she went on to a general attack on Tarbiton.

"I know you Tarbiton lot," she said. "You'd tell any lie to get a moor chap into trouble."

Nevertheless she succeeded in obtaining my father's discharge, mainly, I think, because she was respected as a big farmer and a leading citizen.

103

Some of the magistrates put a great deal of pressure afterwards on Mrs. Coyte to discharge my father and take his cottage in order to remove him from the district. We heard this from Mrs. Coyte herself. She told the whole village about it, and said that the men who thought they could teach her how to manage her farm and her men were bigger fools even than the common run of Tarbiton folk. I think, indeed, this underhanded intrigue did us much good, for during the very anxious time of my father's illness we had at least no fear that he would lose his job and his home. And that would have ruined us all.

We were lucky, I say, to suffer so little by this accident, but it did have a considerable effect on my own youth. For while my father was laid up he could not earn those extra sums so important in a countryman's budget, and I was taken from school to help Fred Coyte, as far as possible, with the horses. From that time it might be said that my regular education came to an end. I did sometimes go to school, but so rarely that I proved merely a nuisance to the teachers and myself. I found myself ignorant of what younger children had learnt long before and, at the same time, remote from them in interest. At eleven I thought myself a man, and gave myself a man's rights to think for himself and to decide for himself what knowledge he would accept. I was now often in sole charge of horses and waggon, and even when my father was capable of work I was obliged always to supplement it. On many days I would be up at five and did not see my bed again till midnight.

How often did I tumble into my bunk without supper, actually without taking off my boots, certainly without washing, and all filthy still with the mud of the fields, the dung of the yards, fall so deeply asleep that Georgina would pull off boots and coat without my waking. And if I did open my eyes, I would gaze at her and wonder at her as at a spectre from some dream and know nothing of it in the morning.

I say I would sleep dirty as well as supperless. It is, I assure you, only too easy for a boy of that age enduring cold and rain, cutting winds and mountain frosts, long hours of heavy toil, or longer hours still of monotony, bringing a couple of carts at three miles an hour from some distant market along the deserted roads, to sink into brutality of thought and act. I lay dirty because to be clean required an

104

effort so great that I could not acknowledge its necessity. I write effort, and I could add pain ; a driver's hands must hold the reins, however slackly, and in winter my hands were deeply chapped. Soap and water were an agony to be borne at most upon a Sunday morning. The grime was bedded in my skin and would not yield to scrubbing except by loss of skin.

I can say from experience that to be dirty and to accept dirtiness are to be halfway to the brute. He who resigns himself to filth in his person will come to delight in the bad thought, the filthy word. In those days labourers have been shocked at my speech when I had reason to quarrel with them in some crowded market over a place for the cart, or feed for my horses.

26

A CHILD brutalised before puberty is a child lost—for all the forces of his growing pour into that rage of appetites. How much I owed in those dark days to the custom of my daily prayer, to the knowledge of my father's goodness, to the care of my sister. I did not, indeed, realise what these things meant to me, I would mutter the few words of supplication already half asleep; my father's reading from some Psalm, as common to my ear as the Shag pouring away through the combe, passed over my understanding like that noise of waters in the whins; but my memory, despite myself, was full of songs. So that on some cold morning of the long cold winter, as, sleepy still and disgusted with the day before me, I would take out the cart with swedes or muck, the dawn was not merely a mark of the weather to me. I had been perhaps an hour upon the road with sacks wrapped round my legs and a sack for hood to catch the night frost, when upon the high moor the first greenish light, itself as green as ice, defined the eastern horizon. All round me that broken landscape has taken form in black and white like a landscape of the moon, and thick frost lying in the furrows of last year's tilth has made as strange a picture on some hillside as the canals of Mars, little more remote from man's handiwork.

And some phrase, half heard in one of my father's Sunday addresses, would rise unbidden in my mind, about the hills that stand about Jerusalem like God about His people, for evermore; or a passage from Ruskin, always a favourite with my father, who had so loved his lonely Highfallow, as when the master writes of the effect of the mountains, "to fill the thirst of the human heart for God's working—to startle its lethargy with the deep and pure agitation of astonishment"—I felt the beauty if I did not know it or use the word.

So, too, when Georgina waked me in pulling off my coat and my boots, I have growled at her to leave me alone. But falling asleep again my soul knew if my mind did not that there was true love and loving in the world.

There was ambition too. I had not forgotten my experience of the fair—or rather, it had not forgotten me. There was planted in this rough dirty boy who spoke now habitually, as in spite against his lot, the broadest and crudest dialect, a vision of glory, of power, by means of the spoken word.

I say that power was a fantasy to me—I had yet no idea of achievement. But the idea can exist without the hope—as a child waves his wooden sword and leads an army of chairs without thought of being a general.

My imagination was not strong enough then to make me an actor, a preacher, much less a politician; the gap between the farm boy and these eminences was too wide for its furthest leap, but I acted all of them.

My first audience was Mrs. Coyte's sheep, or simply the rocks and gorse on some hillside. I began by repeating to them what I could remember of the play, the old parents' complaint against oppression, Corder's repentance and warning against evil ways.

But these practises were as secret as the most shameful vice.

One day, indeed, in the midst of my peroration, when standing on a rock I stretched out my arms and exhorted the people, that is the sheep, to remember that they were children of God, "and as children of God you are each of you free souls born equal in His sight," I was startled to hear clapping and a voice which seemed to say "Hurray."

For a moment I could not have been more startled than was he who heard "the mountain speak"—I stood on my rock quite overwhelmed by amazement and fear.

And when I saw the broad, rosy face of Fred Coyte rising from behind a gorse bush, I flew into an uncontrollable rage, snatched up my crook—a home-made crook of ash, short and thick—and rushed towards him. I should certainly have struck him, for Fred inspired less respect in the village than many boys of my own age; especially to me he was contemptible in being so utterly subservient to his mother.

I say I might have struck him if he had not turned and run, but as

107

he ran he grinned back at me, making gestures as if to protect his head. And when that evening I came into the farm kitchen with my report, I realised by his nods and winks from behind his mother's back that he meant to reassure me—he was not going to give me away.

Fred, indeed, at this time made many overtures of friendship, but I would have nothing to do with him. Not all the advantage of good relations with the son of the farm and one of my father's pet disciples could overcome the habit and tradition of scorning this man because he did not bear the responsibilities of a man.

Yet like so many of his kind, men kept in childish estate to the age of maturity, Fred Coyte struck one as full of clever tricks—his very talkativeness seemed like a trick to avoid responsibility. He would say at the Green Man that he had no money for a drink, his mother did not give him any. So he was always treated. Yet I know he had money—he had been to the fair on two days and spent royally. His whole life was a maze of cunning schemes. And even in his piety we thought that he was plotting to cheat—Georgina said of him that he came to my father's services and expressed belief in the Second Advent not because he expected Christ to come again but in case He might do so.

27

WE were very few Adventists in Shagbrook, but now an event occurred which suddenly increased our number by nearly twice. G, driving a fast young horse home from Tarbiton with Mrs. G on a dark night, and being somewhat in liquor, went into the ditch at the Battwell crossroad and wrecked the gig. Both occupants were thrown out with force, G was unscratched, Mrs. G was picked up quite dead —her skull was deeply fractured on a stone, the only stone, so we were told, for yards about.

That the respected Mrs. G should die because the disrespected G was drunk, this was a fine subject for the village philosopher.

But there was another and a deeper point at issue. My father had been denouncing the Green Man for years, was this tragedy God's judgment on Mrs. G?

You smile with contempt for our primitive religiosity, and it is true that when some months later I happened to notice the site of the crash, it was full of stones, a very dangerous spot—the miracle was that G had escaped. But our people, if they liked to exaggerate signs of God's intervention, did not miss the subtler point that if G had not been drunk he would not have turned into the ditch. It was drink, after all, that had killed the sober and upright Mrs. G.

I do not say that this judgment sent all the village to their prayers, it affected only those who were truly concerned with ultimate things— few at all times and in all communities. And among those, no doubt, of the half score who now augmented our congregation, some were moved simply by fear. But most were tormented deeply and anxiously by a terrible question—if a good woman could so die when a bad man was saved, where was the justice of God, where was any justice in earth or Heaven? And my father offered an answer, an answer which, so he said, and we believed, was to be proved within a few weeks.

The date of the Second Coming had been calculated in London for

109

April 15, 1868, and the local leader and minister of the sect, minister of the chapel in Tarbiton, a young and eager missioner, had chosen for our meeting place the highest hill within reach, Black Man Tor.

My father did not agree either with the date or the place. His own calculations gave the date a fortnight later and the place as Shaghead Down, a great rounded eminence about three miles off from us. But with that reasonableness which was also profound in his nature, he agreed that he might be wrong. He therefore consented to attending at Black Man Tor on the date given.

On that day, therefore, we were roused at four o'clock in the morning and packed into a tumbrel borrowed from Mrs. Coyte. My father, thoughtful of our comfort, had filled the deep body with straw so that we sat warm, like birds in a nest, in the dark, or rather that blue glimmer of starlight which makes the dark seem even more impenetrable. My father's small figure, alone, as seated on a plank he drove Diamond, Mrs. Coyte's mare, was outlined for us by the stable lantern hung from the shaft. It was still an hour before dawn when the track came to an end among the rocks and my father knotted the reins about a hawthorn stump. We had now two miles of climbing through the coarse grass and heather laden with the heavy dew of those moors.

I had slept much of the journey and now, having been turned out of a warm nest, stood among the others with feelings more disconsolate than awed.

Did we believe then absolutely that the world was approaching its last hour?—certainly we did not disbelieve it. My apathy certainly was due not to disbelief, but simply the feeling that whatever was going to happen to me, however fearful the catastrophe, I could not avoid it. It was faith itself that made me submissive, almost bored.

Half-a-dozen lanterns could now be seen approaching from different directions, and two or three assembled together nearby showed a meeting-place of several parties. One man, who had come alone without a lantern, suddenly emerged from the dark and greeted us with the question why we took all that trouble to tie up the horse, for, he said, what did it matter if the horse strayed at this time when the world of horses and mankind was standing at the door of eternity. My father made no answer to this reproach, but we were surprised and startled to recognise in the tall, burly figure, robed from head to

110

foot in white, who stood holding our lantern, the Battwell constable. We children had never attended the central Adventist congregation in Tarbiton, and we had no idea that the constable, a man known for his rough good nature and suspected of a fondness for beer, was one of the elect.

We gazed stupidly at the policeman's garment. And timid Ruth, who had been holding my hand, shrank up against me and uttered a small cry. We had not seen such a thing before. My father had put on no robe. He wore, perhaps as a last protest against the date chosen, his working dress. He had made only so much concession to the majority as to cause us to put on our Sunday clothes. Now he brought out a brush from his pocket, and Georgina proceeded first to remove the straw dust from us and then to brush our hair.

All these various lanterns now began to ascend the hill from their different quarters, and when at last, after a long and most wearisome climb, we stood at the top, we saw that other lanterns were approaching from the far side. And I remember that this silent gathering of the lanterns, roused in my mind, still heavy with sleep and resentful of early waking, some idea of the importance of the occasion, an impression that had not been conveyed either by the long preparation, or even the policeman's robe.

We had been used for years to hearing the end of the world discussed and calculated. My father and the Major indeed, with their papers and their pencils, brought to the calculations the same matter-of-fact attention that I associated with the sale of crops and the stable accounts with their long tale of straw, oats, hay and liniment.

And even now, so strong was custom, so easily does familiar wont dull even the quick imagination of a child, this march of lights, as of a new army of Gideon, converging to the assault, brought me only heightened excitement and curiosity, fed by the gradual arrival of climbers at the summit, and the paling dark, which allowed us to recognise, in this new setting, such well known figures as the Tarbiton minister and his family, Mr. Simons, head keeper at Slapton, two neighbouring families of poor labourers, with eleven children between them, one a baby in arms, and a gentleman from Dollyford, whom we knew as the Professor.

There were in the end between forty and fifty persons gathered on

111

the little plateau of rock at the summit of the Tor, and a large proportion of these was dressed in white. Some of those poor neighbours I spoke of, the Doans, perhaps the poorest of our village, a family always half-starved, had yet contrived white clothes for the smallest of the children. Even as a boy of eleven I was impressed by the grave and anxious looks on the faces of the poor father and mother as they stood there waiting in confidence to be translated into paradise from a world which had treated them so cruelly. Those who deride our folly and credulity might ask why that poor mother among her hunger-wasted children should not believe that if Christ truly loved the poor and the outcasts He would come again to rescue them from misery.

It is often said and believed that only the most stupid and illiterate persons adhered to that sect, but this is not so. I suppose a large proportion of our gathering that day were illiterate; and dependent therefore, as only illiterates can be, upon the instructions of those who possess the mystery of print. But there were also among us men of good and even superior education, such as the minister himself, a college man, and Major Udal, who had brought both wife and daughter. All these were in robes, and it was strange to me to see the daughter's rosy and pretty face above the hieratic dress as she nodded and smiled to her acquaintance in the congregation. Her air was that of any lively young girl attending morning service, and I was wont to see her in a riding habit when occasionally the hunt met near our village. She was a well-known horsewoman and afterwards, I believe, famous in the shires. She married a peer and I had the pleasure, nearly fifty years later, of the assistance of her eldest son as one of my secretaries.

Yet she, as well as her father, was then among the most devoted of that congregation. Her smiles and nods were not evidence of a frivolous heart, but merely of the manners of her caste.

You may say that I should not lay too much emphasis on the judgment of a retired field officer. But the Major had a very good judgment in all the common affairs of life. And the man we called the Professor was Fellow of a Cambridge College and distinguished throughout the world for his mathematic discoveries.

I do not wonder that learned men shared my father's wild hope.

112

What logic will answer the voice that murmurs in the brain night and day, "There is no truth, and goodness is a lie—love a trick." What learning will cure the despair that rages in the flesh like a cancer, eating a man alive.

The marvel is that millions deny all hope and boast themselves wise. Men who for some reason of fear or vanity take care to ask no questions that cannot be answered with a slide rule, who learn nothing, state nothing, but numbers, who, carefully withdrawing their dignity from the arena where men struggle and suffer so foolishly, take their padded seats in the stalls and raise critical eyebrows at the circus which is the agony of the world.

28

Dawn broke at last, the dawn so tremendous in significance for such as the Doans. And as the first pale light made perceptible the wild broken horizon of the mountains about us, and the lanterns began to burn dim, I too felt for the first time with terrifying suddenness the meaning of the phrase "an awful expectation."

I stood, as it were, abashed to an infinite smallness and humbleness —a small ignorant boy waiting upon the doorstep of an imperial palace might know something of my feelings—but my palace was eternity, my emperor was unimaginable in power, and his threshold was the everlasting hills.

It is not for nothing that the Psalmist has said, "I will lift up mine eyes unto the hills from whence cometh my help." No doubt God is in all things. It is His life which maintains the physical world, as the soul of man carries his body for a vesture. But those who choose the mountaintops for that intuition of the numinous in us, in which it seems that we break through the boundaries of the word into the very centre of the Divine Mind, are not deceived. For the word and the works of man, however necessary to his worldly life, hide from his daily imagination the primitive grandeur of creation.

Now, as the light strengthened and the mists fell back, drawing down their heads among the combes like spirits of the night descending sullenly into their narrow graves, I was aware of our isolation in space, a physical exaltation above the daily utilitarian levels of plough and pasture. I felt the distinction of our cause and my own lot —the glory of those who are bound in a private cause, especially one despised of the multitude.

The little poor boy trembling upon the doorstep of the imperial palace knew also the pride of one invited—and the measure of his humbleness was the same with the stature of his honour.

The minister now advanced and called us together for prayer and

114

Psalm. We prayed to be forgiven our sins—believe me, at such a moment one utters such a request with fervour, never does one have so vivid a sense of daily, hourly evil-doing in word and act, in doing and not-doing.

As colour crept up into the light, we rose and sang Wesley's hymn:

> Lo, He comes with clouds descending,
> Once for favour'd sinners slain.
> Thousand thousand saints attending
> Swell the triumph of His train:
>   Alleluia.
> Christ appears on earth again.

The last white head of mist had now disappeared—we stood on the topmost island of a scattered archipelago. The morning was all round us, clear and cold. Only a few very high clouds, small and thin, like the frosty breathing of some genius of the moors, floated through the immense sky opening now before us at speed, as if enormous energies, released below, were gathering power to split the universe apart.

And suddenly, I do not know for what reason, but possibly by some chance ordering of the small clouds huddling upon the horizon, a great sword of fiery light pierced through the hollow air.

The effect upon our congregation was incredible. I can still remember that sensation of mingled terror and elation which seemed, as they say, to turn my bones to water, or rather to abolish altogether the sensation of flesh. I was a mere quivering sensation while I stood there faltering the words of the hymn without the least consciousness of what I was saying. Several of our party fell on their knees, and one woman gave a loud sob. As that great sword flashed still higher to the very dome of the sky, our hymn ceased of itself and the minister shouted, "On our knees." But we were already on our knees—our legs had failed beneath us.

And he began to pray loudly with the words, "O Lord Christ, have mercy, have mercy upon our weakness. We stand here naked and defenceless before Thy judgment. Forgive the fearful meanness and smallness of our insect souls." Here he stopped for a moment and now, as we could all see, another great beam had sprung up outside the first. In a moment there were half-a-dozen of these great rays ir-

115

regularly spaced, piercing far up to the small grey clouds I mentioned which now became like jewels.

The minister had started again to pray, but even I, as I knelt there, knew that what stood before us was not the end of the world but a fine sunrise not uncommon at that season on the high moor. Within a few minutes the sun itself appeared upon the edge of the moor like a row of sparks on a half-quenched brand. The sword-like rays faded from the air and the clouds turned from ruby, amethyst and opal to pale gold.

I do not know how long we knelt and how long the minister prayed. It was my father who first rose from his knees and lifted us to our feet. I know Ruth was so stiff and cold that she nearly fell, and we had to rub her legs to bring back the circulation. She fell asleep as soon as we put her back into the cart.

I, too, was drowning in sleep—I think I slept among the straw all the way home. Georgina's voice, proclaiming with angry defiance to some unseen critic, possibly her own mind, "So father was right—I knew he was right," comes back to me like a voice from a dream.

29

OUR second assembly, fifteen days later, at Shaghead Down, on the date calculated by my father, remains in my mind as a disaster. It was raining—the dawn appeared like a dirty rag, and my father persisted in waiting for his Master until the little band of his personal followers, amounting to nine in all, including Mr. Newmarch, Edward G and Fred Coyte, were so soaked and discouraged that Richard said loudly, "Nothing's going to happen now—it's nearly nine o'clock."

My father turned on him and said, "Ah, Richard, for you it could never happen. Your eyes are blinded with the noise of disputation, and your ears are deaf with gazing on tales."

But in a few minutes after he turned again and said to Edward, "I would not have any man stay here in the wet who does not believe that my Lord will come. For if he stay without faith, then the rain could harm him. And you, Fred, have your earache, you, Edward, have your weak chest."

The Major now spoke up and said that figures were deceptive things, and man too easily deceived himself—it seemed that he, no less than Mr. Nimmo, had perhaps been mistaken in his interpretation of the signs. He proposed to go home and would take any three more with him in his carriage. Fred Coyte and Frank Doan followed him downhill. Edward still remained, but now my father commanded him to go and led us children back to the cart, telling Richard especially to wrap up and get down well into the straw in case he caught cold.

And he never admitted the failure of our expedition; he would repeat, even years later, that those who fixed the dates of the Second Coming forgot one essential thing—that Christ would not appear to those that did not believe on Him.

Richard, as we went to bed that night, did not say his prayers. I noticed the omission and I was disturbed—I said to him, as I might have warned him of a candle left alight and threatening to set his bed on fire, "Dick, you forgot your prayers."

117

"I'm not saying them any more," Richard said. "I haven't really said them for a long time—I only kneel down and make faces. But to-day was too much. Father pretending it was because we don't believe. It's what Fred says—just a get-out. It really is such nonsense."

I was thunderstruck, and asked, "Do you mean you don't believe in God?"

"Do you?" Richard asked with mild contempt. "Where could He live for one thing? We know the sky is only air." And he went on to say that God seemed to him impossible—in fact he repeated all the common arguments which might appeal to a clever boy of fifteen—the scientific one against miracles, and the moral one based on the existence of evil. If there were a God, he asked, why did He not stop wars, and why had He let our good mother die so miserably.

What struck me at that time was not Richard's argument but his indignation, so unusual in my brother. I thought that he was angry with his father for making him feel foolish.

I did not dare to ask him if this were true—I was too overwhelmed by the blasphemy of his talk.

"But aren't you afraid?" I said at last.

"Afraid of what?" he asked.

But I was afraid even to explain—to insult God by suggesting that He might be flouted. I feared Him too much, or rather, I simply feared. But Richard understood me, "Afraid of that poor old God who can't even stop Ruth from coughing or keep mother Weaver out of the workhouse—I'd be ashamed. Why, if He was real, I should have to hate Him."

After these words I dared not speak again. I crept into bed and lay in terror, not only for Richard but all of us. And always after that night I had a special awe of Richard. I did not know if I felt more horror or admiration for my clever brother, but I could not be intimate with him. He had passed finally out of my world.

Indeed, less than a month after, Richard ceased even to live at home. He had been awarded a scholarship at Queensport Grammar School in the previous June, our only doubt was how he would be able to take it up—Queensport was too far for a daily journey. But now our cousin in Tarbiton offered to give him house-room in exchange for occasional service in the shop.

118

This good nature in so churlish a man surprised us, he hated my father as a sectary and an agitator. He may now have thought to see some reflected glory in Richard's scholarship; but the prime mover in this scheme, which alone enabled Richard to take up his scholarship, was again Georgina. She had taken advantage of market days to call on our cousin and tell him the position—a thing that Richard would never have done for himself. For though Georgina had so touchy a pride, and Richard seemed quite devoid of that quality, it was Georgina who in all our young lives would humble herself for our advantage. It was she who begged for us from G and Mrs. G, who bore with Mrs. Coyte's nagging, who now appealed to this churlish old man for help.

I heard that at first he would not listen to her, she stood about for hours in his shop on successive Wednesdays before he consented to acknowledge her as a relation and listen to her request. It is not too much to say that Georgina pestered and shamed the man into surrender.

But in after years she was amused by the recollection—and I believe she was proud of it—her pride was in that humbling of her pride which had brought success.

It was one morning soon after this triumph, when we were still rejoicing in Richard's advancement and he was much in our thoughts, that I spoke to Georgina of his loss of faith.

"What I think," I said, "is that father might have admitted he was wrong. Even Fred thinks so—and Fred is very believing."

"Father wasn't wrong," Georgina said.

"Oh come, Georgy," I said, "you don't really think there's going to be a Second Coming."

"Why not?—it's promised in the Bible."

"Well, it didn't happen, and that's about the tenth time it hasn't happened."

"It didn't happen because some of the people had no faith—that beast Fred doesn't really believe anything. He's too soft. He only wants to be funny."

"Or Dick," I said.

Georgina turned and her eyes flashed but she said nothing. She continued only with more exasperated vigour to chop and beat with

119

two wooden paddles a great mass of saffron-tinted butter just dredged from the churn and now lying before her on a slate slab, to be shaped into pounds for market and stamped with the Stonepit mark, a cow's head surrounded with wheat ears.

Georgina did this work with triumphant precision—she was already known for her skill in all dairy work.

We stood in the Stonepit dairy. Now that G ran the Green Man with a barman, Georgina had ceased to work there, and she had been very glad when Mrs. Coyte took her into the farm dairy. I, having risen also at half past five, was waiting to drive Fred and a cartload of sheep to Ranstone.

The dairy at Stonepit was the cleanest place in the farm—one might say the only clean place—and both Georgina and I took pleasure in the whitewashed walls, the scrubbed slabs of cool slate, the floor tiled in red quarries. It faced east for coolness, but at the moment it was flooded with the early sun—almost as yellow as the butter which Georgina was beating with such violence. I perceived her wrath—I knew she bore criticism of Richard little less hardly than of our father. But in my working clothes, with my whip in my hand and my cart waiting for me, I was in an independent mood. Though in fact I was allowed to drive only old Diamond who could almost drive herself, I was as proud of my carter's status as Georgina of her promotion in the dairy, we met at the farm on equal terms as responsible workers.

And now, perhaps a little jealous of Georgina's loyalty to Richard, I persisted, "Dick said it was just a get-out and that's what I think too—father had to explain somehow."

Georgina jumped round upon me in a rage and exclaimed, "Do you mean that father is a liar?"

She held a butter paddle in her hand and for a moment I thought she would strike me with it. She was in one of her worst tempers, crimson and trembling.

But since that night after the fair, Georgina had treated me with a new kindness, and controlled her temper to us all. She checked herself now and said only that she was surprised that I should agree with a creature like Fred Coyte about my father. But in her view Fred was not fit to lick my father's boots.

120

I said nothing to this—I was startled by the effect of my rashness and I did not want a violent quarrel with Georgina. But Georgina never forgave me on this point—years later she would say something that showed her indignation. In fact, this family disaster which had made my father a laughingstock in the village, had a precisely opposite effect on Georgina and on me—it brought her closer to her father and nearly abolished from her mind all those strong political feelings which she had so suddenly revealed to me after the fair, while it removed from me my complete trust in my father's wisdom and so opened the way to political agitation.

For I had ceased to believe in all those calculations and a special providence. It seemed to me absurd that Christ should be expected to come only to save a few moormen like myself and Fred Coyte. And though I had been shocked by Richard's atheism, though I continued to say my prayers, yet, without having the least idea of it, my faith—the unquestioning faith of the child in what he has been told by his parents—had received a mortal wound. It was already bleeding to death.

30

BUT I was barely aware even of a wound. Children of that age are not used to introspection, indeed, not capable of it. All their energies and senses are turned outwards. Between twelve and fourteen I grew six inches, indeed to almost my full height of five feet six, and while my body was so engaged it knew as little of the state of its soul as a fighting army of the ideals, the dreams, the history, that brought it to war.

I grew from an overworked farm boy to something like a lout, and if the disease at the true centre of my being had part in the conscious roughness of my manners, the deliberate carelessness of my dress, I was not aware of it.

I was perhaps the more ready to be rough and rude that Georgina, in the same time, at least when she was on duty, was becoming cleaner and politer almost by the month—not only, I think, because she had passed the line between girlhood and womanhood, but because she found herself in a trusted and appreciated place.

She was now in charge of the dairy, she had become so good at making and selling Stonepit butter and cream that Mrs. Coyte began to take the stall to Tarbiton Wednesday market. I would often drive them to the place and then make a round with the cart to pick up odds and ends for the farm, according to the season, coal and cake, hurdles and seed.

But I had plenty of time to spare. And one morning as I sat on a box by the stall, replaiting a frayed whip-lash, more to waste time and enjoy the bustle of the market than to be useful, a solemn-looking person in black thrust a pamphlet into my hand.

Pamphlets were much distributed in those days, it was a time of religious and political turmoil. I paid little attention to pamphlets and I stuck this one between my knees while I knotted the lash.

It was Georgina who, turning to get some more butter from the

122

cool box under the stall, noticed the thing, drew it out and said with disgust, "Oh, some more of that stuff." And she was in the act of throwing it away into the market rubbish behind, when I stretched out my hand for it and said, "Let me look."

Georgina gave me a sharp glance from under her sunbonnet as she handed the pamphlet back—she knew very well that I had demanded it only because of her disapproval. But she said nothing, she had begun to allow me my rights as an earner and a man.

I was now obliged to show some interest in the pamphlet—I began by looking at the title and the picture on the cover. The former was *The Great Design*, the latter was a crude representation of a farmer's boy in a smock harnessed to a huge waggon—he had a cruel bit in his mouth marked "Poverty." The waggon was being driven by a bishop in a mitre, and seated in it behind was a party of persons among whom one recognised a judge in his wig, a general in uniform, a peer in his robes, and behind them, in turn, the top of a woman's head wearing something which was not quite a bonnet and not quite a crown—that is, it indicated Royalty clearly enough even to an unlettered yokel like myself, and yet it could have been defended in a police court as the innocent bonnet of an old lady.

I had seen such subversive leaflets before—at that time there was much republicanism in the west. One of our great landowners and liberal leaders was a strong republican. And many of the evangelicals followed him. But these were republicans from religious motive—from the idea that God alone should rule. There were also many who attacked the crown and the state from hatred to religion which they regarded as the instrument of the rich to oppress the poor, what would be called nowadays the opium of the people.

This was such an attack—six months before I should have thrown it away. For I knew my father's views—he was not only deeply religious but a loyalist saying, "Render unto Caesar the things that are Caesar's," and telling us how little those things, taxes and legal obedience, concerned the life of the soul.

But now something had gone from me—from that faith in my father—and so without thinking I opened the first page of the book and read, "Learned men tell us about that All-powerful and All-wise

123

Master who rules the world." It went on in a vein of strong irony to describe the world after five thousand years of that government —especially the lot of the poor.

I will not quote further, the argument was essentially the same as Richard's nearly two years before. Either the omnipotent God was a tyrant and devil or there was no God at all—omnipotence being assumed as an all-embracing power over time and space, to subvert nature itself, to intervene at any moment in human fate.

I say this had been Richard's argument, which had seemed to have no effect on me. But either it had worked in secret and unknown to myself, or I had reached an age of decision—one of those stages of life in which the soul is suddenly laid open to new and powerful impressions. I was now overwhelmed as by an irresistible force—I sat as one "drunken but not with wine," stupefied yet thirsty for more.

When Mrs. Coyte, returning to the stall and noticing my idleness, asked sharply what I was doing there, and had I seen to the horse, I got up quickly and walked off in the opposite direction from the horses and carts—towards the waterside where I knew I could be alone. And turning up the first side street, I climbed a chained gate into the first accommodation land and sat down behind the hedge to read. I read as I had never read before, for the first time I knew the passion of illumination, not only my mind but all my senses seemed to strain forward in eagerness. I was not aware of thought or feeling, the argument seemed to fly by itself into my brain and to find there a place so exactly prepared for it that every sentence fell instantly into the niche that had ached for its coming.

The force of my atheistic socialist in his pamphlet was not in the print but the reasoning. When I had finished the last page, it seemed as impossible to me that God could exist as the pots of gold at the end of the rainbow—more so, for I saw the reason why this great lie had been invented and not why men should invent the other fairy tale.

Impossible, I say, and yet I could not believe it, I could not cry, "There is no God." Something other than my brain, something deeper than argument, recoiled with horror from that thought. Illumination had served to make my confusion a conflict—to turn my dejection into despair.

124

The faith that grows from childhood into the very texture of mind and soul can give it strength and unity which nothing earthly can destroy. It has stood the utmost cruelty that man can invent, it is like the elastic steel of those tall houses which in an earthquake sway each way but will not fall.

But if the steel be flawed and the frame of that house break, it cannot be mended, the sharp ends tear at the fabric till the whole is one wound. Better for that house if it had been built of cob, a low thing that neither dares the gale nor fears to be thrown down, a little mud will make it as good or bad as before.

I had been taught to believe but the frame of my faith had been broken—at the critical age of puberty, when above all a youth needs confidence in his elders and leaders—when nature herself, as if to make up for that physical turmoil that she has injected into his frame, has awakened in him also the power of devotion to a hero or a cause.

But I had no hero; however my feelings, feelings implanted in me from earliest childhood, recoiled from atheism, yet I could no longer respect my father. I saw him only as an ignorant man who had been deceived in a ridiculous manner and had made his family ridiculous.

I returned to the market so distracted even in my looks that Mrs. Coyte accused me of being drunk and said that she would set my father and Georgina after me, "I'll tell that sister Jo of 'ee." She said that she had seen me going to the bad this long time. And, indeed, it is possible that I might have gone to the bad.

31

I was not drunk that day at Tarbiton, but within the next few months I began to drink and to meditate worse things. I was barely fourteen, but, like all my family, precocious in development —and boys of twelve were then fathers, boys of fourteen went a-whoring; it seems that in those days, at least among the poor, as they had short lives, so, like self-sown barley along the hedgerow, they matured too young.

There were in our hamlet boys of my own age whose talk and practise in all vices were evil beyond imagination.

And that might have been my lot but for a chance meeting, a lucky friendship.

I was at this time in a state of singular isolation—Richard had gone from us, I saw him only on a Saturday night, for though he loved his home he avoided the Sunday services. Edward was too old, at twenty he affected the middle-aged man; and Georgina, so close in affection, was not to be consulted about a want of faith. I was lonely at home and bored in the village—it was perhaps natural that as the year went on I found myself more and more often in the company of Fred Coyte.

Fred, I believe, quite understood my state of mind, he was clever at knowing what went on in other people. In his middle thirties he was still like a child in his desire to conciliate—in his search for a friend. So when we found ourselves alone together in some market town he would ask me to drink with him, and I, partly to maintain my superiority as a trusted and confident person, would consent to a beer or cider in the market bar.

I found him now an amusing companion, he had a fund of stories about neighbours, about even his own mother, in all of which he represented himself as the victim and the fool. So while I laughed, I still felt my ascendancy—no doubt Fred, after the way of butts, in-

tended to flatter me in exactly this fashion. And it was very success-
ful in securing my company. I enjoyed being with Fred, for though
I did not treat him with contempt in the old childish way, I con-
descended to him in a manner pleasing to my youth and my private
uncertainty.

Fred, for his part, accepted my grand airs with the utmost good
humour. Indeed, as I look back I see that he was an exceptionally
good-natured and friendly person. And perhaps it was fortunate for
this poor fellow that he had such a disposition, for no other could
have made his life tolerable. Indeed, there is no other that could
have given him that modicum of dignity which the simplest of human
beings requires for existence.

I did, however, discover Fred's good qualities for myself in this
manner. We formed a custom of paying visits whenever possible to
larger towns like Lilmouth, usually to see some special sight, a
regiment on the move, birthday illuminations, or merely a trades
procession, and I think it was about eighteen months after that time
when Richard had left home that Fred and I paid a visit to Exeter.

Fred had been sent to fetch a second-hand wheel plough that Mrs.
Coyte had bought nearby. He was to load it on a train and cart it
home from Dollyford. But this meant a night drive across the moor
and Fred did not care to be alone in the dark—he believed in all
the ghosts and bogies that old moormen told of. So he took me with
him, and I was delighted to see the big city.

And as we were walking down High Street in Exeter we were
accosted by two women from Ranstone, known loose characters who
had been turned out by the minister there, and now carried on their
trade in Exeter. They greeted Fred as a friend and asked us to take
a drink with them in a neighbouring public house.

It was beginning to rain. We had been talking of shelter, and
Fred was obviously delighted as well as alarmed by this meeting,
he kept on laughing at the women's remarks, and yet instead of answering their invitation he turned to me and said, "Go on, Ches,
what do you think of it?"

The women, surprised at having the matter referred to me, turned
round and looked me over. Then one of them took me by the arm,

127

calling me ducky and saying that I was quite the man, she would stand me a pint, and take me home with her.

And I believe I was eager to comply, yet I recoiled from the woman, I tried to pull away from her and turned sulky.

Fred meanwhile looked on and laughed; yet again, when both women in his turn took him by the arms and asked him to come along, he grinned at me and said, "What say, Ches, shall we go?"

I answered sulkily that he could do what he liked, it was nothing to do with me.

I was aware of the poor figure I cut, in my sudden embarrassment, and it made me rough. I threw the woman's hand off my arm, exclaimed that I did not want anything to do with such ——, and ran off.

I had reverted in those few minutes from the arrogant hobbledehoy to the child—my only idea was to escape from those grinning women and the sly Fred—I turned the first corner, then another, in a moment I was lost.

See me then an overgrown boy of fourteen in a Sunday suit of cheap blue cloth, much too tight for him so that his blackened hands dangle from three inches of red wrist, his broken crumpled boots are disclosed in their whole clumsy architecture, as well as the torn socks above, hovering about a street corner in the rain. He has drifted to a corner like others of his kind, because he does not know which way to turn. He has passed along a street because in the street there is no terminus, until the kerb at the corner has asked him, where are you going? He has stopped because he has no answer, there is no reason why he should turn this way or that.

Besides, at a corner the lingerer who has nowhere to go is not so conspicuous—corners are also meeting places for people who have a purpose in their movements. Yet this country boy is visibly uneasy and lost—he glares at passers with defiance and he is ready to cry with humiliation at the shyness, the mysterious drawing back which has made him cut so mean and poor a figure before two women whom he has been wont to scorn, and the friend before whom he has acted a lordly part. He is bitterly ashamed and astonished at his mysterious loss of nerve before that friend.

128

And beneath all these cruder sufferings, the shames of poverty and ignorance, the consciousness of a public failure, there lies the misery of confusion and bewilderment—he does not know even his own mind about this very episode. Has he been a coward and a fool to run away from those women, or is he wise and strong in virtue?

He feels like a coward—he knows that he has run—he is disgusted with himself for not playing the man. He resolves not to fall short again in boldness.

It was fortunate for that defiant and humiliated boy on that wretched afternoon that, looking round him to see where he was, he should catch sight of the name of Leddra on a small poster stuck upon a broken door. It was the name of his father's friend—a well-known minister in Tarbiton—and he approached it as a friend—to read the notice of a meeting for that very afternoon upon the subject of the Brotherhood of Man. The meeting was free and the committee of sponsors included not only the name of Leddra but those of three other ministers.

I did not know these names, but they assisted further to reassure me—I cannot say I chose to go to this meeting—rather I drifted there upon the double impulse to escape from the street where every window seemed to be surveying this uncouth clodhopper from the moors, and to keep out of the rain.

The hall, belonging to a Baptist church, was stuffy and only half full. I was relieved to find it in semi-darkness and to recognise not Leddra on the platform—he did not appear—but two ministers whose white ties alone inspired confidence in me, and two others who appeared to be superior workingmen.

I felt that I could sit at peace under these auspices, but I was not comforted within. My body relaxed in the chair only to give my soul more energy of distress. I heard but did not grasp the words of the opening speech by one of the ministers—the few phrases that struck with meaning on my ear conveyed only the information that we were to welcome a distinguished man, an Italian professor and refugee, who was bringing to us a message of hope and peace, a message of the utmost importance to the whole troubled world.

I had heard this language scores of times—it came often from

129

the lips of my own father—I expected to hear from this stranger, now seated in the shadow behind the speaker, the usual sermon.

And already I had rejected sermons—the word of God had become a suspicious rigmarole—I prepared to shut my ears to what could but increase my despair and confusion of spirit.

What was my surprise when now there sprang to the front of the platform a small fair man who, without any preliminary text, declared that for him there were no churches, no creeds, but only mankind and the soul. Even more startling to me than this unconventional beginning was the man's fervour, his dramatic gestures, the play of his voice, the indescribable spell of the true orator.

I was looking, though I did not know it, on one of the most brilliant orators of that time rich in oratory—Lanza, who began, I believe, actually as a singer.

I am not going to recall the complicated history of European revolution—and Lanza is forgotten with greater names. It is enough to say that he began as a disciple of Proudhon and afterwards became one of Bakunin's most trusted lieutenants in the League of Peace and Freedom.

This association, if you remember, taught that murder, lies, any trickery whatever, was justified in order to bring about the collapse of civilization. It produced a long series of bomb outrages and assassinations.

It was on account of recent outrages that Lanza had now broken with the League and taken a position which might be called Tolstoyan, though it anticipated Tolstoy's conversion by several years.

He was a nihilist, like Tolstoy later, but only in the sense that he believed government and property to be the source of all evil and despised organised religion as a branch of the police.

Lanza had a voice of wonderful tone and flexibility, and though his English was not quite perfect, the unexpected play of accent and syllable compelled a closer attention, and produced more explosive effects. His meaning entered into that chaos of my mind like fire and light—to sweep away the ruins of betrayed confidence, and show among the dark, still firm and fair, the roads of an ancient and noble and to my surprise, a familiar city. It was as though the order, the

130

direction which I had needed so desperately, had been all this time concealed within my own breast.

For he spoke now of love, that family love which guarded over all childhood, the love of fathers and mothers for their children, of brothers and sisters for each other. He spoke, that is, of what I knew, of what was familiar to me as bread; made me know it again for a holy thing, the foundation of all happiness and peace. He asked us what was the place of law between those who loved, did the mother send for a policeman to rule her child? Do children obey only from fear? Why then, he asked, do we who begin our lives in love, in brotherhood and in peace, find ourselves so soon thrown into a world of violence, oppression and cruelty?

But I need not repeat an argument so familiar, I want to show here its enormous force. It appealed to experience, and an experience as deep and strong and true as it is universal. What man does not remember his mother's unselfish affection? Who has not felt the impulsive goodness of a child?

32

Long years after this date, I chanced to call upon a certain lady in a certain villa overlooking the Longwater and its fleet of yachts. I had been co-opted by the Bethel Chapel of Battwell to act upon a certain charitable committee and chosen to take our report of conditions in Battwell to Lord Slapton, the chief landlord of the place.

But my lord was away fishing in Scotland, and so I had been switched to his cousin, Miss Latter, at her residence, Palm Cottage. The very name offended me. This cottage contained ten rooms and had a staff of four maids and two gardeners. It seemed to me a kind of mockery of my own life in a real cottage to use the name for this mansion. Miss Latter I had met once. She was reputed to be engaged to my lord, and took a great interest in the estates. She was then a handsome dashing woman of thirty-two or thirty-three, with a loud voice and a loud laugh. She had the abrupt manners of a man and was extremely popular with the young farmers. I had myself at that time a strong dislike to her.

I had been ushered into a small back parlour which appeared something between a servants' hall and a schoolroom. The table was deal, a shabby upright piano showed on its desk a book of elementary exercises. Here I sat then for twenty minutes with my hat on my knee, listening to the giggling of maids in some neighbouring room, apparently the kitchen, and watching through the window the manoeuvres of about a dozen ladies and gentlemen in yachting dress strolling and sitting on the lawn. It was about six o'clock and apparently these were the relics of a party gathered to watch the yacht races.

I had come ten miles, at great inconvenience and some expense, to see Miss Latter. I had been punctual to my time, and it seemed to me now that I was either forgotten or neglected. I felt, as they say, put upon, insulted not only in my own person but in my position of my class. At the same time I was exceedingly embarrassed. I

132

did not know how to escape from this room, I did not know whom I might encounter while seeking an exit. I saw myself in my Sunday suit, of whose deficiencies I was too well aware, suddenly appearing before that languid group of exquisites upon the lawn.

At last resentment was too much for me. A sudden explosion of laughter from the servants' quarters—no doubt it was not aimed at me, but to my sensitiveness it seemed to express the whole arrogance of which I was the victim—caused me to leap to my feet. I was trembling with rage.

There were two doors to the room, I had entered by one—I tiptoed towards the other which seemed to lead to a passage.

At this moment I heard a peculiar sound outside as of something falling on the floor, and a murmur as of conversation. The door handle rattled and I quickly took my seat again upon the nearest chair. The door handle, after further rattling in both directions, was finally turned, the door opened, and after a pause a small girl entered the room carrying a large book clasped in both arms. The sound I had heard first was the placing of this book on the floor while the owner struggled with the door handle.

She entered without observing me in my place behind the door. She was talking to herself, as children do, with great animation and rapid changes of tone. But turning to shut the door behind her with a jerk of her elbow, she perceived me in my corner and fixed her eyes upon me with a wide unwinking stare.

The eyes themselves were the most remarkable that I had ever seen, large and beautifully shaped, of a deep violet colour—I perceived, indeed, even in my anger and distress, that the child was of an extraordinary beauty. But that beauty, the stare of those lovely eyes, only served to increase my secret rage. To me at that time the children of the rich were even more detestable than their parents, for it seemed to me that they did not even trouble to hide their sense of superiority—their very glance at a poor boy expressed the inborn lordliness of a class difference. The young heir of the Slaptons, a nephew of my lord's, riding his pony along country roads, would shout at our children to get out of his way. He knew that his uncle owned our lives and for him we were serfs. Later, of course, he was

133

taught discretion—he learnt manners, which spread a velvet on his iron; but as a child he did not know how to hide it. And in this infant of five or so I thought to discern the same frank arrogance. I thought too that she intended to disembarrass herself of the too large book by commanding me to hold it, and in my total ignorance of the expected usage towards such sprigs of aristocracy I foresaw that I might be involved in further humiliations.

She did indeed hand me the book—but then, still gazing at me with the same splendid and curious glance, climbed upon my knee and said, "Please will you read to me?"

I perceived then that the candour and confidence of that gaze did not arise from the arrogance of class but from the frankness of childhood, of a soul fearless of man, because innocent of evil.

I felt instantly such a revulsion of sympathy that the tears rose to my eyes. I hastened to obey the command of this princess, and Miss Latter, when she bustled in ten minutes later with a somewhat offhand apology for her lateness—she had been delayed by some of her guests who had wished to see a neighbouring garden—found me in a placable mood.

Indeed, from this meeting arose a political collaboration which lasted many years. It was to Miss Latter, already great in local affairs, that I owed my entry into municipal politics, an introduction which led in due course to Parliament, to my whole national career.

I might say that to the chance entry of that child I owe all the achievement in the world for which, rightly or wrongly, I have received honour. But that would not be true. It was not merely the chance of that small girl's entry which so powerfully affected my destiny—and I might add, not in self-praise but in hers, not my destiny alone but that of my country—it was her nature, the cast of her soul.

Far be it from me to claim that the prejudice of my generation in favour of a certain reticence in respect to the details of private life is a law of the Medes—the more modern practice of, as it is said, coming clean, which so often appears to use the opposite, may be indeed, as it is urged, a salutary blow against a dangerous prudery. And I am well aware that such revelations are often the mark rather of a too trusting than a too sophisticated nature.

134

I am, I admit, old-fashioned in my love of home privacy—my willingness to endure misconception about my private life rather than the limelight. But I am not breaking any confidence—I am giving honour where honour is due when I relate the history of that meeting with Nina Woodville, as she was then, and when I say of her that already she was marked by unusual qualities of thoughtfulness and sincerity. That lucid and candid gaze which so powerfully affected the awkward and embarrassed young man was not only the revelation of childhood's natural innocence but of qualities unique in that child —an inborn truth—an essential generosity of affection which no cruelty of fate, no bitter experience of human perfidy, could ever tarnish. Faith, hope—the profound charity which in the truest sense of the word rests in the love of God, and is indeed the very door of His grace—were innate in that spirit.

I knew it then as in a flash, and though I did not again have the delight of commune with that privileged being for many years— though I could only watch for her passing in the streets of Tarbiton or sympathise with her patient boredom in the back of a dingy office while her Aunt Latter conferred with her estate manager—I have a right to that opinion. For that child, she whom at first sight I had called princess, became my wife. It was she who taught me in daily life, during more than thirty years of happy marriage, to know those bonds of gratitude and loyalty which at once transcend all divisions of class and give the best, indeed the only, promise of lasting achievement to any political enterprise.

What is the purport of all this?—that he who founds argument and policy upon our intuition of human goodness will not be disappointed. True, I had not then in my nonage that other experience so necessary to judge the immediate practicality of a political programme, I had not realisation of the conflicts that arise actually from the good will in different persons having different temperaments, of the complication in all human affairs, of the place of evil in every society. But anyone who wonders at the perpetual appeal of anarchist thought from generation to generation must consider my case of a boy with no possible claim to adult experience and a deep need for some faith to which he could give an absolute and convinced assent of mind and feeling together.

135

Dr. Lanza provided that faith. He appealed to what I knew to be true, the memory of my own childhood—and drew from it a conclusion so simple that it seemed to place instantly within my hands a key to unlock all problems.

I had rejected God and with God, the love, the charity, the assured faith in goodness that I had learnt in my own home. Now under another name, that of humanity, He was restored to His full grandeur and majesty as ruler of the world. For the miseries of that world were shown as the just and inevitable punishment of those who had turned their faces from that fundamental law of brotherhood. How should the world have joy which lived in joyless fear for its possessions?

33

I say again, how powerful is logic, the simplest construction of reason, to the imagination of the young. Once I had accepted Lanza's first appeal to experience, as I did with instant conviction, knowing its truth, I saw rise before me an edifice in which every part was secured by the weight and tension of fact, and every proportion carried the assurance of beauty, a vast and lofty cathedral of the spirit, which united under one majestic dome both my religious intuition and those vague political notions derived from so many sources —yes, and from all the ambition, the resentments, of a poverty-stricken childhood.

For me it was a conversion. I felt my heart beat fast—I wanted to cry out, like those converted whom I had heard so often cry and groan in my father's services. I felt, in short, that violent agitation which renders it almost impossible for those who have suffered such a revolution of feeling to sit still. I was as much relieved as disappointed when the address was over and I found myself among the crowd at the door. I lingered behind in the hopes of finding myself even for a moment close to Lanza; I did not dream of speaking to him, perhaps I might be able to touch his coat. But the crowd behind thrust me forward. At the door two assistants stood one on either side, a man and a woman holding out a collecting plate. Two young girls beyond were distributing leaflets, and when I reached the plate I was glad to put into it all that I had left in my pockets. A moment later I found myself in the street with the leaflets in my hand. I perceived then by the town clock that I was late for my train, but though I had neither money nor ticket I felt not the least perturbation. The world was changed for me, I knew what it was and how it should be dealt with. I was no longer confused or afraid.

Fred had the tickets, and I made my way to the station with the idea of explaining my situation to some railway official. I had no idea that Fred would wait for me, but when I arrived I found him in the street, running up and down in front of the station and peering about for me in the greatest agitation. He had been afraid to go without me. And now, red and sweating with distress, he pointed out that his mother would be expecting him back by the train we had missed.

So I found myself once more in the ascendancy, and said, with the usual injustice that I always showed to the man, that it had been his fault for going with the Ranstone women.

"There you go," Fred said. "What did you leave me for? I didn't want to go with them. They're not my sort."

"I suppose you were frightened of them," I said. But he answered again that women like that were not his sort, and he wouldn't have my father or Georgina hearing that he had anything to do with them. And then, before I could scorn him again, he said that though I might take him for a fool, he was not such a fool as that.

All the way back in the train to Crow Halt where we had left the cart, he lamented my desertion. Obviously he was afraid I should tell tales. He wouldn't for the world, he said, have my father get a bad idea of him—if it wasn't for Mr. Nimmo, he didn't know how he would go on living at Stonepit.

And almost in tears he cried, "And I don't see how I could go away neither, for what would mum do without me?"

Perhaps it was because of my new illumination, the lifting of that deep preoccupation with myself, that, looking at Fred then humped on the other side of the compartment—the heavy stooped shoulders, the broad pink countenance, I did not make the usual jeer, but perceived that what he said was true, he felt his duty to his mother, and I had for the first time an impression of the difficulty of Fred's position.

Yet it was hard to respect Fred Coyte as we lumbered up the moor road in the cart, with the handles of the new plough sticking out awkwardly between us. I saw by the starlight that he had turned his hat back before—a specific against fairies and evil spirits—and for the last two miles of our road he was groaning and moaning in terror of what his mother might say to him. "Whatever did I go to miss that train for?"

138

I assured him that his mother would be asleep long ago. But not so—she recognised our wheels as we came over the hill by the inn and began to scream abuse at us from fifty yards away.

Indeed she was more shrill and violent than I ever remembered —as she grew older she became more nervous, more alarmed for her only son—she fretted for him if he was out of sight for five minutes.

34

WHEN and why does the love of solitude and secrecy come upon the child—the need to be alone? I was much alone at this time—I had lost Richard and my private agonies were not for Georgina. Alone I brooded and tortured myself. Yet I sought loneliness and secrecy not only to practice my oratory, but simply to brood. It seemed that some instinct drove me to be alone with my thoughts even though they were unhappy ones.

I had hated the disappearance of Richard from the kitchen—I had loved to talk with him at bedtime. I had loved the knowledge that he was sleeping near.

Yet now my solitude was precious to me—I waited impatiently till the girls should go to bed, and to their questions about the day at Exeter gave the shortest possible answers. Their affectionate interest, especially Georgina's eager and serious looks which seemed to say, "Why aren't we better friends—why don't you trust me?" only irritated me. And when at last she exclaimed in vexation, "If you won't tell I'll say it's not fit to be told," I answered sharply, "You girls are never satisfied, I've told you—nothing happened."

And yet I was conscience-stricken when Georgina instead of flying out at me only bid me take off my suit so that she could brush and sponge it for Sunday. She kept it in the cupboard upstairs where my mother had kept our best clothes.

At last, but without saying good night, she had gone, and Ruth, who alone of our family insisted on a good-night kiss, had followed her. I could take out the leaflet and read more about that extraordinary event—I didn't need a candle, I could read in the firelight without betraying myself by gleams through the ceiling boards.

I had expected an appeal, and so it was an appeal for a refugees' fund, with an address in London. But it gave also the names of the leaders in the Proudhon Society and a short biographical account of their lives.

I knew only the name of Proudhon—my father had quoted him in addresses as one who believed in the perfectibility of man—but Lanza had mentioned him as the father of the cause, and so already his name was for me a name of power. And now I found to my astonishment that the Proudhon Society had representatives close by, in Lilmouth and even in Tarbiton.

And Tarbiton held one of the leaders, Dr. Dolling—here was the record of his life. Born in France, son of a celebrated Greek scholar; became a student of philosophy; imprisoned by the Bourbons for an attack on the press laws; released by the revolution of 1830 but at once arrested again by the agents of Louis Philippe; escaped to Germany, he took part in the revolution of '48 when for a short time he was Minister of Public Instruction at Hesse; seriously wounded in the suppression of their free government, he was deported to France; imprisoned by Napoleon for two years, and then exiled.

Imagine the effect of such a record on a boy of fourteen, and to know that this hero and martyr of freedom and this fighter for the poor was living within a few miles.

The fire was low and I had to crouch down and hold the paper close to the ashes—but the words seemed to glow by their own confidence, their glorious promise of a great quest and a certain achievement.

"I desire only to prove that society like nature obeys eternal and changeless laws which are not to be set aside at the whim of any ruler."—Proudhon.

I read them till I knew them by heart, and when at last, without undressing, I threw myself on my bed, I could not sleep. My very weariness seemed to make alliance with that vast elation, and the spell of a cause for which I might live and die—the trembling of my nerves, the ache of my limbs, appeared like the pains of that rebirth.

I thought only of my next visit to Tarbiton—unluckily market was four days away.

And on that day, which was the monthly market, Mrs. Coyte wished to buy some young beasts for fattening—we had more skim milk than we could use. This meant commonly that my father, upon

141

whose judgment of stock his mistress had learnt to rely, would drive the cart, and I should be left at home. But as it happened I was told to bring the cart to carry some feed home, and my father took Mrs. Coyte more comfortably in the gig.

They had arrived long before me. Mrs. Coyte's favourite dealer had not yet penned his beasts, and as my father would not enter a public house, they were strolling round the lairages, each limping on a different leg.

Mrs. Coyte, annoyed to be prevented from her beer, yet unwilling to miss the first chance at the stock, was complaining loudly of what she called city people and their laziness; as soon as she saw me she shouted that I needn't have come, there would be no business done that day.

This was only an expression of wrath and disgust, but I thought it would serve me for an excuse if I were found out of the way. So soon as I had tied up the cart I slipped away towards Water Street.

So, at eight o'oclock in the morning, I was gazing at a small terrace house with a neatly whitewashed front and window-boxes, the only window-boxes in the dreary street, when I saw at the window a grey-haired woman and said to myself, "That must be Mrs. Dolling."

I had had no idea of introducing myself to the Dollings. I was as shy of them as I had been of Lanza, as I would have been of any great man, yet I was drawn towards the house. And she must have observed my gaze, for a moment later, when she opened the window to water her window-boxes, she looked down at me in the gutter and smiled and wished me good-morning.

I was taken by surprise, and so moved that I could not answer. She looked at me again, this time with a certain enquiring fixity, an expression which, as I soon learnt, was characteristic of this gentle and thoughtful woman, and said, "Do you want anything, do you want to speak to the doctor?"

I had an impulse to say no, to shake my head and to go away. What had I to say to the doctor? And I do not know what force kept me standing there unable to make even a sign of acquiescence. But Mrs. Dolling had now perceived my emotion. She came to the door and invited me into the house, and here I was able at last to

142

find my tongue, to show her the leaflet, and to say that I had been at the meeting in Exeter.

She was at once interested and sympathetic, saying in a serious manner that Lanza was a very great man, and telling me how much he had suffered in his work for humanity. Breakfast was on the table and she offered me coffee, the first I had ever tasted. Her husband then came in, much older, already white-haired, a tall heavy man with a singularly young face.

Again I was dumb with shyness. Remember that at this time my ordinary speech was Devon, and though I could speak plain English —indeed, thanks to my parents, possessed an unusually large vocabulary—it did not come first to my tongue. But the good doctor had the most perfect method of putting a shy country boy at ease—he did not merely set aside formality, he forgot it. Thus, having seized my hand and asked me half-a-dozen questions, about my home, my work, he broke off in the middle to ask his wife for some coffee, and then plunged into an enthusiastic description of the progress of his mission. To my amazement he let me know that this work of revolution was already far advanced in my own neighbourhood—he gave me twenty or thirty names of sympathisers, several of them already known to me, such as a man called Dodman living actually in Shagbrook, a grocer's assistant in Battwell, a chemist in Tarbiton from whom we bought our Stockholm tar for the sheep, and a small farmer on the Queensport road where I had several times done half a day's work when I was supposed to be at school. Already in twenty minutes from leaving the market the whole aspect of the world had changed for me. I saw it no longer as a place of impenetrable confusion and well-armed oppressors in which a small sect of believers afforded a certain spiritual refuge, and might possibly indicate a way of escape; but as a mass of ignorance and folly already being attacked, already undermined and penetrated in all directions by the heroic pioneers of the millennium.

All this had struck a new silence upon me, but now without embarrassment I was lost in this vision of a new world in the making, a world of brotherhood and peace, when the doctor, perhaps thinking that he had been forgetting his guest in his own enthusiasm, turned

143

his eyes upon me and exclaimed, "What was the name? Nimmo—Nimmo." He tapped himself on the forehead, "Do I know that name? Yes."

Mrs. Dolling said that it was the name of a strike leader who had gone to jail.

"He is my father, but he did not lead a strike, nor go to jail."

"Ah, no." Once more the doctor touched his forehead. "Of course, he was the preacher"—and so, he feared, he would not approve of my visit to him.

"You understand, my dear fellow," he said, "that there are certain dangers attached to my acquaintance."

He meant that it was dangerous to know him, and when I asked why this was so, he answered that he was under surveillance by the police. "So if you do not desire to continue in our friendship, I hope you will leave it while there is time."

I should say that this was an illusion of the doctor's, forgivable in a man of his experience. The English police took no interest in so mild a rebel. But I believed him then, and nothing could have been more attractive to a boy of my age than such a challenge—to defy the established authority of the land was itself a distinction, it gave me the self-respect achieved by an heroic gesture. But to make such an affirmation for liberty and brotherhood—that was a glory of the noblest kind.

The egotism and turbulence of youth—is it not too often merely the need of a worthy cause to absorb the first violence of a responsible will?

I answered the good doctor that I was proud to know him and that I believed with all my heart in everything he stood for—he then grasped my hand with much emotion and said that it was such as I who had encouraged him throughout his life. It was in the heart of youth, uncorrupted by the world, that he found the true shape of humanity and the inheritor of the ages. And he quoted from Mazzini —"Humanity is a man who never dies and never ceases to learn— he is the living thought of God upon Earth as the prophet of a divine law."

It was with this phrase ringing in my head and an earnest invita-

144

tion to visit the Dollings whenever I chose that I returned to the market-place, to dust and dirt, to the haggling and trickery of dealers, to Mrs. Coyte's violent and dominating temper—the whole task of that complicated management and contrivance in which I earned a livelihood, not only by Mrs. Coyte's goodwill but by her continued existence.

35

AND Mrs. Coyte had been ill that autumn; for one week she had actually been obliged to stay in bed, and the village said that she was failing at last. Nobody knew her age, probably she did not know it herself, but it was computed to be in the seventies.

She seemed to recover after Christmas, but was ordered to avoid the night air, then considered very dangerous. And as my father's arthritis also took a turn for the worse that winter, it fell to me to make the last rounds of the yards.

Mrs. Coyte was a nervous woman who perpetually imagined every kind of disaster from thieves to fire. She would jump out of bed at any time of night to run out with a lantern. Neither did she trust Fred to make the last inspection, saying that he would just as soon see her robbed or burnt out as give himself trouble. She always spoke of Fred as one of her principal enemies.

My duty after making the last rounds was to take up the keys and give a report; usually to Mrs. Coyte's bedroom where she would be sitting wrapped in shawls doing her accounts.

To reach the house from the yards it was necessary to pass through the kitchen, a room which seemed smaller than it was because of its great height and the amount of large furniture in it—two immense presses over nine feet tall, the great table at which, in harvest time, twenty persons could sup, a settle six feet high and eight feet long, a huge dresser with its rows of crockery, and numberless small cupboards, stools, chairs of all sizes, bins and boxes, barrels and peat baskets. The corners were filled with whips and poles, spudded sticks, rake handles waiting for new heads, and heads of all kinds waiting for handles. The walls were hung with bags, twine, axes and clippers, Fred's gun, never used, muzzles, straps, some old calenders from seedsmen, a large saltbox and two pairs of fishermen's long boots. Hams, and often whole sides of bacon, dangled from the blackened

146

ceiling beside a huge rack for clothes drying, the whole moved by complicated ropes and pulleys, secured to cleats by the fireplace. This was now occupied by a modern coal-burning range—one of Mrs. Coyte's few innovations—but again, it was of the largest size.

As usual in our kitchens, there was great economy of lighting. This big cluttered room with its high ceiling was lighted usually only by the stove, the storm lantern turned very low hanging by the door, and possibly a single candle.

The winter had been cold, we had had a lot of snow and it was necessary to bring all the beasts into the shippon. This made inspection slower and I would come in sometimes very late, and proportionately sleepy. I was, I daresay, half asleep one night as I tramped off the snow at the kitchen door, when I was startled by a groan. I looked round the room but saw nothing except the large shapes of the furniture in the shadowy light of the fire and my own lantern. I thought that the sound I had heard came either from one of the dogs or out of the fabric itself. One heard there on cold nights, as on hot, all sorts of sounds out of beams and boards, from groans to cries. So I walked through the kitchen, and even when I found Mrs. Coyte's bedroom empty I was not disturbed. I thought she had run out on some private alarm. I left the keys on her table and returned again the way I had come. And I had actually reached the outer door of the kitchen on my way home when I was stopped, my hand actually on the door handle, by an impression of anxiety.

I cannot say where this impression came from, I had heard no other sound, and my first thought was to ask myself if I had forgotten anything in my rounds.

But immediately I remembered the groan. I felt alarm, and went behind the settle. There I found Mrs. Coyte lying half on the ground, half against the corner of a box, bent sideways in a very alarming position, as if broken in back and neck.

I thought her dead, and this was so unexpected and fearful a shock that I rushed out of the room shouting for Fred—if any reader may wonder at my callous failure to go directly to the poor woman's help, he has not understood what this catastrophe might mean to me and mine, the loss of our livelihood, of our home, the complete subversion

147

of our lives. He has not understood the condition of my youth or what dependence means.

And before Fred, that heavy sleeper, had answered, I did return to the kitchen. Now I saw that the woman was still alive—she opened her eyes and muttered a few words. I tried to lift her onto the settle, and she seemed to be protesting that she did not wish to be moved.

Fred had now arrived, but he seemed afraid even to approach his mother; he gave one alarmed glance and said that he would send for the doctor. He then ran out, and I did not see him again.

Meanwhile Mrs. Coyte had somewhat revived, and though I could not lift her—she was much heavier than she looked—I was able to assist her own efforts enough to get her into her usual armchair, one of those great leather chairs with a high domed back, which were called porter's chairs and were valued in farmhouses for their power of keeping out draughts.

The dome of this chair provided a kind of dark cave in which the woman lay, strangely small, as if collapsed into herself. She had directed me to get her some brandy, and she was now talking a great deal in an excited manner, but it was difficult to make out what she said. It seemed like a mixture of anxiety for Fred—she asked every moment what he was doing—and fear that he should come in before she had recovered, she did not want him to see her like that. But there was a great deal that I could not understand, I perceived only that the woman was in great distress of mind and terrified of dying before she had, as she put it, got things a bit straighter.

This was a common anxiety of Mrs. Coyte's, she was always setting out to get something straight. But now it seemed to have a more important significance.

Young as I was and inexperienced in the workings of the human soul, I realised the agony of the poor creature—I knew that I was in the presence of a momentous crisis in her life, and I was shamed and confused by my inability even to comprehend what she needed.

It was a great relief to me when after twenty minutes or so my father came in—Fred, in his passage down the road, had given him the news. And his arrival produced a notable change in the woman's mood —her speech became less urgent and much more intelligible, it seemed

148

that his very presence was a comfort to her. She made him sit close to her and began to talk about Fred and the farm, still in a confused manner but with obvious purpose. It appeared, as they say, that she was getting at something, we heard a good deal about religion.

At last Fred himself arrived with the doctor—he had himself driven to Battwell to bring him back, an action for which he received praise from his mother and my father, but which was put down in the village to his anxiety to get away from her in this crisis. He had been frightened by her deathly look.

Mrs. Coyte in the next months made a slow recovery, but she was quite changed in character. She would spend hours in her chair, reading the Bible or some book of sermons—more often I think just meditating on her life and situation. On Sundays, as soon as she could move out of the farm, she began to attend my father's services. She gave it out, indeed, with some of her old pride, that she did not go to her own chapel at Battwell because it was too far for an old woman, but actually it was obvious that she hung upon my father for comfort and reassurance. Her amens at service were even louder than those of Edward G.

One of the first uses my father made of this new authority was to urge upon Mrs. Coyte the need of giving to Fred a more honourable and responsible place in the management of farm. Fred's humiliating position had long been a grief to my father, it would have been so even if Fred had not been one of the faithful, one of the few indeed who had come back to his services after the disaster at Shaghead Down. For it was the very foundation of his creed that everyone is entitled to freedom as soon as he is old enough to use it, and that children should not only be brought up to responsibility but given every chance to practise it. He liked to quote that pregnant sentence of the Psalms—"And I will walk in liberty, for I seek Thy precepts."

At first Mrs. Coyte resented these appeals, saying that she knew her own son better than any Nimmo, and that he would never make a farmer. And when my father answered that it might be so but that she had never given Fred the chance to show what he was worth, she would say that Tom Nimmo might preach faith in the Lord and she hoped she had it too, but she was not going to trust anyone like Fred

149

to manage Stonepit—it had taken her forty years to make a farm of it and she would not have it spoilt.

To this, of course, my father answered that to trust in Fred was to trust in God, for if God could not make him take thought for his own duty and good, who could?

After some months, that is about the time of the spring sowing, Mrs. Coyte did actually propose to give Fred more say in the management. But it turned out that he did not want the responsibility—he said that he would rather things went on as before.

Some people in the village were scornful of this repentance in a sick woman—they said that Mrs. Coyte, having had a sharp eye for the main chance all her life, was now anxious to secure her place in heaven. And I, in my new revolt against religion, was inclined to agree with them—at least to think that this sudden change in the woman was a symptom of weakness rather than illumination.

But writing now as an old man who has looked his own death in the face, I comprehend how foolish I was and how short the vision of those neighbours. For which is nearer to the truth of existence, the man who says, "I must consider my affairs in the world as if I were going to live in it for ever," or the one who says, "I must not forget that I am going to die and I shan't be able to choose the day"?

And how many do forget it—how easy it is to forget. I can say for myself that I had forgot it for many years—that the sudden reminder of mortality came to me, in my own life, at a very late date with the stunning force of a bolt from heaven, showing me at long last the pits at my feet. It was as though I had lived to that moment in a dream— and wakening did not bring me hopelessness but a fearful start of energy—it did not hurl me into the shadows of despair, but the appalling light, the challenging brutality of truth.

This work is the consequence, and if I do not live to continue it to the end, to the time when I entered on that political career which has earned me so much hatred, then at least it shall stand to show something too easily forgotten by statesmen and their critics alike—the mystery which lies beneath all history, all politics—the mighty and everlasting pressure of the soul seeking by ways unseen, and often unsuspected, its own good, freedom and enlightenment.

150

I was to die, even I, and what then? What had I done with my life, my trust—what would remain of all my labour, how would my ambitions seem to those who came after and asked themselves, "How blind was he, or small? How foolish? Or how mean?"

I say I did not altogether agree with the neighbours who scorned Mrs. Coyte's change of heart—I had been too much shocked by my first contact with her despair. But I gave little enough thought to its causes—and as for its consequences, I was interested only in its effects on our family fortunes. My father was now practically in charge of the farm—nothing was done without his concurrence, and no one, it appeared, was more pleased than Fred to take his instructions.

Apart from a rise in pay and much easier working conditions, this meant for me personally that I was able to visit the Dollings often twice a week—my father was so busy about Stonepit that I had to do most of the errands in the towns.

36

I HAD now begun to read the books lent me by Dr. Dolling. Can I describe the effect of some of the most magnificent writing in the world, the masterpieces of liberation, on a boy in my situation?

"The first true and serious religious belief that erects itself on the ruins of the old worn-out creeds will revolutionise our whole society because all real faith applies itself to every department of human affairs—because the entire history of humanity is a repetition of the prayer 'Thy kingdom come on earth as it is in heaven.' " What intoxication in such words from Mazzini. There were many days at that time when I could not have answered at night what I had done with my day. It was perhaps only Mrs. Coyte's illness and Fred's indulgence that permitted me to be so careless about my duties.

It was, I suppose, characteristic of my age that, after nearly eight months of secrecy and concealment, hiding my books in Richard's empty bed, and reading them often in the Stonepit kitchen rather than at home, suddenly one night I told the whole story to Georgina.

It was haymaking time—in those days, and especially on the moor with its uncertain weather, a task that required all hands available. One night, when rain threatened, we worked actually by moonlight, and since the stacks were not ready for thatching, rick cloths were brought to cover them.

Georgina and I, with Fred, had been working on top of a stack in an outlying field, called the Quarry field, and we agreed that we ought to wait for the cloth, which did not come. Georgina and Fred had stayed on top of the stack—I had slid down to rake over the ground which was thickly covered with hay fallen from the carts. I could hear the two on the top of the stack conversing in their usual style—long and tentative remarks from Fred interspersed with very short ones from Georgina. Suddenly Fred slid down beside me and walked down

152

across the field towards Stonepit below where lanterns now stood in a scattered crowd about the kitchen door—the haymakers had gone in for a last drink of cider, and perhaps a hunk of bread and cheese. I supposed that Fred had been sent by the impatient Georgina to hurry up the cloth. Meanwhile, having finished my raking, I gathered the hay in a prong and called to Georgina to tell her that it was coming. And as she peered over the edge of the stack I had a sudden impulse for her company, I called, "Come on down, what's the good of staying up there?"

She answered that she would stay on top. "They'll need someone on top to lift the cloth."

"You'll not be able to handle the big cloth," I said, "you're not heavy enough."

"Then come up, you too, and help—unless you don't want to."

The stack was secured with straw ropes, very necessary in this exposed field to keep it from being blown away. By the help of the prong slanted against the side of the stack, and the rope and Georgina's hand, I came up beside her and sank down in the warm sweet-scented nest of the hay.

The scent of hay is apt to go to anyone's head. It is not for nothing that, in the village ballads, so many love songs turn on the haymaking. Lying there close beside Georgina I felt the pleasure of her affection and told her of the Dollings. They were, I said, the finest people I had ever known, and she must know them too. I described their house and its cleanness, their beautiful furniture, and Mrs. Dolling's kindness.

But to my surprise Georgina had heard all about my friends. "Yes, I know," she said in a dreamy voice. "They want to turn out the Queen."

I was astonished by this attitude and said that the Dollings were not just Republicans—we had plenty of Republicans, they were as common as crows—they wanted a completely new kind of society.

"Father knows you go there," Georgina said, "he's been properly worried about it. You left a book on the floor too—it was about having everything in common and getting rid of religion."

"What did father say to that?" For in spite of myself I was alarmed.

"He didn't see it—I put it away with the others in Dick's bed. I didn't want him to be worrying any more than he need."

153

"You used to say that you hated the rich, Georgy—it was you that wanted to change everything."

There was a long pause, and then Georgina said, "So I do—but I don't like those Dollings. I think father is wiser than any of your Dollings. Perhaps they know better for France and Germany—I daresay things are different there—but people here are more God-fearing."

I was startled by this lack of appreciation in Georgina, and set myself to make her understand the importance of what I was saying, how much the Dollings had meant to me and how great they were—the doctor was really a great man, far greater than Lord Slapton or even Mr. Gladstone—he was one of the greatest men in the world. And I told about his adventures, about his imprisonments and his sacrifices for humanity.

Georgina did not seem to be impressed. She had taken off one of her boots to shake out the grass awns which had been cutting her feet; and while peering into the boot to see if it were clear, she said in an indifferent tone, "So that's why you think so much of him." I said that of course I admired the man who sacrificed himself to such a noble cause.

"Father has done that," Georgina said.

I said to myself that it was no good talking about any serious subject with girls—especially with Georgina since the Advent disaster. She was simply an echo of my father. And I exclaimed that I didn't want to talk religion but politics.

Then suddenly Georgina pressed up against me—she had lifted herself on her elbow to look down at me, but the clouds were now over the moon and I could not see anything but the shape of her head, tied in a kerchief, against the brown light.

And she asked me why I had gone away from them all. "I know why Richard has gone away from us—he is so full of his books and languages. But you and me seemed to be so close—and now you don't care about anything any more."

I was astonished at this sentimental speech from Georgina, but I was moved by the intensity in her voice—I felt that she was speaking under pressure. I answered that I had not gone away from her—I was very fond of her and she must know it.

154

"You don't know anything about me and you don't care neither," she answered. "But there, neither do I." And she got up from the hay and began to shout down the hill. It was true that Fred and Doan were bringing the cloth, but they were still too far away to be shouted at—one could distinguish only their lantern, winking along through the roots of a hedge.

Then, still gazing outwards, she asked me in an indifferent voice what I thought of Fred Coyte. "You seem to go about with him a lot."

I said that I quite liked old Fred—it was a shame the way people laughed at him.

"So you wouldn't mind so much if I married him?"

This question astonished me so much that I answered only by another, what did she mean?

"It would be a good thing for you," she said, "and father too—and Dick and all of us. We should have the farm. The only thing is I hate Fred so."

"But who ever thought of such a thing?"

"Fred for one," she said in a sullen tone. "He's been asking me for the last year."

This news again caused a revolution in my mind. I had thought of Georgina as a young girl—I perceived that at nearly sixteen she was a woman. I knew too that she was growing handsome, for a long time now the village boys would look at her when I passed with her in Dollyford or Tarbiton. The loungers at the corners would leer at her and call out after her. This was embarrassing to me as well as Georgina. For she did not affect that calm indifference which is the usual defence of girls even younger than Georgina against this kind of notice, she would glare and colour.

I realised that Georgina had become attractive—but it was not till now that I perceived that she was marriageable. I answered after a moment that I could not say what Fred would be like as a husband.

"I can see you'd be quite pleased if I married him," she said, and there was question in her tone.

I made no answer—there are crimes you perform without thought,

155

without reflection. I should like to think that I was silent because I was so preoccupied with my own ideas, my own grievance—because I did not perceive Georgina's trend.

But that remark of Georgina's about the advantages of such a marriage to myself and to all of us, to my father, already crippled, to Richard depending on charity for his career, to myself, had had three minutes to sink into my mind. It was not strange that it should grasp the significance of such a promise—the prisoner offered delivery from an oubliette into the sunshine, the damned soul tempted by salvation at no cost to himself—how should they not comprehend the magnificence of the prospect however remote?

True, I did not say to myself, "I shall encourage this marriage—and as for Georgina's hating Fred, that is a relic of childish prejudice." But did some deep and unregarded partner in my councils, lurking in some back office of my thought but infinitely quick and cunning in knowledge and foresight, tell me that Georgina was seeking support against the pressure of her conscience and that I should withhold it? Did he perceive the enormous advantage to himself, to his own secret ambition, of a settled income, of leisure to read, to think, to study, even to go to the University?

All I know is that I did not speak. I remained, as it were, in a dream, pretending even to myself that the girl was uttering merely a fantasy which was not worthy of my serious attention.

"In fact you don't care what I do or don't do," Georgina said at last, with extreme bitterness.

I affected to come to myself and answered that I did care very much about her affairs—more than she seemed to care for mine.

She was putting on her boots and began to swear at the laces. Georgina was growing up, but when she was not on her best behaviour she could still comport herself like a rough young girl. She could still, when not dressed for town or market, go in tatters. She would let all her moods be seen and even exaggerate them as if to say, "I don't care what you think of me"—asserting herself like a child rather than a grown-up. But the child was a marriageable woman.

I felt the violence of her feelings now—I was even afraid that she would turn on me. It was a relief, I daresay, to both of us when

156

the cloth arrived at last and we could all busy ourselves in dragging the heavy folds across the rick.

The clouds had now moved on and the moon shone out again— Fred said that now we had sweated half the night to save the hay, we could be sure the rain would go off.

But no one answered him, and looking at Georgina's set face as she tugged at the canvas, I thought that it was she who had gone away from me, into a woman's world.

37

THE young, they say, are absorbed in themselves—but as I remember that time, I was not so much self-centred as astonished by the drama of my own soul. If I failed to understand the crisis of another's life, a crisis without comparison, more tragic, more peremptory, than my own, it was because my mind was so wholly preoccupied with its own extraordinary adventures that all else seemed commonplace and ordinary.

I had returned to my own secrecy—never again did I speak of Dolling to my family; I respected Georgina's and did not perceive that it was truly an isolation—the enormous loneliness of a young girl who has to answer questions of terrible importance to her whole life, and cannot even ask for help.

I thought I knew the answer when one day in the next spring Fred came home with a great cut in his head. We had been at Battwell together, the three of us, Georgina and Fred had come from Shagbrook in the trap to bring a side of bacon to the innkeeper, and I had met them walking up from Tarbiton.

Also I meant to look at the latest scandal at Battwell, the new dance hall behind the Battwell Arms—the first dance hall in the moor. It had been built chiefly for the factory girls and their young men, and already there was talk of wild doings there. All the ministers had preached against it as a dangerous modern luxury.

I met Fred and Georgina in the kitchen, and as we passed towards the yard to get out the trap, we stopped to look through the windows at the dancers—they were waltzing at speed to a band of six performers.

The scene was startling even to me, I had never before seen waltzing, or heard a dance band. Our dances, such as they were, in farm kitchens and barns, with nailed boots on stone floors, were always country dances—the music often from our own whistling, or an accordion—rarely a fiddle.

158

The Battwell girls were in low frocks, they wore much jewellery, discreet rouge and powder. The men, too, were mostly in their dark Sunday suits, and some of them actually wore pumps. I myself was so absorbed by a spectacle which seemed at once more beautiful and more daring than anything I could have imagined, that I was not aware of Georgina's fascinated attention beside me, until I heard Fred's voice say, "Come on, Georgy, let's have a turn."

I realised then that her nose had been actually on the pane—she was beating time with hand and foot.

She jumped and turned. But she was still in a trance-like state, and gazing at Coyte she said, "You fool, you've been drinking again, you'll catch it from your mother." This was quite true, Fred had fortified himself with a couple of pints, and he answered boldly, "Never mind the old woman, what about a turn? Just once round the room."

"How could I, dressed like this, and in boots?"

"I didn't know you were one to mind the Battwell girls."

"Neither do I," said she.

"Come on," said Fred, and boldly took her arm. And probably it was as much to his surprise as hers that she allowed him to guide her to the door of the dance room.

"I can't dance," she said, "not a waltz."

"I'll show you." And in fact he showed her the steps and took her slowly up and down the passage, counting one, two, three.

The end of it was that Georgina danced several rounds, not country dances but waltzes.

I stared from the door in confusion and amazement, not unmindful of what my father would think if he had a report, and wondering how Georgina, so attentive to his least wish, could bring herself to conduct that would certainly give him great pain.

But it was easy to see that the girl was quite carried away—a mysterious excitement had transformed even her looks—she glanced at me in passing with a laugh of amusement at my expression. Music, motion, disdain of the Battwell girls and their low frocks, a disdain, as I have thought since, probably mixed with envy, had gone to her head like strong drink.

Georgina had always found it hard to resist any temptation to

159

amuse herself, especially in an active way. As a child she had often danced by herself—one would come upon her jigging and prancing round the kitchen with her skirts in her hands—kicking as high as she could. Let me confess it, she seemed now much more rough and bold than the worst of the Battwell girls, her face grew red, her forehead damp, her hair fell down—some of those standing by me, who stared and laughed and spoke of the wild girl from the moor, had every excuse.

Most of them knew Georgina. There were several couples from Tarbiton, including young Bing of the estate office, who actually asked Georgina for a dance. But she answered with impatience, "I don't really dance, it's only because Fred Coyte wanted a partner and I work for his mother."

The suggestion was that she regarded dancing with Fred as in some sort part of her domestic duty. But I think she was now surprised by her own outbreak—as she stood close to me with fast plimming bosom, fanning herself with her hand, Fred asked her to go into the garden to cool, and she turned on him indignantly, "No—it's time for you to be home."

Nevertheless she went with him down the garden, perhaps simply to escape from the amused crowd about her, and we heard nothing more until after the next dance somebody moving through the bushes heard a groan, and found Coyte lying under the hedge with a cut in his forehead from which he was bleeding freely. In fact he was half stunned, and all his explanation was that Georgina had hit him.

And while they were washing Coyte's head, quite deeply cut, Georgina was discovered putting the horse in the trap. Apparently her intention was to drive off and leave Fred. When one of the girls, very interested in the affair, asked what she had done to Fred, and how she supposed he would get home, she answered that she didn't care. "He can crawl if he likes, he's not coming in this cart. He's not coming near me again anywhere."

"Why," asked young Chadd, "what did he do?" And the girl added severely, "You pretty nearly cut the chap's eye out."

Georgina made no answer to this, she mounted the trap and gave the reins a shake. And when one of the girls made as if to catch the

160

bridle, she lashed out with her whip and shouted, "Don't you try to stop me." She hit the pony then and went off at a canter.

All this I had missed, I had gone to the chemist for my book, and by the time I returned Georgina was already half a mile down the road. But it was lucky I had been there, I was able to take charge of Fred, who was in a very unhappy state. I prescribed brandy, and we spent the night at the inn. Mrs. Coyte sent Doan to fetch us next morning. She was in great agitation about the cut, saying that it might have killed him, and everybody looked forward with interest to her next meeting with Georgina. It was expected at least that she would turn the girl out of the farm.

But not at all, she was furious with Fred. "The silly clot—as if he knew one end of a girl from t'other."

And our next surprise was to see Georgina and Fred going together on the Sunday morning to the new special preacher at the Baptist chapel.

For an unmarried girl to go alone to chapel with a young man was as much with us as the declaration of an engagement—it was especially so in Georgina's case because usually both she and Fred would have attended my father's preaching. The village at once put them together and the usual sly chaff was aimed at Fred.

Fred Coyte received these jokes with delight—he would point to the plaster on his forehead and say, "I've given my luck penny." Then he would utter a loud shout of laughter. He was plainly in a high state of excitement and gratification.

None said anything to Georgina, there was something in her looks that warned the stupidest to be wary of the mildest word. When I said only that I was glad to see she'd made it up with poor old Fred, she retorted that she'd done no such thing and never would. "I couldn't make it up to him for there's nothing to make—that's what he is—just nothing at all."

"Oh come," I said, "he's not such a bad chap."

"He's bad for me—and I wish he were a lot worse. He wouldn't be quite so bad if he were worse." And then flaming at me, "Why do you all go on at me about Fred Coyte—do you want me to kill him right out?"

161

In fact, just after the chapel visit, Georgina picked another violent quarrel with Fred, for coming into her dairy with dirty boots, for a month afterwards she would not go near him. Then they met at a wedding and danced all the afternoon, and it was Georgina who drove the cart which brought Fred home with two more, all too drunk to drive. Next day she was kneeling beside him at my father's service.

Georgina's situation was nothing unusual. There was not much choice of eligible partners about Shagbrook. Men married to get good housewives, good mothers for their children; and girls looked for steady fellows with a good job—some money on either side, even twenty or thirty pounds, was an important consideration.

And who shall say that young people who set out thus to make a home, who relied not so much on impulse as the deeper affection that comes from mutual gratitude, and share the purest love on earth—a common devotion to their children—who shall say that they are sinning? The special interest in this case was the question if so handsome and wilful a girl could bring herself to marry a man she scorned, however eligible.

I admit that I agreed with my father when he said that he was glad to see Georgy taking a hold of herself, for Fred had the makings of a good man.

"Let her get used to him," he said, "and she'll not be so touchy—give her time to be thinking how it will be to have her own place and be her own mistress." And with unexpected humour and pene-tration he said that young women were like young horses—over the hedge at a bit of paper, and rock to a thunderstorm when "they've made up their minds to it."

My father was justified sooner than we expected. A quite surpris-ing change now took place in Georgina. We noticed it especially just after this New Year when she left home for the first time in her life and stayed away a whole week.

162

38

RICHARD was now at the University. He had taken the Gold Medal for Classics and the Slapton Scholarship in the previous June and went up, as they say, in October.

This was a great family triumph. It was recorded in the local papers, and even one Lilmouth paper, that Richard Nimmo was an honour to the west. And it entered very deeply into our situation. I suppose there is no joy so deep and true as the achievement of one you love—it is not too much to say that Richard's was never absent from our consciousness. It gave us not only a sense of distinction but purpose and direction. We felt that through him we had passed into the greater realm, the world of the masters.

Perhaps nobody in these days can appreciate the splendour of my brother's success—it was a rare thing then for a poor farm-worker's son to reach the University. More, it would be impossible for the young men of to-day to comprehend the significance of those words, the world of the masters.

For us the abyss between the masters and the servants of life was as broad and dark almost as it had been in the Middle Ages— the government was milder, the workers had freedom and protection— but power and the dignity of power, the keys of that mystery of state which uttered its commands as from a Delphic cell, these were in the hands of a sovereign caste.

And this was true not only of the magistracy, the political authority, but of that vast dominion of the learned professions. Lawyers, doctors, bankers, the clergy, we saw them then as almost another species of men, a priesthood commanding secrets and speaking them in terms unknown to us ignorant and bewildered mass.

Richard had bridged that abyss—his feet were set upon the path of power, he would become great among the rulers of the nation, those who knew how, as they say, the strings were pulled.

163

Richard's scholarship of eighty pounds was quite insufficient to support him at college, he could not have gone if it had not been for our new prosperity. We were able to give him another fifty pounds, nearly a third of our income, and six prominent citizens, including our landlord Lord Slapton, contributed another fifty between them.

But do not think for a moment that we regretted the need for scraping—it was an actual enhancement of our existence to save for such an object.

Georgina's visit was to Richard. In his Christmas holiday he had been if anything more absent-minded and aloof from us than ever before, but he had remarked on Georgina's good looks, and he had said also one day that it was a shame that she, who had done so much for us, had never had a treat. And the treat he proposed was a visit to him at Oxford where he could find her cheap lodging in the rooms of his college servant, for Richard now had a servant. My father highly approved this plan, saying it was time Georgina saw something of the great world. Richard did not forget his promise—within a month of his return he sent her the fare and said that he was expecting her.

And it was this journey, this visit of eight days in all, that made us see so notable a change in Georgina—she came back, as Ruth said, a real lady.

This change did not surprise the village, it had been noticed before in young people returning from visits in the east. Girls after a few months' service would return on holiday not only in smart clothes but with quite new scorn for what they called our slummocky ways —and earned for reward the accusation of being proper ladyships.

Ruth, and indeed all of us, had then a very elementary idea of what ladyship consisted of—ladies we had none in Shagbrook, my own conception of those days was a mixture of resentment and romance compounded of rich clothes, silk petticoats, scent, delicate boots, a high manner and a town accent. Also we all believed that ladies were given to flattery and hypocrisy—they were cunning and deceitful, false and selective. They would come to one's stall in the market and beg gifts for the church bazaar, and their mouths were

164

full of compliments while they sought to wheedle us out of a pound of butter or a half pint of cream, and going away with their booty they would smile at each other as if to say, "We have tricked them again—these oafs of the moor."

And perhaps there was some mockery even in Ruth's phrase. She was devoted to Georgina, but like many very shy people she loved to laugh at others behind their backs and to mimic them. She would imitate Georgina making the tea, filling the pot with a frown and up-turned eyes, counting the spoonfuls and pouring out the water as if it were some precious draught of magic or chemic value.

But Georgina was not more aloof from us, she was indeed more thoughtful, more gentle, and how this change came about we knew not, we never saw Richard in his mysterious heaven. We could not have afforded such a journey. And Georgina told us little. All I know of her adventure was that she visited some gallery of pictures, which deeply impressed her, went to tea with the wife of Richard's tutor, and to a concert with Richard himself and this lady's daughters, and that Richard had bought her a new pair of boots in which to attend these entertainments—boots so delicate that they were useless in Shagbrook even upon the high road.

Whatever ideas of refinement and social discipline Georgina had acquired among the Oxford ladies, she did not impose them on us —the greatest change we noticed was her new way with Fred Coyte. She seemed for the first time to consider him as a possible husband —she met him as a friend. In the next year it gradually became ac-cepted that they were courting. Georgina, indeed, had obviously re-solved by then not only to marry the man but, in the common phrase, to make a go of it. She became quite surprisingly patient with him —I recall one evening especially, of the succeeding Christmastide.

It had been a bitter winter—Fred and I came into the Stonepit kitchen quite perished from the yards, we had been carting manure.

The women were washing clothes—Mrs. Doan and Georgina, having taken off their bodices, stood at the tubs in their shifts with arms bare to the shoulder, and Ruth was hanging the wrung garments on the drying apparatus lowered for the purpose.

The room was full of steam—perhaps because of the cold, it hung thicker than usual. Fred did not notice Georgina behind Mrs. Doan, and being as usual in high spirits since Georgina's acceptance of him —even rather too swaggering, especially before other women—rubbed his purple hands together and cried, "Ah, on a night like this give me two to a bed—I'll lay you Georgy is warmer than blankets."

Mrs. Doan turned round to Georgina and burst out laughing; Ruth blushed and looked nervously at her sister; I myself felt a deep uneasiness; but Georgina's pale cheeks, little darkened even by steam and heat, changed colour hardly at all.

Fred had meanwhile seen her and was taken with panic—he began to stammer some excuse. But Georgina said to him in the soothing tone with which one speaks to a child, "Poor Fred, you look frozen. Go and dry yourself, and we'll get you some supper."

I told her afterwards as we went home together how glad I was to see Fred so happy with her. She answered with the same tranquil tone. "I hope I shall make him happy—it would be stupid not to try —and at least it makes father happy. It's the first time in his life he's been really pleased with me."

39

THOSE three years while Richard settled happily at Oxford, Georgina got herself engaged, and I grew so quickly from lad to youth—times that seemed so troublous to me—were actually the most tranquil of my life. They were interrupted decisively on January 19 of 1875, the date of the Shagbrook Splash—a light name, probably coined in Battwell, for a considerable disaster.

The moor has always had its floods—the Shag ran brimful every winter. What saved us was its quick fall just below Shagbrook bridge, where the main road crossed the stream about forty yards uphill from the farm. After heavy rain or a sudden thaw the river would swell high at the bridge and perhaps come over its banks at Battwell or Dollyford. But in Shagbrook we were safe.

We had had much snow that year, the river had been roaring for weeks, but we did not take account of it, it was indeed a pleasure to us lying warm in bed to hear that loud monotonous chorus—a combination of deep bass with innumerable softer notes, as of fountains, bringing to one's fancy romantic tales of Arabian gardens under the moon—which sang us to sleep all winter.

But on that evening, the nineteenth, as I was going round the stables about eight o'clock, I was aware of some change in the atmosphere. It was as if a pressure had been relaxed. I was tired and sleepy as usual at that time, and I did not ask myself the meaning of this sensation until one of the boys came running through the yard and shouted that the water was coming into the stack-yard. I could not imagine what he meant, and went out with him. But the moment I passed into the open air I perceived what I had only felt before, that the noise of the river had ceased.

The water at the barn was only a trickle, it had not yet risen to the level of the floor, but it was spreading widely in the field and running fast past the corner of the barn towards the cottages below

167

—before we could realise what had happened two girls screamed to us from the road that the bridge had gone.

We ran then to the road where it crossed the river and saw what had happened. The old bridge, a very rough structure of stone piers carrying a timber road, had collapsed with a great part of the bank on either side so as to form a dam of mud, stone, broken timber and bushes across the stream. The river was already high over its banks and pouring across into the valley.

This bridge, I may say, had been in bad repair ever since I could remember, and all of us had predicted exactly this catastrophe if it should fall down. It was obvious that in that case Stonepit, and especially that part of the village lying below Stonepit at the bottom of the valley, would be flooded. I sent the two girls to warn my father and the village and call up some men who might work on the bridge. Mrs. Coyte was in bed, she had been in bed since Christmas, and I feared to disturb her—Fred was not back from Tarbiton. I felt responsible for taking some immediate action till my father should come.

Still I had no idea of the magnitude of the disaster, not that I didn't perceive that the lower cottages might be flooded, but that my imagination did not spring to the size of remedy required.

It was my father and Mrs. Coyte who, in the graphic phrase, rose to the occasion. My father was fortunately on his legs—in twenty minutes he was directing a gang of men with spades and crowbars, working at the ruin of the bridge. Mrs. Coyte, as soon as she had the news, sent to Ranstone for a miner with dynamite, and all about for volunteers to strengthen the river bank.

Meanwhile the water was rising fast in the lower valley; it was already three feet deep in a dozen cottages along Back Lane, and the women, many of them just out of bed and half-dressed, were carrying their furniture to the road, which fortunately stood high above the windows on its embankment.

My father's plan was to loosen the debris of the bridge from below. Here the water was no more than three or four feet deep, for though large spouts were gushing through the dam, the overflow ran quickly away in a side channel. He ordered me to bring the horses

168

down into the bed, harnessed with plough chains. These chains were then wedged among the stones and rubbish with crows, and the horses set to drag at them.

This operation was growing more dangerous every moment as the water rose behind the debris of the bridge, at every pull the people on the bank would cry a warning "It's coming." But though great stones fell from the ruin, and sometimes a beam would splinter and bend outwards, though suddenly a new gush of water would spout from a fresh hole, though once or twice the whole heap seemed to be tumbling in upon itself, yet after every alarm stones, earth and timber remained seemingly even firmer than before in their new shape, and the total amount of water escaping appeared rather to diminish than increase.

Mrs. Coyte herself now took direction of the work. Although there was no danger of flooding in the upper storey of the farm, she had insisted on getting out of bed, and as she could not walk she had herself carried in the porter's chair. Doan and Kimber by her direction had thrust a short ladder under the seat, and using this as a lever, and taking one of the boys to steady the whole contraption, had brought her safely to the river bank just below the bridge. Here she appeared only like a dark bundle sunk down in something between a rajah's howdah and those strange conveyances for Oriental women seen in old pictures of the flight into Egypt. It was only by her loud and rasping voice that we knew our old mistress.

Her first command to me was to bring the horses out of the river bed. "What are you doing down there with my horses—do you want to drown 'em."

I handed over the horses to the men who were moving furniture out of the cottages and joined the crowd trying to build up gaps in the lower bank of the river above the bridge.

Meanwhile a cartload of volunteers had arrived from Ranstone, and some of them went down at once into the place from which I had just been removed—the central pool below the main ruin of the bridge.

The water there, partly in consequence of their own vigorous work with heavy crowbars, rose fast, and my father suggested that we should deepen the bed of the river below the pool to relieve the

169

men working there—the cry was, "Anyone with boots or waders."

I had already borrowed Fred's waders—he was still within the house carting chairs and carpets out of the lower storey, and I was standing on the bank with two more waiting for a lantern when Georgina came to join us. My father had lent her his seaman's boots —bought in the days of our prosperity—such boots or waders were greatly prized on the moor for just such work in the deep ditches or bog bottoms.

Georgina had tied a muffler over her hair and tucked up her skirts —as a moor girl she knew how to give them all the convenience of trousers for such an occasion—though she was touching my arm, I did not recognise her till she spoke and asked who were those fools down under the bridge. "They'll get themselves killed any minute."

"I don't know, Doan was there for a time."

"Doan's too thin and crooked."

Just then the boy came with the lantern and told us that the men in the pool were some of the foreigners from Ranstone, and we followed him down the bank into the river bed. His answer had satisfied even Georgina. This may seem strange to those who did not know the moor in those days. But certainly I thought no more of the four men still in the pool with fifteen feet of stones and broken timber shaking over their heads, and the flood piling up behind. They were foreigners, that is, from some village beyond the moor, and so not to be reckoned as an anxiety to us. To do us moormen justice, I might suggest that the idea behind this indifference was partly that foreigners, having no pressing reason to risk their lives, could be supposed to act on their own responsibility. As Georgina said, "I suppose they know what they're doing."

Presently these four men, all foreigners, came to join us—the pool was getting too deep for them to work their crows.

Only one of these men had boots, all obviously belonged to the poorest class of casual labourer—men whose lives were indeed cheap and usually, at least in those days, short.

It was, as I say, a cold wintry night, a light but keen east wind was blowing across the moor; Georgina and I with all our wraps and big boots were shivering and chattering—our noses and fingers were swollen and purple with the cold.

170

I do not know a more miserable task than fumbling and stumbling in the mud about freezing ditches—and now the first excitement had passed. After hours of work the ruin was still firm. The lower cottages in Back Lane were slowly filling and there were now two feet of water on the floors even of the farm—only the high staddles saved the ricks from floating away on the current.

Along the river bed, therefore, we were working in weary and sullen silence, and the arrival of the foreigners plunging about in their rags, shouting remarks to each other and the onlookers, did not improve our mood. We felt that their liveliness and boisterous noise conveyed a kind of contempt of us in Shagbrook—men who had risked their lives in the desperate work below the dam—their shouts towards the watchers above on the bank conveyed this opinion, and one said to another that those chaps were afraid of getting their feet wet.

Those chaps were women and grandfathers—the men working on the breaches above the bridge or on the road culverts in the valley—I was stung by the words and said that our chaps knew how to do the job in the right way. It was no good pecking at the stones with crows, nothing would shift them but a shot of dynamite.

One of them, a big powerful fellow, answered promptly, "Why, it's Ches Nimmo—well, I thought so too, but I couldn't be sure. So this is Miss Georgina grown up to be a woman."

Georgina said nothing to this, which made me know that she had already recognised the newcomer.

40

THIS young man, Wilson, was a year younger than Richard. He had been at school with Richard and had been a friend, or rather dependent admirer, of his—Richard had helped him with his work, and sometimes he had brought him home to tea.

We had thought him rough and rude—he was the only son of a labouring couple living then in a loft over the stables at the Green Man—the Wilson parents were decent, hard-working people, but not in line for steady jobs or good cottages. For though as a rule they took no more than their pint with the rest, they belonged to that number, small but constant, which would get very drunk on holidays or feast days, and then the father was apt to be dangerous. He had been twice in gaol and each time he changed his village.

This kept the family even poorer than they would otherwise have been. They were a very united couple, devoted to their only child as he was devoted to them. There was, however, bitter conflict between them on one point, his going to school.

The Wilsons, like so many of the poorer families in Shagbrook, saw no use in the school and fought against the new school law. Many fought with success. The law was not strongly enforced, almost any excuse—illness at home, harvest work, the need of earning the rent, or bad weather—was accepted for non-attendance; and the children themselves, taught by their parents to despise what was called a scholar, were delighted to be saved from education. On the other hand, even among this opposition, there were four or five children who were determined to learn, who could not be kept from school even by threats. Young Wilson was one of these. It was extraordinary what hardships he underwent to get schooling. For as he was fond of his parents, who loved him so much, he would take work in the fields to make a little money for the household, and then try to catch up at school by working at night. The Wilsons, like

172

most of their kind, went to bed almost with the sun, unless they could afford a pint of beer—the price of light and warmth at the inn. But I had seen young Wilson even in winter standing outside the kitchen window of the inn reading his book by the light through the pane.

I remembered that he had been a very ugly boy, pug-nosed, with very small eyes, and a wide mouth, with thick black hair growing low on his forehead. In the village he was called Monkey Wilson.

Wilson met Richard at school and had an immense admiration for him. When his parents moved to Shagbrook he would travel with Richard to and from school, and often he came to our house to ask Richard's help with his work. He was not a clever boy, we thought him rather slow at his books, but he had this passion to know, and immense industry.

Soon after he began to come to the house, Richard who was protective towards this disciple, asked Georgina one day to mend his trousers for him. But Georgina did not welcome Wilson, she said he was noisy and dirty—above all he despised girls and said so, a thing no girl of eleven could forgive.

When, therefore, Richard, sitting by the fire with his friend, said in what we called his lordly way to Georgina, "I say, Georgy, have you got your needle? Monkey here has got a hole in his trousers," Georgina made no answer, but simply came to the fire and stretched out her hand towards Wilson.

The two boys looked at her in surprise for a moment, and then Georgina said emphatically, "I can't do them while you've got them on."

Wilson, quite unaccustomed to girls, and especially sisters, was obviously very startled by this peremptory air, and Richard said impatiently, "Can't you wait a minute—or do them on him without all this fuss?"

We were accustomed to having repairs done, when possible, by the way—a button sewn on or a hole sewn up while the garment was in use. I had seen Richard only that week reading his book, a mere novel, while Georgina knelt at his feet sewing up a rent in his knee. This had more excuse than mere convenience—our only spare trousers were usually our Sunday ones, kept in the drawer and not to be ex-

173

posed to week-day dangers even for five minutes. Georgina herself was the first to enforce that law, and she was right. The loss or damage of a Sunday suit has kept many a poor boy from chapel and made him find any excuse but the true one—for it is one that even poor boys do not care to admit. "I was ashamed of my clothes," who will admit that for a cause of action? But it is a cause that has driven many a boy to idleness or theft, and put many a girl on the streets.

Georgina, it is true, took more than a motherly and prudent care of Richard's clothes—and she would kneel at his feet quite as much to express her love and pride in him—a passion that could not find expression in endearments—as to save his trousers. She was not going to allow to others even the semblance of the same privilege.

"Come on," she said to Wilson impatiently, tapping her foot. "Take them off, I haven't time to wait—I've got to be at Stonepit in five minutes."

I imagine that Georgina expected this to finish the affair—that Wilson would not care for the humiliation of removing his trousers at her command and in her presence. But suddenly he accepted her challenge. He jumped up, tore off his trousers and threw them at her.

For a moment I thought she would throw them back at him. Then Richard said smoothly to Wilson something about the work, about the history they were doing together, and Georgina, thus excluded from their affairs, retired to the corner and got out her work-box.

When she had finished, she passed between the two boys and the fire, dropped the trousers in Wilson's naked lap, and, without a word, walked out of the house.

We boys, thus interrupted, looked up, and Richard made that slight gesture of the head which meant, "These girls, what do they care for our important employments." But Wilson, again, was obviously taken aback. He had no means of understanding that Georgina, who seemed to be our slave, was also our proud queen and our dangerous enemy; he, an only son, could not understand our family bonds, so complicated and so strong, full of tension, of secrecy, of deep knowledge and indifference, of love so natural and unbreak-

174

able that it needed no sign, of conflicts that belong to every close community, especially where there is love to exasperate every issue.

And for the few months of that year when Wilson came to the house, he and Georgina carried on a war which was all the more lively that they had the same kind of temperament, impulsive, downright, and inclined to strong feelings of both affection and dislike.

Georgina had expressed much satisfaction when the father, going to gaol for a longer spell than usual, made his wife and son move to Lilmouth where he had a brother who was charged to keep an eye on them. This disaster had finished Wilson's education. When Richard had gone to Grammar School, he, at fourteen, had gone out as a labourer to support his mother.

I had been surprised then when Richard had said that he was sorry for Georgy's sake—she was losing her best beau; I was irritated now by the man's talkativeness. I thought he was, as they say, showing off before the women, and especially Georgina. It was in an unfriendly tone that I asked him how he came to be there.

"Why," he said, "you know I had a bit of bad luck last September —just started as a carrier—my own horse and cart—when the horse spiked himself on a harrow and I got sold up."

It was typical of Wilson to expect everyone to know about his affairs, he threw himself into his various enterprises with such a sense of their importance to him that he imagined they were equally interesting to others.

I found out later that after his mother's death, two years before, he had invested a few pounds of savings and some credit in a very old horse and a decrepit cart and quickly gone bankrupt.

"Just when business was looking up about harvest time," he said, "so I been looking for a foreman's place. But there never was a worse winter for work—and a bad time too. I tell you," he said, with his old grin, a grin that invited not so much sympathy as an equal amusement at the queer tricks of fate, "I was damn glad of Mother Coyte's offer of a shilling and supper tonight for a job on the river."

"You'll catch your death for your shilling," I told him, but he answered with a serious air that it would take more than a little cold water to do him any harm. As for my suggestion that we could do

175

no more in the dark, he declared that if they could get back at the stones they would soon have the thing down.

"Now we know where the master is," he said, "all we want is to get our crows under 'un."

I doubted this hope and went on with my scratching at the river bed—it was in fact half an hour before the new cut began to run free. And all this time, as I noticed, Georgina and Wilson, standing close to me under the bank, were talking together with great animation. In fact they did not pretend to work. I gathered that a general exchange of news was taking place, I heard the words "horse" "Richard," but little more under the noise of scraping shovels and Mrs. Coyte's fire of instructions from above. I thought little of the encounter—Georgina, like the rest of us, had a warm welcome for any old acquaintance, any news from outside our isolation—until, happening to glance up to reach for a lantern, I had a full view of the couple in the light, of Georgina's intent, curious, appraising gaze, her smile that seemed to anticipate the word before it was said—and Wilson's sideways turning eye and rather foolish crooked grin. I had seen that face on many a young labourer meeting his sweetheart behind a stack, an expression of mingled excitement, daring and fear.

But it was Georgina's look that most startled me. I had not before seen her so interested in any young man's presence, and so unguarded. True, the lantern had surprised her, but that was no consolation if it told the truth. I felt a moment of deep uneasiness. The water was now lowered enough in the pool to let the gang go back below the dam—Wilson left us, and I heard Georgina asking her neighbours, "But what's going to happen if it comes down? They'll all be killed."

I thought her anxiety too particular, I was glad that others showed it also; the foreigners, of course, the elected heroes of the occasion, were reassuring. "Don't you be afeared," one of them said to the women generally, "we'll keep our eyes skinned. It's that big stick will tell us." And Wilson's voice called back from the darkness, "When that wags its head at us, Miss Georgina, you'll see us run quick enough."

"You won't have time," Georgina called impatiently. "It's foolish."

176

We had got out on the bank to drink some tea and thaw our fingers, but Georgina was protesting still to all and sundry that the foreigners would be killed. "They ought to be stopped going down there under the bridge."

The stick which was to be their warning was one of the bridge beams whose splintered end could be seen standing up obliquely ten feet against the sky. The dawn was now breaking, a grey-white dawn like old snow, and this stick was clearly perceptible against it. The four men, who had now been joined by Doan the father, were splashing about in the shadow of the ruin, making as before a great deal of noise as they encouraged each other and swore at the obstruction.

Everybody was now watching the men at work, and I think all of us were uneasy—but even in this moment, I noticed Georgina's agitation, and so did others, for a woman just behind remarked to some companion in a voice meant to reach my ear that Jo Nimmo didn't seem to have forgotten her old beau Willy Wilson yet awhile.

The words were plainly audible to Georgina also. She half turned her head, then faced forward again with an indignant jerk of the shoulders.

I paid no attention to the spiteful gossip, I thought that Georgina had done everything possible to deserve it. I determined to warn her that Fred could be jealous.

Meanwhile I continued to gaze at the stick. A voice had cried out, "It moved—it's moving," but I could see no movement. Georgina turned to me and said urgently, "Get father to call them back. They really will be killed. I know they'll be killed." And at that moment the beam slowly leant towards us. There was a sound as of heavy waggons rumbling over a hollow road, and two or three splashes; then with a roar the whole debris of the bridge collapsed into itself and the river poured over it in a foaming broken wave.

I was alarmed to find that Georgina was no longer beside me— she had run down the bank. But I found her at the water's edge, and when I caught her arm and told her to come up again because the bank might fall in, she yielded to me, saying only that if those fools were drowned it served them right.

177

I said that I did not think Wilson would be drowned, he was such a big strong fellow.

"Nobody here would care," she said in an angry tone. "I do hate this place." And I said that Shagbrook was not much of a place, but what was wrong with it was not the people but the poverty, and that it was our job, as people who knew the remedy, to try to rouse the people up and cure the poverty.

Georgina did not answer me for a moment—I expected some rude retort about the Dollings. But instead she repeated with still more violence that she hated the whole place, the people as well as the poverty, they were mean tattling cowards of people.

I said nothing to this, and luckily, even before we had scrambled to the top of the bank again, Wilson's loud voice was heard shouting from low down in the darkness on the opposite shore. He was safe. In fact his promise was justified, all the foreigners saved themselves —the only man killed was Doan, who had gone down the bank with a lantern, partly out of curiosity. But we made much of our hero, you can still see his memorial in the churchyard. And this is not written in mockery. Doan was nearly sixty, and he knew the real danger of his position far better than the reckless and boastful foreigners.

41

WHEN I went to the yards next morning I was surprised to see a light in the barn. I was alarmed in case of fire, and hurried to the door to find Wilson scraping the mud off the floors.

He was still very muddy himself; he seemed to have slept, if he had slept at all, in his wet clothes, his face was streaked with dirt. With his two days' beard he looked like a tramp of the roughest class.

My first idea was that he had come there on a rendezvous with Georgina. Indeed, whether it was arranged or not, he was with Georgina in less than half an hour when she came to the first milking, so that my suspicion had some justification. I asked where he had stolen that lantern—I had recognised the one from the Stonepit kitchen.

"Well, I needed a light to get on with the job." I had never quite liked Wilson's pushing ways as a boy, and I said shortly that there were no jobs open at Stonepit.

"Doan's gone," he said. "Why shouldn't I get his job?"

I said that this wasn't the way to get the job, and a Shagbrook man ought to have first chance at it. He laughed and said he'd been a Shagbrook man once—how was my father, and did he still work for the tinners' union? How were Richard and Ruth? Was it true that Georgina was going to marry that slob Fred Coyte?

When I told him yes, as a warning not to force his attentions on the girl, he answered that he had heard so but could not believe it. "I took the chance last night to come up and see." And he asked what we were thinking of to let such a fine girl as Georgina rot away in such a hole.

I answered that we did not consider Shagbrook a hole and that everyone was not like him, everybody didn't think of life in terms of grab.

He laughed again at this and said that he was a union man too, he belonged to his own union. "Work for Wilson—and down with scabs."

179

All this time I had felt that Wilson was, as the phrase goes, up to something, and now I asked him what he was talking about. The tinners' union? My father wasn't a member of the tinners—only the honorary treasurer.

"I wasn't meaning the tinners," he said, "I meant up here."

Then we looked at each other, and he said, "It's only what they say."

"What do they say?"

"That something's going on here too—with old Bennet and Dodman."

Here were two problems thrown at me—firstly, did this man know anything, or was he shooting at a venture and had nothing to go upon but the vague suspicions of gossiping, watchful neighbours? Secondly, a fundamental question in politics, now for the first time presented to me, when and where is one justified in telling a flat lie?

For it was true that there was a union in Shagbrook. It consisted at the moment of no less than fourteen members, but they had joined on my promise that it would be kept a secret. It would have been impossible in those years of fierce reaction to organise a farm labourers' union on any other principle. The men were too much afraid of the masters and rightly so. Neither Mrs. Coyte nor G, probably no farmer in the district, would have employed a union man.

"What are you talking about?" I said.

"That's all right," he said, "I shan't tell on you."

"There's nothing to tell."

Wilson winked at me, and then said, "It's a pity though, it won't do you any good and you won't do them any good. They're no good those chaps in the unions, or they wouldn't be there."

I said that I didn't know he was a Tory. When did he go in with the landlords?

"Tory—It's nothing to do with your old politics." He grinned at me as if to say that he had heard that kind of nonsense before. "I don't bother about all that."

"Then what's wrong with you?"

"Why, common sense. Of course if you're going to be a union boss, that's different. There might be something in that—but just one of the chaps. It's stupid."

180

"I see you're a regular born scab."

But he only laughed in my face, and I came away from the man in case I should lose my temper with him.

I was surprised at my own rage—I was trembling with passion. Indeed this short conversation made such an impression on me in that cold dark morning that I have never forgotten its circumstances; the lantern hanging high on the shaft of the gig; Wilson with his dirty unshaven face and tousled hair; a dirty red handkerchief round his neck; his stained corduroys strapped below the knee; enormous boots on his feet; the picture of a working labourer, leaning on the shovel with which he had been clearing the mud; the depths of the barn behind and outside the strange new sound of the Shag pouring over the ruin of the bridge.

I had met Tory labourers—there were plenty of them, church and state men, old soldiers and their sons—but I had not yet found one who expressed such calm contempt for his own class, as a class.

I swore that, hero or not, I would not have Wilson in Shagbrook. He was a danger as well as what I called a scab, a traitor. I asked myself who had betrayed us to Wilson. Who was the spy?

I went over the names of my followers, I called up their faces, and all seemed to me equally trustworthy—and therefore equally deceitful. For it seemed that looks, and long acquaintance, went for nothing.

What of the wives, of thin cottage walls, of families sleeping together in one room, of innocent or mischievous children who would repeat half-understood hints?

It was barely three weeks since these men had promised secrecy, with a very good knowledge of how much depended on it. But I go too fast for my story.

42

EARLY that month the tailor had arrived on his usual round. He came twice a year, in spring and autumn, and put up at the Green Man or at Stonepit to carry out village repairs and alterations on the spot, if he had a suit to make he would stay till it was finished.

This year he stayed at the Coytes' to make a suit of black for Fred —it was acknowledged that Mrs. Coyte had not long to live, and she not only knew of this order for Fred's blacks but had them tried on in her presence as she lay in bed, and made some strong comments on the cut. In fact the tailor threatened to throw up the work and sue her for the cost. It took Fred and my father together to pacify him.

This tailor was a little bandy-legged fellow called Gomme, bald and gay-seeming, he always wore a grin, but his temper was notoriously short. It was, as the people said, always on simmer. He was a very old acquaintance of mine, he had made my first breeches out of a coat of my father's, and I had always looked forward to his visits.

Like all such roundsmen, he was a great gossip, indeed, an important news-bringer. Through him illiterate labourers, who could neither write nor read a letter, had news of relations as far away as Exeter where he went to buy stuff, and Lilmouth where he had customers. He was a great radical, a republican, a single taxer, a disciple of Henry George, and he had the greatest contempt for lords and ladies, for squires and magistrates.

You think this is unusual in a tailor; tailors are mostly Tories, it is the cobbler who is expected to be a Communist.

But though this tailor boasted that he had made a suit for my Lord himself at Slapton, yet he was a revolutionary of the most extreme type.

All this I had known all my life, and it had made no impression at all upon my idea of the world. It was only in the last three years, since my friendship with the Dollings, that I had begun to understand the

182

man. I thought him crazy and ignorant, one of those whom the Dollings regarded with pity, as deceived by Bakunin's theories, but I understood his arguments.

A newsman must have news—a fact not to be ignored by those who trace the fall of empires—and Gomme had his yearly tales, scandals about great names as well as small ones. He had told us of Napoleon's mistresses and hinted that Mr. Gladstone walked the streets by night. He told us that the Prince Consort had been poisoned to prevent him from sending the British army to fight for Germany—this year he was full of mysterious hints about a revolution in Britain. He had been to Lilmouth to make a suit for the secretary of a friendly society there and he had penetrated all the secrets of a great conspiracy.

It seemed that some big man, called Pring, had come down from London to meet the local leaders, and he had started a plan to join all the workers in the kingdom together. Then he would call a general strike, and end the society of privilege—the workers would rule the world.

This big man, Pring, so Gomme said with relish, was a real boss. He didn't stand any nonsense—if anyone said a word to him he put the boys on him and they knocked him into mummy.

I was sceptical of such a plan and revolted by the suggestion of violence, which ran counter to all my recent instruction from the Dollings.

"Dr. Dolling was in Paris at the time of the Commune," I said, "and he'll tell you it put back the cause of the people for fifty years—with its burnings and murders."

Gomme's little bloodshot eyes, ruined by sewing in bad lights, fairly glowed with spite. He hated every distinguished person. "Do you mean the German bander—that old fool? He's only fit to blow bad air down a dirty pipe."

Dr. Dolling was an expert on the oboe and played in the amateur band at Tarbiton. He had founded the band and sometimes conducted it—the reason why, I suppose, he was thought to be a German.

"What's he do for any of us?" Gomme demanded. "Just talk. Why, fat old Brodribb at Tarbiton is more use, he does get the chaps into the union."

183

He then suggested that Dolling was not an anarchist at all but a police agent who had run away to this country because he had betrayed so many comrades to the police that his life was in danger. And what was he doing in Tarbiton—spying on Brodribb. Let me ask Brodribb about him.

"And where's he get his money from? He don't work, catch him. He don't get no pay for his banding. And lives like a lord all the year round. Looks funny to me. And a lot more. Go on. You're a bit simple, an't you? or what?"

I have noticed that such questions are common among the poorer agitators to whom any income except money paid in wages, money that is seen and handled, has a mysterious air, so that it is easy to imagine it arising from fraud or treachery.

"The doctor has means in France," I said.

"The good old tale. If he's on the square, why do the police let him get them? I tell you what, young feller, a lot of our chaps have taken notice how you go with that nark. I been surprised myself—very surprised."

I said that all this was stupid lies, and yet such is the terrible force of suspicion, when next I met the Dollings I found myself uneasy and embarrassed. I mentioned Pring to them and they told me that they had met him—he was a very bad man who aspired to power by every kind of deceit and violence. He had already betrayed certain London comrades, turned them out of the London committee and actually taken away their livelihood.

I asked if they thought him sincere, and they said that on the contrary he was almost certainly in league with the police. And this answer increased my suspicion of my old friends—a suspicion of which I was ashamed and yet I could not remove it. For I had heard from themselves for years of the cunning and endless deceits of the police, of their penetrating into the most secret counsels under every kind of disguise—of one who actually murdered a Russian General to establish his reputation with the Communist chiefs.

An inner voice that I could not silence asked me why, if the mark of an agent was his cleverness in advancing the most extreme opinions, Dr. Dolling should not be one. How was it, after all, that he lived—

184

and why did the government permit him to receive an income if he were truly a refugee?

I did not condemn Dolling, I simply became unsure of him—the whole joy of my friendship, the candour, the confidence, was gone—I took care of what I said to him and regarded everything that he said to me with a double mind.

I asked him about Brodribb, for though I was familiar with the name I knew nothing of his activities. The doctor laughed and said he was now the branch chairman of the Tarbiton dockers, a man of small education and narrow views, a gradualist of the meanest type.

He meant that Brodribb was not for world revolution; but for some reason that I cannot explain, except by saying that once more the hour had struck for me, once more I had reached a crisis in my growing, I had been stung by Gomme's question—what did Dolling do for the poor—and I went to see Brodribb.

He turned out to be a typical middle-aged docker, a heavy solemn man with a heavy wife and four children—a Methodist and the local secretary of the dock workers' union.

He was highly suspicious of me till he discovered that I was the son of my father whose intervention in the tinners' strike was not forgotten. Then he was very friendly, and showed me all the workings of his organisation.

He took me into his back room which he called the union office, it was furnished with a kitchen table, two kitchen chairs and an enormous safe.

This ancient iron safe with its three locks impressed me very much. I believe it was kept for the impression it made, for it held only a few notebooks and three or four pounds in small change. The union funds were at the bank.

Brodribb kept me to tea—I found myself in the midst of a family life I understood, among kind simple people devoted to each other and their children, honest as the day. And when he asked me what I was doing for the cause, I was ashamed—it seemed that I had done nothing but read and talk, collect a little money for refugees and pass happy afternoons at the Dollings, being petted by Mrs. Dolling as their one genuine field labourer, almost a moujik.

I asked Brodribb what I could do, could I work for him. He pointed out that I was not a docker. But why not do something for my own class—the farm labourers?

The great union founded by Arch was now in decline—its enormous success had been followed by an equally strange and sudden decline. But it had proved that field workers could be brought into a union.

And he showed me how to begin a branch by approaching a few reliable men well known to me, and warned me that the first beginning should be secret, so that these pioneers should not be victimised.

I had begun at once with surprising and intoxicating success, Doan was my first recruit, and at that time of the Shagbrook Splash I had twenty-seven members in all, including those from outlying farms.

43

How many can even imagine the agonising anxiety of those pledged to some secret enterprise, dangerous to others as well as themselves, who find suddenly that there is a traitor at work.

I tell you there is no discovery more corrupting. From that morning in the barn, I never escaped from the gnawing fearful thought that someone among my men was selling me and the rest of his comrades.

Times were bad, the depression of the seventies had set in, most of the hamlet depended on the farmers, who had already laid men off—and I had promised security.

Even in my sleep I could not throw off such responsibility—I waked one night to find Georgina standing over me with a candle. We stared at each other. I was startled by this apparition, by something new and wild in the girl's look.

"You were shouting things and then you screamed out—I thought you'd been murdered."

This was a new fear—I talked in my sleep. I answered carelessly, "It was a bad dream, that's all."

"What's happened to you, Ches? Why are you so different?" Suddenly she kneeled down by the bed and asked me why I was angry with her. "Father is always angry at me, and Dick has gone from me long ago. Now you are going from me too and I shan't bear it."

She leaned her breast on mine across the bed and I felt the immense force of loneliness and constraint, banked up for years, that had driven so proud a girl to such an appeal. She put her arms round my shoulders and looked into my eyes, trying, as women do, to make me feel the love and need that she could not express in words.

"What have I done—only tell me?"

But I, obsessed with a new danger, was thinking, "It might have been at Stonepit, I often doze off there, waiting for Fred." I was ashamed too for my fright. And I blamed Wilson for that too. I

187

answered Georgina only with another question. What did she think of Will Wilson?

"Willy Wilson," she started back, "what do you mean?"

"I think the sooner he's out of here, the better."

"I suppose Fred's been talking to you." She was scarlet. "Fred's a jealous fool. What would Richard say if I turned my back on his old friend?"

"It's not only Fred's been noticing—it's everybody."

"So I'm not to have a friend anywhere—I'm not even to speak to an old friend. And you agree with them." She jumped up and said in a trembling voice that I was worse than Fred.

"When I give my word—I keep it. Even Fred knows that." I answered that I hoped so. Georgina stood gazing at me, her dark blush had faded, she seemed pale and hollow-cheeked—she picked up the candle and turned away without another word. I daresay she could not have spoken. I thought only, "So Fred's jealous—that might help to get rid of Wilson."

How did I show such cruelty to a beloved sister? I felt her anguish of loneliness, I perceived a crisis in her fate. The only excuse I can find for that raw frightened youth is that he took the girl at her word —the word she believed of herself. He did not conceive the evil that could flow for her from the night of the Shag floods.

I went to Fred next day and suggested that Wilson could be spared even before the cleaning up was finished. If we wanted another man it should be Kimber.

Fred warmly agreed with me and burst out with all his complaints against Georgina—she had not been near him since the flood, and Wilson was always in the dairy. They had been dancing at Tarbiton together and come home by the combe. Georgina was mad about the fellow. To say that any young couple had come home by the combe after a dance had the worst implications.

I told him that Georgina was not that sort. She might be too fond of dancing—she was no jilt. But the affair was making talk. Wilson was a bad friend for any girl. "Why don't you speak to your mother? She'd soon shift him."

But my poor friend was a helpless soul in all dimensions, he was terrified by my suggestion. Mother was too ill to be worried. And she had a high opinion of Wilson. She said he was the only man about the place who knew how to work. He was worth any three of the rest.

"You go to your father. He's the real guvner, now."

So he flattered me. And in my desperation I did go to my father. I found him, to my surprise, quite aware of Georgina's infatuation, and more disturbed about it than I. He said that Georgina was a scandal to the family and the place. He had appealed to her but she had only gloomed at him.

I had seldom seen my father so agitated. He limped about the room at speed pouring out his fears, and in the midst of them he stopped to light a pipe, always a sign of extreme distress. He had long waged a battle against this craving and gave way to it only in moments of great stress.

Startled by the storm I had raised, I murmured that the old women were making too much of the thing, Will Wilson was a nine days' wonder and all the girls had lost their heads over him. But he wouldn't last—he'd be forgotten as soon as he left the place.

"They say she's with him half the day. It might be a fancy, but Georgy is so stiff in her fancies. If she breaks her word to Fred she'll do a wicked thing. How will she forgive herself a thing like that?" And then when I did not answer, he said, "They say she was too young, but she chose for herself. It's too late to change. Cissy Bennet was only fourteen when the cart knocked her down and lamed her, but she has never complained of that fate, she has been a good honest girl and given thanks to God for her life."

My father, in short, took a view of Georgina's obligations that would now be thought severe by those who do not believe that this world is but a testing place for the soul. But when I now urged that it would be a good thing for Georgina if Wilson were sent away, he answered that the girl's bad conduct was no reason for depriving a poor man of his job. Wilson had done well at the bridge, it would be a wicked thing to put him out on the roads in mid-winter.

And now I cursed my folly in raising this question with the man. I had provoked in him that conscience, those scruples of justice and

189

right, which might cause him actually to favour my enemy—to, as our transatlantic friends say, lean over backwards in obliging him.

I am not pretending anywhere in this book that a man so scrupulous as my father was not often a cross and burden to his family. As we shall see, his scrupulosity went far to ruin us all in a material sense. And then I almost hated him.

But I do not think I was ever quite unaware that that rigidity was but the somewhat heavy and wooden scabbard of a precious steel which was for us all the very mirror of truth, the bright star of our faith. And how shall such honour admit a flaw—the least speck of rust within the sword and it is no longer a strength but a fraud and a danger. For in the day of decision, the crisis of fate, it will break in the hand.

I trembled before my father, but I said boldly enough that though Wilson might be deserving, Georgina was young, we were taking a risk. He answered only with the same furrowed brow that it was for Georgina to recollect herself, a girl could always put a man from her if she chose. And I did not dare to press the point, I went away in angry dejection.

I daresay, indeed, that Wilson would have had permanent employment at Stonepit if it had not been for the hand of fate. Mrs. Coyte, who had seemed greatly better for some days, was found one morning dead in bed.

And Fred's first action as master was to sack Wilson, or rather to ask my father to do so.

My father was careful to support the authority of the new master. He agreed to pay Wilson off, but he recommended him to a better job. My father had plenty of influence when he cared to use it, he enlisted both Mr. Newmarch and Mr. Simons, head keeper at Slapton, to pull strings. Wilson went straight from Stonepit to a very good place under the Slapton estate office—and I daresay he owed much of that promotion to my efforts in his disfavour. One might say that I was the first begetter of his remarkable career.

As for my proposal that we should now take on Kimber, the most troublesome of my union men, it failed completely. For my father was himself inclined to Kimber, a devout Methodist, but not a very steady worker and a quarrelsome wrong-headed sort of man, and therefore deferred the matter entirely to Fred.

Fred, when he found that he could not extract definite advice from my father, said peevishly, "But there—I don't mind—it don't matter now Cousin Cran's coming—and I'll ask him."

This was the first we had heard of Cousin Cran for some years, his name excited some gloomy prognostications in the village. At every death of an employer people see bankruptcy at hand—they cannot be blamed for uneasiness when their livelihood may depend on the twist of a will or the folly of an heir. And the funeral had already gathered a collection of extraordinary relatives. An ancient cousin from Bristol, two spinster sisters of the late farmer Coyte from Bournemouth. Cran came last. He came in his own smart dog-cart, and though he was dressed in dark grey with a black band, even his mourning had a sporting and flashy air. In fact he immediately imposed himself upon the whole gathering, and most of the village except my father.

I do not know why in England even the poorest excuse everything to what is called a sportsman—very often a swindler, a petty crook, the lowest type of self-seeker.

I do not say that Cran was dishonest in a strict sense. He was, I believe, never discovered in any fraud during his career as a bookmaker, but he was tricky in all his dealings, you could not trust him to tell the truth in any affair—about a horse, about himself and his own actions, about anything at all. He said what suited him, that is, suited his advantage.

He behaved, too, with astonishing arrogance. He would swagger into the Green Man and lay down the law—anyone who dared to contradict might expect the most contemptuous reply. I have heard him say to a poor boy who doubted his statement that he could tame a poor pony in ten minutes, "Who are you, ragged a——e, and what do you know about anything?"

Yet our moor people, who would not have borne so much as a careless glance from my Lord, not only took such sayings with equanimity, but repeated them afterwards as good things.

It soon appeared that Cran was comfortable at the farm and had no intention of leaving it. Within a fortnight of Mrs. Coyte's death he and Fred went to Lilmouth races. A horse-coper called Beal was now at the farm almost every evening to play cards, and it was rumoured that Fred lost large sums.

And Fred had begun to drink. During those last months at the farm I doubt if he was ever quite sober. He would get up at midday to go down the street to the Green Man where he would stay till closing time. He would describe his last day's racing, tell everybody who came in what a fool he was to go with such as Beal and Cran, and when he was very drunk he would weep and say his mother had been quite right, that he was no good, it was no wonder that Georgina had jilted him.

My father was very indignant at these proceedings. He said that Fred would ruin himself and the farm, and reproached him severely for drinking and gambling. He even denounced him publicly at service. Fred cried and promised amendment but immediately went back to the bottle.

My father, night after night, would come home in extreme perturbation of spirit and say, "It can't go on like this—the house is surely a byword and a trap—a place of corruption for the whole village."

But I was hardly aware of these lamentations. I was living in another dimension where nothing was sure, nothing was dependable.

44

ONE evening in that March as I stood in the corner of the yard looking at the clouded sky, wondering if the frost would break, a small boy came slipping along underneath the wall and said that his mother wanted to speak to me.

I said, "Let her come in." But the boy answered that she did not want to come in, she was afraid. I went out then, and in the shadow of the barn found widow Doan.

She was a thin little woman who had had a hard struggle since her husband's death, but two of her sons were doing job work for a farmer called Mann on the Battwell road. Now she told me that both the boys had been turned away. She was in great agitation and burst into tears as she spoke.

"But what for, Mrs. Doan?" I was fearful she would ask me to call a strike which would have been impossible. But both the Doans were members of my union.

"It's this union of yours. Mr. Mann knows all about it." And then she began to abuse me for getting her boys into trouble. Also she wanted something from the union fund.

The union fund had once had a balance of four pounds, but most of this had gone on expenses and grants. We had paid Dodman's fare to Exeter to see a union organiser there, we had bought a cash-book and cash-box, we had entertained a delegate from a Somerset branch and given Bennet half a crown relief after the flood. At the moment there was less than two shillings in the box. I gave Mrs. Doan half a crown—and warned her to keep quiet about the union. I promised to see Mann and intercede for the Doans.

I went to Mann in a fury. I meant to find out who had betrayed us —to threaten reprisals; I meant to use mystery against mystery, telling myself that Mann would not know how weak we were.

But when I asked him why he had turned away my friends the

Doans, he answered that he had sacked one for idleness and the other for impudence. And he asked what business it was of mine.

"They say," I said, "that there's been talk among you farmers about a union."

"I don't know nothing about any union," he said, staring hard at me. "What's this about a union?"

I stared as hard at him, but how could I tell if he were lying or not? How could I tell how much or how little he knew? I dared not risk disclosure if it were not necessary.

"Whose union?" he repeated. "Where?"

"That's what I want to know," I said, and went hastily away—I could not tell if I had been the greater fool to go to the man or to lie to him, and meanwhile I could not forget Mrs. Doan's tears and outcries, the fact that my union fund was exhausted.

It was with this scene on my mind that one afternoon in April I came into the stable and found my father at work. It was typical of him that he preferred to do his repairs in the stable among his beloved horses rather than in the workshop where there was a comfortable chair.

Here he was obliged to prop himself against the wall on a tub and a horse blanket. His leg had been bad for some days in the east wind and he could not walk without a stick.

He was sewing harness—work which he preferred to do himself rather than entrust it to a Tarbiton saddler. In the course of years he must have saved Mrs. Coyte many pounds by his expert work on cart harness.

This is the kind of task, spread over years a little at a time, which is rarely adequately assessed or paid upon a farm. The labourer who will stop to poke out a drain, to tighten a clamp in a gate latch, to stop a hole in rabbit wire, to set a prop under an apple branch, is worth twice the pay of another who does only his stint. My father was the kind of man who had put sympathy as well as conscience into his work. He had a feeling for the broken gate as if it was a wound in himself. So, too, he would restuff a horse collar, or sew a trace, as if he were responsible not only to his master and the horses, but to God.

Upon seeing him in these days I was always startled by his thinness, and his smallness. He had aged very much in the last five years since that day upon the Tor. We are not a long-lived race, for apart from the family scourge that killed two of my sisters, there is something impatient and fretful which wears us out before our time. My father's arthritis too had much increased upon him that winter, there were days when he could not walk more than a few yards and then with much pain. And this afternoon was the first time for a week I had seen him out.

I did not make any remark. Since in the last two years I had ceased to attend the Sunday sermons regularly there had been some embarrassment between us. And now he did not seem to notice me as I wisped the cob. Yet so soon as I had finished he said, without raising his eyes from the trace in his hand, "If you have time, Ches, I'd like to speak to you about things here."

I went over to him and he took off his spectacles as if to greet me, and asked me to draw up a bucket and take my seat.

But I preferred to stand, in case I should want to excuse myself and escape.

He then took up his awl in his blackened fingers and proceeded with his work. "It's like this, son," he said, and he told me about Cran and asked me what he should do.

My father had consulted me before in a formal manner, for instance, in a political question, for I was supposed to be the family expert upon politics, as he would ask Georgina's advice about the planting of vegetables or Richard's upon a point of grammar. He was completely modest and even humble in his relation even with children.

This was the first time he had asked my advice upon an affair of conscience, but in my troubled state of mind I was more startled than flattered.

"It's like this," he said. "If I should tell him that things can't go on in this way then he may say to Fred to let me go."

I saw at once why my father had asked my advice; for him, in his half-crippled state, to lose his employment at Stonepit would be to ruin himself and us. He would never get another job as foreman, and he would almost certainly lose his cottage.

"I don't see it's your fault," I said, "if Fred plays the fool."

195

There was a pause while my father fixed a bristle to a new length of thread, and he passed it through the hole before he answered that this house had become a place of drinking and gambling, and worse. Then, raising his eyes to look at me over his spectacles, he said, "How can I stay in such a place and say nothing, do nothing to stop such wickedness?"

I felt already a fearful impatience with the old man. Why should his ridiculous scruples come in now to make my position still more difficult. While I was earning, I could at least afford a little help to such as Mrs. Doan, but what if I lost my job?

"If you leave Stonepit," I said, "the place will only go to ruin, and we might all lose our jobs. Georgina as well."

There was a long silence and my father raised his eyes to my face as if seeking pardon. "I have prayed," he said, "and God tells me to speak."

"Perhaps you think so because it will ruin us."

"It may be so," he answered, with another sigh. "Often I have thought so myself, but how can light come save we seek it, and where can we seek it but with God?"

There seemed no more to be said. As I went back to my work I said to myself, "The old fanatic will ruin us all with his cranks, and Fred too."

In fact, on the very next day, my father went to Fred and told him that if the gambling and the drinking continued he could not stay. And Fred cried and answered that he could not mean to leave him.

But afterwards he went round the village telling this story and asking the people what he should do. Must he send Cran away or should he let my father go? It is a cruel truth that, as we were soon informed, many in the village whom we had thought devoted to my father both as man and pastor advised Fred not to be put upon.

This action caused us equal disgust and astonishment. For many years I thought it a sign of the ineradicable evil in men's hearts. Now after fifty years, I think it arose not from evil will towards my father, but simply from a primitive sense of human dignity. These poor labourers and cotters felt, obscurely enough, that it was degrading for a man of forty to remain in tutelage.

196

But the consequence for us and for my father was grave. Fred, after many waverings, accepted his resignation, and my father at one stroke lost his income and the cottage. For Cran and Fred now brought in a new foreman, a man called Meakin, who would require the cottage at Midsummer.

It seemed now that our family, like so many others in the same circumstances, must break up. I, indeed, could sleep in the loft over my horses, but there was no cottage in the village available for my father and the girls.

Georgina and I were divided and yet we were closer than friends. I stared with surprise when she exclaimed thank God for the Shagbrook beasts—now we could escape from Shagbrook. But I felt her rage against the place in my own nerves.

"You stay at Coytes' if you like," she said. "But I'll take father to Newmarch's. At least he'll be among friends and warm and dry and properly respected."

She went at once to suggest this plan to Newmarch who, again showing unexpected generosity, was delighted with it—it would be an honour, he said, to give houseroom to his revered pastor.

On that same day, Bennet, one of my men, was sacked by old G. who had employed him as shepherd on the moor for more than twenty years. G lived now in Tarbiton over the shop he had inherited from his wife's father. We hardly ever saw him in Shagbrook, but the rumour was that he was going to the bad in his old age. He certainly kept a very young and lively housekeeper.

I had to ask myself if this unscrupulous old rake, ten miles away at Tarbiton, was in league with Mann in quite another direction at Battwell, and if some traitor had betrayed the whole list of our members throughout the countryside, if the farmers everywhere were waiting their chance or convenience to throw us all out to walk the roads.

I was like a man in some quiet town carrying a secret treasure in his pocket who is suddenly lost among the dark unlit streets, and now he hears himself followed, a voice calls from the distance, a dark lantern flashes. He stops abruptly and the footfalls behind also stop, he tells himself they were only the echo of his own, that he is imagining these terrors—suddenly a whistle sounds and is answered from far ahead, he rushes on in rage and confusion saying that at least he will die game.

And my treasure was the livelihood, perhaps the very lives, of forty or fifty poor wretches who had trusted me. The Bennets had four small children, Mrs. Doan three under seven; now all homeless. I felt the bitterness all about me. And suddenly I agreed with Georgina that the sooner my father and she and Ruth were out of Shagbrook the better.

All I objected to now in Georgina's plan was that Ruth should go into service. Ruth herself hated the plan. On the day when Georgina announced that she would apply for a place, I found Ruth in tears, she could hardly speak in her misery.

45

I HAVE written here little of my younger sister Ruth, though it was Ruth who for a long time now had been our chief support at home. Without her neither Georgina nor I would have had freedom to earn, for when my father was in bed he needed the most careful watching and nursing—he would try to get up and do things for himself when he could not stand. Once already he had fallen and broken his wrist.

He was restless in bed and impatient when any of us tried to keep him there, saying that doctors were no good. But he was more patient with Ruth than with Georgina or myself. Ruth, after Richard, was his favourite, and her gentleness put him on his mettle not to be a trouble to her. I have never known anyone so self-effacing as Ruth, nor anyone so contented. Her life seemed completely filled within the family circle, she was happy if we were happy.

This does not mean that she was stupid or wanted humour. As she was like Richard in her fairness and her good looks, so she had something of his detachment. She read very little, indeed, and had small education, but what she knew she knew well and she had a lively sense of humour.

She was an extraordinary mimic, and even as a small child would throw us into fits of laughter by pretending to be Mr. Newmarch, who was a great fat man, coming in to service and looking for a safe place for his hat, and kneeling down, slowly and cautiously, on the stone floor.

She would clear her throat like Newmarch and she would give a sermon like Dr. Leddra.

My friend Edward G, at the age of twenty, had surprised us all by falling in love with Ruth, who was then only just thirteen. Edward was a very shy young man, and yet excitable—he would get very excited about small matters and shout. Since his mother's death many

199

people regarded him as slightly mad, and it was true that with his red face and strange gestures he had an odd look. But he was a good man of business, and an efficient assistant in the Tarbiton shop.

He had met Ruth when he came to my father's services. Now he began to drop in at odd hours in the hopes of seeing the girl alone.

It is true that Ruth at that age was already like a little woman, much more so than Georgina had been. But she was not less shy. When Edward came to the house she would throw her apron over her head and burst into giggles; she had always found something amusing in poor Edward—she was apt to be amused by much that seemed only too serious to the rest of us.

Ruth was self-effacing but she had plenty of character. I had not realised how much this affectionate and undemanding sister meant to me until, for the first time, I saw her in real misery.

I was highly indignant with Georgina as I went to find her—she was, as I had expected, cleaning out her dairy after the morning's work. And I burst out at once, "What's this about forcing Ruth into service against her will? It's a wicked idea."

Georgina looked up at me from the floor where she was scrubbing and asked me if I thought it would be good for Ruth to go to Newmarch's with our father. "She'll have nothing to do there except be a farm servant, and Newmarch's is just a rough place like this."

"Ruth is crying her eyes out at the very idea of going into service, and I don't blame her."

"It isn't the service, it's the going away by herself. Ruth don't know what's good for her, service is just what she needs, you know how shy she is—she'll never be anything at all if she's let go on in a place like Newmarch's. She'll go all stupid there or get married by some lump. And Ruth is so pretty and clever, I'm not going to have her dragged down any further."

"Dragged down—it's you who want to drag her down. I always thought you were the proud one."

I think I felt that, even at that moment, Georgina was in truth the proud, the independent one—that is why I was so angry with her.

But she did not trouble to answer me, she got up from her knees and wrung out her cloth as if squeezing the folly out of my argument.

200

Neither, as it soon appeared, did she give up her plan, even when the excuse for it was removed.

My father's disciples about Shagbrook had been much concerned at the thought of his leaving the neighbourhood, and some of them now formed a committee which pointed out that there was a cottage available in the village. True, it had been empty for years, it was half ruined and it stood off the road, next the muddy footpath behind the Green Man. It had been, however, a free cottage, not tied to any farm, and the committee offered to repair it. Its name was Ladd's House or Ladd's Corner.

Georgina and I were strongly opposed to the scheme. The place was miserably small and in the dampest part of the hollow. We considered that if these people wanted my father so badly they ought to have more consideration for his health. Georgina raged at their selfishness, and pointed it out to my father, who answered only that poor men could not be choosers.

"They might choose to let you go to Newmarch's."

"It's a long way for them on Sundays and I can't come visiting as I used to."

My father did hesitate for a few days, but then he had what he called a strong indication that he ought to accept the call. The committee went to the Slapton agents, who approved their scheme—it was of great advantage to them, for the whole of the work cost only ten or twelve pounds for materials. The labour was given.

We moved into Ladd's House just before the middle of June.

46

MEAKIN was now in sole charge at Stonepit. Fred and Cran were away for weeks together and the foreman behaved like the owner. He was, as I realise now, a good farmer, up-to-date for that time—he brought in various improvements. And this was his excuse when he paid me my harvest money and said he would not need me after November, which was my contract date. He was going to use less horses, and put down some of his arable.

I asked him if this was his real reason and he gave me a look, not so hard as Mann's but more inquiring. Mann had seemed to say, "You can't take me in"—Meakin to ask if he would risk telling me the truth.

Instead he said, "I tell you now so that you can look for a job. Of course I can recommend you."

And I began to hunt for work whenever I had a day off. But no one seemed to want a horseman, or even a labourer, after they had heard my name.

The farmer would say, "Nimmo? From Shagbrook? Son of old Preacher Nimmo? Yes, I thought so," and he would look at me for a moment as if trying to see my wickedness in my face, before saying that he did not need me.

One man, a corn merchant, went further and said that he didn't want any trouble-makers on his place.

Not only Dodman, the Doans, and Bennet were now out of work, but three more in Shagbrook itself, and two on the Slapton property.

The idea of class war has never taken hold in England. The reason is perhaps that in the hard times before the unions grew to power and learnt to value negotiation, the more obvious battle was between town and country—countrymen saw their interest rather with the squires than the factory workers.

And perhaps I myself came so late to the conception because Mrs.

202

Coyte had protected us, and the Slaptons were reckoned good land-lords. My Lord, for instance, had subscribed to help Richard to Oxford, and his sister, Miss Mary, used to bring Christmas presents of invalid port and blankets for the sick poor. My mother had had both. But now these considerations merely increased my bitterness. I saw in these charities merely a trick to keep the poor contented with their lot, to buy their servility with their own money.

Was it surprising that I hated all lords and squires, and called Georgina a class enemy when now again she proposed to send Ruth into service—actually to old Lady Slapton at the Court, who wanted a sewing maid.

"But Ches, it really is a good chance for Ruth, and I don't worry you about your union, do I?"

"What union?"

"Why, everyone knows about your union. How could you keep it secret in a place like this?"

"I knew you'd be against unions—like Will."

"It depends on the union and what it does."

"And you're the girl who used to want a revolution."

But since I had failed her, Georgina never quarrelled with me. She seemed even especially gentle with me.

She had her way with Ruth, who could never withstand that strong will—as for my father, he was persuaded that his dear Ruth was in danger in the new house with its damp walls. Wilson brought a Slapton cart for her just before Christmas—she was wanted for Christmas preparations at the Court—and she was driven away in such a state of despair that her whole face was swollen with crying.

All the village agreed with me that Georgina was a cruel as well as a wicked girl. It was said that once a girl goes wrong as Georgina had done in jilting Fred, she takes to all kinds of evil courses.

"It's the spite in her," they said.

I must confess that I believed them, I was astonished by Georgina's hard persistence, her indifference to Ruth's tears—I said too that since her meeting with Will Wilson she had gone to the bad.

I found pleasure in the news that Ruth was wretched at the Court, in her unhappy letters. When six weeks later she wrote urgently to

Georgina saying that she must see her or me upon a matter of importance, and Georgina remarked that no doubt I would not want to go
near such a wicked place as Slapton, I answered that on the contrary
I was determined to go. I did not intend that Ruth should be bullied
into staying another week in servitude.

One afternoon, then, after Tarbiton market, Georgina and I walked
to the Court and were directed by a kitchen maid up the back stairs
to an attic corridor, to find Ruth seated alone in a small room among
a mountain of sheets, which she was mending.

I looked with surprise at my young sister's tranquil air and rosy
cheeks—I had expected a pale broken creature. But before I could
say a word, she sprang up to embrace us; she was laughing with joy.

When Georgina asked her how she did, she answered that she was
very happy, that Miss Colton, my lady's maid, was very kind to her,
and that old Lady Slapton had complimented her on her sewing. This
kind of conversation continued with great animation for at least
twenty minutes; Ruth seemed to be giving a full account, with illus-
trations, of all the inhabitants of the house from my Lord downwards.
She acted the old lady threading a needle, the butler's pompous walk,
the lively swagger of some footman or groom, and Georgina as always was highly delighted by the performance. The two girls laughed
so much that they grew red and hot, their cheeks shone as much as
their eyes. My amazement can be imagined—after a moment, I
shrugged my shoulders, so to speak, at these girls who could never
be steady for a moment in any direction, at Ruth who had so quickly
reconciled herself to such a lot, and fell back upon my own preoccupations.

I had plenty to worry about. I had indeed at the moment no idea
how I was to live. I had no job, I was sleeping on the floor in the very
small attic which was all that Edward G was allowed by his father in
Tarbiton, and earning only odd shillings at odd jobs and a little cler-
ical work for Brodribb and the dockers' union.

The girls had now been joined by a smart, dark, neat young man in
a white stock and a cotton coat, the undress of a groom. In fact I
recognised him after a moment as one of the Slapton grooms—he was
the lively young swaggerer whom Ruth had just been mimicking. I

had seen him before on my Lord's second horse, and in a racing party with Cran. As I looked more attentively at him, so self-assured and easy with the girls, I thought, the typical arrogant lackey, the Tory parasite.

He was presented to me and gave me an easy handshake—confident, as it seemed to me, that I should admire his brisk address, and said that he was pleased to meet me. He asked if we would like to see the house—this was a good opportunity because the family had been on a visit and were not expected for another two hours. Georgina accepted this offer with gratitude; the young man, whose name was Geoffrey Simnel, then fetched a friend, one of the footmen, and we were conducted through certain of the rooms.

I was familiar with the house from the outside. As a boy I had been a beater in the woods, as a man I had delivered dung for the garden and wood for the fires. It was a plain square house of the early eighteenth century, its façade, its lawns and gardens were not remarkable among country houses even of the middle sort. So, too, its state rooms could have been excelled by those of many a city man in the home counties. But to me, the place was a palace, the rooms with their Persian carpets and gilt-framed mirrors, their silk hangings and polished floors, represented the utmost of magnificence. I had never seen anything like them, and reflected on the immense cost, as I thought it, of this luxury and splendour only for the enjoyment of a family consisting then of three persons—old Lady Slapton, her son, at present abroad, and his sister Mary.

Do I dwell to excess upon my bitterness in face of these differences in wealth? I am writing of a time when many of the poor in any winter season were actually short of food, a time when a labourer's wages were twelve shillings a week, and there was a numerous class enjoying between fifty and a hundred thousand a year, and paying for it the smallest of tax.

But above all what enraged me at that time was the idea of conspiracy, the belief that behind all the façade of law and justice, hard enough as it was upon the deprived, there was a secret compact between owners, the rich and their hangers-on, against the dispossessed.

It is this suspicion, I tell you earnestly, this belief, that works like

205

madness in the blood. The machinery of the law, of government, of economics, are themselves complex and difficult enough to comprehend for the poor man compelled to spend his best hours at manual labour, condemned to tremble every day not only for his livelihood but for the future of his helpless dependents. But when they wear the face of a plot, a conspiracy, you cannot blame him if he answers with the same arts, and if he makes the sharpest division between those who serve this cunning and relentless enemy and those who give their loyalty to their own people.

I listened to Georgina's exclamations as she admired the beauties of Slapton, displayed to her so proudly by Ruth and the two young men, with angry contempt for them and sad wonder at my sisters; I said to myself that as soon as girls turned into women and involved themselves in women's affairs, they lost all political sense and the stability of mind necessary to take part in any important enterprise.

I did not say this again to Georgina as we drove home, I did not trouble once more to call her class enemy, and I listened without surprise while she congratulated herself on her luck in being able to see the house, and then asked me what I thought of Geoffrey Simnel.

I said that he seemed to me an ordinary kind of groom and small gambler, and probably he was the usual kind of lackey and snob.

Georgina smiled at me and asked if I had not realised why he had been there, and why Ruth had sent for us.

"You think he's after Ruth?"

"Of course he is, but Ruth is afraid we won't approve and that father won't approve. For one thing, it's true that he bets a little, and of course he's not a teetotaller. And for another, he's Church of England."

I said that if Ruth could bring herself to marry such a fellow I had no objection.

Georgina looked at me for a moment then said, "Why bring in politics—politics isn't everything."

"They come into everything."

"I'm not going to let them come into Ruth's life just to spoil it. If you and father don't approve of Simnel, she won't marry him. And I'm sure she's very fond of him, and I think he's probably her best

206

chance too. The betting is nothing, all grooms bet, and he wants to get on, he has already tried for a coachman's place in Bath."

I answered nothing to this, for all I could have said would merely have exasperated Georgina. And when it turned out that, just as the girls had feared, my father knew something of the young man and did not like it, I stood aside from the battle.

I saw Georgina walking about with a pale tragic countenance for weeks, oblivious to all considerations but this love affair, or rushing eight miles to Slapton with secret news or advice—I saw Ruth brought to Ladd's one day in Will Wilson's trap, in such a state of mind that in the end she could not face her father, so good and gentle, but hid in the Stonepit dairy.

Lady Slapton was brought into the fight. She wrote that Simnel was a worthy young man and an excellent match for her dear Ruth.

All this, I thought, because a groom has a fancy for a sewing maid of eighteen, the whole women's world high and low is agitated as by an earthquake.

47

LAST week I had a heart attack, today, the ninth of April, is the first on which I have been allowed out of bed. I sit here by the window and look at those fragile buds of spring that may outlive me, yet never have they been more delightful to my eyes, more powerful with the grace of courage and hope. And she who has been my wife, my nobler soul, the close and secret comrade of my darkest hours, who has given to me more than her youth, her life and loyalty—the perpetual knowledge of a truth that is truth's very substance, the faith of the heart—who has sacrifced all to me over thirty years—sits before me, pen in hand, eager to render me that last service of interpretation, anxious, as she says, to dispel through these memoirs a cloud of misunderstanding which has thrown so black a shade upon my last hours.

Her once most beautiful hair is grey; the face which charmed London in its most splendid years is worn and lined with long suffering; but never has she been more lovely in my sight, never has her presence and support been more necessary to this poor atomy.

One flesh, how magic and how terrible is this phrase to those who love—one flesh for good and for evil—one flesh and one soul in which the nerves, the sympathies, speak as across a common heart, with meanings not to be expressed in words.

She is part of me as I of her—she is my woman's part, and through her in all those years of our joining I came to know the other half of the world where women live and feel—no, it is not a half world but the whole world seen through a woman's soul. Through her I look back fifty years to that time when Ruth laughed at her lover, but wept because she could not have him, and Georgina wondered and raged at me and said, "Everything isn't politics." And I understand how little I knew of the real world in which people actually live, and make their lives.

208

I know now that those two young girls, whom I thought so frivolous and small-minded, whom you would think almost uneducated,
were wiser than I, with a far deeper wisdom—Ruth in her want of
envy, Georgina, who could indeed feel envy, but refused bitterness.

It has been said by a cynic that womanhood will be the last thing
civilised by man. Is it not more true to say that she has that within
her, in her heart and soul, which can never be corrupted by man?

This is not a mystic doctrine, a claim for superiority in one sex or
another, I leave such doubtful and heady eloquence to the demagogue.
A woman has a like brain with ours, a like power of reasoning. But
she applies them from earliest years to a different matter, to her own
place and function in the world.

The small boy sports to show off his muscle and practise his
strength, he has no object beyond himself and the pastime of an hour;
the little girl plays with doll and pram and stove and imagines herself
already a mother and a house mistress.

How often is it noticed that at sixteen or seventeen the youth is
still more than half a child, full of impulse, irresponsibly reckless in
idea and action. It is impossible to predict his actions; his sister of the
same age, or younger, is already a woman, reserved, thoughtful, cir-
cumspect in all her commitments.

It is not instinct that tells a young woman in love that politics deal
with the ephemeral, the passing situation—while she is concerned
with a permanent truth, with problems of loyalty and responsibility
that never change their essence, with family duty, with the heaviest
and most inescapable of responsibilities. She knows it by imagination
and experience.

The cynic had before his eyes the frivolity of dress shops, and in his
ears the triviality of tea tables, he might as well have spat upon the
sea because it sparkles in the sun and because its ripples on the sand
send holiday makers to sleep. The lands of the earth rise and fall, the
ice advances and recedes, but if all the life on earth should be overwhelmed in an afternoon, the womb of ocean would still hold the
teeming seed and in its own time, a million years or so, bring forth
another race of man, other cultures.

The empires die and are succeeded by more ruthless and cunning, more mean and evil despots, the kings depart and presidents set new and crueller prisons for more efficient oppression; the rack and boot are abolished, the scientist takes charge of the torture chamber; masks and catchwords change, the same mobs of fools and thugs, of hysterical boys and greedy lying opportunists rush through the streets and cry, "Down with the government—down with the law"; autocracy with a sword is followed by democracy with a Cheka; the capitalist with his wage slaves gives way to a minister of production and the concentration camp; but thug, student, minister, each has somewhere a home, and in every home, throughout the centuries in all the world, women ask themselves the question—How shall we ensure peace, how shall love be served?

Their politics are the everlasting politics of love and truth, beauty and cleanness. Georgina admiring the curtain stuff at Slapton, under my surprised and contemptuous gaze, was obeying a more profound impulse of social conscience than I. She did not even notice the conception of class loyalty which to me was law.

Ruth, after a year at Slapton, and seeming quite resigned to my father's doubts, showed independence even more unexpected. One day we had an anxious enquiry from the Court—she had disappeared and so had Simnel.

We did not hear from her until a week later when her father had a remorseful note to say that he must not be troubled for her, she had married the man she loved and they were very happy. The letter was from Bristol, where apparently Simnel had work—it was followed by others full of affection and remorse and assurances of happiness. In our astonishment that so shy and gentle a girl should do so bold an act we had a fearful doubt, how far had the recklessness of passion carried her? The village, of course, said at once that both the Nimmo girls were bad lots, my father was to be pitied for this misfortune in his declining years.

But Simnel put that doubt at rest, he sent us a copy of the marriage lines, possibly in scorn of our anxiety. The misfortune of the marriage was more ordinary, Simnel could not settle to a job. He was the most ordinary and foolish kind of gambler, a layer of odds, unlike Cran he made bets with his own money. The couple wandered from town to town, Ruth's postmarks were always different.

210

48

FOR some time now it had been an accepted thing that Georgina was going with Will Wilson. It was not so much that she at last openly abandoned Fred Coyte as that he abandoned Shagbrook —in this year he gave up the lease to Meakin, and from that time we heard little of him and less that was good. He ended, in fact, by wasting his whole inheritance and died in a workhouse infirmary.

Though Georgina never spoke of Fred, I think his fate was always present to her imagination and conscience. The village that called her cruel one year praised her the next when Ruth married a smart young man with a good place, but they had detected something reckless and desperate in her mood. At this time she had no friends in Shagbrook, none apparently anywhere except Will, and as on holidays she drove about with Will in his smart trap—flaunting herself, as the indignant village said, not without truth—she had the air of scorning the very sight of the people.

Will Wilson's known plan had always been to go to America, as soon as he could afford the journey, with some capital to spare. We realised that Georgina had the same ambition when advertisements and price lists of shipping lines catering for emigrants began to arrive at the house. Georgina, as if to warn us of her intentions, allowed them to lie about—my father would pick them up from the table and silently hand them to her—but in that mood of aloofness which she had shown to all the world since her entanglement with Wilson, she said nothing about them even to him. Her air defied us all to interfere in her concerns. We, too, had reason to think her grown scornful and unfriendly.

Will Wilson himself, in spite of his genial ways, was not popular. He was getting on too fast for country neighbours who had known him, as they say, in the gutter. He was now foreman of all maintenance work on the Slapton properties, he drove round inspecting roofs and drains, gates and fences, and he was not to be cheated. Also

211

he worked too hard for the easygoing westerners, he harried his gangs, he would turn up at the most unexpected moments to see how the work was going.

I was wrong to hate this man—our difference, as I said, was temperamental—but I was not altogether wrong in my criticism of his idea of life. I undervalued his courage, his enterprise, his good nature, his loyalty to a job or a friend, but I had reason to think of him as a danger to social order and peace. He was in essence a buccaneer, a man who fought always for his own hand. He was like one of those elemental forces of nature contained in steam or petrol whose properties are highly necessary to the activity of the machine but need the carefulest management or they will blow it to pieces.

Indeed, he could not bear any opposition. In this spring, soon after Ruth's marriage, he differed with the office over some contract for road work and threw up his job. He came to Georgina and proposed to marry her at once and take their passage to the States—he was not so well off as he had hoped but he had enough to make a start.

My father, rather to my surprise, quite approved of the plan. He said that Georgina had always wanted to escape from the moor and now was her chance. But Georgina answered that since Ruth's marriage the situation had changed for her—she must stay at home while my father was liable to spend weeks together in bed, he had been ill and helpless half the winter, he could not be left alone. And when my father protested vigorously that he could look after himself very well, that if he should be ill there were several neighbours who would be glad to come in every day to see to his immediate needs, she said that such a casual scheme was neither safe nor right.

The only solution of the difficulty would have been for my father to move to Newmarch's, the arrangement that Georgina and myself had always desired, and this was well understood by all parties. But my father would not contemplate the desertion of his flock. And Georgina told Will that for the present she could not come to him. He must go to the States if he chose but she would not marry him first. It would not be fair. Let him send for her if and when he wanted her, and she would come if she could.

I was with Georgina on the evening of this decision. Will had just

212

passed me on the Tarbiton road and told me the news—I had never seen him so angry. "Those two," he said, "they're always fighting each other and they'll never own to it. Why shouldn't Jo let the old man do what he likes—it's my belief he'd be glad if she went. She gets on his toes all the time."

I answered that Georgina was her own mistress, no one more so. But seeing Georgina so visibly wretched, having on her face what Ruth called her dark look, I told her of Wilson's anger and said that he had some reason for it. "If he goes to the States alone I doubt if you'll ever see him again."

"I know," she said, "but what else can I do?"

"There are three or four women in Back Lane who would be delighted to come in every day and look after father."

"You know father wouldn't allow them. He hates to be looked after by anyone. He hates me to look after him. But it has to be done."

In the upshot, Will behaved much better than I had expected. He agreed to put off the marriage, but he cancelled his passage to the States, losing his deposit on both tickets, and spent his savings on a share in a Tarbiton firm, Beck and Son. Becks' were old established carriers and shippers, but they had been in a declining way for a long time. Will's investment was regarded as a speculation.

He wanted to stay in the neighbourhood to be near Georgina, and he met her often as before. He ceased only to come to the house—he would not forgive my father for, as he saw it, keeping her from him.

The village was divided on this point, according to their religious views. Some considered my father a selfish and narrow-minded old man who was wrecking his daughter's life, others that he was a saint for whom it was a privilege to work. But no one found Georgina's decision strange. All took it for granted, like Georgina herself, that in the circumstances there was nothing else for her to do. She had had a piece of bad luck such as happens to thousands of women—nothing more extraordinary than had befallen Cissy Bennet when, as my father had said, she was knocked down by a drunken carter and lamed for life.

It was so ordinary, so commonplace a thing, that I scarcely considered it then except as a woman's affair. When Ruth, ten months later, was expecting her first child, in a London lodging, I had the same sense of dissociation as Georgina perpetually worried about her, wrote her long letters, made me take one of Ruth's short misspelt notes to a Tarbiton doctor to consult upon some symptom, and even wired for news when Ruth omitted to answer questions.

And when the child was born, quite safely and quickly, how wearisome I found the confidences, the discussion, the excitement. Babies, I reflected, were born every hour—I looked at my sisters as hand in hand they bent over the cradle with a kind of wondering boredom.

Not a year past, just before her elopement, I had seen Ruth all but a child, laughing and crying in the same moment, swayed by every impulse; now her every gesture was full of purpose, her mind was preoccupied, concentrated. But we have all seen such a transformation, it happens every day, it is a bore even to mention it. Love, it has been said—not the appetite of the flesh but the true unselfish passion of the soul—is as common as air.

A dying London sun filtered through rain and fog to fall upon the shabby lodging, the grimy chairs, the sordid carpet; from the street below came the noise of thousands of boots scraping on pavements, it was time for the insect prisoners of this vast ant heap to make their way home. A brutal and squalid world surrounded us with its enormous overwhelming meanness—a hell the more fearful that it was so calm, so subdued, that all the faces of its damned expressed only a gentle resignation.

With those doomed faces in my mind, those sounds of weary subjection in my ears, I stood aloof and asked myself if women would ever break out of their coop. Ruth appeared ten years older, her cheeks were pale and thin. Her life had been hard with a gambling husband, and already it was a question if she could stay even in this poor room. Simmel, always smart and confident, had put it to us but a few minutes before that it might be a good plan to take Ruth home with us for a while till he got things a bit straighter.

Ruth had cried then—there were still the marks of tears on her cheeks as, with raised eyebrows, she now gazed downwards at the cradle. But her mind had passed already from that new grief, her expression was a compound of wonder and anxiety, it seemed to

214

ask, "Have I really accomplished this miracle? And how shall I, Ruth, ever be fit for such an enormous responsibility?" Georgina, on the other hand, seemed like a young girl again. Those lines of suffering so deeply cut in her face during the last months since her quarrel with Will had vanished, her hollow cheeks had taken the roundness and colour of a young girl's, she was smiling with the complete self-forgetfulness of a child. At that moment she was pure delight.

"Yes," I said to myself in my gloomy rage, "they are children—the eternal innocents of the world, daughters of nature. They may play at thought, at politics, they may run a few yards from the nursery into the real world of men—but nature has them on a string, she gives one pull and they are back beside some cradle."

And I did not see the meaning of my own thought. For what is nature if she teaches love and duty, what is goodness that was before all teaching, all doctrine? Was it the churches and the parties who showed these poor girls how to devote their lives—or the God who was before all churches, all states, and will be after them in all eternity; the God to whom all churches are as the stammering words of children playing upon His doorstep, the God who is love and beauty at the heart of things, the Lord of creation whose freedom is the breath of the soul and the life of all existence?

I say that love and duty and freedom were in the world before the thought and name of any god, before ever they could name themselves, for God is and was and always shall be, or there is nothing at all.

49

I CAN forgive myself for my blindness then—I stood in the profoundest dejection of spirit that I had ever known. For I was a fugitive. I had run away from my first battle, and nothing can go so far to break a young man's heart.

In the month before this date, during February, I had left Edward's attic at Tarbiton to visit the Brodribbs, and took a short cut by a lane behind the waterfront. The lane consisted chiefly of small warehouses. It was, as usual at the time, quite empty, when suddenly three figures emerged from a doorway and stood in my path.

I hardly observed them, I was still in the innocence of my apprenticeship as an agitator. I had not acquired those nerves which observe, which feel, as in the subconscious, every movement of unrecognised persons even at a distance.

I stepped off the narrow pavement to avoid them—they also stepped off and closed about me, I recognised three of my union men, Kimber, Dodman and young Frank Doan.

There was a moment's silence while I stared at them in amazement—then Doan jostled against me and raised his arm. I saw that he carried some kind of weapon, a short iron bar or box opener. Dodman thrust him aside and said, "No, no—not yet—give the b——r a chance."

I asked them what they wanted, and Kimber, speaking with extreme anger, as if under a pressure of rage that he could hardly contain, answered that they wanted to know how much I had sold them for. Then immediately he rushed off on another tack and said that I had been talking about him and calling him a scab and he was going to break my neck for it.

Kimber was actually in work, he had taken my place at Stonepit. But though I suspected him of betraying us, I had never called him a scab, I had learnt some discretion in the last two years.

216

But before I could answer this unexpected charge from the man, Dodman broke in again and told him to hold his mouth. Then he and Doan took me by the arms and pushed me through the doorway into a small enclosed yard.

The yard itself was unlit but there was dim light falling from a lunette opposite, the window of some stable or cart shed, and this light showed me the faces of my judges: Kimber's heavy powerful features, not so much stupid as mad; young Frank's long countenance, wearing now an expression which could not be read, perfectly calm and assured; Dodman's, that of an old man already, so wasted and fallen in that I could scarcely recognise him.

Both Frank and Dodman had left Shagbrook some time before— I had not seen them since. All I had heard was that Dodman had no work and was being kept by his wife, and that Frank was at the docks.

"What we want to know," Dodman said, "is if it is true Meakin gave you a pound for each name in that union you got us into."

"And said no one would ever know it till you were strong enough to look after us," Frank said.

I answered that the story was an obvious lie—didn't they know I myself had lost my job at Stonepit, and that Kimber here had got it?

"Never mind Kimber," Dodman said in his heavy slow way. "We know what you've been saying about Kimber but we know it an't true."

"It's to cover up his own dirty tricks," Frank said.

"You've got money, you've got a job," Dodman said. "I'm not asking what happened to the money we paid you but you're going round in style now wet or fine. Look at that overcoat you're wearing —that cost a bit. All right, wait a minute. I'm telling you what they say, and if it's true I shouldn't stop Frank again not if he knocks your skull in. I'm an old man—I hadn't so long to go anyhow, what I don't like is my kids going in the workhouse. And now the missus is dead, it seems there's no place else for 'em."

"And you did it, Mister Nimmo," Frank said.

I realised now how much suspicion had gathered about me since

I had put on a whole suit of cloth and gone to work in an office instead of the fields and ditches of the moor. I may say that it was Georgina and Brodribb together who had supplied money for the suit, and an overcoat—Georgina from her earnings and my chief by an advance of pay. The outfit had been absolutely necessary to make me decent in the new job. I told them this but they said it was a lie, they demanded proof that I had not betrayed them.

How could I give proof? I could not propose an appeal to Meakin. It seemed to me that he was a deadly enemy. There was only my word—and probability. I pointed out again how wild and foolish was their suspicion. I was actually employed at that moment in a union, I was with them still. But Dodman answered in his slow reflective way that old Brodribb might be in it too. No one ever saw his kids with holes in their boots.

Suddenly Kimber and Frank lost patience and took hold of me, they pushed Dodman aside and began to drag me towards the dark end of the yard—it was only providence that caused two dockers who were passing along the street outside to hear the struggle and imagine that someone was being robbed. They suddenly appeared in the archway and shouted, Hi, what was going on there? Dodman, standing near the gate, ran past them, Kimber and Doan let go of me and disappeared through a gate in the back wall that I had not noticed. But as they did so Doan aimed a blow which would have killed me if it had struck straight upon my skull. Luckily, as they let go of me, I had reeled aside, and received it only at a glancing angle. Nevertheless it laid me unconscious on the stones.

My rescuers fortunately knew me by sight—I had collected their dues. They carried me straight to hospital where I was soon revived and my head stitched up. And when they wished to know who had attacked me, suspecting that it had been some gang in the pay of the dock owners, I answered that I had been set upon by robbers who had hoped to find my weekly collection on me.

The wound to my head, in that affray, was superficial, I can truly say that the wound to my soul has never healed. It was the first time I had been made to understand the fearful condition of political

218

life, the fundamental want of all security, the appalling risks of those who accept any large responsibility for their fellows.

You say that these three men were illiterates, half-savage natives of a half-barbarous hamlet as remote then from civilisation as central Africa or they could not have swallowed so preposterous a tale.

But already I knew that well-educated persons, learned gentlemen, could swallow tales quite as wild, that there is in many people, with every right to be considered intelligent, a total want of sense in dealing with any political matter. I have only to mention my friends the Dollings. For a long time now Brodribb and I had smiled at their delusions about England and its rulers—the doctor seriously believed that the real government of England was in the hands of a secret police and certain courtiers near the Queen, that Parliament was only a false front to deceive the people.

He would say, "Your cabinet meetings are held in secret, and no one is allowed even to take a note of what happens at them, why?"

And when I would answer that our committee meetings were also private, he would say with indignation, "Yes, because of the police—because of this hypocrite government. It is just this hateful necessity that we must destroy for ever."

I did not tell him of the attack upon me. It would have brought forth only a stream of nonsense about agents provocateurs, about police spies, and I was not in the mood for such romantic talk. When my rescuers innocently reported the affair to the police, I refused to prosecute. I said that nothing had been taken, which was true, and that I had recognised none of my assailants.

I told myself that the ruin of those poor men was not my fault, but I could not forget their misery for a single waking moment—Dodman, that big hearty countryman, brought down to the wreck I had seen. I knew some of the rest were no better off.

Only two persons knew the truth of that affair—Edward, who took me in that night from hospital, and Georgina, whom he sent for next morning. Georgina fetched me home that same day after market, to Ladd's, and put me in her own bed. She would sleep on the floor.

I will not say that Georgina saved my sanity. I was certainly half

219

mad when she carried me away from Tarbiton—I talked sometimes in a very wild way. But I think there is no doubt that I had some concussion and my nerves were not calmed by Edward's insistence that providence had sent this judgment upon me as a punishment for my unbelief.

Edward, in those days, since his mother's death, and especially since his father had taken a young and rather gay housekeeper, had been more and more extravagant in piety. He was only prevented from becoming a preacher by a fear of his own unworthiness.

I was angry with Edward and complained that he was as unreasonable as my father—the world was bad enough without fanatics to make it worse. I was in a rage with the whole world and for some reason I wanted Georgina to join in my hatred, a bitter disgusted fury that I can't describe. For it was not hatred of people—how could I allow myself to hate the poor men who were starving on my account—it was more like a hatred of the whole situation in which people lied and intrigued and distrusted each other, of that vast darkness which had suddenly descended on the neat bright world displayed for me, like a French toy, by the Dollings and their heroes.

I told Georgina that neither of us had had a fair chance—it had been a cruel thing to induce her, at sixteen, to pledge herself to Fred Coyte. How was it her fault if Fred was a weak fool who was drinking and ruining himself? And now our father had spoilt all her hopes of marriage. Will would never agree to share a house with any man, he wasn't that sort of fellow. He liked things his own way.

But Georgina listened to me with the tolerant, absent-minded air of a nurse whose patient is in mild delirium.

50

SHE had got up from her palliasse beside the bed to fetch me a drink. I was feverish and thirsty in that stifling room, hot with the ashes of the kitchen fire, and when I had drunk, she rested my head in her lap to sponge my forehead. I told her to go back to bed, she would have to be at Stonepit by half past five for the first milking, but she answered that she could not sleep.

"Why shouldn't you sleep?" I asked her. "You don't mind anything."

"Why do you want me to mind?"

"I only want you to see what's happening to us."

"I see that somebody has been trying to kill you—was it Doan or Kimber?"

It seemed that she knew all about my affairs—both Doan and Kimber had been heard to threaten me. I said that Kimber was the traitor who had sold us to Meakin for a job, but she answered that Kimber was not like that. "He's only a stupid kind of man who always gets things wrong, it would be easy to make him tell you anything, and he wouldn't even know he'd given it away."

"You agree with Will. You think I've been a fool with my union. I ought to have kept myself to myself and saved money."

Georgina answered, still with provoking patience, that Will had never said any such thing and would not say it to her—he was not the man to forget that she was my sister even if she let him.

"He doesn't say it but he thinks it, and you've gone over to him. You're all against unions both of you. And what are you doing for yourselves—just waiting till father dies."

"Why do you want to put everything so crooked?" And now Georgina did grow angry—she burst out in something of her old style, "You've no right to say such things of me, or Will either. After all he's done for us getting Ruth that good place and timber for this house and the new stove, and after the way he risked his life for all of us in the flood and never made anything of it."

"But Georgy," I tried to stop her before she grew outrageous. I wanted her ministrations.

"All right," she said, "tell me it was for money and a job and to get up in the world. What if it was for a job—I honour Will for doing so much to get a job and to make his way. It's for me, too, he wants to get on. I tell you Will is an honester man and a truer man and a braver man than the whole of the fellows round here rolled into one—you only have to look at him."

She stopped and I perceived in her voice that she was very near crying with indignation and her feeling for Will Wilson. But she caught her breath and after a moment asked me if I wanted another drink.

"No, but don't go away yet."

"And as for unions," she said then—her anger stayed in her voice as a kind of groundswell of urgency, "I daresay some of them do some good. But all I know of them round here is they nearly killed father, and ruined his life, and now it seems they're trying to do the same for you. I think you were quite right to want to start something for the men, I'm sure they need someone to push them along. Only it isn't any good starting anything in Shagbrook or Battwell, and I don't choose to have you killed for nothing at all."

"How can I help what they do? It seems they'll believe any lie."

"You haven't got to blame yourself—that's the great thing. It's not your fault if they turned on you. It wouldn't have happened at all if you'd just sat about like the rest of them and done nothing for anyone. It's because you're another like father that they turned on you. And as for being killed, you've got to be got away from this place and Tarbiton too. If you don't get away they will kill you. Why shouldn't you go to the top union men in Lilmouth or Southampton and say what's happened, that you've been working here for the unions but it isn't safe for you any more, and get a job with them? It would be a disgrace if they didn't do something for you."

I said that I would not run away, I could not leave my men. But the truth was that I longed to run away, to escape from this situation

222

which I could neither control nor understand, this desolation of fear and misery.

And when Ruth's child was born six weeks later, and she begged us to come and see her, Georgina very easily persuaded me to accompany her to London. We did not say that now was my chance to escape, but it was understood between us. It was, indeed, tacitly admitted when Georgina suggested that I should get an introduction from Brodribb to a friend of his in London, a man called Dennis, chief of a small craft union among warehousemen. Brodribb was glad to write the letter; he, too, had been anxious for my life since that attack; and Georgina took charge of it, she was not going to let me repent of the scheme. She also found money for our fares. I've no doubt from Will.

It was in this new strange alliance with Georgina that the visit to London was planned—and it was she above all who, in her ambition for me, her will to serve my will in spite of her own, brought me to know the man who, after my father and Dr. Dolling, most powerfully affected my whole life.

51

It is said that great cities terrify the contemplative soul but intoxicate the ambitious. London had a double effect upon me—I was both terrified and inspired. I had conceived its vastness, but not its lowness, its streets were no grander or cleaner than those of our country towns. And that magnitude of extent, which, they say, appalled the zeppelins—I could not see it then, and if I had had that Pisgah sight would it not have served only to multiply my sense of a spreading littleness, of a creeping disease blindly eating its way into the flesh of a stricken land?

What I had not dreamed was the dirt, the ugliness, the sense of insignificance and helplessness conveyed by the anonymous crowds which jostled by without a glance—the train passengers who sat in rows gazing straight before them with eyes utterly indifferent to every other existence. Nothing in my experience had prepared me for this world of atomies, mere corpuscles or droplets of life, whose difference from one another had no importance, whose dignity as individual human souls was, even to themselves, lost in the moving tide which alone had purpose and meaning.

Inconceivably depressing then in the strictest sense, degrading to my own humanity, were these streams of men so slowly, darkly flowing through ditches of brick and stone, beneath the dark fields of roofs, ridge and furrow, as if cut by the ploughs of some demonic monster, to yield crops of poison smoke, blinding fog, under skies that flared or sulked night and day like enormous cinder heaps.

It is the noise of thousands of boots scraping on stone that remains with me from that first visit, a sound which still conveys to my nerves a special disquietude. No doubt a hundred impressions join in that heart-sinking movement—of refugees dragging along a dusty highway, of battle-worn troops going to their death, of convicts trailing monotonously in some prison yard, of factory workers stumbling

224

at dawn towards the factory gate. But the deepest is still of London humanity—that is what rises again like the very voice of mortality as background to the triumph of Ruth. That was what sounded in my ears, a louder, grimmer note, as I gazed with wonder and dismay at the precipice of grimy brick behind one of whose rain-streaked windows Richard was pursuing that great career that we had imagined for him.

Richard had passed out from Oxford nearly two years before with a second-class degree, which we understood was due to his uncertain health. He had been given at once a good post in the University College in London, but after a few months had resigned and taken a place in a wholesale firm of textile merchants.

He had explained his unexpected move in one of his rare letters home as following upon his need for more leisure to pursue his own work. He was writing a book about the influence of Greek on English literature.

The clerkship, he said, gave him not more leisure or pay but more uninterrupted leisure. He needed, above all, time to himself.

I do not know what visions of bank parlours and rich guildhalls had risen in the imagination of Georgina and myself at the news of our great man's new enterprise, but in face of that gloomy wall we looked at each other, and asked a silent question.

I said to myself, "But in this city it seems that the richest firms live in just such squalid barracks, the most important persons have their offices behind such dismal walls."

We clambered up then many flights of dark and broken stairs smelling of dust and, as it were, an ancient staleness, to a landing surrounded by dark and blistered doors. These doors bore various inscriptions, we agreed that I should be the first to enter one marked ENQUIRIES. It was with doubt and nervousness that I knocked upon this door and entered at last without an invitation.

I found myself in a compartment not much larger than a sentry-box, with a single chair in the corner, and in the wall on my right a hole like that of a booking-office. It was closed by a slide. I looked at this slide, and the slide seemed like the drooping eyelid of some giant from whom my entry meant less than the buzzing of a fly. At

225

last I knocked. There was no response. But to a second knock the slide was dashed back and a young man with peculiarly worn and peevish features asked me what I wanted.

I said that I wanted Mr. Richard Nimmo.

"Mr. who?" he said.

"Mr. Richard Nimmo. He's a clerk in the firm."

"Never heard of him. You sure he's in this firm?" I assured him on the point, and he said that he must be in some other department. "Anyhow," he said, "you can't see him now. You'll have to wait till twelve."

"But he's my brother."

This remark equally surprised and irritated the young man. He looked at me with scornful amazement, and said, "What's that got to do with it? I say he can't see you now."

I explained that I had come up a very long way, that I was staying only two days, and that it would be enough for me to see Mr. Nimmo for a couple of minutes. The clerk's only answer was, "I told you, if he's here he'll be coming out at twelve," and he shut the slide.

With what feelings of humiliation and wonder we lingered in the street for the next hour until, in a gush of black-coated clerkdom, poured from the gloomy door into the drain of the street, Richard came to us. And then we saw that he was still the Richard we had known, paler, thinner, but calm, aloof, carrying with him still that natural distinction which belonged to him throughout his life.

At lunch in the dirty little chop-house, blue with fumes and smell, where we ate, we listened once more to his confident speech, the words of a man who seemed always to know both what the world was and what he wanted from it. Under that old spell we were not astonished to find that though Ruth had been six weeks in her lodging Richard had never yet managed to visit her—Richard who had been so devoted to Ruth. As soon as he saw her he began to talk of the old days when he had taken refuge in her room to read in peace.

"I never had such good reading since—why did I ever leave Shagbrook?"

Georgina remarked gravely that there was not much room for reading in our new cottage at Ladd's Corner, but Richard seemed

226

not to notice her, he was smiling upon Ruth as upon some vision of past delight. "I was so pleased when I heard you were coming this way," he said to her. "But, after all, if I had come to see you, I should only have had to go away again."

He spoke with a smile, and we laughed as at a joke, glad to think that Richard could joke. But the joke, as with much of Richard's casual talk, was not very clear to us—it was many years before I saw in the phrase a key to Richard's character, so enigmatic to us, so transparent in fact—the mind of a man which made of itself and almost without thought the sharpest division between the permanent and the transient things of life.

But that was far beyond my comprehension at twenty. All I perceived was that somehow the brother I so admired was here in London treated as a nobody, that his great talents were neither appreciated nor made use of. As soon as the spell of his presence had gone from us, I asked in amazement what Richard had thought of in taking such a job.

"Perhaps it's better than it looks," Georgina said in a hesitating voice. "People have to start low in new jobs. They'll soon find out how clever and honest he is."

"Will they?" I burst out. "Have they got the sense? That fellow at the wicket didn't even know his name."

"There are so many of them." We looked at each other again and realised our mutual thought, that there was some strange flaw in Richard—that he might fail.

"And what did he mean about being sorry to leave Shagbrook, he hated the place," Georgina said.

"I'm not surprised if he hates London." And I broke out into rage that was half fear—fear of this terrifying mechanical world that devoured man as a thrasher swallows corn to beat it into straw, and grain, for sale: I cried that Richard was lost in this filthy place, London was killing him.

52

Lᴏɴᴅᴏɴ, I say, threw upon me an immense depression and terror—but also an excitement. The idea of it can still alarm a mood of doubt with a sense as of a brainless monster, escaped from all possible control by the millions who are compelled to endure its evil whims—it stood, and stands too, as a challenge. In the same moment that my heart recoiled, my will sprang up, saying— Here are vast wrongs to be set right, here is proof enough that humanity has plunged off its road, and as for putting it back again with pretty speeches and philosophical pamphlets, you might as well try to stop a landslip with wind.

My will sprang up, but only to remind me that I had no notion of what was to be done, no idea of a policy. I put out my hand—a young man must affirm his courage or admit himself nothing—I reached for a tool, a weapon, but there was nothing there.

"Now for Mr. Dennis," Georgina said, taking out Brodribb's letter from her petticoat. Her mind had followed another track from mine. If Richard was not the one to make the best of his chances, I must not be wasted.

"Yes, I've looked up the trains, we can get a train from Victoria."

Georgina did not hand over the note, instead she read out the name and said in a critical voice, "I wonder, is he anybody? Now you're here why don't you go to see the top man, the one tailor Gomme is always talking about—what's his name—who was in prison for the fighting at Manchester?"

"Pring, that's nonsense, he's one of the biggest union men in England."

"A cat can speak to a king, and you've been in the fighting too. I daresay you were more hurt than ever he was. If you won't see him I will."

"You wouldn't be let, and I'd just be thrown downstairs."

228

"Still, they'd have to notice you—and you could come back."

"Apart from all other objections," I said, "I haven't a notion where Pring lives."

"If you'll go to him, I'll find him."

"How can you among these millions of people?"

"Will you promise?"

I did not promise, but Georgina suddenly turned aside and walked into a chapel; from the chapel she went to a minister's house; from there, by his advice, to a post office; and thence to the office of a dockers' friendly society where the clerk in charge was delighted to furnish us with Pring's address.

And now there was nothing for me but to show my sister, as in the old days, that her plan was absurd. I walked with her to the address in a mean street of Southwark, knocked on a blistered door and asked for Mr. Pring. The woman who opened, young and handsome, simply but well dressed, asked me suspiciously what I wanted. Who was I? Had I an appointment?

I began to explain the position, but after less than a minute the girl was obliged to stand aside to let two persons from within pass outwards. They stood then at the doorstep, the one giving instructions, the other answering at intervals, "Yes, Mr. Pring—I see, Mr. Pring."

"There you are," Georgina said loudly. "Shall you speak to him or shall I?" But I stopped her with an impatient gesture. I was startled by the appearance of this leader to whom my hopes had flown. To me, indeed, even before I had the barest notion of his plans, his ideas of life, he was a leader, because I was young and lost, bewildered by my first defeat, because I needed a leader as desperately as any traveller benighted on the moor needs to find a guide before he walks over some precipice, or sinks drowning into some bog.

At this first sight Pring seemed no different from the ordinary type of dock worker or general labourer to be seen in scores about any port. He was square and short, with rather a plump pale face and dark hair cut very short, growing in a widow's peak on his forehead.

But already in my eagerness I found something remarkable in him,

229

something different. I noticed his bright blue eyes and their lively and curious expression, and how steadily he kept them fixed on the face of his interlocutor—a young man whose whole appearance was in sharp contrast to him. Tall and thin, he seemed like a gentleman, both in dress and speech. His respectful politeness to Pring served again to excite my interest.

All this time I was standing at the kerb two paces away. Pring did not seem to have noticed me at all. I was extremely startled when he turned his gaze my way and said, "You want to see me?"

I could not believe for the moment that he was speaking to me, and looked around. Pring then dismissed his companion with a nod, stepped up to me and gave me a clap on the shoulder, saying, "Well, what is it—up from the west are you?"

This seemed to me like magic and completed my confusion. I did not know then that Pring prided himself on such Sherlock Holmes deductions, or realise how much was told by my country boots, my complexion, my gaze, or Georgina's accent when she had asked, "Shall you speak or shall I?"

It was she who now answered Pring, saying, "Yes, Tarbiton, and this is Mr. Nimmo of the dockers' union in Tarbiton."

"Ah, you've come to the right place."

Pring shook hands with both of us and then laid his hand again on my shoulder. "You're the man I want to see—Tarbiton is a place that's a bit on my mind just now."

"My brother started a union of his own in our village and they set on him and nearly killed him," Georgina said, and she went on to tell the whole story of the Shagbrook union as she understood it, giving me a very bold part.

"And as it isn't safe for him any more in Tarbiton Mr. Brodribb said he would get him union work in London instead."

This wasn't quite true. Brodribb had only recommended me, and I broke in at last to explain how small and feeble my first efforts had been. I was somewhat surprised when Pring agreed with me. "A good try," he said smiling, "but you han't a chance that way, it does more harm than good. Lets the men down and gives the whole movement a bad name. But Tarbiton's different—you've got a good body of members there and a fighting fund. So you work for Brodribb,. do you?"

All this time he kept his eyes fixed on my face—Pring was the first of his type—the conscious and practised leader in whom I had encountered this habit. But unlike some of the others, he took off from its offensive effect by a certain ease of manner and a friendly expression. His stare was made to seem like a flattering interest rather than the trick of a despot trying to intimidate, or the watchfulness of a detective.

As he asked me about Brodribb, I knew that he was in fact inviting me to say what I thought of the man. There was a little pause in which I was actually aware of an impulse seeming to arise within myself to say that I thought Brodribb too old and dull for his job.

I did not do so. An instinct of prudence as well as loyalty prevented my youthful desire to seem independent and critical, and how glad I am of it now. I said that I did work for Brodribb and described my collecting and recruiting duties.

But I felt that Pring's gaze detected both the temptation that I had suppressed and the reason—what was more strange, I was pleased by the impression of his power.

I must not enlarge on this first meeting with a remarkable man. It's enough to say that my weakness and frustration were drawn to his self-assurance as irresistibly as the starving man by a well-furnished table.

It is not for nothing that nations in disillusionment fly to a dictator —that young men, seeing their road dark before them, seek an infallible guide—that revolution brings in the police state. I desperately needed my master, my Napoleon, and though I was ready no doubt to find him in any man possessing authority and a policy, yet I was not altogether deceived in my estimate of Pring. He had elements of greatness and it was not his fault that he did not achieve great things. One of his more important qualities, unrecorded, I think, in the biographies, now completed my conquest. He asked me what he could do for me and, instead of saying that he could give me five minutes, asked me how much time I could give to him. I said that all my time was his, I wanted nothing so much as to know about

231

his policy in the face of bad times and my own failure. At once he answered that in that case I had better come with him, he would show me what was being done in his own organisation—went into the house for a moment, no doubt to say that his plans for that afternoon must be changed, and immediately we were strolling down the street together in deep and earnest conversation, like old friends.

It was not till now that I discovered Georgina's disappearance. Pring smiled as I looked round and said, "Your sister went some time ago, you've trained her well," and I did not explain that Georgina's abrupt departure was not due to respect for man's affairs but disrespect and suspicion towards political agitators generally.

But before I could gather the import of his remark, Pring went on to speak of the problem of the workers' women. Several recent strikes had failed because the women put pressure on husbands and sons to go back to work. Talk about the value of women as good material for revolution applied only to young girls and spinsters— the majority, the married women, and especially the mothers, were always against action even if they pretended to be sympathetic.

"The wives are a weak spot and we have to find some way of bringing them into line."

It was typical of Pring that he never answered his own questions, he suggested the answers. When I went home that night, after a couple of hours during which we had paid visits on half-a-dozen branches and perhaps a score of officials, after a great deal of casual talk which did not seem to lead anywhere, yet I found in my mind, for the first time in months, some clear impressions—that union policy, like all policy, was a matter for experts, and the ordinary rank and file were far from experts. They knew nothing either of organisation or economics. That we did not want talk of revolution, we were not out to smash the machine but to take it over and use it. And we wanted a pretty clear idea of what we were going to do with it when we did take it over because government was a tricky job.

I need not say that Pring was a Marxist. Most of the English union chiefs then subscribed to the International—they found no difficulty in combining Marxist manifestoes with constitutional tactics and devout Methodism. Pring held these muddleheads, as he

232

called them, in scorn. He was a convinced and consistent Marxist.

But he did not then instruct me in this dogma, he gave me only a plan of action towards a material and definite objective, the taking over of all government by the workers, or rather, by the workers' leaders—a programme extremely attractive to an ambitious and frustrated boy of twenty.

And he completed my conquest by what I now know to be two well-tried moves, he gave me information which was, so he said, a secret between ourselves, that a dockers' strike was already contemplated for that year through all the ports, and that it would almost certainly lead to a general strike—and he offered me the hope of promotion. If, he said, the strike broke out that year, he would call on me for extra work at headquarters.

"But not in London—there's no work here for you."

I must have shown my disappointment, for he answered it at once, "The place for you is the place where you know the people and they know you."

"What, in Tarbiton?"

"Tarbiton or Lilmouth, unless you're afraid." And before I could answer he said, "That beating up won't do you any harm among the men, they'll like you all the better."

"Of course, if you think that's the place."

"Ah, you're the man for me." He gave me a clap on the shoulder and, "I'll see if I can get you to Lilmouth."

So I returned to my attic in Tarbiton, but not to terror and bewilderment. I found that I could now defy my enemies, that it was a pleasure to defy them. I had a reason to do so, an object in life. I was set apart from all those poor fools, chosen for a front-line post.

53

I AM not going to tell the story of the Lilmouth strike. Like
many political events which made a great noise in its day, it has completely vanished from all but local and party history. And this book
is not the history of political events but of a boy's mind and soul, of
one who came so near perdition that his escape still seems to him like
a miracle. And if perdition is a word that makes you smile, a
preacher's word out of date even among preachers, I must urge that
I use it in a strict sense, for the state of one who is lost. In those
days I was indeed lost, and each time I seemed to find the path
again it was merely another by-track in a maze of bewilderment.

Pring was better than his word. I was transferred to Lilmouth actually three weeks before the strike was called in that October. At
a pound a week and a lodging allowance I was to act as assistant
clerk in the office, and liaison officer between Brodribb and the Lilmouth chief, a man called Banner.

But soon after Pring himself arrived, I became in fact his chief
aide-de-camp. He liked young assistants, especially when they were
absolutely devoted to his ideas—I was now a fanatical Marxist and
he had had a good deal of trouble with local leaders like Brodribb,
who did not even call himself a Marxist, and who liked to tell his
men that they were Christians first and workers second, whose trades
union cards had embossed upon them texts like these:

> Thou shalt not oppress an hired servant that is poor and
> needy.   Deuteronomy 24:14.

> At his day thou shalt give him his hire, neither shall the
> sun go down upon it . . . lest he cry against thee unto the
> Lord, and it be sin unto thee.   Deuteronomy 24:15.

Pring said of Brodribb that his god was an employer, and I
certainly agreed with him that no Marxist could be a Christian.

See me then on a dark morning of November walking along the
234

dockside at Lilmouth beside a huge stevedore, my bodyguard. I am just twenty-one, three months before I have been the most insignificant of persons, at whom this very stevedore, humble toiler as he is, would have scorned to look twice. Now I am a man so important that I am never allowed out without a guard, now it is not my shame but my glory that I need a guard. It is my pride to have enemies—in truth, everything about me turns to my pride.

The docks all around me are dead. Not a winch sounds, not a truck moves, as far as the eye can see. The cranes point crookedly towards the sky at chance angles, crazy and motionless as gibbets already struck with rottenness from which the very bones have fallen. The mist that hangs over the sea is like a winding sheet, cold with the death sweat; the pale sun gleaming low through the fog is like the glazed eye of death itself, or, as one might say, of commerce mortally wounded.

Half a million pounds' worth of freight along fifty miles of coast is held up in two million pounds' worth of shipping, and I am one of those who have commanded this death, who have wielded this spell.

I walk into the office and the young clerk, a boy from the Grammar School, jumps up to receive me—I am ushered straight to the chief. I give my report and receive my orders, confidential orders from Pring himself. At night I go to my lodging in India Street, a dockers' street, and as I appear faces turn towards me, conversation is hushed, men give me a respectful nod, the women's eyes follow me with anxious enquiry. I enter my lodging, with a docker's wife, landlady and daughter hover anxiously about my supper table to know if the food is good, if I am satisfied.

Will himself attends my lightest word. Indeed, it is highly important for Will to know how my mind is working, for my mind is the mind of the committee, and the committee can be masters of his fate as a businessman.

Carters who depended on the docks, like Will's own firm, had expected bad business, if not ruin. Some of the biggest laid by horses and men. But half-a-dozen of the smaller, especially about Tarbiton, held on, and after the first ten days found themselves growing busy. Wilson and Beck was one of these.

We had expected increased traffic on the roads. What surprised

235

us, like other strike leaders before and since, was the resourcefulness with which the public, as if by spontaneous contrivance, extended and organised it for its own service. Goods, and especially coal, ordered by rail, were collected at railhead in every kind of vehicle from hand barrows to old hansom cabs.

The new firms who had carried on were now short of horses and carts. Wilson threw himself into this unexpected opening; he was one of the first to bring horses in by rail. In a fortnight after the strike began he was delivering coal round the clock up to ten miles inland.

Will had always said that he needed only a foothold—give him a hundred pounds and he would make it into thousands. Now he showed how right he had been, how wrong were those who laughed. He did not even need his hundred pounds, he worked on credit, promises, all kinds of strange alliances, he borrowed carts from Newmarch in exchange for a special delivery of cattle cake. He controlled the cattle cake because he could promise immediate coal to a warehouse. He had in fact that kind of genius for organising exchange of services which had made so many fortunes.

And now his plans for marriage took a great jump forward. Ruth was at home on a visit that promised to last many months, until, that is, Simnel found a job that satisfied his demands for an easy life and much leisure. Meanwhile, Georgina was free. As for her question about the time when Ruth might have to rejoin her husband, money had solved that problem as it solves so many in real life. Wilson had undertaken to provide a trained nurse at Ladds', and even Georgina could not deny that such skilled help would be better than her own. She and Wilson were already exploring all the coast between Tarbiton and Lilmouth for a house.

And whether Georgina had not expected this release and it carried her away, or whether she considered herself already Will's wife and bound to him in loyalty, whether perhaps she was simply reckless as usual, she would not listen to me when I pointed out the danger of Will's operations. "I suppose your Pring wants to freeze the poor people as well as starve them—it might do in London but it won't work here. He won't frighten Will anyhow."

She was even more outspoken than Will in scorn of the committee, and that January, in the ninth week of the strike, I had to give Will the gravest kind of warning.

Things were not going well with us—London had refused to come in and it was only now that I had found to my naïve astonishment that the London union was most miserably weak. The dozen branch chairmen and organisers to whom Pring had introduced me had, many of them, little more than a dozen men behind them, the whole membership was but six or seven hundred out of as many thousands. The London union then could scarcely pay for postage stamps. And our men were hungry and wavering—there were threats of a break. Pring's choice of winter for a strike, because in winter it is more easy to excite public sympathy, was under severe criticism by several of our leaders including Brodribb. Above all, many of the wharfs in the smaller ports were doing a considerable traffic, loading and unloading at night with volunteer labour—warehouse clerks and quayside loafers.

Many of the schooners and brigs that then carried a large proportion of the coast trade were manned by the owner and his family, wife, daughter, a son or son-in-law, and perhaps a nephew or two. And they would land a cargo in some creek directly into farmers' carts.

Wilson, I heard, was picking up such cargoes and also working in with a wharfinger at Tarbiton, a man called Barret who was notorious for his spite against unions and his boast that he would smash any attempt to close his wharf.

Barret was a magistrate—one of the bench that had tried to convict my father ten years before—he was a much hated man. We had our men in Tarbiton who watched him all the time, and we were waiting to pounce. Our plan was to concentrate such a crowd of pickets from Lilmouth that his carters would have to drive half a mile between two lines of half-starved men and women very ready to express their opinions of such traitors.

It was on the report that a coal brig from Swansea was being unloaded into Barret's warehouse, and that the coal was for Wilson, that I made my visit to the wharf at Tarbiton.

54

Old Bull Wharf is on the opposite side of the Tarb from the town and the parade. It belongs to a confused mass of small docks and crowded tumbledown buildings surrounding two creeks between the bank of the estuary and the main Queensport road. It was dusk when I took a boat at Tarbiton. I hired a striker and I was accompanied by my bodyguard, a man called Rattray. Pring himself had ordered me to take a guard in case Barret attempted to carry out his threats against any strike leader who came about his wharf.

January had been surprisingly mild, as often in the west at this time. Leaves still hung on the oaks, and though the sun had long been hidden by the hills behind the town, the brilliant sky threw down a golden light in which they burnt dark red. The tide was high, for the moment the water was a smooth and gently undulating surface of quicksilver in which sky, clouds, trees and buildings were translated into a picture of sleepy animation and a soft brilliance.

But the silence, the peace, meant only war to me—the evidence of our success, so hardly maintained.

"There they go," said Rattray beside me in the stern. "That's old Barret's."

His ears, quicker than mine, or more intent upon the one object, had caught in that silent hour the click of a lever, the next moment we heard the rattle of a donkey engine.

Old Bull Wharf stood in a tidal creek which was dry in the neaps, but now full. The wharf itself was then an old and tottering construction of rotting timbers flanked by even older and more squalid warehouses, which were, however, kept in good working order. Barret was a man who spared paint but oiled wheels. The warehouse yard opened upon the main road behind.

As we approached from the estuary we could see the single crane lifting the first sacks of coal from the hold of a small brig that had just been warped to the quayside; the sails had been cast loose but not stowed, the topsail flapped languidly in the light breeze, which we at water level could not feel at all. I was startled and angered by this open act of defiance, and said to the man, "Has Barret been doing this all the time?"—you could hear the engine half a mile away.

"He thinks we're beat," said the rower.

"Ah," said Rattray, and I thought there was a nervous enquiry in both their exclamations. I felt that fear which had been growing upon me for weeks. A fear which, like a man with a cancer, I dared not acknowledge. And like such a man I flew out at anyone who made me feel its deep harassment.

"I see you're one of the scabs who'd like to get out," I said sharply. "Just when we're winning too—as men like this Barret will soon find out for themselves."

To my surprise neither of my companions answered. And this silence, too, worked upon my nerves. I felt that these older men were judging me, perceiving my motive. Probably they were only startled by my outburst. I said, in the same tone of menace, "Keep in the shadow of the bank, d'you want us to be warned off?"

We had, of course, no right upon the wharf, which was private property. My excuse was a visit to Will, and that was why we had made sure of his presence. We took care, too, not to go near the brig. Already at one small port we had had a boat staved by a sack of cement dropped over the side. We made for the outer end of the wharf which lay in the shadow and where a ladder inclined to water level.

Up these steps then I climbed, with all the desperate feelings of a man who may receive a knock on the head the moment he shows it—and found two large figures waiting for me at the top, Will Wilson and Barret.

Barret had a pick-handle in his fist and raised it at me. I leant back as far as I could from the steps and said loudly, "Is that you, Will?"

"Hello, Ches," and he pushed Barret's hand aside. "It's all right, Barret—friend of mine, Ches Nimmo, just the man we want."

"Aye," Barret growled, "if you can trust him." And Wilson explained to me, "It's this Allsend offer."

The Allsend offer was one that had come in two days before from

239

certain small owners at Allsend and Tarbiton. It was a highly confidential offer, handed to Pring himself, because it represented a breakaway in the owners' association. The small men, threatened with ruin, had offered to settle by giving a rise in pay—two-thirds of what we asked.

It had caused us a good deal of embarrassment, because we knew that the men in the smaller ports would certainly wish to accept it. It would break the strike. What's more, Brodribb for Tarbiton, and three others of the committee representing the smaller ports, would almost certainly vote for acceptance or at least further negotiations. This had appeared forcibly at our last committee meeting.

I say that the strike was already causing hardship. Contributions had not come in as we expected; after nine weeks strike pay was down to half a crown a week. It was one of my duties to attend the distribution in order to mark off the list, I looked at each face to check the claim. Shall I ever forget those thin grey cheeks, the eyes that were beyond resignation—sunk in apathy—the shuffling feet, eloquent of languor and weakness—or the crowd of shawled women standing outside in a cold January drizzle to receive those half-crowns as soon as possible?

They were not apathetic, their eyes glared fiercely, they murmured loudly, one shouted out something about the damned Londoners. They did not stand aside even for Pring as he came out, he had to push them aside while they cursed at him.

It was with this scene in our minds that immediately afterwards we attended the usual weekly full committee meeting, to decide general lines of policy.

Our office was in a bare front room over a saddler's shop. The saddler was a sympathiser and let us have the place free, he had been doing very good business with the cartage firms. We were nine in the room, sitting on packing cases round a kitchen table—Pring, Brodribb, Banner, the Lilmouth chief, a big heavy man, who was always very bitter; Pittway, a Socialist intellectual and Pring's devoted supporter—he was the young man whom I had seen with Pring at our first encounter; two from Allsend, two from Queensport area, and myself.

I read the report. It had been discovered, to my surprise and grati-

240

fication, that I had a certain flair for such writing, and Banner was quite illiterate.

I gave a picture of the whole situation. On the one hand some of the small firms were in a bad way, on the other, a lot of the Tarbiton men were ready to go back on any terms. They were afraid the port itself would be ruined by the strike. Our Lilmouth people were grumbling about the strike pay and we should make every effort to keep it from going lower. The tale of contributions from the chapels showed a slight improvement and we might try a special appeal.

In short, my report, like all such reports, offered no large conclusions.

But our leaders, experienced men, who had heard hundreds of such reports, knew exactly how to get the truth from them. That slight degree of optimism, raised in my mind by my own reading, vanished at Pring's first words.

"We're done if this breakaway gets hold."

"Ah," said Banner, "three-quarters of them are ready to chuck it up this minute."

Pring said then that we needed a more active approach, more activity in the pickets, especially at warehouses. The wives, too, were a weak spot, they might lose everything for us. "In Sheffield," he said, "the grinders broke some windows and smashed a few parlour chairs, and that had a very good effect."

"That game wouldn't do round here," Brodribb said. "Our chaps in Tarbiton wouldn't stand for it." But the rest of us were silent in our mood of anxiety.

Did we realise that this was the moment of decision, that we were being asked to make a vital choice?

I cannot say. Such moments pass too quickly and usually at a time when the mind is confused with half-a-dozen issues. I had just been overwhelmed by that word from Pring, done, the first word from him that had spoken of defeat.

"Where are we getting at?" Brodribb persisted in his slow heavy way—he would writhe himself slowly about in his clothes as if it needed a kind of private earthquake to expose his thoughts. "What's the plan—is it something new?"

"I'm not talking of a plan. All I said was that something happened

241

in Sheffield and when it did happen it happened to have a good effect. They pushed a wharfinger into the dock last week at Rotherhithe but no one planned it either—there isn't even a strike."

Before Brodribb could grasp the meaning of this rapid and impatient utterance, Pittway began a long speech, summing up the whole position from each aspect, the financial, the local, the national, the political, what would now be called the ideological, and finally the disciplinary, a favourite subject. Discipline was all-important. If we did not manage to restore discipline the strike was doomed already—morale was very low. The only real question, therefore, was how to induce the men to stay out. Could we put pressure on the weaker elements, and if so, how?

Pittway was the son of a judge. He had been at a public school and the University. He had studied logic and philosophy and he had done good work for the cause in London.

It is not true that such attainments are negligible beside practical experience. Such as Brodribb and the two Allsend representatives, who took no trouble to hide their impatience and contempt, are grossly mistaken. The power to marshal arguments, to arrange facts in an order of importance, is a great and often decisive one—when Pittway had finished, Banner and I were convinced that some further steps were necessary to keep the men in line and that they were urgent.

Notice that Pittway, in putting forward this policy, Pring's policy, did not use any word like violence, still less did he speak of smashing windows, he used words like discipline, pressure and private persuasion. "We should get the names of a few individual weak brothers and get their neighbours to reason with them."

Brodribb interrupted several times, saying that he wasn't going to have any of that at Tarbiton. But his angry excitement looked foolish in this calm logical atmosphere. Banner asked him if he wanted the strike to fail, and he had no answer except that Tarbiton wasn't Sheffield.

When Pittway asked for a vote, five of us voted at once for more activity on picket and more private persuasion, and we agreed to leave the details in Pring's hands. And I can remember nothing but relief that a decision had been made.

242

55

THIS book would be worthless if it did not show how men, especially young and ardent men as I was then, come to do evil in the name of good, a long and growing evil for a temporary and doubtful advantage. And I may say here that those who have accused me of extreme and doctrinaire pacifism are deceived. I was not then, and never have been, a pacifist. I believe still that there are occasions of oppression and despair when violence, even war, can be justified. But I know, I think I knew then, that it had no real excuse at Lilmouth. The compromise offered was fair, the victory in sight was reasonable. Pring's motive in the so-called active policy was violence for the sake of violence, cruelty to make hatred, in short, class war and revolution.

And in the final resort, I supported him because his gospel had become my gospel, I would have supported him even if I had fully understood what Pittway meant by pressure and private persuasion.

The committee then broke up, and I went as usual into the back office, Pring's room, to write up my minutes. It was there that Pring joined me, told me of the Allsend offer and pointed out how dangerous it could be to our purpose.

"It's in my pocket, but I kept it there. It would split the committee, and the men too. It would mean the end of any effective union down here for years. On the other hand, if we can keep the men together and get the carters out, we're bound to win. The small employers are finished already, they'll break away on their own, and the big men will have to follow or they'll lose all their trade. We've got a big victory right under our hand."

It was with these words in my mind that I faced Barret and Wilson that evening on Old Bull Wharf. I asked them what offer they were talking about.

"Our offer, the Allsend offer. Haven't you heard of it yet? Do you mean Pring hasn't passed it on?"

I thought quickly, and answered that I had heard of the offer but that it had not yet been before the committee.

"What are you waiting for?"

"Till the next committee meeting, but it won't be accepted, I can tell you that. Why should it? We're winning all along the line."

"That's all right, Ches, you can keep that tale for the soap-box. You know as well as we do that the men are sick of the strike—they'd go back for nothing if you'd let 'em."

As I fully believed this myself I retorted that no doubt he would get a good deal of satisfaction out of such a disaster, but it wasn't going to happen.

I thought this interview so important as showing the urgency of the position that I went straight to Pring that night. But he reassured me with the news that the new policy was already in hand. In fact on the very next afternoon three carters at Allsend were ambushed with a volley of stones and the men turned back.

I heard of this from a passing striker on my way to meet Georgina. It was the time of my regular Sunday visit home, and Georgina would drive me across the moor in the Stonepit trap. She asked me at once if I had heard of the attack on the carts. I said, yes, and she answered, "Did you set them on to it?"

As I climbed into my seat, I answered no, but I was glad that my face was hidden from Georgina. I even felt a momentary discomfort in my breast, such a pang as that which comes when one is called upon to destroy something precious and irreplaceable.

But in the same instant there arose in me a sense of glory and triumph, something quite unexpected in its force and puzzling even to myself—I had lied to Georgina for the cause.

While I was still bemused by this sensation Georgina gave a flick to the cob and said gloomily, "Will thinks that toad Pring has kept the offer to himself."

"You mean the Allsend offer? But that's just a trap. How do we know the owners would stick to it?"

Georgina kept silence for a long time. She said at last in the same tone of exasperation, "Will is very worried. He counted on the men going back, and if they don't he'll lose a lot of money."

"Your Will is a bit too sharp. Some day he was bound to cut himself."

"If you abuse Will I'll take the bank and put you in the road."

I laughed at this sudden explosion, but I did not retort—Georgina in a rage was still capable of upsetting the trap. Besides it gave me pleasure to see that I had frightened her at last—a pleasure added to my exaltation at the news of the attack on the carters, and their flight. "This is the turning point," I thought. "We've saved the day and we deserve it. We took the bold line. We risked our necks."

I felt like a Napoleon. How mean and small the hamlet seemed to me as we topped the last rise by the shop; how remote and uncouth, a place where men scarcely came to life, where life itself was a slow corruption. The cottages in the valley—our own cottage—seemed to be sinking into the ground as if half dissolved already into their natural elements of mud and mould, as if the effort to be something more had been too much for them.

We wheeled aside into the rough lane that skirted the paddock, and Richard came out to hold the horse's head and to greet us.

Richard had turned up a week before to take, as he said, a Christmas holiday, but it had leaked out since that he was not going back to London, that he had been sacked from the textile firm and did not want any more office work. Meanwhile he spent his time, as of old, lying on Ruth's bed with a book or strolling thoughtfully about the moor roads.

In the evening he would go to the Green Man for a pint of beer and talk in his calm sagacious manner to the labourers assembled there. He was treated to his face with respect as a learned person who had seen the world, and behind his back with amused contempt as a jumped-up educated native who had failed even to support himself.

I will not say that it was part of my glory in those days that my admired elder brother should hold the horse for me while I got down. Indeed, Richard seemed entirely unaware of what was happening in Lilmouth, and he would have held a horse for anybody. But Ruth's anxious enquiry about how I was feeling and Georgina's request, five minutes later as she came out from attending on her father, that I should go in at once because "he's been worrying himself to death about you," these were true compliments to my new importance in the family circle of the Nimmos.

My father had been in bed all the winter, always in pain, and I found him lying flat on his back with compressed lips, gazing at the rafters. He was now a very little crooked man with thin pearl-white hair and moustache. His eyes had disappeared into deep holes beneath their arches of bone. His long peaked chin below seemed to make up half his face, he was all forehead and chin.

A rope hung from a beam so that he could pull himself up. As soon as he heard me, he grasped this rope and dragged himself into a sitting position. I dared not help him. As his helplessness grew, so did his disgust at being helped.

I greeted him and asked him how he had been, but he did not answer the question. He asked me instead if it was true that the strikers had attacked the carters. He was obviously full of this news and very excited about it.

I answered that I had heard a rumour to that effect. "That's bad," he said, "that's very bad—if they were set on to it. They say this man from London is scheming for trouble—in the Paris style." He was referring to the commune still in recent memory—a fearful memory of senseless destruction and assassination followed by equally fearful reprisals. "And what about some letter from the owners offering to negotiate. Georgy thinks he's made away with it. That's worse than all—the worst. Tricks like that poison all confidence. And if there is no trust how shall there be peace? But I know you see that as well as I do." And then, of course, he set to work to make me see it, repeating all the arguments usual in such a case; that fighting led only to more fighting, and trickery to more trickery, until there was no peace or truth anywhere and everybody suffered including the poor—the poor most of all in the latter end. I had heard it before in several of his addresses. He ended with a favourite quotation from, I think, Isaiah, "Their webs shall not become garments, neither shall they cover themselves with their works: their works are works of iniquity, and the act of violence is in their hands."

This expected view of the matter, this expected quotation, only

246

made me impatient. I said nothing. My silence in the circumstances expressed my feelings very plainly.

My father, looking fixedly at me, said then, "You think that's not true, but it ruined them in Sheffield, it's ruined France—it will ruin you here. You get an advantage for a few months, a few years, and lose everything in the end. How can you have any settlement if no man can take another's word?"

And perhaps because his reasoning gave me some secret uneasiness, I felt only the more impatient, and still kept silence.

"And what about this letter, this offer of terms?" he asked, looking keenly at me.

"Georgina has the story."

"I can't ask Georgina for anything, she never tells me the truth—not all of it, at least." And then when I did not answer, "She said your committee had nothing to do with the stone throwing, is that true?"

I found unexpectedly that I did not want to tell him even so much of an untruth as I had told Georgina. I said indignantly that he was not fair to Georgina. It made her very unhappy.

He saw my evasion and paused a moment, pulling impatiently at the bedclothes.

"Georgina is unhappy because she has done evil." And he fixed his eyes on me. "Because she turned away from what she knew to be right. That was a cruel thing she did to poor Fred Coyte, a fearful thing to have on one's soul—the ruin of another. And she never repented of it."

Even in my anger and prejudice I saw that there was some truth in this. It was an exaggeration to say that Georgina had destroyed Fred—his own weakness had done that—but her jilting had taken away from him the will or strength to fight against that want of self-confidence. I had wondered before this that Georgina had never shown any pity for Fred, had never admitted any fault towards him.

"It is her temper," my father said, as if interpreting my thoughts. "She always had that proud temper. It is her temper that has cut her off from God."

And he told me that my mother had warned him against Georgina before she died—that as she had had a hard birth so she would have a hard mind—"obstinate in evil."

Just then Georgina herself came into the room—she brought the hot flannels which were used to relieve his pain. He broke off in the middle of a sentence while she turned back the bedclothes and stripped off the old dressing and laid on the new. We remained in silence throughout this process. It took a long three minutes.

This silence expressed, certainly to me, certainly to Georgina, and I believe to my father also, with great force, the tension of feelings between father and daughter.

"I'm just going," Georgina said, as if apologising for her presence, "and then you can talk about me. Only it's no good if the flannel gets cold." She tucked my father up again in his blankets.

Neither of us spoke, for there was nothing to say. My father was not a man who could utter those polite denials and face-saving taradiddles which ease such situations in more polite society. For him such statements were merely lies and could only increase the evil for which already we were paying forfeit. He reached for his pipe—the short black pipe which was all that remained to him of the old trooper, and Georgina lit it for him before she went out of the room.

Do I seem to picture a house full of hatred? Nothing could be more false. These two wished only each other's good; their conflict, even to themselves, seemed nothing beside their devotion. Their very battles arose from their love, their passionate concern for each other's welfare.

248

56

WHEN Georgina drove into India Street on Monday morning to set me down at my lodging, we were instantly surrounded by a crowd of men and women. They ran after us, they pressed so closely to our wheels that I could not get down at my door till I had answered their questions.

What was going to happen next? Were the carts all stopped? Had the police any clue? Would the cartage firms force the dock owners to make a settlement?

One man handed me up a newspaper to show the heading— OUTRAGE AT ALLSEND. ATTACK ON MESSRS. GADDS' CARTERS. POLICE CALL ON STRIKERS' LEADERS.

I was startled. I had not thought that a few stones could cause so much turmoil. The people, like my father, had been quicker than I to interpret the signs—to know that they meant war.

But again, as I sat there above that excited crowd—the faces coloured for once with something like health if it were only a fever of wonder and anxiety, the raised eyes imploring comfort and guidance from me, Chester Nimmo—I felt a glory, I said to myself, "If it is war then let it be war. I'm not afraid."

And at the committee room I found the same elation, the same feelings of defiance. Banner, Pring, Pittway and half-a-dozen more of the section leaders were all there discussing an answer to the police, and a manifesto for the press.

But we need not follow this common tale through its usual course —public outcry, police arrest of pickets, attacks of growing savagery, men beaten up, increasing bitterness—both sides declaring that nothing would satisfy them but total surrender. Above all and beneath all, the fear that comes with bloodshed; on one side fear of anarchy and universal ruin, on the other of a crushing revenge by frightened authority.

It was after a month of the active policy that I was sent one night to visit the scene of what we called an incident.

This was an unusual task for me. We kept a man, one of the clerks who had come out on strike with the labourers, to make such visits and give us an accurate report of them. We leaders were instructed to keep away from the scene so that we could deny complicity.

But the clerk was taken ill within an hour of an important action, and as I was in the office at the time I was chosen to take his place. I was to keep out of sight as far as possible—my duty was not only to report, but to see that what Pittway called the active elements did not get out of hand.

So with the big silent Rattray, I walked through the ill-lit streets of the dock quarter, streets which now seemed to smell of misery, streets unnaturally clean because there was no litter of paper or peel to be thrown there, the children had not eaten a sweet or seen an apple for months.

So I came to a little open space where three streets met, and one broken gas-lamp gave a flickering and smoky light.

Two houses at one side of this place had been wrecked. All the windows were smashed, the torn curtains hung from them in rags, and the street was littered with broken furniture—the pitiful furniture of very poor people.

There was blood on the pavement, and in the gutter opposite a man was lying.

One of the two men chosen for an example had run away, he had been stopped and beaten, but not so severely that he had not been able to walk to hospital; the other, the one I saw, had tried to defend his home. He was now lying insensible among the broken crockery and splintered wood, the torn shreds of stuff which had been his household possessions. His face seemed like a pulp of blood, no features could be recognised. His wife, with two small terrified children beside her, was standing among a group of women on the pavement. They were holding her and trying to lead her away. She was struggling with them and shrieking something. Nothing could be understood, but I gathered that she was denouncing the committee because at sight of me the others tried to silence her—the looks they

250

threw in my direction were full of terror. Two of them threw their aprons over their heads and ran off.

I should have liked to say that I was sick with horror at this spectacle of my work so coolly arranged in the office. But my own words contradict me—they have been preserved for nearly fifty years in a column of the Lilmouth *Advertiser,* luckily for me an obscure and long defunct sheet.

"The women were obviously much alarmed in case I should recognise them—there is no doubt that the new policy has had all the success we anticipated in bringing the scabs into line. B and L and party deserve high praise for the efficient manner in which the assignment was carried out. The whole operation took less than six minutes and the police had no chance of interference. The last of our men had been withdrawn from the action five minutes before the first copper arrived. And it is noticeable that he received no information except from one young girl, daughter of the man dealt with."

This letter reached the press on account of a police raid at our headquarters, on the morning after the incident. It was thought that the man would die, and the magistrates granted a warrant on the ground of conspiracy.

Of course we took counter-action and claimed damages for illegal entry. We described the letter as a police forgery, and I was instructed to deny authorship.

Fortunately I had signed the note only with an initial—fortunately too, our counsel, a clever man sent specially from London, managed to perplex the local constables so much, and to cast so much confusion and doubt into the minds of the magistrates, that we escaped the assizes.

My friend Edward probably saved me here by his evidence that I had always been strongly opposed to violence—he swore, too, that on the night of the attack I had been with him.

Edward G was highly respected. Do you wonder that he, a convinced and extreme pacifist, swore to a lie, a lie in defence of such bloody work?

The answer is that Edward G, in his devotion to me, to my sisters and my father, managed to believe me when I swore to him, under

251

orders from my colleagues, that I had no hand in the crime. And then very easily persuaded himself to give the evidence which alone could establish what he believed to be true—an alibi.

He did this the more readily because, so law-abiding in fact, he was in religious theory, or rather, assumption, an anarchist who thought of all government as an usurpation of providence, a concession to the devil, and the police especially as sons of Belial.

The press were then threatened with libel and the *Advertiser* published an apology. No one has dared to raise that old charge from that day to this.

Edward and our London counsel saved me and the committee from a desperate situation. The case had reached the national papers—it was compared with the outrages in the north still very present, in these revolutionary times, to the public nerves.

Luckily our side, the very women who had recognised me, starving as they were, refused all offers of reward for information, and Pring behaved with the greatest coolness and courage. The men responsible were slipped away without suspicion and the committee itself opened a subscription for the injured man.

For the moment we abandoned the active policy, but it had had a great success. The two days for which we held back the Allsend offer had been decisive. When those owners, in desperation after the attack on the carters, made their terms public, we had no difficulty in getting them rejected. Brodribb had resigned from the committee immediately after the first ambush, and we carried the rank and file with us; they were both encouraged and terrorised, there were no more breakaways and all carting had stopped.

To add to our triumph, the Allsend owners were turned out of the owners' association and two of them went bankrupt at once—even Wilson and Beck in Tarbiton were obliged to close down and Wilson was in London trying to raise capital to carry them over a long stoppage. There was no more house hunting.

57

RICHARD was often with me at this time. He came to Lilmouth for the bookshops, better there than at Queensport or Tarbiton. He would ride in free on G's grocery cart and stand reading in one shop or another until the shopman asked him if he wanted to buy. Then he would lay the book down and go out—I would find him sitting on a bollard by the quay gazing severely out to sea. Richard never seemed to dream but always to reflect.

I would avoid him if I could. I did not care for his indifference to the strike and to my own position. But if he noticed me he would get up and meet me.

I remember one such occasion especially because of a conversation that has stayed with me ever since. It was a wet morning in late January, not cold but overcast, with thin clouds in many shades of silver and grey through which the sun appeared now and then, but of a pearl colour, almost as pale as a winter moon.

I was on my usual patrol with Rattray when I caught sight of the well-known figure, in cap and overcoat, seated with crossed arms on the iron bollard which was actually an ancient cannon, sunk to the trunnions in the ground. It used at that time to be called the armada cannon or Drake's gun.

Richard, apparently oblivious of the drizzling sea mist, sat quite motionless. His form was repeated upside-down in the shining yellow surface of the wet paving stones, accurate even to the square bulge of a book in his overcoat pocket and the slightly lighter colour of a patch on its skirts lately inserted by Georgina.

As usual he did not seem to notice me. I was about to turn aside to pass behind a crane and some empty rusting trucks when he turned his head and leisurely rose to approach me.

It struck me then for the first time that Richard sought these meetings, it was his characteristic reserve or consideration that prevented his suggesting them. He preferred to wait on my convenience—I was the busy man. I was ashamed now to escape from him, and waited till he should come up.

He nodded to Rattray and said to us both, "How are you? How's your strike going these days?"

"Very well—we have the owners beat out of the field—another bankruptcy in Allsend yesterday."

"D'you mind if I come along?" and he would turn to walk beside me. Rattray, a man of natural politeness, fell a step behind.

Richard on these walks, which happened at least once a week, would discuss what I thought very small and stale matters, village gossip, family affairs, the latest phase in our father's growing helplessness, Ruth's wayward husband, who was said to be running after girls as well as horses, or Georgina and her strange passion for Will—"a nice enough chap in his way but a bit ordinary for Georgy."

Richard, in fact, had developed an absorbed interest in family news, and this was always exasperating to me for none of it was good. Naturally the case had excited the most excited feelings all about, but especially in Shagbrook, I was one of the best-hated men in the west country and most people were convinced that I had written that letter. My friends, on the other hand, Edward G and my family, my father and Georgina, took my word for it that I was much maligned. My father had indeed preached a sermon on slander and backbiting, mentioning Newmarch and two more by name, which had deprived him of half his congregation.

Georgina, too, had abused Newmarch. She seemed to be in perpetual quarrels on my account. She was ready to fight anyone on mere suspicion. Lately she had accused Meakin of calling me a liar and a crook—this was the story of the suit and the overcoat bought with union funds, and Georgina knew that she herself had contributed to this purchase—while Meakin said that Georgina had deliberately picked the quarrel by demanding an apology for words he had not uttered, that the girl was mad.

I think perhaps that Georgina was a little mad, she was very depressed by Will's affairs and his absence in London. But the story of her whims did not encourage me.

254

When Richard told me one afternoon that Georgina had finally thrown up her job at Stonepit, I was very angry. I knew what the dairy meant to Georgina—the great success of her life. Her butter and cream were known as far as Exeter. I asked what the family was going to live on. My pay was very small, Richard had no job, and though Simnel had lately, to Ruth's great joy, sent her an affectionate letter with money and clothes, he had also announced the chance that he might soon take himself and her to the farm of a bachelor brother in Australia who badly needed a woman in the house.

"I wish Georgy had more sense," I said. "Why can't she mind her own business?"

But Richard, as I say, had his own angle of view. He answered after a moment, "Well, I suppose—for Georgy—it is her own business."

"I don't see it."

"If she feels that way about it."

"Then she might have more consideration for me—doesn't she realise that it's not exactly helping me to carry on here if I've got to worry about the weekly bills at Ladd's. How do you think we're going to pay our way and keep father out of the workhouse?"

This was a direct hint to Richard to feel some responsibility towards the family. But his mind was still preoccupied with Georgina's character. He went on musing about her violent pride in all that she had to do with, the dairy, her father, the family, and ourselves, Ruth's good looks, Will's enterprise and cleverness.

"I suppose the truth is that father's right—he usually is right—what Georgina loves is success and glory. Do you remember the kid boots from Oxford and the silk petticoat she bought with her own savings?—look at the way she sits up with Will when they go driving in that gig of his. You can see she feels like a queen. She's never forgotten that time when we had our own farm, or got over the come-down when we lost it. I can understand that too." And he began to talk once again of our old days at Highfallow.

This was, of all subjects, the one he seemed to enjoy most—he would ask if I remembered this or that incident, the glorious time at Christmas when we were snowed up for six weeks and ate all our own

255

chickens, the night when the oak tree by the cowshed was struck by lightning and our mother ran out to the cows through the freezing rain in her nightdress and with bare feet. She had said that she was easier to dry than clothes. "But she liked walking about in bare feet —there was something in her that liked to break rules, Georgina didn't get all her character from father.

"But mother was happy in her life. I think she was the happiest person I have ever known. I suppose it was because she had everything she needed for happiness and knew it, and knew how to enjoy it too."

I was impatient with my elder brother. I disdained even to ask him for the news I wanted, about finances at Ladd's. I said to myself, "No wonder he is a failure, no wonder he accepts it so easily—he lives anywhere but in the real world." I said now with some roughness that my mother had suffered a great deal in her last illness, "She was fearfully unhappy when she died."

"Well, if you have all you want and enjoy it so much, of course you don't like losing it. It's something that can't be helped."

"She hadn't much to lose in Back Lane."

"She had us and she had father. Naturally she was worried about what would happen to us without her."

I made no answer to this. I let my disdain be felt in my silence. Why did I avoid Richard that winter—why when I could not avoid him did I oppose to all his thoughts a bored contempt? I think now that I was deeply afraid of my brother because for all his vagueness and failure in what I called the real world, he lived in a much more truly real world than I.

I said to myself with amazement, "How can he occupy his mind with the boring trivialities of family life, questions of family conduct?" But the man who is bored by the fate of his own kin, how shall he escape the final boredom even in the place of the rulers, and the pleasure gardens of millionaires?

Bills meant little to Richard, but he understood Georgina's strong attachments, which were part of her imperious temper. He understood why her fierce defence of me was necessary to her soul because I was

256

part of her soul. She was all of a piece in her sense of honour and truth, like Richard himself.

If I had admitted the truth of my brother, I should have known that my own life had become a lie. If I had recognised his success I should have had to accept my own enormous failure. And in that phrase, so common, so true, I hardened my heart.

58

I say my heart was hardened. This is a true image if it is remembered that hearts are not metal but flesh. By work, by the blows of fate, the flesh can grow a surface as hard as horn, but not hard all through like steel. The cruel man need not have a hard heart. How many torturers, agents of despotism, experts with the rack and the thumb-screw, have been tender fathers and loving husbands. The hard heart is that which turns aside the blows of truth, the arrows of conscience, and often it is hard above because it is soft and fearfully weak below.

Perhaps that is why the young are cruel, because they are afraid. They harden their hearts against the memories of goodness done to them, against the natural kindness of the flesh—the more they are to be moved the more they need hardness.

My case was then a common one. It was easy for me to walk about the streets and scorn the angry glance, the muttered curse, but it was hard for me to wipe out of my mind the memory of that scene in India Street. It was because of that hardness that I was hard.

But the heart that takes to itself a shell can die within its shell, for the heart must breathe, and its breath, its very life, is the give and take of human sympathy.

So my heart might have died, my whole life have been twisted, if it had not been for an accident.

Brodribb, I say, had resigned from the committee immediately after the first attack on the carters. He had now sent a letter to the press dissociating himself from the whole policy of the Pring committee and proposing a conference with the employers. Two of the Allsend strike leaders had now joined with him. It seemed likely that the whole of the Allsend-Tarbiton district might go back to work.

I deplored this weakness and treachery in Brodribb as much as the rest. I spoke of it to Rattray on my usual rounds of inspection,

258

and Rattray answered with meaning, "Aye, and I saw B and L last night coming from the station."

B and L were two of the thugs who had carried out the last attack. Their return to Lilmouth and the danger zone could have only one meaning. I did not ask Rattray whether he was sure of his facts, because I could not bear to let him suspect that I was not, as they say, in the know—I, a leader, and supposed to be in the innermost counsels of the strike committee.

As soon as I could get rid of Rattray I rushed to the office. I was in a fury of suspicion and injured dignity. In the office I found, as usual at this time in the morning, Pittway dealing with routine papers, appeals and accounts, and Banner walking about the room, smoking and growling.

I demanded to know at once if it was true that anything was intended against old Brodribb. Pittway's cautious expression as he looked up, Banner's growl as he spat into the fireplace and demanded what it had to do with me told me at once that Rattray's guess had been correct.

Pittway began to explain that Brodribb had been warned repeatedly, that his latest action was in absolute defiance of the committee and threatened to lose all the fruits of victory just at the moment when it was finally at hand—victory, I may say, according to us all, had been at hand for more than three months.

"That's not the point," I said. "The point is that since Brodribb resigned I represent Tarbiton here, and that I wasn't told anything about a decision affecting Tarbiton. Who gave these orders?" And I looked at Banner.

Pittway began a long smooth speech about an emergency meeting and an omission on the part of the clerk who should have notified me. I pointed out that if Brodribb had had several warnings, the matter could not have been dealt with at one meeting.

"Oh get out," Banner said. "You and your Judas overcoat. You've sucked all you can out of this job, or do you want a top hat to go with the other duds?"

Banner had always hated me as a young upstart, brought from a junior post at Tarbiton to act, so he believed, as Pring's spy upon him.

259

I ignored the man, for I despised him. I was more infuriated by Pittway's smooth periods, his polite evasions. Prejudice against what is called the intellectual is foolish, and often damaging to the cause of progress, but it is comprehensible, it is founded on a truth. For me Pittway's very coolness was the mark of one who had no knowledge of real life among the poor. It seemed to me, therefore, that he had no right to enter the discussion. I asked him if he had lived in these parts, did he understand what effect it would have if a man like Brodribb were hurt?

"I told you," Banner said, "that he was one of Brodribb's rats."

I turned upon him then and said that the most dangerous rat was the one that had not the sense to know what was the best thing to do and when to do it. Banner, as bad-tempered as he was stupid, made a rush at me, and Pittway hastily placed himself between us—all three of us were talking at once. Indeed, one might say that Banner and I were shouting.

Pring now appeared in the doorway, from his private room at the back of the house, and asked to know what we thought we were doing. As both Banner and I naturally tried to explain at the same time, he silenced us with a gesture and turned to Pittway, certainly the coolest man there.

Pittway stated the case in a reasonable manner but, I thought, did not make enough of my claim to represent Tarbiton—I broke in to emphasize it. Pring interrupted me in my turn to tell me to keep calm. "The resolution was passed unanimously so what did it matter if you were absent? It's only a technical point." His voice, as he said this, expressed his hearty contempt for what he called technical points and those who made them.

But what had startled me still more than this scornful attitude towards the whole principle, as I saw it, of our democratic and representative constitution was his glance at me as I attempted to explain my grievance. In the cold stare of his blue eyes flashed upon me, his expression of bored and angry contempt, I perceived the truth about the man; a truth I had always known and even gloated upon, but never applied to my own case, that no one on earth counted with him beside the cause.

260

I knew in that moment that I was less than nothing to Pring, I had become a nuisance to him, to be quietly got rid of, from the time when, by some intuition or guess, he had decided that I might oppose his will to make an example of Brodribb. And I knew it most intensely in my nerves. I attempted a reasonable air and I began to explain my point about representation.

Pring broke in impatiently to say that if I did not agree with the committee, I had only to resign. I answered, with such dignity as I could manage, that such was my intention, but meanwhile I wished to record a serious warning, based on my special knowledge of the local conditions, against any precipitate action at Tarbiton. Banner interrupted with the noise known, I believe, as a raspberry. And I believe I tried to strike him. The next moment all three were pushing me downstairs, and, to my own horror and amazement, I was shrieking that there was too much boss in this strike and too little democracy.

I spoke the words in hysterical anger. As I raged for the next hour and more—I know not how long—through the lanes among those squalid warehouses, the only place, at this time of stagnation, where I could be alone, I said them again a thousand times and recognised their truth. I told myself that Pring loved power too much and men not at all.

When I returned to my lodging an hour later, I found all my goods, the smart new bag that I had bought in town, the old carpet bag of my mother's father, and my few books, piled on the pavement. The door of the house was locked—an extraordinary event during the daytime—and no one would answer my knocking.

At last, when I persisted, the daughter of the house, a girl of fourteen, opened the bedroom window a few inches and said that some men had come to put my things out and they threatened to smash the windows if I was let in again.

She said that she was sorry but her mother was in bed with the worry, and would I please go away at once. I made no answer. These people had been my friends and now they were afraid to speak to me. I went to find a cab, but when I told the man where to drive he refused to enter the district, the dock area was too dangerous for drivers. I therefore stopped a young boy and gave him sixpence to

261

take a note to the Shagbrook carrier asking him to send a hand barrow. The boy was very willing—children, thank God, were still treated as neutrals in this civil war.

I returned then to guard my belongings. They had not been touched. I myself had given strictest orders against looting. And there I sat for that whole afternoon alone among bricks and mortar, I might have been the only man in the world.

Hours passed. Still not a soul had appeared in the street—I was aware only of an occasional face peering cautiously from a window. As it began to grow dusk I began to wonder what was going to happen in the night. But I had no thought of leaving my place. It seemed impossible to me.

This was not courage or even obstinacy. Can anyone who has been in the same position describe the feeling of the man who has been betrayed, and says to the world: do what you like to me now, I cannot give way, it is impossible for me to accept this thing.

And when I write betray, I am expressing something beyond human treachery. It seemed to me in this disaster of my youth that I had been tricked by fate itself, by a conspiracy of circumstances. To abandon my goods in the street would have been not only to run away from my enemies but to proclaim that circumstances had been too much for me.

Yet I was in a position from which I could not extricate myself. The very silence of the street, usually full at this time of women's voices and playing children, seemed to join in with the falling dark like an approaching doom—as if a vast dark mind was gradually thinking itself to the point of crushing me out, a bug, a nothing, a creature rejected.

59

Now again, at the other end of my life, an old and broken man, I am thrown into the gutter, I sit and wait for the night, the last darkness.

I am told that my whole career has been a disaster and a fraud. That great party, called so truly and proudly the liberal party, the party of freedom, to which I gave forty years of my life, in which I rose to honour, lies in ruins, and those who lately filled the streets to cheer me on my way long only that I should die. I am an embarrassment to them.

But nothing shall persuade me to believe that the generous youth of my country, that these young men who hate and revile me, like those old ones of Lilmouth long ago, practise evil for evil's sake. They are only deceived—they are under a spell of words.

The world itself is young, we are but little removed from the time when writing was a wonder, when any written speech was magic. Words printed in books—Rousseau, Proudhon, Owen, Marx, what power they can wield. But it is the power of sorcerers—the spell they cast is abracadabra. And the fruit of their sorcery is egotism and madness, war and death.

So evil is the brood of the slogans that the most splendid and noble battle cries, Liberty, Equality, Fraternity, bred nothing but new and more cunning, more hypocritical despots, better organised murder, popular nationalism drunk with the conceit of hooligans, militarism as the tool of demagogues, hatred not to be assuaged by the blood of millions and a century of tears.

Trace now the record of another, a modest and unconsidered force, an influence little more noticed by the learned and the propagandists, the word-wielders, than the play of the English weather—the daily, weekly ministrations of fifty thousand servants of the Lord. I speak not here of the mighty Wesley but of those humble and poor men who gave their lives to oblivion. Yea, and among them not only the so-called dissenting pastors, but many a vicar and curate of the English Church, as poor and as ungratefully forgotten; above all, that great anonymous crowd of witnesses, teachers of children, speakers in the way, lay preachers and readers, men like my father, who went among their neighbours speaking mercy, truth, kindness towards all men.

I have related the tragedy of my Shagbrook union, the Lilmouth strike was a far worse calamity. Within a week of my expulsion, the men were back and the union itself had dissolved in bitter recriminations. And this was but one of many such failures—in those days of the seventies, it seemed that the unions were finished. That poor society which, ten years after Lilmouth, in desperation started the London dock strike of 1889, had but a few hundred members and almost no funds. Its material power was as nothing, it was a joke among its enemies.

But to the amazement of those scorners, money and encouragement poured in from every side, from all classes, in three days ten thousand men were out, the docks paralysed. The dockers won a victory that was more decisive in history than the storming of the Bastille, it was the end of the old regime of the tyrant capitalist, and an end which bred no tale of revenge, reprisal, and reaction, but rather a new understanding, a new drawing together of classes, a new peace.

How did such a strange thing come about? The country saw the justice of the dockers' case, it detested and condemned the abominable conditions of their work—the dockers' victory was won not with cannon but by the conscience of a nation, the active soul of a people.

Man is a mystery and his destiny is hidden in a depth of time beyond imagination. A million, two million years, what do such computings mean to human sense? And why speak of years and numbers, how shall we divide the courses of eternity?

To bind man's future in a coil of words is to put an iron cage on the tender limbs of a child. I do not repent of the liberalism which inspired that great government in which I served, I do not stand in a sheet, much less a winding sheet, for our creed—for tolerance, for freedom, for private rights, yea, even for private property—tolerance which is room to learn, freedom which is room to grow, private rights

264

and private property which are the only defence against public wrong and public breach of trust.

I say that, as I lie here in my bed, an old man condemned to a double death, of his body and his name, I am full of faith, of hope. Forty-five years ago, in the full strength of my youth, I was bankrupt of both. Such was the despair of my anger, I did not know even how to save my body.

60

I CANNOT describe that strange mixture of feelings, of irritation and relief, with which at last, as the lamps began to shine, I heard a rattle of cart-wheels on the setts and saw Georgina driving down the street. To leave was surrender, but I had no object in staying, no principle to fight for, no purpose for anything.

Georgina was standing up, in her old style, with a rein in each hand, driving like a man, and she called out from some yards away, "So you've left them at last—and quite time too."

"What are you doing here?" I asked. "I sent for the porter with the barrow."

"He was frightened to come, but they sent to tell us you were in the street so I got the cart from the shop."

I will not say that Georgina was enjoying herself. I don't think she could enjoy herself at that time when Will Wilson was away from her and their future was so uncertain, but there was about her that air of energy and recklessness which, from a little girl, had marked her answer to any challenge.

As she pulled up and threw me the whip from her right hand, she said with great satisfaction that she had known I should never get on with "those London beasts. I always said that Pring was a brute." And jumping down with the reins in her hand she poured out a stream of abuse against "the Londoners," how glad she was I had broken with them. "Now you can come off to Shagbrook."

I was not prepared to admit that my late hero was no longer in that position, I answered that it was I who had resigned from the committee—and on a mere question of procedure. But for Georgina this was nothing but a fight between her brother and the foreigners, in which I was bound to be in the right.

In the long drive up to the moor, through gusts of thin rain, the tired horse plodding at the hill, she continued to burst out at my late

266

colleagues—she had always known they were beasts, and I was well quit of them. They did not deserve me. And now what I needed was a holiday. There was plenty of room for another mattress next Richard's, beside father's bed. What's more, I would find the room as I liked it, nice and warm, because Will had begged coal from the estate office.

I listened in silence—I wanted no obligations, even of sympathy. I could not bear them, I had too much to bear already.

I shall not relate the further history of the strike. It broke within the week, the Allsend offer was accepted at Tarbiton, and the Lilmouth men drifted back on the same terms. Pring, Brodribb and three other leaders all issued statements abusing each other. The only point on which they agreed was that I had betrayed both sides. Banner informed a large meeting at Lilmouth that the letter signed C was mine, and sought to lay upon me alone the whole responsibility for the pressure policy.

There was no prosecution, I had already been acquitted. And the strike was over. No one wanted to recall its bitterness. I was not even asked for explanations, and I offered none—not even to my own family. And this was not from pride but a strange indifference. I told myself that the world was too vile, the treachery of my colleagues, the fearful humiliation inflicted on my father and sister, these were beyond speech, I did not want even to think of them. I did not want, either, to be reminded of them. For the first months after Banner's disclosure I hardly stirred from the cottage save to walk on the moor. I did not show myself even in the village. At home I was safe from the least hint of reproach—my father's prayers for the repentant sinner struck on my ears as mere routine, for I did not call myself a sinner.

I was ill that spring. The Spanish influenza, which swept the country again in that year, affected us all, and in spite of Georgina's nursing, I made a slow and poor recovery, I do not know that I wanted to recover. Perhaps I owe my very life to my family then— their plan was the old one of distraction, of finding me something to do. In June, thanks to Wilson, I was found a place in Bing's estate office at Tarbiton. I was to lodge once more in Edward's attic.

So I went to work and passed some hours every day copying and filing letters, making out bills and schedules, and it seemed to me that these operations were conducted by a second person, an automaton, whose company I endured only for the sake of a pound a week, and because it was too much trouble to get rid of him.

I shall not describe my life in the next year. No one could understand that prostration of mind and feeling who has not passed through the same experience of an intense lethargy which is yet a torture. The confidence, the enthusiasm, the hero-worship of years, had run into the sand. I no longer hated Pring, I only ceased to regard him. But deprived of loyalty I was an emptiness that yet agonised in its vacancy, a nakedness that disdained to be hidden from contempt, and yet quivered like a bare nerve in the wind.

During my youth in that time before I knew the Dollings, a house fell down in Tarbiton—a house that had a bad name—and with many others I went to see the ruin. The fall was pronounced a judgment, two of the women had been killed. But I was attracted by a different curiosity, to see the inside of a house of pleasure thus exposed to the air.

I do not know what I expected of magnificence, what wicked glory, but I saw only the inside walls and furnishings of half-a-dozen rooms exposed to the afternoon sun in a dirty squalor which was even more pitiful than it was contemptible. As I gazed I felt only a stupid confusion.

So I myself was now a ruin with all my secret places laid open, and I was astonished at their mean appearance. My glory had ended in this pitiful rubbish heap, I turned my eyes away from it, it said nothing to me of good or evil, only of sordid failure; I had no meaning even to myself.

It might have been said of me with awful truth that my webs had not become garments, nor did my works cover me.

I was restless as well as weary. After three days at Edward's I moved to a lodging; after a week at the lodging I went home. I preferred to take the long double journey every day in order to sleep on the moor.

I now had Richard's company on the road. In the spring he had taken a post at the Battwell school teaching village children their ABC's, and he would walk each evening to the crossroad to join me in the carrier's van.

I remember still his long stooping figure as he leant against the sign-post and gazed at the jagged horizon towards Highfallow, the sound of his stirring at night when, with a turn of the head, I could see in the early light from the thin-curtained window that he too was awake. He had turned on his side and, with head resting on hand, his eyes close to the page, was reading in one of the books that always lay by his pillow.

My father, too, was a bad sleeper. In the smallest hours, with a stealthy stroke of the match below the bedclothes, he would light his pipe, and then for a long time he would sit propped against the bed-head, smoking with deliberation—by the glow of the bowl we would see upon his eyes, at the bottom of those dark pits of their orbits, two steady gleams of reflected light, fixed in contemplation of the fate of souls, or perhaps only of some neighbour's dilemma.

In the next room we would hear the women, Georgina's unmistakable cough, which Ruth said was like a swear—Georgina hated coughing as if it were an indignity put upon her by fate; or the baby would cry out and Ruth would hush her, murmuring sleepily, probably telling her a story, or assuring her that her daddy was coming to her soon.

61

I SAY we had all been ill that spring, I and Ruth so much
so that the doctor was called. But he was most concerned for Georgina,
who had only her usual winter cough, and had not even gone to bed.
An old patch on her lung was active again and he prescribed the
usual remedy of an immediate removal to southern France or Italy.
Ladd's, he said, was the worst possible place for any Nimmo.

It was impossible for us, even in our improved circumstances, with
Richard earning, to think of Italy, we urged Torquay. But Will
Wilson, much concerned, wrote from London to say that he would
pay for Italy, he could well afford it for he was already doing very
well in London. He was, indeed, upon that line of universal carrier
which brought him in thirty years to his imposing fortune and a
baronetcy.

Wilson himself did not come at all, and Georgina had refused to
go to him, even though he hired a housekeeper for her father. London,
she said, was too far to be married away, while he was so ill and
while Ruth and myself both needed watching. Italy had even worse
objections than London, and it wasn't necessary. The doctor was a
known fusser—had she not been coughing every winter for years?

As for Ladd's being a death trap, as long as it was her father's
home it must be hers.

I cannot say if Georgina would have been cured by a removal in
that cold spring from the mists and piercing chill of the moor. But
the doctor believed it. Will Wilson has never ceased to believe it,
and has never forgiven us for her death eighteen months later.
Certainly when she decided to stay she condemned herself to death.
But I am sure that she did not choose to do so. She was not tired of
life, she had never been so eager in her living or, I dare to say, so
happy. That remark about Ladd's which might seem like a renewal
of the old battle with her father was, I am convinced, merely the

270

statement of a fact. For the question of my father's domicile had been settled for the last four years.

And one reason, I suspect, for that serene happiness was her decision not to marry the man she loved so much, especially after her increasing illness made marriage impossible beyond argument.

This is only a guess—Georgina did not discuss her private affairs with anyone. But Ruth has told me that the day she wrote to Will and told him she would not come to London, that he must consider himself free, she said she had always known that she would never be Will's wife "because of Fred's dying like that."

The village certainly took this view—they went beyond it to see Georgina's illness as God's judgment on a proud and wicked girl. Blood will have blood, they said. Had not Fred cut his throat, and was not Georgina bleeding to death?

It was not true that Fred had cut his throat; his death, announced more than a year before, had been from drink and pneumonia. Neither had Georgina seemed to take much stock of it. You can say if you like that her thought about Fred was the superstition of a girl born and bred on the Moor.

My own view is more prosaic, that Ladd's killed Georgina as it nearly killed me and finally killed my father. What feelings, known or unknown even to herself, constrained the girl to stay at Ladd's in spite of all—that no one can tell. But I do know certainly that if she were moved at all by some deep consciousness of evil doing, and the devious courses of retribution, it did not drive her to misery or despair. It brought her rather peace, the peace of those who, in the presence of death, can give themselves with single-mindedness to the tasks of their devotion.

Never had she attended so anxiously to her father's needs. And never had he found her services harder to endure—for he would have been helpless without her.

Home as always was full of strains and pressures, not only my father's everlasting struggles with his pride and his pain, but the gradual realisation that Georgina was gravely ill.

Richard was deeply absorbed in problems that we could not share. It was still five years before he published, by local subscription, his little book on Greek aesthetic. And Ruth was desperately asking if her husband had any intention of returning to her. Was not his continued absence of over a year the attempt of a good-natured easy-going man to slide away from his marriage?

Why, in this year of my emptiness and frustration, did I cling to my people? Why did I stay in this atmosphere electric with tension? Georgina's care was a trouble as well as a reproach, the serene faith and self-forgetfulness of my father and Richard, so different in form, so close in root, gave me nothing. For I know all the arguments, the experience from which it sprang—they are present somewhere in every soul. To me they were all old tales among the worn-out lumber of the past.

And as the months passed that strain, familiar as it was, grew rather worse than better, Georgina wasting beneath our eyes, but a thing not to be spoken of; my father concerned for both the daughters, and Ruth more agitated by hope and fear. At Christmas, there was a fine present for her; at New Year, a wire asking for money, the man had lost his last pound and couldn't pay his lodging, the week after a letter to say that he had finally decided to accept his brother's offer. He had borrowed two pounds from Will Wilson for a cable.

The brother did not give him time to change his mind, he took the tickets for the family and wired journey money—the next we heard from our smart and gay brother-in-law was that he would arrive on the following morning to carry off wife and child to Southampton.

Poor Ruth did not know whether to laugh or cry at such news. Her husband was coming back to her, but only to carry her away to a country so far in her imagination that it might have been in the moon. She was almost hysterical all that last day at home while she tried to pack, and at prayers that night she could not control her sobs.

Once or twice my father stopped in his reading and glanced at her through the back of his chair.

My father would always get up for prayers if he could do so without assistance—on this important night he had even allowed Richard and myself to help him. He knelt now at his usual chair in the old horse-blanket he used for a dressing-gown, and each time he straightened himself to peer at Ruth, the blanket would slip a little. I was

272

afraid it would fall off and wondered if I should adjust it at the risk of seeming irreverent. I was still more afraid that he would reprimand Ruth in her misery—I had never felt so acutely the torment of this life at home, the incessant exasperation of the nerves.

But it soon appeared that my father's mind was directed upon a different matter, Simnel's known indifference to religion. He made a little homily on the duty of the Christian parent to see that children comprehend the uniqueness of God and give thanks for the love that surrounds them, "as with a strong wall." And he quoted once more from a favourite Psalm—"Except the Lord build the house, their labour is but lost that build it; except the Lord keep the city, the watchman waketh but in vain. Lo, children and the fruit of the womb are an heritage and gift that cometh of the Lord."

And as, relaxed perhaps from that fear of some painful scene, I listened with an idle mind, or rather allowed those musical sounds familiar from earliest childhood to fall of their own weight into my consciousness, suddenly something deep beyond thought or will responded with great force.

Once when I was passing Battwell quarry just after a big fall of rock, the little tin chapel behind me began to ring for some special service, and I was startled to hear how the sound echoed and multiplied itself among the raw surfaces of the limestone. The familiar tinkle was transformed to a peal of commanding beauty which I never forgot.

And for me the music of that great Psalm brought with it a thousand remembrances, my soul stirred and rose to it as to an old trumpet. And as the trumpet brings with it to the soldier more than he can speak or even analyse, vast regions of history, of his nation's glory, so I felt the release of a man who becomes for that moment greater than himself. I did not know then what had happened to me. I might say that it was years before I grasped the full significance of that profoundest of truths not only for the man but for all his endeavours—not only in his family life but in his political activity—that unless he aim at the life of the soul then all his achievement will be a gaol or a mad-house, self-hatred, corruption and despair.

I say I knew not what had happened to me. Six months were still to pass before I returned to faith and, to my father's great delight, preached my first sermon to his own flock, nearly a decade before I returned to the political arena. At the moment I felt only the upsurge of a mysterious excitement, tears came to my eyes, my heart beat fast and strong, I could scarcely stay upon my knees, as soon as amen was said I slipped out into the lane to be alone and to examine this strange convulsion in my soul—the thoughts which were struggling to be born, the feelings which had not yet taken shape.

The moon was high—a cold moon of early spring—the night was frosty but I did not feel it. Then, in my rapid pacing up and down, as I turned back at the hawthorn, I saw Georgina coming towards me. She was carrying my overcoat, that same one they had called the Judas coat.

She had not seen me yet. As she looked about, the white beam from overhead shockingly revealed her emaciation, the deep hollows of her cheeks, the eyes grown too prominent in the shrinking of her face. The rich and shining abundance of her black hair springing from that pale forehead brought back moor tales of the dead whose hair lives after them, and who walk from tombs to enchant and twine the living in its coils. Georgina then seemed indeed a revenant—her face as she searched, frowning, had the impatient feverish expression of one released only a little while from the grave to do her work on earth.

I felt a sharp annoyance at this typical family interruption at such a moment, and stepped back further into the shadow. But pity held me, Georgina had the privilege of the dying. I waited for her and silently allowed her to help me into the coat.

Then as I turned again she smiled at me in that serene and tranquil manner which quite contradicted her tragic looks, "Why are you so unhappy? Don't you see how proud we are of you?"

She was consoling me and it broke my heart—I felt then an indescribable shock of anguish and of exultation. And instantly among the turmoil of my senses a darkness fell away, great presences were revealed, things absolutely known and never again to be obscured, grief that I knew for love, love that I knew for life, joy that I knew for the joy of the Lord.

274

62

Nearly a year has passed, since, finding unexpectedly an absent friend's car and driver at my disposal for an afternoon, I went to Shagbrook Church where Georgina is buried.

I had not been to the place for forty years and more. For in my first and only visit after the funeral, to plant some bog myrtle, a bush she had loved, I had felt too bitterly the sense of loss. And I thought, why this empty ceremony. It only falsifies the truth. She lives and must live in my memory. There is nothing of her here.

What impulse took me now? I was myself as a dying man, in body as in spirit. My life lay in ruins and, as it seemed, all that my life had meant. Was it perhaps the thought of my own death that sent me, that afternoon, to see where Georgina lay?

The day was fine for November, a few gulls planed high overhead but made no sound, the shadow of the little church, a mere box without tower or turret, and half ruinous at that, lay stretched on docks and nettles, on frost-cracked tombs.

Georgina's last request to us was that no stone, no mark should be put on her grave mound. She said that it was a needless expense. She would not have us run into debt for her. She showed such intensity in this desire, exacting from us the most solemn promise, that we obeyed her. We knew that, as usual, she had more reason than she cared to tell.

Was that injunction more proud or more humble? The Mogul emperor, who lies nameless under bare clay and open sky—was he not the proudest of them all and his monument the most arrogant?

Looking down on that mound in the farthest corner of Shagbrook churchyard, now no more than a gentle swelling of the turf, hidden under the long grass by the moor wall, I asked myself if it spoke more of pride or humbleness. For it said more plainly than Georgina had ever spoken in life. No one knew my bitterness and I would not tell it.

I wept in secret and learnt in the night of desolation. I made myself nothing and the world was nothing to me.

The humbleness of a saint? A boast so proud that no Mogul could surpass it? Or are they one in such devoted beings?

Suddenly my blood quickened. I perceived that my memory of Georgina had failed and deceived me. It was here, in the vast silence of the moor, that her spirit lived, silently awaiting me whether I came or no. I had come at last and my heart was beating again strongly to a heart that could not know despair because it forgot itself in the duty of its love.

And my way was made plain. "Here," I said, "the story began and here it shall begin again, in the things I lived with this forgotten one, in the young cruelty of the world, in the making of our souls."

AFTERWORD

WHEN *Prisoner of Grace,* the first volume of Joyce Cary's "Second Trilogy," was published, Cary was startled by the failure of most critics to understand the politician Chester Nimmo, the book's central character. "The critics seem to think Chester is an exceptional blackguard," Cary wrote to Dorothy Muir. "He is only a lively, democratic politician."[1]

Cary revealed both his own sympathies and the reason for the misunderstanding in a letter to Elizabeth Lawrence, his editor at Harper's. "What I believe, of course, is what Nimmo believes, that wangle is inevitable in the modern state, that is to say, there is no choice between persuading people and shooting them. But it was not my job to state a thesis in a novel, my business was to show individual minds in action and the kind of world they produce, and the political and aesthetic and moral problems of such a world."[2]

There is evidence that Cary did not decide to write a second trilogy until after *Prisoner of Grace* was published. Urged to it by his friends, however, Cary soon began a book about Chester Nimmo's childhood and the events which shaped the politician. As he wrote to Lady Megan Lloyd George, "The book I am writing now will, I hope, correct a good many misconceptions about this hero."[3]

The reader who is acquainted with *Prisoner of Grace* will know that Nimmo is purportedly dictating *Except the Lord* to his ex-wife, Nina, in the home she shares with her new husband, her cousin Jim Latter. Nimmo has four reasons for writing the book. First, he wants to celebrate his memories of childhood. Second, he wants to convince Nina that it is her duty to return to him. Third, he wants to teach his readers an important lesson, "that liberal ideals of tolerance and freedom are rooted in our religious history and that state systems of socialism which deny private rights are the enemies of religion and God himself."[4] Fourth, Nimmo hopes to be re-elected to public office.

Unfortunately, the critics who thought the Nimmo of *Prisoner of Grace* an ogre thought Nimmo the narrator of *Except the Lord* a hypocrite. "Obviously some of the reviewers are suspicious of my intentions," Cary wrote to Evan Owen, "and others have simply lost any sense of the religious atmosphere and don't know what I am writing about."[5]

In fact, Cary hoped that the reader of *Except the Lord* would take Nimmo at his word. As he wrote to Elizabeth Lawrence, "I don't want to start the reader with too much of the notion of the old Nimmo, Nina's Nimmo, in his head in case he gets this book wrong and thinks the man is writing with his tongue in his cheek."[6]

Wherever Nimmo's tongue, *Except the Lord* is a fine novel about the formation of a mind, the shaping of moral and political beliefs. Nimmo's prose is both sober and graceful, alternating smoothly between auto-biography and a rhetoric more suitable to the pulpit. Like a good preacher, Nimmo draws a lesson from each incident he relates. Far from boring the reader, however, these didactic interludes continually reveal more about why the politician acts as he does. Every aspect of Nimmo the man is a natural extension of Nimmo the boy.

In *Prisoner of Grace* Nina betrays her frequent annoyance over Nimmo's class consciousness. In *Except the Lord* Nimmo describes his boyhood in a squalid Devonshire hamlet. Although his life has not been without happiness, money, clothing, and food has been scarce. His sister Georgina, who has worked for the grocer G., has submitted to G.'s sexual abuse in exchange for gifts of food and necessities. His mother and several siblings have died of tuberculosis exacerbated by their damp lodgings. It is small wonder that Nimmo bears a grudge against those landlords who might have eased his family's poverty.

Nina is also put off by Nimmo's religious zeal. *Except the Lord* is, to a great extent, the story of a religious pilgrimage. Nimmo's father is an Adventist preacher who sacrifices both his family's welfare and his own advancement for his beliefs. Chester Nimmo takes these beliefs for granted until his father, having predicted the date of Christ's Second Advent, takes his family in the night to a hill to await Christ's coming. Following their disappointment, Nimmo loses his faith. He feels empty inside until he discovers Dr. Dolling and a new faith, anarchism. This captures his imagination and leads him to "evangelize" farm laborers in his district, urging them to form a union and demand higher pay. His efforts, to his dismay, cause a great deal of suffering among these laborers and their families.

Nimmo then turns to the Marxist leader Pring and his more muscular ideas. Pring teaches hatred and violence. Nimmo is at first taken with these ideas and becomes one of Pring's lieutenants, but is disenchanted when he discovers that Pring's goal is dictatorship.

Finally, as the book closes, Nimmo returns to the religion of his youth and becomes a preacher.

One of the turning points of Nimmo's life is his attendance at the play *Maria Marten,* in which a rich young man seduces and murders a farm girl. This play strengthens Nimmo's dislike of the privileged. More important, perhaps, is his realization of the actor's power to change opinion. This leads Nimmo to practice the rhetorical art by preaching to sheep and prepares him for his later careers as preacher and politician.

It is Nimmo's experience of poverty that leads him, in *Prisoner of Grace,* to join a political party which forces social legislation through Parliament to help the poor, the aged, and the unemployed. It is Nimmo's nonconformist religious background which inspires his love of freedom and democracy and his dislike of all forms of totalitarianism. It is his sense of his family's affection which leads him to believe that "Except the Lord build the house, they labour in vain that build it,"[7] and to extend this from his family to his country.

The course of Nimmo's Christianity from *Except the Lord* through *Prisoner of Grace* is a rocky one. Nimmo is elected to Parliament on the strength of the Evangelical vote in his Devonshire district. As his importance grows, he gradually loses touch with his constituents and assumes the "vices" he has condemned. He learns the necessity of creative lying. His commitment to the poor is diluted by his new grasp of international policy. It is when Nimmo forgets his old beliefs that he makes ethical mistakes which damage his reputation. Each slip on the ladder of success, however, brings him back to his religious faith, though only for a while. When he loses an election following World War One, he regains much of his original vision, but this time it is difficult to separate it from his desire to be re-elected. It is also sobering to realize that this chastened Nimmo is fondling his ex-wife at the same time he is dictating his autobiography.

Nimmo's intentions are often honorable, but never pure. He is unable to live up to his ideals, though his ideals do, perhaps, sometimes keep him from worse crimes than those he commits. His is an inevitable dilemma for which he ought not to be condemned. Despite Nimmo's faults, those readers who recognize his basic decency and compassion (especially when they compare him with Jim Latter and Jim's intolerant ravings in *Not Honour More*), will gain from *Except the Lord* insight not only into Nimmo, but into the thousands who share his understanding of reality.

Edwin Ernest Christian

[1] From the James Osborn Collection of Joyce Cary Manuscripts, Bodleian Library, Oxford. MS. Cary Adds. 4/fol. 179, Cary letter to Dorothy Muir, 21 September 1952. Thanks are due to the U.S.-U.K. Educational Commission for the Fulbright Scholarship which allowed me to study Cary's papers.

[2] MS. Cary Adds. 9/fol. 18, letter from Elizabeth Lawrence to Harrison Smith of *Saturday Review,* 12 May 1955, in which she quotes a letter Cary wrote to her.

[3] MS. Cary Adds. 6/fol. 49, typed draft of letter to Lady Megan Lloyd George, 9 March 1953. As the parallels between Nimmo and the late Prime Minister David Lloyd George had been noted by critics—though Cary denied them—he had worried about a libel suit. Cary was greatly relieved to find that Lloyd George's daughter—herself a politician—had enjoyed *Prisoner of Grace.*

[4] MS. Cary Adds. 3/p. 137, letter to Elizabeth Lawrence, 25 May 1953.

[5] Cary collection, uncatalogued letter to Evan Owen, 12 December 1953.

[6] MS. Cary Adds. 3/p. 163, letter to Elizabeth Lawrence, 29 July 1953.

[7] Psalms 127:1.